C

EXCEPTIONAL

A NOVEL

ROBIN READ

A CLOSE EMBRACES BOOK

This is a work of fiction. Names, characters, places, and incidents either are the product of the author's imagination or are used fictitiously. Any resemblance to actual persons, living or dead, events, or locales is entirely coincidental.

For more information, contact: robinuread@yahoo.com.

First CLOSE EMBRACES paperback edition 2022

Cover Illustration by Daniele Fabbri
Book design by Veronica Scott
Edited by Larry O'Connor

ISBN 978-0-578-34119-4 (paperback)
ISBN 978-0-578-34120 (ebook)

www.robinuread.com

For the faculty, staff and students at HGP

Awaken, doomed city, that thou mayest save thyself. Awaken from your heavy slumbers, heedless ones, lest you be slain in sleep; awaken, for the walls are crumbling, and will crush you.... Awaken, awaken!

– from *Jeremiah*, a play written by Stefan Zweig in 1917

Now up rode royal Camilla with her files of Volscians; just at High Gate she leaped down from her horse, and all her cohort followed her, slipping from mounts to earth. Camilla spoke: "Turnus, if merit give boldness to the brave then I am bold. I'll meet Aeneas' men and ride alone against the Tuscan horse. Let me and my horsemen risk the first encounter: you keep to the rear, afoot, and guard the walls." The girl meant terror!

– from Vergil's *Aeneid*, Book XI

How the story ends? That's completely up to us. One thing is certain: your actions, inactions, and interactions are now being recorded.

– Creators of Earth's Black Box, a 33-foot-long steel structure located on Australia's island state of Tasmania that is designed to aggregate and store climate change news and research in real time for posterity.

1

NORTHEAST OF EDINA

Camilla Borlaug, whose family and childhood friends called Cam, had recently earned the nickname Cahmie-kaze, a tongue-in-cheek moniker bestowed by fellow activists in Minneapolis. Raised on grilled steaks, iceberg lettuce soaked in ranch and baked potatoes slathered with butter, she subsisted these days on lentil soup, veggie hotdishes and green tea while dwelling in self-imposed exile a dozen miles northeast of Edina, the lovely suburb of her All-American upbringing. One snarky post she ran across had her hometown pegged:

> **Mad Metic_803**
>
> They say you don't move to Edina, you earn it! New money from rising professionals, not trust funders. Once a white-flight haven made safe by sundown laws and racial covenants. Now moderate to liberal elitist but with a strong NIMBY streak. They support more housing for low-income residents—just as long as it's built elsewhere. Not a blade of grass out of place. Masklanders, fer sure.

In Cam's neck of Northeast, she could walk to the bus stop and food coop in five minutes and bike to the riverfront in ten. While the sawmills and factories were long gone, plenty of older Polish families still called "Nord'east" home. In recent decades the area's neighborhoods had drawn Latinos, Somalis and other immigrants. A vibrant arts district and ethnic eateries galore led more than a few students at U of M to stick around after graduation. Her city block wasn't hip, but that made it affordable—at least for now.

Cam did miss Giles and worried her sudden departure during the pandemic might prove too stressful for him, especially if her parents began fighting again. While being on the spectrum cramped his ability to cope at times, he was high functioning both at school and among other gamers online. When mom ordered him off screen, he'd tinker with another model rocket, re-arrange his impressive rock collection for the hundredth time or hang out in her room with the fish. She had always been there for the meltdowns. Twice he'd left a scar, though neither were noticeable. Love bites, she called them. Absent a crash pillow he'd hurl himself at the nearest wall a few times and then wear the bruises without a care. She, and only she, called him Tramp for his endless hours bouncing in the backyard and the way he scurried about wide-eyed like Chaplin in a pickle whenever he misplaced the remote. They texted daily now.

u up

u should
be asleep
tramp

where r u

in bed silly
[yawning face]

where in
the city

nordeast

u should be
in north loop
can walk to
bullseye field

gucci
where i am
[sunglasses]

where in nordeast

near st anthonys
cemetery

geez you live
in a cemetery???
with dead people!!!

haha
get some
winks
luv ya

gn

For his sake, she made a habit of posting pics of her comings and goings. Just no images of the street action, despite his curiosity. What was shared with a smart, curious twelve-year-old had to be filtered. Still, he kept surprising her in his annoying-little-brother way with how much he knew about the uprising.

seen any
boogaloos

where did
u hear
about them
[open mouth]

all over net
wear gas mask
go all black

so not funny

antifas like u
need protection
dontcha know

nice try
not antifa

wanna play
fort fite

another time

u never play

[pouting face]

not my thing
u know that

tom signed in bye!!!

have fun!!
[heart-eyes]

Coming out of high school a house share in the city with no job wasn't where Cam was supposed to land, according to her parents. She certainly wasn't supposed to be lobbing tear-gas canisters back at the police in the dead of night. During the last millennium her mother Zoe had met her father Erik at a karaoke bar on South Street in Philly. Tall and angular, his performance of "Born in the U.S.A." blew her away before the Yards lager on tap evened the field. They dated while he secured an MBA at Wharton and she finished at La Salle. An athletic on-the-go couple, they often jogged Forbidden Drive along the Wissahickon and skinny-dipped once in Shakespeare Pool, to date the biggest dare of her life. He won her heart with frozen peas tossed to the geese and ducks in residence at Valley Green Inn. Eventually they married and moved back to his home state.

When Cam reached school-age her mother insisted she attend parochial Our Lady of Lost Lakes and later Friezelda-St. Mitten's Prep. From their spacious Colonial Revival overlooking Minnehaha Creek, she was shuffled year in and year out from one activity to another by her soccer mom in the family's Ford Emissionade. Her executive dad drove his Toyota Flexus daily to Warbill's HQ in Waygonza, where he kept watch over the corporation's global R&D networks working on animal nutrition, specialty oils and something called food innovation. On weekends come shorts weather he made for the first tee at the country club while mom swam with Cam and Giles at the pool. Summers were spent with her too, sailing and water skiing up north at Lake Vermilion. Dad drove up to the cabin on Friday night if no member tournament was scheduled the next day.

Zoe and Erik invested all they could in their daughter's happiness. Reporting a 4.04 GPA to top-tier schools, she was as fit for admission as any parent in the Land of Lake Snowbegon could expect. Classmates envied her unbeatable list of extra-curricular achievements: standing in the family tradition by winning a blue ribbon for a science exhibit on soil health at the state fair; placing first in the hundred-meter butterfly five years running at sectionals, her flutter as strong as any dolphin's tail; earning a black belt in Taekwondo by age fourteen, the youngest ever to do so at Master Moon's; and superbly playing Anne Sullivan in *The Miracle Worker* her senior year. Clearly, she could attend any college and pursue any career her heart desired. Enduring an increasingly strained marriage, each whispered to themselves, had been worth it.

Only now Cam had gone off the deep end with her dangerous save-the-world fantasies, proclaiming herself a social-justice warrior—whatever that was. Zoe was furious with her impulsive decision to move out, a decision made only a few days after the shocking death of George Floyd. Her abrupt departure became one more argument between husband and wife.

"I can't believe you're letting her waltz out of here just like that," protested Zoe at the time. "Have you bothered to check the news lately? The cities are going up in flames!"

"She's eighteen and hell-bent on going whether we say so or not. Finals were last week, and they've postponed graduation until late July. By then the whole thing will have blown over," replied Erik, sounding like some middle manager desperate to mollify an SVP irate over a bonus-threatening dip in the division's quarterly performance.

"She's on a bender all right, and all you can do is enable."

"Fer cryin' out loud, she'll be back by forty-joo-lie, if not sooner."

"Yeah. Sure."

On the last Sunday in May, day six of the uprising, the Borlaugs had watched Mass together in the living room. No one said a word during brunch. After Cam finished packing, Erik drove her over to Richfield to pick up a futon and bean bag she'd found online. He insisted she let him foot the bill, but she'd already free-mo'd $135 to the seller. Purchases in hand, they drove up the expressway across Saint Anthony Falls Bridge, passing by another Amerizon van en route to the rona-spooked. Glancing down at the waters of the Mississippi, he resisted the urge to remind her of the risks one incurred with online exchanges. Catching a glimpse of BLM protestors amassing on the river's far side, she suppressed her excitement. The less mom and dad knew, the better.

They exited at Bronson, turned left onto 27th and then pulled into the driveway ten blocks later. As Cam unloaded her bike and other belongings, Erik snooped around outside. While scruffy out front, the rental property was surrounded by tidy homes and its backyard was blooming. A young mother pushed her newborn down a well-swept sidewalk. Though closed due to covid, the small park down the street sported shiny new playground equipment. For the first time that day, he exhaled. Then he walked over to where she was waiting, arms folded, and extended a wad of $20s. "Here ya go." She shook her head no-thanks.

"I'll be fine, dad. Tell mom not to worry." She managed a faint smile before bouncing up the front steps.

"Still have the credit card I gave you?" She nodded yes. "Ya wore number ten for the occasion, I see. Skol! Purple is still your favorite color, even if ya could give a fig about the Vikes. Flopped around like a seal in that sweatshirt for years before ya grew--"

"Yah, two sizes too big." Now perched on the top step, she shuffled her feet and looked past him.

"Geez, it seems forever ago now, watchin' Tarkenton with your grandfather and uncles. Hasn't been a better scrambler in the whole league since Frantic Fran hung up the spikes."

"Dad, memory lane is that way, don't cha know." She pointed down the street. Erik looked where he was told. White oaks and Valley Forge elms shaded one sidewalk. Telephone poles lined the other, interspersed with trash cans. A few lawns could use more weedkiller and the neurotic terrier four doors down needed muzzling, but all in all the neighborhood passed muster. An Amerizon van pulled up next door. He shrugged and then looked up at his daughter, blonde hair blowing all about, full-grown and fleeing the nest at first opportunity. At once proud and petrified, he could not take his eyes off her chest. "Ya grown into it, fer sure. Ten is just the right number."

"Thanks for the lift, dad." She smiled blankly and waved before shutting the door behind her. As soon as her father left, she switched into a tie-dye and was off to join the crowd gathering at the bridge.

At the occasional light Erik glanced toward the empty leather seat where he'd tossed the untaken cash. Now what? He was used to solutions and always had insurance in case things went south. He'd delivered everything to his daughter. To whom or to what had he delivered her now? Feeling helpless and no longer needed was strange new territory. Time for the 80s station. Yes, "Hungry Like the Wolf"! What a great concert Duran Duran had given at the Mann Center! Still Zoe's favorite band after twenty-five years. As he drove back over the bridge, head filled with old lyrics, he failed to notice the swarm beneath. Fifteen minutes later he was back in Edina, safe and sound.

After an early dinner, while Zoe sat out back with the still creek and fading sun, he watched Pox News. The lead story: Minnesota State Troopers and the National Guard stand ready to defend the capitol in St. Paul against rioters. Dozens of armored vehicles ringed the building; armed-to-the-teeth phalanxes blocked every point of entry. Finally, after days of mayhem, they've got it under control. His call to the governor's office had made a difference.

A moment later his heart dropped into his stomach when the anchor switched abruptly to a live cam showing young demonstrators on the bridge dodging a tanker truck barreling down on them. He texted Cam. No response. Was she there? No one had been hit. Only the driver was injured, accosted by irate protestors after the rig came to a stop. Still no text. Minutes crawled by, yet each time he picked up the car keys he froze and then let them drop back onto the kitchen table. Waves of regret fell over him followed by panic and another reach for the keys. He stifled the urge to scream, punch a wall, tell his wife. He decided to finish the dishes but cut himself while rinsing a steak knife. For several minutes he stood by the sink staring at the blood dripping from finger onto dishes and down the drain. An hour later Cam texted back.

just saw this
im fine
tell mom
not to worry

This is a huge mistake.

Let me come get you.

sorry im
staying

I can be there
in half an hour.

gotta blast
[waving hand]

Please let me
come get you.

Hello?
Hello?

He kept messaging for another two hours before giving up. The next morning he cancelled two meetings and proceeded to stand cheek by jowl with the great unmasked for three hours outside Every-Ready Rifle, a duck out of water in his oxford polo, khaki shorts and shiny loafers, the lone shaven face in a lot filled with stubbled, bearded mugs. After his device unexpectedly died, he started to notice other gun seekers in his midst. On the backside of the broad fellow just ahead, a huge pig with Spam Museum stenciled into its belly. Emblazoned in bold letters on the next swayback was Jesus Is My Savior, just above the stars and stripes, while below it said Trump Is My President. On the burly chest behind him a Betsy Ross with an I Don't Kneel declaration above it. Looking down he noticed his left shoelace loose but thought it unwise in the moment to bend over for it.

The long, winding line moved slower than the Minnehaha. Around eleven am, after spotting a vintage VW Beetle parked across the street in front of Cannabis Row, a state-sanctioned dispensary, he slipped on shades and wafted into the past. Growing up he'd played Slug Bug with his older brothers during long car trips to Niagara Falls, Yellowstone and, best of all, the Nevada Test

Site. Olav the oldest always reached fifty first, but it was Gunnar who yelled Slug Bug! the loudest and pounded the hardest whenever he lucked out and beat Olav to the punch, as it were. Why could they knock him into the middle of next week, while he never could do likewise? He reached puberty in one piece only because Gunnar always ran a distant third and their dad, a Korean War vet who sold farm equipment for a living, limited them to one round per leg. In high school he drove all over the county playing strip Padiddle with Tula, who saw burned-out headlights at every turn and loved losing as much as winning. What a back-seat driver she was!

Father banned firearms from the house after ten-year-old Gunnar, having mistaken the neighbor's cat for a gopher, blinded it with the 17-caliber he'd received for his birthday. While it felt invigorating to line up for a Glock G19 after all these years, by eleven-thirty Erik's ankles began to ache. Riding a cart on weekends had left him unprepared for this ordeal. To take his mind off things he decided to count shirts sporting flags with the aim of reaching fifty before scoring a handgun. Just the Don't Tread on Me's, Southern Crosses and Jolly Rogers brought him to twenty-six within a few minutes, but his hopes began to fade as the line's pace picked up. Should flag tattoos count? Too easy. When he stepped out of line for a wider view the ugly, porcine stares locked on and drew him, like a Klingon tractor beam, back into place. At high noon he was up to forty-eight flags and just two yards from the front door when a rotund store manager waddled out. After tugging at his praying cowboy belt-buckle he announced Ever-Ready Rifle closed for the day. "Sorry, folks, we're out of stock in every category. Bullets and vests all gone too. But we appreciate the business! Come see us again real soon. Can't be too prepared these days, don't cha know."

A month later Zoe still had not forgiven Erik for aiding and abetting Cam's reckless escapade, nor had she forgiven herself for not stopping her firstborn from flinging herself into the lion's den. For the second time in her life, she was filled with regret for not putting her foot down when it really mattered. Just out of college, her fear of losing him led to the worst decision she'd ever made. Would falling early into the mommy track have been as horrible as he made it sound at the time? She still harbored the suspicion that he'd projected his own insecurities, having no fast-track offers in hand despite the famous name and blue-chip degrees. "Timing's bad," he kept repeating for days until she finally relented. He kept saying it while driving her to the clinic, his words hacking away at her sapling faith until nothing but a stump remained. She told him to wait in the car after he paid the bill for the procedure.

It didn't help that Cam ignored most of their texts and calls, replying only on occasion with brief patronizing assurances. "As independent as ever," he kept saying in reply to her fretting. While he marinated the meat, she chiseled at stains on the tablecloth with a fingernail. "This is insanity. Does she know how dangerous it is? From what I've seen on TV these protests are super-spreader events."

"They're all young, and they're all wearing masks," he observed in a vain attempt to calm her nerves.

She stood up and began pacing. "Masks aren't vaccines! They say we're six months away from having them."

Fourth of July came and went. Two more weeks went by and still no word, even as the Amerizon vans kept coming and going like clockwork. The delayed graduation was now just a week away, and Zoe was livid with them both. "Is she even going? If she doesn't, you are as much to blame as she is, I swear. That she hasn't been arrested or caught covid yet is a miracle." How wrong he'd been about her returning soon!

"For Pete's sake, she may not have aced every course this spring, but she still wound up with a 3.92." She didn't know or care if he was talking about her cumulative GPA or some penny stock's inflated number on the exchange, she just wanted the two of them the hell out of la-la land. She shook her head in disgust, collapsed onto the couch and nursed a cabernet. Erik felt a buzz in his coat pocket. After reading the text he stifled a sigh and refrained from rubbing his eyes. When he tried to show her the message, she waved him off.

"This is as much your fault as hers." She stood up to leave the room.

"Does it really matter? With the masks and distancing it won't be the same." He regretted every syllable the second they'd left his mouth.

"Does it really matter?" echoed Zoe in contempt before she stormed out.

After four years of babysitting gigs, three summers lifeguarding and a habit of stashing away cash from two childless uncles, Cam had managed to bank an impressive $4,567. Her father, a lapsed Lutheran, thought savings and sanctity were synonymous. And since dad knew best when it came to money, that's what she had done. It was as close to a theological stance as he ever came.

First of August she paid for her room, the smallest in the house. Buried in her bean bag, she stared at the screen: a balance of $3,210 equaled at best another five months of rent and lentils. She pushed the laptop aside and gnawed at a fingernail. Spotting an unwary cockroach scuttling by, she popped to her feet and a second later brought her heel down. "Ope!" Her eyes darted to each corner. "Where there's one there's another," she whispered to herself.

Spying no other intruders, she picked up her backpack and headed out the door. She enjoyed her morning ritual of meandering through the arts district, stopping often to peek through a gallery window before bending south on Carwall down to Ruff Love Dogs where she picked up the bike path along the river that brought her to Boom Island Park. There she liked to sit by the water and sip tea before stretching and practicing her hook, axe and crescent kicks. Then it was time for a stroll. As she wandered about, all who crossed her path wore masks and waved. Each day she checked the bubbler. Still off. With restrooms closed, she stayed for as long as her bladder allowed.

Among the park's regulars her favorite by far was an older albino fellow with a long pointy beard who bumbled along with a limp passing out crumbled crackers to the many pigeons flocking about him, a beret always atop his thick mop of wavy bright-white hair. In appearance he resembled El Caballero de París, a street person beloved by many Havañans and memorialized with a bronze statue located in San Francisco de Asís Square, which she and her classmates had seen while on a service trip to Cuba. His name was Antoine, but in her journal she dubbed the feeder of five hundred birds Godol—a makeshift abbreviation of Jesus' parting advice to the Torah scholar who asked about eternal life and was told a parable of mercy.

Word of Godol inspired her housemates to place a jar on the kitchen table and take turns making small donations she delivered more-or-less daily. Upon her approach he always smiled kindly before pulling up his weathered bandana, while she always waved before stopping six feet away. Each time her gaze met his she fell into a cavern filled with light, so deeply inset and luminous were his ocean-blue eyes. While few words passed between them, he always held eye contact for as long as she did. With each passing week their shared gaze grew a little longer—and more loving. After she handed him a few saltines and stepped back he would bow slightly and murmur *merci* before returning to his almsgiving.

What she found most fascinating wasn't the albinism or entrancing gaze or how the rock doves seemed to come in droves from out of nowhere just when he entered the park, always from across the footbridge on the north end. Nor was it how every child on the swings and slides would stop at the same time, as if on command, and wave as he and his flock slowly passed by. Rather, it was how not one bird among so many would depart even when he sometimes arrived empty-handed or was left crumb-less within minutes. Some mornings a half-hour might pass without a speck falling from his palm, yet the chirpy followers at his feet remained ever faithful, taking flight only after he reached the south-end footbridge and bid them adieu with a tip of the beret.

She never could divine if he was homeless or heaven-sent or both. She wondered whether come winter he would come to the park--or if she would. Perhaps ice or an empty checking account or both would end their encounters. No matter. In her heart his warm eyes would always meet hers and stay as long and lovingly as she desired, a gazing without end.

2

LANDING ALONG RIVERS

After meeting with Godol near the playground, Cam walked back toward the boat launch. Better to spend mornings on her own before the strat-chats, banner-art meets and demonstrations. The rippling water evoked visceral memories of similarly aimless hours mucking about the edge of the Minnehaha and taking in Vermilion's crimson surfaces at twilight. Mud between her toes, stones beneath her feet, splashes across her cheeks, loons beckoning one another--these elemental recollections were like keel and compass, she sensed, indispensable for navigating the turbulent uncharted seas ahead.

Returning to her favorite spot along the Great River, she wondered how she'd landed by its edge. Instantly she thought of Sr. Edna, the flyweight nun everyone at school called Sister Yoda. With impish glee she provoked insights simply by asking the right questions. The Yodic method, a devoted coterie called it. In a poll taken for the yearbook, Cam and most every other senior voted her the teacher they'd miss the most.

A raft of books had brought her to this riverbank too. On the reading list for Mr. Pierwink's AP Am History class was Zinn's *A People's History*. Seeing the past through the eyes of victims and those who fought against injustice was both compelling and unsettling, for it meant the comfortable in every generation are confronted with a query labor activist Florence Reese framed as simply and powerfully as anyone: Which side are you on? Cam was determined not to side with the executioners, as Camus put it, whether by settling into silent complicity or blindly calling for law and order amidst the uprising.

On the day before Thanksgiving her junior year, Cam's father had insisted she read an editorial in the *Gall Street Journal* he found moving. Titled "A Hideous Wilderness and a Beauteous Land," a footnote indicated the op-ed had appeared every year on that day since 1961. Serving as a mission statement for the paper's elite audience, it opened with Governor Winthrop's mythical account of the white settler founding and then celebrated the march of progress without a whiff of irony. Before she was done it had dawned on her: deep down her dad believed in manifest destiny and a secular version of the prosperity gospel, and this was his lame attempt at evangelizing her. Another thought arose: he was clueless about the full cost of the affluence he was convinced he'd earned fair-and-square and enjoyed as a matter of birthright, if not divine blessing. Mom, at least, did thank God and the saints for all they had.

Cam also realized she was as complicit as her dream-hoarding parents. Born on third base but no longer sure--as many of her classmates still were--she'd hit a triple. Back then, though, the cost of refusing to conform seemed daunting. In the wake of Black Friday, she felt a nagging sense of helplessness and hypocrisy, mocked daily by the Amerizon deliveries. The orgy of over-consumption--good news for retailers and investors—was near at hand. Part of her wanted no part of it, yet part of her could not part with it.

On the Sunday before Christmas, she watched her mother light the last purple candle on the advent wreath and joined her in a Hail Mary. Two days earlier she and Giles had festooned two silver maples in the front yard with mini-white lights. He dressed the tree, a Norway pine stationed in the living room, with the same. Tinsel was tacky, he declared at age eight, and that was that. He also made the hanging of ornaments and arrangement of nativity scene his sacred mission, neither resting nor eating nor relieving himself until baby Jesus was tucked in and each bauble was perfectly positioned. He set the Star of Bethlehem on high with a precision no Swiss watchmaker could match. Pope Francis sometimes evoked a geometric image—the polyhedron—to convey the ideal of unity-in-diversity amidst a divided world. What Giles wrought was polyhedric: from every angle of vision the tree's symmetry was evident even as myriad shapes and colors bedazzled the eye.

"You always light the white candle on Christmas Eve," noted Zoe. "Your favorite holiday."

"Maybe it's time for Giles to take the torch. I'm not feeling it this year." Her mother wrapped a blanket tight before kissing her on the forehead. She drew Cam close and whispered: "Keep looking for the light. Angels will appear when the time is right."

"So now you're a poet? Please." She nuzzled in closer and closed her eyes. At the time her mother's embrace was the closest she'd come to heaven.

Cam looked up from the Big Muddy at the city skyline. Certainly not Chicago, yet still an impressive downtown anchored by the Capella Tower and fifty-seven story IDS Center where pedestrians could stroll through the largest skyway in the world. Within the Mississippi's vast watershed, stretching from western Pennsylvania to eastern Montana, cities small and large prospered for over a century. Those days were gone for dozens of Midwest towns people were leaving in droves. In 1968, the year her father was born, the country's thirty most prosperous metro regions included five midwestern locales. Now only Chicago and Minneapolis appeared on the list, with the rest all on the coasts. Over the years she had seen more than one mall ghosted by shoppers. Her favorite haunt attempted a face-lift after the Great Recession but failed miserably. No one wanted water slides, jungle gyms and arcades getting in the way of window shopping. Still the cities thrived, though recently they'd slipped out of the Top 20 in the Best Places to Live rankings.

She turned her gaze toward the small lighthouse on the north end. When she was very young her parents took her for a riverboat cruise on the Anson Northrup, a huge side-wheeler that returned to the park's boat launch each night guided by the modest beacon. The riverboat attraction had disappeared years ago after the city decided to slow the spread of invasive Asian Carp by closing St. Anthony Lock. Somewhere in mom's mammoth scrapbook there was a pic of the lighthouse, still painted white with a blue stripe mid-way up its walls. Once she told her a bed-time story about a riverboat lost in a terrible storm and a faint yet steady glow that brought them to safe harbor. The little lighthouse that could, she called it, echoing another favorite tale of hers.

Saving lights. Cam now remembered how floored she'd been watching fifteen-year-old Greta going off on the grown-ups, shredding every excuse they made for dithering on climate action, calling out their betrayal of future generations and demanding they step up or get out of the way. With the world house on fire, she sounded the alarm. The power of one: an autistic teenager who began her lone quest in front of parliament holding a sign that read School Strike for Climate soon was speaking at the United Nations and galvanizing a fast-growing climate-justice movement.

Inspired by Greta and the Sunrise activists occupying the halls of Congress, Cam had written a Valentine's Day love letter to Sister Earth in her journal and vowed to go vegetarian. Later that month she turned seventeen. She already owned a well-stocked aquarium, and for her birthday her father bought her a ferret—another step toward making her room a menagerie. She named her new ball of energy Taz after he took just five minutes to demolish her room. A day in the life of Taz was four hours of total mischief followed by twenty hours sacked out. It took a while to box train the little beast, but eventually he caught on. Giles loved to play with him—for about ten minutes. In March she purchased a ball python and a chameleon, at which point her mother invoked a moratorium. All she cared about was the odor, and Taz could be a bit much. When dad called her Cam of Arc at the dinner table, no one found him funny. Dessert that night was a late-arriving present from her grandmother, who always sent two boxes of Oh Ryan's Irish Potatoes--coconut-cream balls rolled in cinnamon—as soon as they hit the shelves at Acme's in Philly just before St. Patty's Day.

During the spring of 2019 she'd posted hip climate-action memes, lent friends her copy of Klein's *This Changes Everything* and talked up the idea of boycotting school on Fridays to anyone who would listen. While many of Friezelda-St. Mittens' brightest feigned interest and several seemed genuinely enthusiastic, only her signature appeared on the pledge sheet. Walking down the hall, she strategized with her best friend Goldie.

"Forget the Friday strike, Camster. Let's make Earth Day a truly awesome event instead."

"Earth Day, again? That is so last millennium, something our grandmothers did. It's like King's holiday, just another hoop we jump through without knowing why."

"We'll make it all about climate justice, you'll see. We can cast Greta on the wall above the cafeteria door. Oh, I know! We'll get everybody to abstain from meat for an entire week, and we'll get Charles to calc up the greenhouse-gas emission savings each day and announce the running tally each morning. Once everyone sees what a difference we're making, we'll make meatless Fridays a thing. It's *totally* Catholic, don't cha know."

"Seriously?"

Goldie halted suddenly and placed her hands on her hips. "Tough tomatoes, Borlaug, the whole school knows we're frying the planet, but no one is going to blow every Friday off. Not even you." Golda Bloch was among a handful of Jewish students at Friezelda-St. Mittens, which some Reformed families found preferable to Bais Yaakof where more tradition-minded parents sent their daughters. She and Cam had met while taking a modern-dance class at Wellstone JCC and been close since sophomore year. They shared a blue ribbon, won at the state fair for their nifty report on the rhizosphere. It was Goldie who convinced her to become a vegetarian. The grand-daughter of Ernst Bloch, a prominent German-Marxist philosopher, her parents were successful architects and active in Minnesota's Democratic-Farmer-Labor Party.

Sullen in defeat, Cam kicked a locker. "I hate you, Bloch. I really do."

"Love ya too!" she clapped back before ducking into Doc O'Donner's room for AP Am Lit. An aspiring journalist, she edited the school newspaper and constantly shared the latest livestream. What Cam knew of breaking news usually came from her. Despite her pragmatic stance on Fridays for the Future, she had more sisu than most. A real one. Someday Golda Bloch would be reporting live from the front.

Cuba had been a real turning point, Cam now realized. She and her classmates helped organic farmers prune fruit trees, repair windbreaks, spread mulch, lay out new driplines, build raised garden beds. They planted chayote and chard, dug up carrots and potatoes, picked mangos and papayas. Twenty-three farms, none larger than four hectares, grew thirty-two different crops each year. The produce sold well in nearby towns, and all proceeds were shared equally. On their last day volunteering, the students ate lunch at the community center with Chano Guillen, a permaculture expert whose institute supported the coop. After introducing Chano, a balding middle-aged Afro-Cuban with big cheeks and a bright smile, Sister Yoda gave a blessing. It wasn't long before the criollo stew and fried plantains were gone.

Chano stood up to speak. "Forgive my English, it's as cold as Montreal where I studied a long, long time ago!" He paused for the polite laughter. "This coop is named after Antonio Guiteras, a Yanqui revolutionary from Philadelphia. In the 1930s he founded Joven Cuba, the student movement that overthrew the dictator Machado and agitated against Batista in the 1950s. The Castro brothers and Che succeeded with militant support from many students and peasants. I come here often to collect data, exchange ideas and train local leaders, but I work most closely with a bigger coop in Duhrsey, about fifteen kilometers to the north."

The students looked at each other quizzically. "Duhrsey? Like the chocolate?" one asked.

Chano lifted a foot to the bench and began tapping a beat. "Yes, before the revolution the company shipped sugar to their Dollops factory in Pennsylvania. Then the Fidelistas set up state-owned farms and exported sugar to the Soviet Union, but when the Berlin Wall fell the oil from Russia dried up. That was the beginning of the end for the Green Revolution in Cuba."

A junior named Vibol voiced everyone's confusion: "Pardon me, Mr. Guillen, but what do you mean by 'end of the revolution'? Aren't the communists still in control?"

Chano lowered his foot and waved a hand, as if erasing a blackboard. "I'll start again. In the 1960s the American embargo was strangling the revolution in its crib, so the Soviets sent oil and tractors. Back then the Green Revolution promised bigger yields. You mechanize, plant new seed varieties, spray lots of chemicals and scale up production of export crops. Buy whatever you don't grow from other countries. Both the capitalist West and the Soviet bloc adopted this industrial monoculture model--"

"Oh, I get it," interrupted Goldie. "When the Russians pulled the plug in the early 1990s there was no way to fuel the factory farms, so the government gave the land back to the peasants and encouraged them to go organic."

Chano smiled and raised both arms high, as if joining a wave. "Yes, precisely!" He put his foot back up and resumed the beat. "During the transition lots of people lost weight. Fried grapefruit rinds passed for steak. Many urban gardens and rural coops sprang up. The permaculture method they adopted takes more labor, but when done right it's just as productive as industrial farming and kinder to the earth. Our organic farms weather blights and hurricanes better too." He patted his belly playfully and pointed to the empty pot. "Best of all, the stews taste better. Cubans love to eat!"

"Did the whole country go organic?" asked Mr. Pierwink once the chuckling subsided.

Chano brought his foot down, shook his head and waved his arms low, like a referee signaling a missed penalty shot. "We still import lots of wheat and still run state farms with oil from the Venezuelans. But the number of coops is growing. Since 2014 the government has distributed land-use titles to 300,000 farmers. Our goal is to show them agro-ecology is the future. You aren't free when you have to depend on others for food, energy and other essentials."

Vibol, whose Cambodian father had escaped the Khmer Rouge, could not let his comment go unchallenged. "Mr. Guillen, I don't mean to be rude, but isn't it also true that you aren't free in a one-party state? Isn't your country's transition to democracy long over-due? My grandparents were killed by the communists simply because they were Catholic, could read French and ran a productive rice farm."

Chano nodded and smiled sadly. He picked up a clump of red dirt, held it out and turned it over in his hand. Everyone watched the wind carry loose granules away as the dirt-clump quickly shrank to marble size. Then his fingers gently enveloped what was left. He lowered his arm and spoke directly to Vibol: "I am sorry your family suffered. My people fought and died for independence, yet nothing changed after the Spanish left. The dream of José Martí was betrayed. We still cut cane and washed clothes for whites as we always had. In 1912 Afro-Cuban veterans, mambis they were called, revolted in the province of Oriente. U.S. Marines poured in to protect the sugar mills and copper mines, while the army crushed the rebellion. Afterwards, they hunted down and killed members of the Partido Independiente de Color. Think of them as Cuba's black panthers—slaughtered for daring to organize and speak out. That is how my grandfather died."

"*Black Panther* was the bomb!" blurted Todd.

"Uff-da, you *didn't* just say that," sighed Cam. Student eyes rolled. Mr. Pierwink covered his face and turned away.

Chano waited a moment before returning his foot to the bench. "Fidel was no Pol Pot. He was educated by Jesuits. Catholics are building new churches here. Three popes and President Obama have come to the island. If farmers take care of the land they've been granted, their land-use titles will be honored."

"But they still don't own the land they've been given," countered Vibol. His classmates spun at once toward him, caught by surprise at his insistent tone. Rarely did their well-mannered, door-holding friend turn combative—especially with elders. When matters of principle were at stake, though, a pillar of iron appeared. All eyes remained on him, while his remained locked onto their host.

Chano did not blink. "You are forgetting the bigger picture and greater danger, my friend. The conquistadors took the best land by force, wiped out the Indigenous peoples and brought in African slaves by the millions. That story you know from your own history, but our experience has been shaped by Yanqui imperialism and other powerful forces. For centuries the Catholic church sanctified private property and told peasants to pray, pay and obey. Bishops blessed colonial troops sent to put down uprisings. Priests and nuns ran private schools and hospitals for the rich. There were exceptions, of course. Bartolomé de las Casas, some Jesuits, the revolutionary priest Miguel Hidalgo—they defended the poor. But in the 19th-century Bolívar and the liberals wrote property rights into their constitutions once they won independence. That was Cuba in 1898. Weak governments across Latin America allowed foreign companies and the banks in London and New York that funded them to buy up vast tracts of land for next to nothing."

"Banana republics," interjected Goldie.

"Yes, exactly!" replied Chano as he resumed the beat. "During this time a single U.S. company, Fantastic Fruits, owned millions of hectares throughout

Central America and brutally exploited their workers. If peasants revolted and the dictators ran scared, then in came the Marines. Smedley Butler, one of your most decorated commanders, finally resigned in disgust. When a reporter asked why, he said he could no longer be a gangster for capitalism."

"And you're afraid of a re-play if Cuba ever let the corporations roll in and have their way," cut in Cam. "They might modernize production and increase yields, but control over the land would be in foreign hands."

"That's right. Look at what is happening to Puerto Rico after Hurricane Maria. The disaster capitalists are descending on the island. They'll turn it into another playground for the rich if they can."

"Sounds like what New Orleans went through after Katrina," noted Mr. Pierwink. On campus he kept his political cards close to the chest, but all his students knew where he stood. At one morning meet he'd played along with a script provided by Goldie and other editors of the Lampoon. Getting Mr. Pierwink to out himself as a socialist was great fun.

"These companies always find a way to re-invent themselves and target new territories," said Chano. "Fantastic Fruits is now Banana Guapo. Not long ago they were caught paying murderous paramilitary thugs to protect their holdings. They're still in court pretending they had nothing to do with the atrocities they financed."

"Wait, did you say Banana Guapo? My mom buys their bananas all the time!" exclaimed one shocked student.

"Mine too!"

"And mine!"

Sensing things were getting out of hand, Sister Yoda attempted a re-direct: "Before we return to Havana tomorrow, we are going to early Mass in Jaruco."

The collective groan drew a smirk from Chano.

"What happened to your people after the revolution?" asked Vibol.

"Things got better. The Fidelistas put anti-discrimination laws in place and set up literacy programs. But decrees don't change hearts and minds. Whites still deny Afro-Cubans access to good jobs. The government keeps saying there's no race problem, and so people don't talk about it. They yap about baseball and Beyoncé instead. This denial of reality does not help the situation."

"Sounds like a revolution within the revolution is coming," mused Cam.

A wide grin flashed across Chano's face. His foot-tapping went up-tempo. "You may be right. Internet use is growing on the island. I got my first cell-phone last month! In San Isidro now there's a movement of Rastafarians, artists and journalists pushing for more freedom. I hope they will succeed." Then his smile began to fade while his foot fell silent. He raised his arm and opened his fist. All eyes fell upon the red marble teetering in the breeze. "We know our past. A true social democracy can't grow in soils controlled by dictators and the wealthy. They push the poor off the land for sugar and cattle. They decimate the wildlife draining wetlands for resorts. It comes down to this: we must protect our gardens from invasive species, or we will lose everything." He closed his fist and remained still, like a statue in the square. Only his dark eyes moved, from one student to the next. Though Cam's gaze met his for only a second, it seemed a century passed between them. Finally, he spoke: "I'm told the homeless in your cities are free to sleep under bridges. I hope you can see why we do not envy them." A moment later his affable manner returned. He brought his foot down and took a few steps away from the tables. "Building up good soil is hard and sometimes boring--as you discovered this week!" The students laughed heartily, grateful for the levity. "I must return to the fields. Thank you for coming. You are always welcome. We need more friends in America!" As he turned to go, everyone except Todd stood up and waved farewell. Cam caught up to him and flashed a warm smile, which he mirrored.

"Chano, any chance we can stay in touch? I promise I won't pester you."

"Of course!" They exchanged numbers and a hug.

Internet was available for tourists at the airport in Havana. Before boarding Goldie sent a group text with a link to the website of a watchdog group for the global chocolate industry.

over 1M kids
in west africa
work on cocoa farms
95% under dangerous
conditions some
as forced laborers

u mean slaves

dirty duhrsey
[angry faces]

totally sucks
[crying face]

i still like dollops
dontcha know
[smiling poos]

thx for sharing
[cowboy hat face]

says warbill
makes a killing
off the exports

cams dad
works there
[open mouth]

now that was cold
outing him like that

sorry cam!
[person bowing]

ya he works
at warbill
will ask
him about this

but u wont
cancel him
if theres blood
on his hands

so not funny

time to go
fair trade

ikr
[hundred points]

i still like dollops
dontcha know
[smiling poos]

really todd???

No [heart]

Once the Airbus dropped under the clouds, Cam looked down from her window seat at the winding rivers below. Soon they landed just a few hundred yards west of where the Minnesota and Mississippi meet. Disturbed more than she had let on by the possibility that Warbill was complicit in the exploitation of children and destruction of the environment, she was eager to speak with her father.

3
FATHERS ON THE GRILL

On the drive back to Edina from the airport, Cam now recalled, she had interrogated her dad on Warbill's business in West Africa. He didn't know the details but assured her the company operated within the law.

"Honey, ya may not know, but foreign corporations are the gold standard for employment in developing countries. In the bush you're a hero if ya land a job with a Warbill or a Beastlé. The money you make supports a dozen family members! Many villages wouldn't survive if we pulled out. As for the Ivory Coast and Ghana, I know we recently signed on to the Cocoa & Forests Initiative and have an action plan. I'll send ya a copy. Sound good?"

"Maybe a little too good. The activists say it's been twenty years since promises of reform were made, but nothing much has changed. Dad, I want you to take this seriously. No PR run-around or corp-speak."

"You betcha. The Warbill Way means something. My R&D group is all about the future of food, a future that works for everyone."

"I saw a different future for food in Cuba, one that doesn't depend so much on the Warbills of the world."

"Well, don't forget it's the paycheck from Warbill that pays for trips to Cuba and private-school tuition and--"

"That is so unfair, and you know it."

"Just remember, you're a Borlaug."

Cam grew silent and looked out the car window. She thought back to the blue ribbon at the state fair and how those clapping also were pointing to the statue of her granduncle, the Nobel Prize-winning father of the Green Revolution. It wasn't the first time she'd stood on his shoulders. Among her earliest memories was a family trip to visit him in Texas. She had straddled him, still strong after ninety years, and kept squealing giddy-up as he whinnied and swayed back and forth until mom pulled her off. Her father took immense pride in his uncle's work and believed he was carrying forward a legacy of saving the world from hunger. She wondered why Chano had recounted one of the great stories of the twentieth century but left out so central a character as Norman Borlaug.

"Dad, I'm just saying the latest science doesn't solve all problems. At some point the technological treadmill will be seen for what it is: a false hope."

"Geez, just like your mother: always the last word."

"Don't forget to send the document."

During free period the next morning she poured over the company's action plan. Only one brief reference to women and youth in a vague section on promoting community development. Lots of action steps to protect old-growth forests, but nothing about due-diligence standards, nothing about paying a farm gate price sufficient to cover a living income for the smallholders, nothing about greater transparency in the supply chain. According to the latest Cocoa Beat report, Warbill was dead last among the six major buyers in its ability to trace bulk cocoa purchases back to the source. So much for conscious capitalism.

After school she hung out with Goldie, who as usual was in the know ahead of her. "It's not just dirty chocolate, don't cha know. Greengroan has been taking Warbill to the woodshed for quite a while. They signed an agreement to protect rainforests in Indonesia from palm-oil plantation expansion and then didn't follow through."

"Another empty promise. Sounds familiar." She stood up, pulled off her Frantic Fran sweatshirt and nodded to Goldie, who tossed a couch pillow that she swivel-kicked into the recliner across the room, the thwacking noise drawing a nervous bark from Goldie's black lab Luna. Bullseye. She tugged a bit at her athletic bra and nodded again. Thwack. Bullseye.

"Get this," said Goldie. "Warbill built ports along the Amazon and roads into the rainforest--all to grow and export soy, most of which is for animal feed. That infrastructure gave farmers the green light to slash and burn."

"No pun intended, of course."

"Of course. In 2014 the company committed publicly, at a UN Climate Summit no less, to go deforestation-free by 2020 but then went back on their word. Just blowing smoke."

"Touché, darling." Another nod, another bullseye. She retrieved the pillows and plopped them next to Goldie before hopping over the coffee table and curling into a love seat.

"I'm just getting started. Bolsonaro, the new Brazilian president, vowed to open Indigenous lands and other protected areas to unrestricted development. This is a guy who said not long ago, and I quote, 'It's a shame the Brazilian cavalry wasn't as efficient as the Americans, who exterminated their Indians.' No cap."

"So the green light to blow tons more smoke into the lungs of the planet just got, dare I say it, even greener."

"Yep. And here's the sad part: Warbill had complied for the most part with the previous government's soy moratorium. Before Bolsonaro the deforestation rate was declining. By the way, any time ya want to break open the smacks, be my guest." She kept tapping her index finger on the edge of her laptop.

"All in good time, my pretty." Cam ripped open the bag, pulled out a dollop, peeled back the gold foil and sunk her teeth into delicious darkness. "Always *so* good…"

"That is *totally* wrong. You *know* how much I love them." A few seconds later Cam lobbed a goodie over.

"Just one?" She paused before unwrapping. "This calls for meelk."

"Be a good Goldie Retriever and bring me some." Goldie flipped her the bird on her way to the kitchen, returning with two glasses and a gallon jug. She poured with a look so sour Cam thought the milk would prove undrinkable.

"How about you share a pair this time, if it's not too much to ask." Cam tossed one over.

"Borlaug, you can be *so* niggardly at times, I swear."

"Uff-da, you *didn't* just say that." She grabbed a handful and flung them across the table.

"Works every time!" She gathered half a dozen off the floor. "So, what are we going to do? Maybe your father has some pull."

"Warbill is way big, and he's not *that* far up the totem pole. Plus, he doesn't have an activist bone in his body. Grey flannel suit guy. What can I say?"

"Then we'll go after them ourselves. We love tilting at windmills!" Excited at the thought of a children's crusade, she quickly undressed three dollops, popped them in her mouth and chased them down with four big swigs followed by a long burp.

"Isch! That is so…"

"I believe the phrase you're looking for is wretched excess. Anyway, I'm all out, so fork over--"

"Liar, I yeeted half the bag at you!" A minute later Goldie began to whimper--just the way Luna did when she had to go pee--and would not stop. The dollop eventually thrown over disappeared instantly down her throat. Only four were left now, but Cam concealed the fact. She sat up and poured some more milk. "Warbill knows how to fly under the radar. Huge as they are, they aren't publicly traded and don't own any visible brands we can lean on."

"Facts. We can't start a divestment campaign or a consumer boycott." Her finger was tapping hard again on the laptop's edge.

"Yah, they seem to have no pain point. We could try an indirect approach and go to the bigger companies that buy in bulk from them and demand they pull the plug—or else."

"Good luck with that." She ran a hand through the creases of the couch in hope of finding lost treasure. "Guess your dad is off the hook, at least for now."

"I'm afraid so. I don't want to troll him if there's nothing he can do. But I am going to make him squirm, don't cha know."

"There's got to be another way, we just haven't figured it out yet." Suddenly she squealed with delight. "Found one!" She sat up quickly, ripped off the foil and shoved the glob down her gullet. Cam looked with horror as the Cheshire-cat smile widened.

"Seriously, Bloch, you need help."

"Actually, I've never been better." She poured herself another glass and drained it so fast Cam was tempted to look up the Guinness World Record then and there.

"Oh my God, another one!" she shrieked a few seconds later, yanking her hand from beneath her bottom.

"Thanks for sharing, Gloop girl."

"Don't mention it." After belching she adjusted her bra, which now seemed a bit tight. She stared across the table. "Tell me friend, tell me please, is Duhrsey a fiend or a disease?"

"Wagging our tail after that witty one, aren't we now."

"I was born to wag, baby." She stood up and bent over, ready to twerk.

"Down, sick puppy." Goldie gave her a few quick shakes and then complied.

"There is one other option, but it's a long shot: the U.S. could work with the EU to make Warbill, Duhrsey and the rest clean up their act, even if it means you and millions of other chocaholics have to pay a higher price."

"Well, if smokers can cough up more dollars for their death sticks, surely we can find a few quarters for our fix! It's not like chocolate is a necessity," pronounced Goldie as she devoured the last dollop in her possession.

"You're so full of it, Bloch. Soon you'll be in withdrawal, on your knees shaking like a leaf and drooling as you *beg* for just one more." Cam withdrew another from the vault and took her time removing the gold foil before placing it delicately on her tongue and slowly licking her fingers. "Last one is always the best…" A moment later she had the wet chunk on display between her front teeth. With her tongue she rolled what remained across her lips.

"I so hate you right now. How can you torture me like that and live with yourself!"

Cam smacked her lips and jumped up, bag in hand. "Sike, there's three left!" she cackled before racing out of the room. Too bloated to take up the chase, Goldie stared into her empty glass a long second before closing her laptop and sagging into the cushions.

A moment later she clapped back hard. "Screw you, Borlaug! I've got your smelly old sweatshirt and I'm *not* giving it back! Ever!" Luna bounded into the room barking and jumped on her. "Down dog!" she yelled, only to land flat on the floor amidst a flurry of paws and frothy licks. The over-excited lab finally relented after sniffing out a stray dollop and absconding with it.

"Luna, no! Cam, the dog's got one! It'll kill her!" Seconds later she heard a yelp and the sound of frantic scratching on polished hardwood. Cam walked into the room with Luna right behind her. Between middle finger and thumb lay the treat, a bit tattered now and dripping with drool but still edible to the desperate. She dangled it near Goldie's nose and nodded to her sweatshirt on the couch. "Fair trade?"

"Isch, no way!" She looked up at Cam defiantly. "You still have three left. By rights I have at least one more coming."

Cam glared at her contemptuously. "By *what*? Nice try, but no cigar." Being in a commanding position was even better than commanding the moral high ground. Luna sat obediently next to her. Dogs always knew what side to take.

"Just one more, I'm begging you."

"This *is* the last one. I ate the others."

"You did not."

"No cap." She waited a moment before slowly lifting her other hand. In her palm lay a crinkly gold marble, the compressed remains of three wrappers. She let the evidence drop onto the oriental rug. A still prostrate Goldie reached for it, but a firm foot came down first. "Ope!" The gold marble was now a gold coin.

"Final offer: the last morsel for the sweatshirt. You have three seconds to decide."

"Deal," she muttered a moment later. Cam bent over and retrieved her property. She glanced at Luna and whistled sharply. The dog trotted out dutifully. Then she flicked the drippy dollop into a far corner of the room; it came to rest after collecting lint and hair of the lab. "Go fetch. And be sure to get your goop before the dog does. I'm *not* doing this again."

Since the service trip Cam often thought about whether Chano's agro-ecology cooperatives were a viable alternative to the chemical-based Big Ag her granduncle and father championed. That June the rains kept coming throughout the Midwest and turned the Corn Belt into one giant mud pit. Thousands of farmers working millions of acres delayed planting. They saw ephemeral gullies form on bare fields as the relentless downpour swept tons of topsoil away. Many filled in the fast-forming gullies with precious loam one week only to watch more rain wash it out the next. Watching the downpour out her bedroom window as Taz sniffed about, Cam shared what was happening with Chano, whose downpour of text she found both amusing and erudite:

Civilization depends
on ten inches of topsoil,
yet soil levels across Iowa
and other breadbasket
states
have dropped from sixteen
inches to just six.
Despite the Dust Bowl,
most of your farmers
still don't plant
soil-conserving
cover crops or use
no-till planting.

Just as your buffalo
and prairie grasslands
have disappeared,
so will the tractors
and combines.
Not overnight,
but sooner than
you think.

big yikes
btw u ever
heard of an
agronomist
named Borlaug

Are you joking?

he was my
dads uncle
dontcha know

Why didn't you tell me
during your visit!
I would have given him
a big shout out!

even though
you believe
everything hes
made possible
is wrong

Unintended consequences
come with every
innovation.

including
agroecology

We shall see!

lol

Good to chat, ciao.

Bye!
[heart]

At the end of June, Goldie had sent Cam a two-word text with a link:

must read
https://www.earthroar.org/whompwarbill

The press-release title was blunt: Warbill - The World's Worst Company. Cam skimmed over the corporate crimes going back decades, recognizing some but not others. She wasn't familiar with the group either. Earth Roar? Did they really go by that name? She read on:

> The release of Earth Roar's exposé kicks off a multi-year campaign demanding Warbill eliminate deforestation and human rights abuses from its supply chain. Earth Roar called attention to Warbill's irresponsibility with a rally outside company headquarters in Minnesota at which they awarded the race-to-the-bottom winner a thumbs down placard.

Had her father seen the demonstration? How could she get involved? A reply to her inquiry came quickly:

> Hi, Cam:
> We meet every Tuesday at U of M. 7 pm in the Student Center, Room #362. Next action is still in the works. Come help us figure out how to Whomp Warbill!
> For the future,
> Heather
>
> Thanks, Heather. I'll be there!

Excitement turned to disappointment when she realized that, with Goldie heading off in two days to her summer gig as a counselor at an overnight camp, she was on her own. A driver's license never seemed that important. Vibol ferried her to FSM most mornings, while mom picked her up after play practice. Goldie drove them to MOA or another party at Clare's boujee house. During the summer she rode her bike to the club, and at the lake it didn't matter in the least. In a pinch she always could count on dad, a plow parent if ever there was one, but asking him to taxi her into town and wait around while she trashed his company was a bit much. Ditto for three buses over three hours, or even the price of an uber lift both ways. As she stared at the email to Heather saying she couldn't make it after all, the words of Chano rang in her ears: you aren't free if you have to depend on others for essentials.

As the summer of 2019 had come to a close, Cam now remembered, she read *When They Call You a Terrorist*, a memoir written by BLM co-founder Patrisse Khan-Cullors. She barely made it through the stories of Patrisse's mentally ill brother Monte. During one manic episode he was shot by police with rubber bullets, tased and charged with terrorism. His experience was at once familiar and utterly foreign to her. She grappled with the disquieting notion that blind luck, another spin of the cosmic roulette wheel, had placed Giles within a supportive cocoon while Monte was left to the wolves.

After finishing the book, America's original sin seemed like a permanent stain. Weren't the advances made by every anti-racist movement—from slave revolts to abolition to reconstruction to civil rights and now BLM—inevitably rolled back by black codes and lynch mobs, racial covenants and redlining, mass incarceration and Driving While Black? These days Jim Crow was rebranded as James Crow, Esq. and now operated through gentrification, voter role purges, ID requirements and gerrymandering. Tomorrow her senior year would begin, and Cam wanted to hear what her diminutive mentor had to say.

After the final bell she walked into Sister Yoda's classroom and unburdened herself, beginning with an emotional reprise of what the Montes of the world face and ending with the question of theodicy. The spry nun listened patiently and then responded as always with a question.

"Is this a crisis of meaning for you or a crisis of faith?"

Immediately Cam grasped the question's import, her mind racing back through last year's discussions. For any thoughtful person of faith, Sister Yoda suggested, occasional crises of meaning are inevitable and necessary. One learns to let go of old metaphors so that one can image and experience God as, say, a mother, lover and friend instead of stern Father. What if God is not "up there" with a skyhook lifting the righteous into heaven but rather continually "out ahead" inviting all creatures to become more alive and more beautiful? In both theology and science, such questions spark insights that transform one's vision. It follows that sin and evil are at root a refusal to learn and love as God intended, a fearful clinging to limited conceptions of self and reality that distort one's capacity to care for others and the world.

Even more profound is a crisis of faith, suggested Sister Yoda. At stake is one's basic trust in and openness to Absolute Mystery. The reality of God grounds all reality—even if one's grasp of the real and true is always partial, always a seeing as through a glass darkly. *Ecclesiastes* said it best: "God set eternity in the hearts of humans, yet none fathom what God has done from beginning to end." But what if no Source and Ground of Being exists, and humans are nothing but "a bunch of chemical reactions running around in a bag," as Dean Hamer put it? Then nihilism is the only alternative, not secular humanism, for the latter is simply a distant cousin in the family of faith. On the one hand, both theist and secular humanist find goodness and meaning woven into the fabric of things, even though at times the fabric may appear frayed almost beyond recognition. On the other hand, the nihilist sees only loose threads lying about, some of which she may find to her liking as she fashions her own self. When nothing but one's own will matters, what is sown this way or that may be tossed aside, ripped to shreds or burned to a crisp without a care. Each day, then, every human being faces a fundamental choice: open one's life to God and live under a higher law, come what may, or make one's own way amidst the absurdity, ever tempted to fancy oneself a god.

"I'm not sure," Cam finally said. "I believe there's a point and purpose to it all, but so much suffering seems meaningless. Evil never goes away."

"That's right, it never does," replied Sister Yoda, her own memories of Maryknoll mission work in war-torn Central America now returning to haunt her. So many disappeared, so many dismembered by fascists armed and trained by the U.S. military at Fort Benning in Georgia. Despite all the protests, the Pentagon simply changed the counter-terrorism school's name and then took the tactics they'd honed and applied them a few years later in Iraq and at Guantanamo Bay. Principalities and powers. All you can do is bear witness and wait upon the light, even as you work as if everything depends on you.

"I'm choking on the idea that history is a vast training ground for soul-making," said Cam. "It turns life into an obstacle course, with the blood and tears worth it in the end if we become stronger, nobler souls who inspire others. For the martyrs you told us about, it makes sense. But that still leaves too many nameless who just get run over and left for dead."

"Perhaps all we can do is cast our lot with the oppressed, stand in solidarity with the poor. That's a choice we can make. Here at Friezelda-St. Mitt's, it's going to involve a journey beyond privilege that requires uncommon courage."

"Yah, I've been thinking about that. Privilege means freedom from fear, freedom from want, freedom from paying full freight when you mess up. Around here we get involved when it's convenient, not when it's costly. Yet activists like Khan-Cullors don't waste their time guilt-tripping. They say white allies should be motivated by a passion for justice and a desire to dismantle a racist system that degrades all people. Despite everything, they still dream—only without illusions."

Sister Yoda smiled kindly at Cam, the best student she'd had in a decade. "Where's your dream taking you these days?"

"I haven't forgotten what you said after the Parkland shooting about focusing one's time and energy without going OCD on any one issue. The Line 337 pipeline, the abortion industry, the prison-industrial complex--on and on it goes. I'm seeing more clearly what the culture of death looks like, and it's scary. I still think climate justice needs to be my priority. There's a big event at the state capitol in a few weeks."

"I'm planning to go with my green-sister brigade."

"See ya there!" She blew a kiss on her way out.

A few days later Cam and Goldie had played dead with fifty other Earth Roarers in the long, quiet hallways of the Minneapolis Art Institute, which included a wing donated by Warbill and thus was deemed a strategic target. Cam was thrilled to meet Heather in the flesh. As tall and athletic as she was, Heather could be naturally effervescent one moment, kindly diplomatic in another and edgily indifferent in still another. The supple young organizer put her and Goldie to work holding the lead banner: There's No Art on a Dead Planet. The die-in was ER's first major action since the Whomp Warbill campaign kick-off back in July. While Pox's camera mostly passed by the bodies strewn about, the reporter saw fit to interview telegenic Heather at length. Afterward the event was deemed a resounding success by everyone except Jordan, an aging Roarer with a grisly beard who had brought his five-year-old granddaughter along to die with him.

"Jordan, I understand your concerns, but this *was* a local broadcast," noted Heather. Engaging yet firm, Cam thought. And such poise. She was an event unto herself.

"Pox will send the footage straight to New York where they'll doctor it beyond recognition. They'll paint us as pinkos and cast the movement as a vast conspiracy to deprive red-blooded Americans of their right to eat meat whenever they choose, God's good earth be damned," he warned, both arms flailing.

"Bubbee, I gotta pee," insisted the young girl bouncing up and down beside him.

"Not so fast, Jordan. Our message was heard by moderate Minneapolitans who watch Pox to stay abreast of what's happening in the community," observed Ruth, a petite tie-dyed boomer with long braided hair who, instead of drawing media attention by feigning death, had garnered eight petition signatures from passers-by.

"Pox is state media, and the state exists to protect corporate miscreants like Warbill. Whoever among us invited them to cover our action did more harm than good."

"Bubbee, I really gotta go." Now the little child looked like she was skipping rope.

"I'm almost done, Rachel. Just be patient, will you."

Ruth was out of patience. "We heard you, Jordan, now take her to the restroom before it's too late."

"Who's handling media outreach? I want to know--"

"Enough! The child is nearly in tears!" Ruth took the squirming girl by the hand and marched off to find relief. Sensing the debrief had out-run its usefulness, Heather tried to close out the evening on a high note by inviting everyone to let loose a primal scream. "On my count, let us bring forth the Earth Roar we wish to hear in the world! One, two…"

For Cam the release at three felt volcanic. No one else roared with such gusto. Still, the collective effort was rather mighty, if not deafening. But as their volume began to fade, Jordan suddenly clutched his chest and collapsed, his wizened cheek coming to rest on the grill of a storm drain. Once the gasps and scuffling about subsided, the only sound heard before the sirens arrived was Rachel weeping.

True to her word, Goldie followed up the Earth Day event with a meat-free Friday campaign, which at the time was received with enthusiasm by the school's elderly chaplain Fr. Albert B. Creamer, known to all as Father C, who was fighting his own uphill battle to interest the student body in morning rosary, advent novenas and other traditional observances. By finals week, Charles calculated, total hydrocarbon-emission reductions had equaled an impressive

683 Whoppers uneaten. Come the fall, however, Father C was less excited when Goldie, together with the popular new student group Tran Vegans for Life, proposed re-branding Fast for the Future as Fire Grill Fridays. TVL also was pushing the school to cancel cafeteria vendor Terramock, a food-service corporation tied to farm-animal abuses, rainforest destruction, plastic-straw peddling and other patently anti-life activities.

"Golda, our students were just beginning to get the idea before summer break. You'll sow confusion and undermine the whole effort with this gratuitous name change. It takes time for these kinds of things to take hold," counseled the old cleric.

"*Time* is running out, Father. There won't *be* a future if we don't light a fire under the student body and cut our fossil-fuel emissions in half by graduation."

"I fear your proposal is too provocative. I'm trying to engage with all student groups and bring everyone together. The Young Benedicts agreed to endorse the fast because it affirms their Catholic identity. I imagine their contribution to the cause has been considerable."

Aalia Bhargatya, TVL's spokesperson at the meeting, was done waiting. "Father C, may my voice be heard now, or does your male gaze attend only to Goldie?" Two inches taller than the avuncular priest, she told Goldie she'd give him five minutes—and not one nano-second more. A descendant of Brahmins from New Delhi and shoe-in for valedictorian, her stateside relatives included a billionaire entrepreneur and dark-money lord for the tea-party crowd in Michigan. Amerizon had thrown six figures and a hefty signing bonus at her older brother Fitan, Friezelda-St. Mitt's 2015 valedictorian, to join the company's secretive R&D group in data science. After a few years slumming in Seattle, he planned to study number theory at Princeton with his celebrated cousin Maanas, a recent winner of the Fields Medal and the youngest tenured faculty member at the prestigious institution.

"Oh, how rude of me, Alibi, for not--"

"It's pronounced Aalia," she snapped.

"Yes, of course. So sorry, my dear. This tinnitus of mine--"

"I am *not* your dear," she declared, the urge to lecture him on micro-aggressive language intense.

"Aalia, yes. I do apologize. Please, tell me how you see things." Father C found ministering to youth more trying with each passing year, their texting endless and argot indecipherable.

The Brahmin with jet-black hair, bushy eyebrows and hourglass figure pulled a large piece of paper out of her bookbag. "Our research shows the Young Benedicts and their kind are responsible for a whopping sixty-nine percent of our school's ecological footprint. This is male entitlement of the worst kind." She placed the spreadsheet on his desk, stepped back and folded her arms. Goldie folded hers in solidarity.

"It's all there. And be assured, the methodology Charles used is flawless." Aalia's reginal bearing, not to mention her bling, never failed to impress Goldie; everyone thought her diva drip iconic.

"Heavens, our boys do eat a lot more burgers than the girls," muttered Father C after perusing the data.

"Did you just say *our* boys, and then say *the* girls?" The flummoxed priest, palms now pressed together and positioned just below his collar, did not know what to say. He stared past them at the portrait of Saint John Paul II hanging on the far wall, no longer wondering why there were so few altar girls these days.

"Father, are you ignoring me on purpose?" While waiting her visage had turned Kali-esque.

"Of course not! I'm just amazed at how much information you have here." He picked up the spreadsheet and studied it carefully, holding it in both hands, his frail physique soon rocking like a rabbi at the Western Wall. "So many categories! This one on plastic-bottle usage is particularly revealing. Who knew! I confess I use them on occasion." He put the parchment down, picked up a bottled water and took a polite sip. "Life is so hectic around here. We save time where we can."

"Actually, *we* don't use them," corrected Goldie, holding up her hydro-flask.

"We don't use plastic straws either," added Aalia.

"You certainly are setting a stellar example for the under-classmen—er, younger students. Tell me, why Fire Grill Fridays? It's catchy, I grant you, but don't you think it a bit, well...alarmist?"

Aalia leaned toward him, now up on all toes and another inch higher. "Seriously, Father C, what part of the climate emergency don't you understand?"

"OK, I get it, but then why not just say Fire Drill Fridays?"

"Like you said, Fire Grill is catchy. Plus, we want to keep the abstention from meat front and center as we transition to a grilled-veggies-only menu and a new food-service provider whose values align with ours."

"Your group's values, or the school's?"

"We read *Laudato si* in Sister Edna's class last year. She told us many Catholic schools are going solar and sourcing their food from local farmers. Friezelda-St. Mitt's should be a leader on this front, not a laggard. Wouldn't you agree, Father?" countered Goldie.

"Well, if our parents can afford it, I suppose so. What you're proposing sounds costly, though. Financial sustainability does come first."

"It's affordable--*if* one does a full-cost analysis and doesn't discount the future. Our generation can't afford to wait any longer for yours to wake up and do the right thing," asserted Aalia. She really was quite good at playing bad cop, thought Goldie. The close would be a breeze.

"Father C, how about this: I'll talk with Todd and the other Young Benedicts. If they agree, will you give us your blessing?"

"You betcha. I just want our school family to be happy."

"Thank you for your time, Father. We know you're very busy."

On the last Friday in September, Cam had skipped classes with Goldie and Aalia to attend the Climate Strike Action in St. Paul. Her parents let her go on the condition all future Fridays would be spent in school; she had to choose between performing in the play and protesting. While not her first large demonstration, being part of a global event—an estimated four million young people at over 2,500 locales in 163 countries on all seven continents participated—evoked a thrilling sense of possibility. If Greta had demonstrated the power of one, the Climate Strike unveiled the power of a multitude. Among the many placards on display that day her favorite read End Patriarchy, Not the Planet.

"Gotta text from Fitan," mentioned Aalia. "He and a thousand Amerizon techies just walked off the job and joined two thousand others in the streets. They gathered eight thousand signatures from fellow workers demanding the company get serious about going green."

"A mutiny on the mother ship," observed Goldie.

"Facts. And not just in Seattle. He said lots of engineering and computer-science students are fed up with the digital monopolies and VC junkies desperate to find the next killer app. But you can't live in a cool city on the coast and pay off student loans without serious cash, so they sign their non-competes and jump into the lap of Bleudough, Eizenberg and the like."

"Well-trained and well-fed dogs."

"But some won't be tamed easily. Today thousands of them aren't rolling over, they're picketing the boss. On Primo Day two months ago a delegation of tech workers flew to Minnesota and stood with strikers at Amerizon's warehouse in Shakopee. Annual turnover rate there is a hundred percent, the work is so brutal. Every move they make is monitored. Fitan said the techies and quants are tired of designing algorithms used to grind people of color into the ground or ID them for deportation by ICE."

"Aren't they afraid of getting fired?"

"It's a game of fear, all right, and lots of new hires knuckle under. Fitan isn't afraid of anybody, though, because he knows there are worse fates than losing a job. Our great-grandparents stood with Nehru and Gandhi against the Brits. In our family the deeper worry is what happens to your soul if you betray dharma."

"Karmic justice."

"Exactly."

After the Climate Strike, Cam and Goldie limited their activism to promoting Fire Grill Fridays and canceling Terramock, but when Heather told them Earth Roar's next action was to take place in Edina of all places, they had to re-think priorities. The situation called for a sleepover summit at Casa Bloch.

"Once mid-terms are over and we've knocked out our applications we'll be free and clear," reasoned Goldie. She slipped her first-choice Columbia U. t-shirt over her head and pulled down the sheets.

Cam pulled off her gold-striped running pants and tossed her sweatshirt on the floor. "Speak for yourself. Rehearsals gear up in November. I can go to the protest, but there's no way I'm joining the action-planning team." Droopy eyed after a long day, she felt the luxurious bed calling to her. She had dubbed it the Silver Queen after an all-nighter during which they'd gorged on half a dozen ears apiece under the makeshift teepee they'd made with the comforter and a lacrosse stick. They'd mimicked and mocked one another and descanted till dawn so many times in this grand snooze-cruise. Let Dickinson claim there is no frigate like a book. The worlds explored between these silky sheets were as wonderful as any novel or traveler's tale—at least any she'd read so far.

"I still don't get it: how does a whiny ingrate like you end up in the queen's quarters? There is no God."

"What part of JAP don't you get, goy girl? Or should I say goy toy."

"Enough with the pathetic word play, I need to figure some things out, don't cha know. This role is the most demanding I've ever played."

"A miracle worker? What's so hard about that?"

"Remind me to pillow you in your sleep."

"Stone-cold murderess. You were born for that role."

"Deadass, I don't see how I can get involved with Earth Roar right now."

"How can you *not*? This event is practically in your backyard!" It was true: the planned spotlighting of Warbill CEO Mack Leland at his McMansion on Moreland Boulevard was, as Cam's father might say, just a driver and three-iron away from her house. The rigors of the role aside, what made the choice before her so hard was Heather. The question wasn't what dad would say if he discovered she'd called out his boss, it was what Heather would think if she didn't step up. Her head said a no-go was a no-brainer, while her heart and hormones said go for it. As close as she was to Goldie, she decided to keep her own counsel.

Whenever she turned pensive, Goldie couldn't resist trying to tease her out of it. "Face it, Borlaug, you suck at life decisions. Like the time you bought the Convex All-Raws instead of the Alibaskas. Now *that* was an epic fail. Or the time you told Chris you were too busy and couldn't help her with A&P after she suggested a study session in the band's storage room. Talk about a bruh moment!"

"Mmm...whatevs."

"Look, I'll volunteer for the two of us. I know you've got your eye on Heather and don't want--" Cam abruptly sat up and swiveled. "Liar! I'm not interested in her in the least."

"The lady doth--"

"Don't even. I may suck at making choices, but you totally blow at flirting with boys." Goldie grabbed a pillow and began to wail on Cam, who retaliated in kind. A half-minute later the bed was a blizzard of feathers as they throttled one another to the point of exhaustion and fell giggling into the sneezy mess. They were quite the pair: a stocky buxom Jew-girl who couldn't swim beside a Norse dolphin with a black belt who couldn't drive.

As soon as Cam caught the hiccups Goldie sat up, took her hydro-flask from the side table and handed it to her.

"Drink it upside down. Never fails."

"Yah, you've told me a thousand times. What a little Jewish mother you are."

"Call me that again and you *will* die ugly."

"Yes, mother." Cam got out of bed, bent over, placed the flask under her chin and let the water roll across the roof of her mouth and down her throat. The trick was to keep drinking while inhaling through the nose steadily. Six gulps and the hiccups were gone, guaranteed. She stood up straight and finished what was left. "Speaking of mother, I take it yours will not be amused by our antics."

"Eema will never know. Tomorrow first thing we smuggle the evidence out and hit MOA for a spendy replacement."

"Oh, fer cute!"

"I drive, you pay for the pillows. And the Concrete Mixers."

"Don't sleep too soundly, Bloch, there are still plenty lying about."

"Bet."

In mid-November three dozen Earth Roarers had marched from a nearby park to Big Mack's abode. Heather and Cam co-led the contingent through a tree-lined neighborhood populated by Edina's most successful. An early snow the night before made the march a slippery affair. While the chants left something to be desired, Cam was right where she wanted to be, close to yare Heather.

"Dirty business!"

"Agribusiness!"

"Dirty business!"

"Agribusiness!"

"Hey hey, ho ho!"

"Warbill has got to go!"

"Hey hey, ho ho!"

"Warbill has got to go!"

Goldie and Sue, a granola girl wearing a winter cap adorned with velvety moose antlers, carried the day's banner: Warbill, Keep Your Promises. Upon arriving a wheel-chairing demonstrator did three-sixties on the well-shoveled sidewalk, while the colored-chalk squad filled it with #smackmackdown, #warbilltheworst, #dontbuythebigmacklie, #forkingovertheplanet and other messages for the man of the house. One activist held a large portrait of the CEO labeled Mack the Piker. On the trees out front protestors taped an array of disturbing photographic images: orangutans in a cage, refugees from clear-cutting on the island of Sumatra; an Indigenous mother holding her sick newborn, poisoned by pesticide run-off; a drone shot of São Paulo at noon, the city so darkened by smoke from rainforest fires it looked more like dusk; five young black boys staring plaintively at the camera, machetes in one hand and cocoa fruit in the other. Two young Roarers made snow angels in the front yard. No one in the patrol car at the end of the block seemed to notice the trespassing. An Amerizon driver dropped off a package without incident.

Heather and Cam took turns with the megaphone reading from ER's exposé and calling on the CEO to come out and face the music. A large school of protestors waved dead fish cut-outs as Cam intoned: "The agribusiness giant Warbill, recently named the Worst Company in the World, released eight million tons of raw sewage into the Mississippi River last year. Massive marine carnage resulted." Cut-outs plunged into the snow next to the angels. Two demonstrators took a knee to pray for the endangered and mourn the extinct. After a moment of silence, Heather led the group in several provocative chants.

"Time's up! Time's up!"

"Can't sneak out the back, Mack!"

"Yo, Mack! Can't sneak out the back!"

"Warbill comes in first!"

"At being the absolute worst!"

"Warbill comes in first!"

"At being the absolute worst!"

"Big Mack, heart attack!"

"Big Mack, heart attack!"

He never did show his face. Several curious neighbors seemed sympathetic, but they were certain Mr. Leland was a very nice fellow. Two signed the petition after chatting for twenty minutes with Ruth. One sympathizer's dog—a Pekinese with an eye-patch and a slight limp--lifted a leg in solidarity, marking the scene. All the action was livestreamed for ER's online following, which peaked early at seventy-nine but dwindled to eight by the time Heather closed out with a primal scream open only to those who had signed a medical release form prior.

During the debrief at the park Heather accented the positive. "Mission accomplished, people. We let Big Mack know *we* know where he lives and lit up that sleepy 'hood with an earth roar they'll not soon forget!" Cam slipped her hand into Heather's, raised it high and let loose a long wolf howl.

"We have a pair of new petition signatures," added Ruth. "There may not have been any news coverage, but one-by-one we will reach moderate Minneapolitans receptive to our message."

"And nobody died!" blurted Sue, still traumatized from September's tragedy and on edge after the cardiac-arrest chant. All agreed to a moment of silence in memory of Jordan before heading to their Toyota Priyatas and Honda

Civil Hyphids. Goldie turned to Cam. "Take your time, I'll go warm up the car."

"OK, I won't be long." She glanced Heather's way, smiled coyly and then averted her gaze. She had no idea what to do next. Her veins were running white-hot while her feet felt frozen.

"See you soon?" inquired Heather, an eyebrow lifted. Her penetrating smile left Cam speechless. She ran a finger from Cam's shoulder down to her wrist and back up again. In an instant she realized she was the one who sucked at flirting.

"Yah…well, maybe. I'm super-busy from now until Christmas." What a sniveling idiot I sound like, Cam thought to herself. She's gonna ghost me, I just know it!

Heather took a step back, lowered her eyes a moment and then gave Cam a look that suggested the door hadn't closed forever. "No worries. You and Goldie have a lot on your plates right now, I get it. We all do."

"Fer sure."

"We're going to take things to the next level in the coming--" Suddenly Cam was hugging her. She did not want to let go—ever—but she also didn't want things to become awkward. After releasing her hold and stepping back, she avoided eye contact.

"See ya soon, I hope."

"The sooner the better, eh?" Eva stepped forward and kissed her lightly. Tongue-tied by the amatory advance, she smiled and waved goodbye. The walk back to the car felt like forty miles. As they drove away, she leaned in between the front seats and looked out the back window. Heather was still standing in the snow, effulgent as ever, an event unto herself.

4

FROM CANCUN TO THE CRATER

Sitting by the river, her tea drained, Cam pondered whether Heather was her first love or just a powerful infatuation. That fall had been a blur of college visits, rehearsals and protests. She settled on Georgetown as her number one and was accepted early. Much deserved were the standing ovations *The Miracle Worker* received. She channeled all she'd learned from Giles into feisty Anne and found the right chemistry on stage with Toni, who was wondrous as Helen. After the Sunday matinee, Giles ran to her with a bouquet and hugged her so hard it hurt; the play had released a torrent within that surged toward the one who knew him best. Zoe and Erik kept clapping furiously--until they saw how many people had stopped to look at them.

On Christmas Eve Cam curled up on the couch to enjoy the tree's glittering array, another masterful dressing by Giles. She thought back to his huge hug and her proud parents making a scene. She noticed he'd placed manger and magi on the far side of the fireplace opposite the tree. Ox and ass were now standing forlorn at the far corner of the barn rather than nestled close to the golden child. A feeling of gratitude mixed with sadness set in as she realized the past fall had been the family's happiest in years.

Over the holiday break, she spent more time with Giles and Taz. They crafted a Frosty in the front yard and snowballed dad whenever he ventured outdoors. Burrowing deep into a huge snowbank left by the plowing, they vowed never to leave their icy lair. As gamesome as they come, Taz couldn't wait to get outside and pounce about. She and Giles took turns manning the leash that kept him from escaping into the cold white world. Mom always had hot chocolate ready when their toes grew numb. They sipped slowly and thawed out by the fire dad tended faithfully.

A familiar comfort, those crackling flames, but that winter they had reminded her of the horrific bushfires burning out of control in Australia. A territory larger than Portugal torched, vast billows of smoke blowing across the ocean to other continents. Kangaroos and koalas, wombats and wallabies, countless other critters all perishing under hellish-red skies, as stark a warning of greater destruction to come as any imaginable. She had wondered whether this shocking event--like Hurricane Katrina or Cyclone Idai or the Great Midwestern Flood of 2019—would become just another ripple across the bow, a ripple soon receding from memory as the ship of civilization kept to its coordinates. Would Greta, Sunrise, Earth Roar and other mutineers grow in number and find a way to seize the bridge? If the climate scientists were right, then the decade ahead was humanity's last, best chance to chart a much different course, one that just might allow homo sapiens to slip through the Great Filter.

To escape Midwest winters and spice up her birthday celebrations, Cam's parents flew her and Giles every February to a different Caribbean resort. For her eighteenth she'd lobbied for something different: Great Huts Resort, just east of Port Antonio on the northeast coast of Jamaica. Billed as "glamping at its best," the treehouse resort sat at the edge of a cliff overlooking Boston Bay, where surfers enjoyed some of the island's best waves. She was out-voted on New Year's Day after enduring another good-parent bad-parent routine.

Dad always played the soft sympathetic one. Glancing over her shoulder at the screen, he pretended to be impressed. "Looks like a cool spot, honey. That's one spectacular view of the water. Comfy little huts too, and so much art on the walls!" He grew genuinely excited when Cam clicked open a window into his past. "Stop right there. Port Antonio was Erol Flynn's favorite hideaway? God, he was great! *Captain Flood* was his best, don't cha know." He quaffed the last of his lager and took in the tall tree and many gifts still lying about, like a pirate surveying the latest booty. Cam clicked away. "Look, dad, says here your hero was infatuated with Fidel. This critic gives Flynn's last film, *Cuban Rebel Girls*, four stars. Can we rent it?" Not waiting for an answer, she whipped out her phone and shot Chano a text:

hey ever heard
of erol flynn

Nunca, señorita.

didn't think so
my dads hero
big movie star
way back when

Does knowing who
Ricky Ricardo
is win points?

i love lucy!!!
gotta go

Happy New Year!

heres to 2020
being the best!!

Will I see you
all again

in the spring?

yeet, yeet
cant wait!!!

[three thumbs up]

Erik was not amused by her flip request. Their recent arguments over the dreaded S-word and the candidates—Cam was ga-ga over bomb-throwing Bernie, while he had settled on Uncle Joe—had run on much longer than he liked. "I don't think so, Cam. We only have a week to celebrate your birthday, and this place is just too out of the way. Perhaps next year." Ah, the velvet glove dangling a delectable treat just out of reach.

Mom followed with the iron fist. "That's right, it's too remote and too rustic. A four-hour drive on bumpy, dusty roads isn't anyone's idea of fun. Besides, it could be dangerous. They stop you, out in the middle of nowhere, and you're never heard from again."

Cam clicked to the State Department's travel advisory site. Jamaica currently was at Level 1: Exercise Normal Precautions. "Mom, I really don't think we have to wor—"

"I don't care if the government says it's safe. We are not going to risk our lives traveling for hours on end through a third-world country. Period."

"Ya let me go to Cuba."

"End of discussion. You'll love the Paradisus Cancun, it has everything. Right now, a little gratitude might go a long way." Mom's wariness was understandable: she had lost her younger brother Leo in Afghanistan during Operation Anaconda in 2002, the year Cam was born. While on patrol his jeep hit an IED. Under heavy fire it took his unit forty minutes to retrieve the shattered body. Two friends were wounded during the extraction. Both helped carry the casket from church to grave three weeks later.

"OK, mom. I'm sure it will be great, it always is."

"That's the spirit! Now, would anyone like more hot chocolate? And are we going to play Jenga tonight or what?"

Doubtless the destination her parents had pre-determined was lovely in the usual sun-and-sand-and-sangria sort of way. Still, she found herself chafing under what seemed too much a color-between-the-lines approach to the world at times. A moment later she remembered Cancun sits on the Yucatan peninsula, as does the Chicxulub Crater, a world-historical site evolutionary theorists say triggered the fifth great extinction sixty-five million years ago. Excited, she pulled up Booble Maps and punched in the locales. Her heart sank when it showed the drive from Cancun to the crater took four hours over remote roads.

Her eighteenth birthday fell on Fat Tuesday. They'd been at the five-star resort two days. She loved the festive beads handsome, bare-foot waiters tossed out before dinner, not to mention the sextet that played her favorite reggae upon request. While feasting on jambalaya mom re-told the story of Leo joining the Mummers and strutting down Broad Street in Philly, the wings of his feathered costume ten-feet wide. Dessert seemed the best time to suggest a side-trip to the crater, but the idea was dead on arrival. She and Giles spent the week bodysurfing, riding bikes and tooling around bayside in a Sunfish. Neither noticed the absence of rancor between their parents, who had agreed to a cessation of long-running hostilities over politics and other bones of contention—at least for the duration of the vacation. Not spending much time with each other—Zoe sipped on margaritas by the water while Erik snuck off to the executive course with his sticks—helped to keep the Cancun Accord intact.

During the return flight Cam overheard several passengers talking about the first confirmed case of covid in Minnesota. The forty-minute lay-over at O'Hare felt like four hours. Dad kept letting Giles beat him at thumb-wrestling just often enough to keep him playing; after ten minutes they switched to rock-paper-scissors. Clouds and runways, terminal walls and floors, window reflections and waiting-area chairs—all were grey. Minute by minute the Caribbean buzz faded. From smiles to stone faces. Every head buried in a device, a vast cemetery of the cyber-anesthetized. Soon hers was as well. She was wading through a week of texts when Goldie's arrived:

	r u back
boarding for last leg to tcs	
	covid has arrived [worried face]
so sucks	
	hear about palo alto
???	
	amerizon van blew up no one hurt tg
[open mouths]	
	just happened

She looked up from her phone and noticed travelers glued to a TV. The explosion had occurred during a delivery to a residence near Stanford. Not much remained of the blue-grey van. Firefighters were hosing down its charred chassis; EMTs were attending to a bewildered driver holding both arms over his head. Boarding pass scanned, she dropped her eyes into the grey carpet and disappeared into the tunnel.

Her birthday getaway behind her, Cam turned her attention to the audition for *Newsies*, the spring musical. With only an above-average voice, she likely wasn't first in line for the lead. Still, her dance background gave her a leg up, the role requiring someone who could learn quickly how to tap—no easy feat. Unfortunately, choosing her would reek of typecasting--the lead character Katherine was as strong-willed and independent as that of Anne—and Mrs. Philsmeier was adamant that actors must stretch if they expected to excel. In any event, Goldie was stage managing and all her drama-geek buddies were stoked about the play, which seemed just the right pick for an election year.

Super Tuesday was followed by the shutdown. Cam and her friends bucked up, but tele-learning was the worst. All service trips cancelled, so no seeing Chano. Playing Katherine Plummer, playing frisbee in the parking lot with her crew, playing coy when Chris came sniffing around her locker, playing Charles off against Ron, playing one last April Fool's joke on Mrs. Bruno--everything that mattered obliterated by the covid meteor. She only wanted to visit a crater, not live in one!

5

ON THE HOME FRONT

Easter afternoon, Cam now recalled, she had ambled down to the creek to clear her head. One could only spend so much time inside the glass cage scrolling and clicking.... In the still water she saw cloud reflections drifting along the surface like lost shrouds. "Take me with you," she murmured to herself as they slipped around the bend into oblivion. Not one to indulge in pity parties for long, she welcomed the geese that came honking, feathered heralds announcing the arrival of an early and unusually vibrant spring. Around the world wildlife were returning to urban spaces freed for now from the incessant noise and smog.

On the other side of the creek, she spied a blue heron tiptoeing stealthily along the water's edge in search of minnows and tadpoles. What a focused, patient creature! Joy seeped into every sinew. She turned around and grew still, a transparent eyeball intent on taking in all: fox squirrels scurried over rotting leaves and exposed roots, the hungry among them daring a raid on the feeder as red-winged blackbirds took flight; on the garden fence bold-jumping spiders prowled before pouncing upon unsuspecting larvae; patches of pussy-willows flirted with the fickle breeze; jonquils aproned the shed and accompanied the wooden fencing separating yards. Alongside the patio a huge forsythia shrub was on fire with stunning gold, bell-shaped flowers. Everywhere she looked the bloodroot blossomed, each rhizome sending forth eight white pedals surrounding a gold ring of florets. Was any place on the planet more alive, more blessed, more beautiful?

A deep sense of abundance beyond measure remained for several days. Yet nothing gold can stay, she soon sensed, the lines from Frost returning with a shiver. The relentless undertow of the pandemic began to take hold and pull her down into a mild depression. Living in a large house amplified the isolation. Dad hid in his study and mom camped out on the living-room couch, while she hung with Taz upstairs and Giles occupied a finished basement decked out with ping-pong table, an 85" flat screen and mom's rowing machine.

Amerizon drivers dropped off provisions daily, and a wise addendum to the Cancun Accord--no politics and religion at the table--kept an uneasy peace during family dinners. Come week six of the shutdown, however, one snippy sarcastic comment led to another. Soon the testy back-and-forth escalated. While the strict ban on profanity and ad hominem attacks held, neither party was inclined to ratchet down the increasingly heated rhetoric. Thursday night the first shot was fired by Zoe when she clicked on Pox and turned up the volume as Erik made the usual: a cut of porterhouse and a simple salad anchored by a buttered-up baked potato. The provocation violated the Accord, and she knew it. At present he was a captive audience.

Pox's attack dog was taking Chief Justice Roberts to task for a cowardly, traitorous vote supporting abortion rights. Zoe didn't much care about politics—except when the Right to Life was at stake. Erik had tried to convince her that single-issue voting wasn't smart, and wasn't even very Catholic at that, but gave up around the time Obama was re-elected and a lefty bishop from Buenos Aires became pope. Three years later, he was at first amused by her increasingly vocal support for candidate Trump, mocking her newfound fealty to the orange knight of the unborn. The more he poked fun the more strident and resentful she became. After the Donald won, she took both kids to DC for the annual March for Life. Stunned by the outcome, he was left behind to watch the Women's March on TV.

Now, despite a tax break that did wonders for his portfolio, he could not stomach the idea of four more years. Trump's unforgivable sin wasn't the blatant misogyny or crude self-dealing or daily Pinocchio's or any number of other transgressions against decency rightly leveled against him. No, what was unpardonable was his pandering to the biblically brainwashed know-nothings who would take a sledgehammer to the one true pillar of American prosperity. The way to MAGA wasn't WWJD, it was STEM. In his view, the We Believe lawn signs sprouting in Edina's front yards contained only one fundamental article of faith: Science Is Real.

On Super Tuesday he'd rejoiced when it became clear the adults in the party had put Sanders, Warren and other wild-eyed progressives in their place. The sensible center's craving for normalcy would prevail. With Uncle Joe in the White House, America would reboot after removing the bug. Tax benefits for the college saving plans--Cam's now totaled $210K--would remain in place. The Dems would reinstate the SALT deduction. American leadership in the world would be restored, and that would bode well for Warbill's overseas operations.

While cooking he tried to tune out the right-wing ravings, but when he saw he'd left the steak on too long after fiddling with Cam's tofu he returned fire. "For cryin' out loud, how can ya believe anything Pox says? That isn't news, it's propaganda. Carlson, Hannity and the rest, they tell more lies in ten minutes than Trump tells in a week. It's a disgrace, don't cha know."

"Somebody has to call Justice Roberts and the rest of them out. The liberal media never do. Just a smug silence as the daily massacre continues." He was too hangry to go the rounds yet again on real reporting versus the hijacking of pro-life sentiment for higher ratings. Aggravated the meat was irretrievably medium-well done, he hollered down to the kids: "Come and get it! Now!"

Giles winced instantly and began pacing, hands over ears. In his world an alarm clock reaching sixty decibels equaled a shotgun at 120. They stared glumly at each other. Dad's harsh tone meant they were already at DEFCON 2. Slowly the two trudged up the stairs, each step heavier than the next. Cam did not want to see him shut down again--staring blankly at the fork in his hand, as if frozen in ice--but it was better than a meltdown if he was armed with ranch-drenched lettuce and a drippy potato. The past three nights she had tried to buffer in the hope her parents would come to their senses. So far nothing had worked. She'd leaned the gym mat, which she used to hold him down when he did blow, on the wall close to her chair at the kitchen table.

Mercifully, Zoe clicked off the TV when the kids appeared. She walked over to the sliding-glass doors and gazed out at the water. After a day of managing accounts and making lunch and keeping Giles on task with schoolwork, she would check out around five pm with a cabernet, bundling up in a blanket next to the heat lamp on the back patio--her own happy hour. The bracing wind and glistening creek evoked fond memories of crew mates, regattas on the Schuykill and the pavilion between boathouse row and the art museum made famous by Rocky where she and Erik used to make out well past midnight.

These days she found it harder to let go and drift back. Arguing in front of the children was wrong, but she couldn't figure out why she kept butting heads with Erik. Was it spring fever or the shutdown or both? Did the election-year animus between them matter that much? At least she'd dialed it down before dinner was served. Some things were sacred.

The cease-fire was filled at first by awkward silence. Erik broke the ice with the usual questions about school and summer plans, all of which struck Cam as ludicrous since no one knew when life-as-usual would resume. She seized the opportunity to ad-lib as a ditzy stan going on about freeing Britney from the money-grubbers. Her parents found it amusing, but her brother would not budge from his bunker. Still, a resumption of the Accord was a W. Dessert now dished out, Cam and her parents smiled at each other when Giles suddenly laughed out loud. "I'm dead," he declared, the delayed reaction signaling a dialing back to DEFCON 4. He plunged his spoon into the caramel swirl made with cashew milk that by some fluke was now the family fav.

Zoe marked the occasion by pulling another pint out of the freezer. While no one took her talk of resuming daily workouts on the rowing machine seriously, all lauded her resolve. Cam knew Giles didn't want her down in his den, that much was certain, but she played along on the assumption her mother's determination would dissipate soon enough. The art of domestic diplomacy, she thought to herself a few hours later as she lounged in bed and thumbed through black-and-white photos of the Belle Epoque in her European history textbook, oblivious to the ball python stirring beneath her pillow. Somehow it had slipped out of its terrarium while Taz was sacked out and found just the spot to do likewise. "Ope," uttered Cam as soon as she felt the slither along her shoulder. She quickly gathered the five-foot snake up. The hiss she heard next came from Taz, who kept his distance. A few seconds later she locked the latch cover and placed her textbook on top. It took several minutes to calm the frightened ferret down. As they nuzzled in bed, she realized he was still alive and hissing only because the apex predator turned escapee had swallowed its weekly mouse whole only yesterday.

Soon Taz was back to his playful self and dooking for a game as she tickled his belly. She formed tunnels with sheets and pillows and let him go to town, his energy and curiosity endless. An ever-ready maze runner. These days the little rascal was her only pick-me-up. As he darted this way and that, she told herself things would turn a corner. Mom and dad would kiss and make up, she and Heather would be re-united, a vaccine would deliver all from the lock-down, college next fall in DC would be a blast. She just had to wait for all good things to come.

On Memorial Day a few weeks later, Giles woke at dawn and went to the back-yard with his uncle Leo's flag. He unfurled it slowly, taking care not to let it touch the dew-covered grass. Then he hoisted it to the pole's peak and paused a moment before lowering it to half-staff. At noon he raised it back to the top. Regulation. After an early, uneventful dinner Zoe pulled out her jam-packed scrapbook. Fading photos of her Pet Rock and Cookie Monster puppet, a list of Frankford Gang members, Smurf stickers, Girl Scout badges, stubs from *Star Wars* and *E.T.*, a crayoned birthday wish from Leo, a fake Sting autograph, her confirmation certificate from St. Bartholomew's and acceptance letter from La Salle. She told stories of grand-daddy playing linebacker for Joe Pa-terno when Penn State went undefeated and won the Orange Bowl, and how he held little Leo over his head like a trophy and paraded through Torresdale bare-chested with fifteen other hockey fanatics after the U.S. Olympic team upset the Soviets, and the time he took them all to a Phillies game at the Vet and almost dropped Leo off the 700 Level trying to snag a foul off the bat of his favorite player Greg Luzinski, and how they nearly froze to death in that same foul-mouthed, God-forsaken section later that fall as the Eagles lost again to the Cowboys.

Two hours of reminiscing seemed like two minutes. Outside the sun had dipped below the tree line. "Let's bring Leo down now," Zoe said to her children. "The time is right." Once unclipped, Erik secured the rope while Cam helped Giles fold their late uncle's flag. He handed it to his mother and then embraced her, the triangle-shaped cloth nestled in between their chests. Cam wrapped her arms around them both.

Once inside, Giles suggested they all watch *1917*. Everyone chuckled and then froze, realizing instantly what their unscreened reaction might trigger. "Not tonight, my boy" was all his father could think to say. Cam gave him a bear hug and then cajoled him into playing ping-pong instead.

The Borlaug house exploded the next day. This time it was Cam, who blew up in tears and anger ten seconds before the bystander's video ended. A moment later she screamed into her pillow, threw her sweatshirt on and bolted from her room down the stairs. She slammed the front door shut and flew down the street out of sight. Her panicked parents rushed outside and looked at each other dumbly. Zoe dashed back into the house to find Giles downstairs, lost in a speedrun. Erik went to the backyard, yelling her name. He returned a minute later to find Zoe standing on the front walk, one hand cupped over her mouth as she watched the now-viral video a friend had texted her.

"Oh my God…something terrible happened."

Erik approached her. "What is it? Show me--"

Clutching the phone to her chest, she met him with a stiff-arm. "No! Go find her! Now!" He jumped into the car and sped out the driveway. After searching the neighborhood to no avail, he turned onto West 50th and drove up and down the street past City Hall several times before jumping onto State Highway 100 heading north. A mile up the road, he saw her running like a wild horse. She was staying on the right side of the white line—for now. Rather than pull up beside her and honk, he decided to drive ahead about fifty yards and pull over.

When she saw his Flexus skid to a stop, she slowed to a jog and came to a standstill twenty yards away from her father, who had yanked the emergency brake, hopped out and begun to walk hurriedly toward her. She was still panting and held both hands over her face. As they walked back to the car, he thought it best not to ask--at least not yet. He opened the passenger-side door for her, but she paused before getting in and now stared at him intently, as if about to accuse him of something. The mood shift caught him off guard.

"Dad, I want you to take me to Goldie's house."

"I don't know what's going on, but I think you should come home."

She gripped the car door with both hands and pulled it toward her, as if holding a piece of armor. Eyes still locked on his, she let loose. "Last night the police killed a black man…they had him down on the ground and he wasn't resisting, but one cop put a knee to his neck while others just stood there…he kept saying he couldn't breathe and begged them to stop and called out for his mother…then he went unconscious, but the cop kept the knee on his neck…he died before they got him to the hospital…the whole world's seen it…I need to go to Goldie's house…this isn't right." She stopped, nearly out of breath, and pushed the door out toward Erik, who already had taken a half-step back onto his heels. While at work he usually navigated the occasional crisis well, here he felt completely at sea. Never had he seen his daughter so distraught. Keep her safe and calm, he thought to himself. Be patient and ride out the storm.

"I understand you're upset, honey," he finally said. "Let's go home and sort this out with your mother." He waited, but she said nothing. Her whole body turned taut. She glared at him fiercely, like a shield-maiden girding herself for a charge. Unnerved, he stood there awkwardly, his own eyes darting between hers, the door she held firmly and the number ten on her chest, his search-and-rescue mission now a nerve-wracking stand-off. How to scramble out of this collapsing pocket? What would Frantic Fran do? Nothing in his hero's latest self-help playbook *Every Day Is Game Day* had prepped him for this situation.

She let go of the door and stepped away from the car to check her phone. Goldie was gushing texts.

chief of police
just said
being black
in america
should not be
a death sentence

omg this is
so wrong!!!
[angry faces]

makes me sick

we gotta do
something!!

people are
gathering
ill drive

parents let u?
[open mouth]

not going to
tell them

[winking face]

btw elijah
just got back
from nyc

[fire]

so they went
to the cabin
for two weeks

to quarantine

ya my dad is
seventy now

big yikes

what r u gonna
tell the rents

wont tell either
just say im
sleeping over

sounds like
a plan
pick u up?

dad will drop
me off soon

k elijah wants
to go too

bet

Cam turned toward her father and repeated her request, which now sounded more like a demand. "I don't think it's a good idea," he responded weakly. She took a step forward and pressed. "Goldie is upset too, and I really need to be with my best friend right now." When he hesitated, she took two more steps toward him. "It's just a five-minute drive from here--and only a half-hour run if you won't take me. Either way I'm going." She wasn't surprised when he relented. Without mom running interference, he wasn't that tough to tackle. They drove in silence to Goldie's house in St. Louis Park.

6
TO LAKE STREET AND BACK AGAIN

By the time Cam, Goldie and her older brother Elijah arrived the street was filled with mourners. At the intersection of Chicago and East 38th lay a wreath memorial. After adding flowers to the outer ring, they walked slowly through the growing crowd. Already the pavement was awash in chalk messages: RIP George, White Silence = White Violence, #CHANGE, Say His Name, #8cantwait, I Am a Man. Bobbling heart-shaped balloons hung from street signs and telephone poles. One street artist sketched Trayvon and Breonna with George; another drew a row of raised fists, each one a different color. A young girl with braided locks wearing a pink Hello Kitty sweatshirt and matching sneakers held up a cardboard sign—Please Don't Kill My Daddy—for all to see. Next to her a teenage boy's sign, dangling on string from his neck, said Freedom Over Fear. The grieving formed circles and held hands while praying. On the corner across from Sup Foods four teenage girls sat on a sidewalk and wept as they watched the witness video. An "I can't breathe" chant rose and fell every few minutes, growing a little louder each time. A half-hour later the refrain became "It could've been me." Two ancient Red Power activists took turns holding up a large American Indian Movement flag.

By five pm the crowd had doubled in size, a swell of off-work and laid-off millennials joined by zoomers home from school. Word was out that a march to the Third Police Precinct would begin soon. At the edge of the memorial ring a BLM organizer held up a bullhorn and invited everyone to gather around.

"Thanks for coming out, y'all. My name is Maya Fortier and I'm with Black Lives Matter Twin Cities Metro." The crowd clapped respectfully. Cam wasn't the only one struck by her magnetic presence. Atop an orange milk crate, she stood eight feet tall and was looking thicc in blue jeans worn, not distressed by design. Shirt sleeves rolled tight. Feed-in braids with cuff beads and bright brown eyes that looked straight through the lot of them. Definitely a main character.

Maya confirmed the plan for a two-mile march, reminded them of BLM's commitment to nonviolence and then issued a stirring call to action.

"Now is the time to raise up another black life that mattered, say his name!"

"George Floyd!"

"Now is the time to take back what is ours, whose streets!"

"Our streets!"

"Now is the time to demand justice, no justice!"

"No peace!"

"Now is the time to walk the walk, whose streets!

"Our streets!"

"Say his name!"

"George Floyd!"

"Now is the time to confront the killers with their crime, no justice!"

"No peace!"

Cam's heart began to hammer, the call-and-response evoking an unfamiliar frisson. In a flash she knew what she had to do.

"I'm going, anyone with me?"

Goldie nodded yes right away. Elijah paused before responding. Four years back he'd spent six months at Standing Rock. "OK, let's do this. But you both need to know it could get ugly. We're going to get up in their face, and they don't like that. At the Oceti Sakowin Camp we faced attack dogs, water cannon, mace. They even had skunk spray, which the Israelis use against Palestinians in the Occupied Territories. Under the DOD's 1033 Program, cops across the country have been getting hand-me-downs from the military since before Abu Ghraib. Have you seen what Atlanta's finest are wearing these days? Storm troopers 2.0, I kid you not. Before we go, let's at least get some milk."

"I say we grab a bottle of pop and some munchies," replied Cam. "Definitely a bag of Dollops."

"When your eyes begin burning so bad you want to rip them out of their sockets, you'll be glad you brought milk."

"Wait, what?"

"Tear gas is a euphemism, don't cha know. So is rubber bullets. So is less-lethal launcher. One friend of mine lost an eye and another had to have reconstructive surgery on her wrist after they unloaded. They used black permanent marker on forearms to number the water protectors they arrested before throwing them overnight into kennels. When activists finally got their confiscated belongings back, everything from signs to sleeping bags to ceremonial pipes was soaked in piss."

Goldie admired her big brother's activism and was thrilled he'd decided to pursue grad studies in political economy at the New School in NYC, but he could be a bit much at times, dragging the un-woke at every turn. Nothing a little humor couldn't cure, though, and she never passed on a chance to needle him.

"OK then, down the yellow brick road we go!" Cam giggled at her mock resolve. They locked arms and skipped around Elijah, tilting their heads his way. Goldie offered him a free arm. "C'mon tin man, let's bounce!"

"I'm going to get milk. They'll be sold out soon." He wanted no part of their silliness.

Goldie kept at it. "Yes, and buy some Wonder Bread while you're at it." Now it was Cam's turn. "Yes, and don't forget the Dollops for Wonder Woman as she goes forth to vanquish Ares!" Improv was a favorite pastime of theirs, and recently they'd dabbled in cosplay.

"My lasso and god-killer, they're gone!" cried Goldie, looking about frantically. Cam grabbed her. Neither could stop giggling. She took hold more firmly and turned her toward Elijah, as if to present an Oscar nominee. "Goldie Gadot is awesome, wouldn't you agree?"

He scowled at the Marilyn Monroe pose she struck. "What we're walking into is deadly serious, and you two making light of it makes me wonder whether you're ready."

Goldie flipped on a dime from giddy to flinty. "Go get the meelk. And some water, too. And grab my shield—er, umbrella--it's in the trunk." Elijah shook his head and trudged off toward the convenience store. On its roof the billboard reminded everyone not to text and drive.

Most everyone at the memorial site decided to march. BLM activists handed out placards, offered masks to those without and answered questions about pepper spray and legal aid. While waiting a large circle formed around three B-boys who took turns displaying windmills, air-flares, hand-hops, deadman floats, buddha flies, baby spins.... After a local pastor offered a blessing, organizers signaled go-time and Maya sent them forth. "Let's move, people, let's move!"

The marchers headed north on Chicago, others joining along the way. Marshals stopped traffic, and at every intersection waiting drivers honked in support. Homeowners waved from their porches. On a chalked sidewalk three tweens showed off their cheerleading moves chanting "no justice, no peace." Arriving at Lake in larger numbers, they moved east through the street's working-class section sandwiched between Uptown's trendy restaurants, boutiques and luxury condos on the west end and the brewpubs, hip diners and coffeehouses popping up near the river. At one point a motorcycle club rolled through revving engines and raising fists. Near the front Maya was leading the pack.

"Power, power!"

"Power to the people!"

"Power, power!"

Power to the people!"

"Black lives--"

"Matter!"

"Black lives--"

"Matter!"

"Show me what democracy looks like!"

"This is what democracy looks like!"

"Show me what America looks like!"

"This is what America looks like!"

Several hundred protestors had converged on the police station before the marchers arrived. Elijah was worried from the get-go. "This crowd is ticked off, ready to rumble. We're out of here if things get out of hand. No heroics, are we clear?" Cam surveyed the scene. The signs alone confirmed his take: Fuck the Police, Am I Next? Murderers with Badges are STILL Murderers, Again??? WTF!!! This Shit Ends Now, Perps Gonna Pay, KKKops, Drop Dead 12. Atop a metro bus shelter two scrawny antifa types held a large graffiti banner proclaiming ACAB—whatever that meant. She spied one burly white guy carrying a crowbar wrapped in a towel and another with a piece of pipe clumsily tucked under a sleeve. Provocateurs? The unarmed did vastly outnumber the armed, a fact that felt comforting until it occurred to her the many smartphones pointed at police could be categorized as weapons of a sort in some quarters. Most lugged nothing more than milk jugs. One pushed a Bullseye cart full of them through the street and offered one to all comers. How clueless she'd been back at Sup Foods!

"Elijah, thanks for bringing the meelk."

"No problem." He handed her the carton. "Don't drop it."

"Yah, not to worry." The stony look he gave her suggested she ought to be.

Within minutes Maya had the crowd chanting in unison.

"Hands up!"

"Don't shoot!" thundered the throng, all arms raised.

"Hands up!"

"Don't shoot!"

"Say his name!"

"George Floyd!"

"Say his name!"

"George Floyd!"

"Money for schools!"

"Not the police!"

"Money for housing!"

"Not the police!"

"Stand up!"

"Fight back!"

"Stand up!"

"Fight back!"

"Hey Hey! Ho Ho!"

"These racist cops have got to go!"

"Hey Hey! Ho Ho!"

"These racist cops have got to go!"

By dusk the demonstrators had fired off about eighty rounds of chants—a constructive channeling of righteous anger, a magnified voice reaching well beyond its immediate, uniformed audience. In between chants the protestors heard a dozen or so speakers, most representing BLM but a few self-appointed. Cam found the latter voices alarming, with one loud soap-boxer coming dangerously close to inciting a riot: "We're here to let twelve know this shit won't stand! This fucking place is gonna burn if they keep killing us day after day!" He pointed to the banner behind him. "Never forget, all cops are bastards!" ACAB. Each time some loner went off, BLM leaders attempted to calm them down. Maintaining a militant yet disciplined nonviolent presence under these conditions required constant vigilance. The line distinguishing legitimate protest from mob violence could be erased quickly, regardless of what movement organizers did or did not do.

Many who had marched began to scatter when the rain arrived. "I say we stay for a little while longer," declared Goldie, popping open her umbrella. Cam quickly took shelter beside her. The two looked at Elijah, who was trying to size things up as he blinked and wiped water from his bushy beard, soon a soaked sponge hanging from the chin. "The darker it gets the more likely it'll go haywire. If we lose track of each other, let's meet in front of Bullseye. We'll walk or bum a ride back to the car from there."

"Aye, captain," saluted Goldie, drawing another giggle from Cam.

Elijah glared at his little sister. "You just can't help being a smart-ass, can you?"

"Don't look now, brother, but you're all wet."

Once the downpour subsided three dozen officers appeared in riot gear. A chopper swung in low, its deafening chuff-chuff-chuff and rotor downwash pressing protestors into the pavement. After it pulled away, some started hurling rocks, bottles and assorted obscenities. Others spray-painted squad cars. Maya and her marshals pled with the vandals, but their appeals fell on deaf ears. Soon after, bricks shattered two station windows. Police fired tear-gas canisters and flash grenades before advancing on a crowd that now numbered four hundred. Minutes later a paddy wagon in the precinct's parking lot went up in flames, a police cruiser's lights were smashed and rubber bullets were beginning to fly.

"Fall back! Fall back!" marshals yelled. Most did so, though some stood their ground fielding hot canisters and flinging them back at the cops while others went to their knees and raised hands high. Cam froze, horrified by what was unfolding around her. Another volley of tear gas landed close by and set her eyes, nose and throat ablaze. Goldie and Elijah were nowhere to be seen.

Then a flash grenade exploded only a few yards away, the concussive blast rendering her blind and deaf for six terrifying seconds. Bent over, both arms wrapped around her head, she lost all bearings. Disoriented by the afterimage and ringing in her ears, she struggled to stay on her feet. Lights blinking blue-red-blue, sirens and screams, wet pavement and puddles, unbearable burning sensations—all swirling about a brain ready to burst. Hunched over and hacking, she staggered this way and that, driven by an overwhelming panic. "Goldie! Elijah!" No answer. She dropped to one knee, fighting the urge to collapse and go fetal, the pain from sternum to forehead intense. The milk carton, where was it? Must keep moving, she thought, but which way? She managed to stand up and wobble forward, like a zombie stunned by a blast but stumbling blindly onward. A moment later someone grabbed her by the arm and hustled her out of the miasma. The milk splashed on her face offered some relief.

"The burn takes time to fade, anywhere from fifteen minutes to a half-hour." Cam recognized the voice immediately. It was Maya.

"Thanks for pulling me out of there." She never felt more foolish.

"No problem, it goes with the territory. Glad I saw you when I did. Boys with batons were moving in," she remarked with a battle-worn matter-of-factness Cam found unsettling. Had she been spared a beating she'd witnessed others enduring just before she'd buckled under the bombardment?

"I should have dropped back as soon as the call went out."

"Shell shock happens, don't beat yourself up about it." Maya handed her a bottled water. Another newb to babysit for a bit. So be it. "Flush your eyes every few minutes and take a few sips. Are you flying solo?"

"I'm here with a friend and her brother. I'm sure I'll be able to find them." She wasn't sure at all but didn't want to appear pathetic. She stood up straight, as if coming to attention for inspection. Maya looked her up and down: a soppy mess of blonde hair, a shoelace untied, a little pale and shaky yet still on her feet. Good enough. "OK, I need to get going. Keep your mask up, and next time bring a pair of these," she instructed, holding up goggles. "Ear plugs too." Cam watched her stride back toward Lake Street, her silhouette finally slipping into the night. As she wiped away tears, her mother's soothing words washed over her: "Keep looking for the light. Angels will appear when the time is right." How sappy, she thought to herself a second later. Fatboy Slim said it better: right here, right now. This became her mantra from then on. No slinking back to Edina. Faith without justice was fake, and she was determined to be for real, come what may.

To Maya's surprise the cake eater from the suburbs came back. One fiery night after another, she showed her how to read the street and schooled her on what BLM veterans expected of white allies. Nonviolent discipline and no ego were table stakes. She caught on quickly and displayed more sisu and savvy than expected. Soon she was trusted with marshaling and other roles usually reserved for older and more experienced activists. One night on Lake Street, now a boarded-up war zone, as riot patrol tried to kettle and mass arrest several hundred demonstrators, she seized the moment and led a large contingent through a gap in the police line. The next night, she shot past baton-wielding cops and smoking canisters to a skinny young activist overcome by tear gas, slung him over the shoulder and whisked him away. Cahmie-kaze, or just Cahmie, they all now called her.

Almost overnight Maya became the big sister Cam never had, though she didn't see herself that way. An oldest child herself, her Creole parents had sent her to St. Mary's Academy in New Orleans before re-locating to Chicago after Katrina. She went to Howard in DC where her vision of the African diaspora, and the world, expanded a hundredfold. After college she served as a Jesuit volunteer in Haiti and then pursued grad studies in public health at U of M. Steeped in the black Catholic tradition of social activism, she'd been involved with BLM for several years before her path crossed Cam's. When she invited her to move in, it was simply a young sister in the struggle to whom she made the offer.

"Really, ya have a room open?"

"A small one, yes, but that makes it cheap. Asking $425. Includes utilities. I share the house with Rayna and Diego. Both twentysomethings, you'll like them. Best part is you don't have to sign a lease. Month to month. Rent is due Monday, so I need a decision by--"

"Yah, I'll take it!"

"Sold to the impulsive white chick! Should have asked $550," she teased. "Let me text them, call off the search."

A few minutes later Cam heard a ping.

hi cam rayna here
welcome to
movement house

thx cant wait to
meet u and diego!

trust me u can
wait to meet him

[open mouth]

jk hes chill
best bartender ever
[goat]

free drinks
love it already!

fyi we dont mask
and distance in
the house

np

no furry pets
i hope

allergic?

2 of us

ferrets too?

fraid so
sorry

ill deal

[thumbs up]

ball python and
chameleon?

just our type

[thumbs up]

c u soon

bet

A personality test taken in AP Psych class had confirmed what Cam already knew: she had a bias to action. *Self-will, run riot* is how mom put it when she'd shared the results with her. Pulling the trigger on Movement House had been easy, figuring out what to do with Taz--not so much. Giles liked to watch the zebra danios, bettas, neon tetras and other fish dart about, and he was old enough now to take care of the tank. Check. She speed-dialed friends from school, mostly juniors and sophomores, in hopes of arranging a quick adoption. No luck. Musky odor, tough sell. Desperate to find the ferret a new home, she decided to go door-to-door. A neighbor down the street who'd watched her grow up saved the day, and not a moment too soon.

"Oh, my, what a pleasant surprise! It's so good to see you, Cam! And hello there, little rascal." Taz nose-twitched in reply while looking for escape routes.

"Hi, Mrs. Barnes. How are ya?"

"Oh, gosh…I'm getting by. These are times that try the soul. Just grateful for one more day." Cam noticed the strong cat smell that always wafted out the front door was less pungent than usual. Over the past year, she had stopped by weekly to pick up a dead mouse for the royal python's pleasure, the tiny carcass reliably deposited on the back stoop by Whiskers and then kept frozen in a baggie. During the shutdown, visits to the Barnes residence for rations had been less frequent.

"How's our favorite feline?"

Her query wilted the widow. "You didn't hear? Whiskers passed away three weeks ago. I do miss him so."

"I'm so sorry, Mrs. Barnes." Taz was now running circles around her and soon had the leash looped twice. As she reached down awkwardly to untangle herself, the little devil redoubled his efforts.

"Oh, careful now. My, he *is* rambunctious!"

Cam finally brought him to heel and turned back to her host. "I loved Whiskers and his ball of string. What a hunter he was!" Looking past her elderly neighbor into a living room she knew almost as well as her own, she saw the grandfather clock still stuck at three-twenty, the overstuffed couch she'd napped in so many times and the late husband's boat of a recliner—all just where they always were. The large aquarium was still stocked to the gills but had grown a little grimy and green of late. Years ago, she had given Cam a hand-me-down starter tank and shown her the ropes. One time, when she was just four, she'd reached a little too far for one of the goldfish in the pond out back and nearly drowned while mom and Mrs. Barnes got carried away gossiping. Always the same line when, years later, she'd show up on her doorstep to show off another blue ribbon won at club meets: "Now isn't that a beauty. I'm so glad you learned how to swim!"

"Yes, you were as fond of the old fellow as I was," sighed Mrs. Barnes. "Every time he tickled your rosy cheeks, I knew I'd picked out the perfect name for that cat. You two used to play for hours on end. Lord, where have all the years gone?"

"Have you thought about another pet?"

"Of course, but with the shutdown what's one to do?" Bullseye. She was thrilled when Cam explained her dire situation and made the request. Taz was truly heaven sent!

"Oh, Cam, you've made me so happy! Of course, we'll miss you dearly. Anytime you're home, you really must come by. You and Taz can play with that old ball of string," she said with a wink.

God bless Mrs. Barnes.

7
MOVEMENT HOUSE

With all the uncertainty surrounding covid, and having made new friends in town, Cam's decision to defer college wasn't hard--especially after Goldie said she planned to put studies at Columbia on hold. In late June her dad had fallen ill suddenly and died four days later, at the time one of over 131,000 in the country taken by the virus. Vibol drove Cam to the funeral. The two stood close to Goldie, who covered her head and wiped tears away with a dark maroon scarf. After the rabbi tore black ribbons and handed them to the bereaved, they pinned them on their clothes. Goldie, Elijah and their mother sat Shiva for three days. Friends and relatives stopped by to offer condolences and drop off a hotdish.

They now talked every few days by phone, usually around noon after Goldie climbed out of bed and she was back from the park.

"Cam, I'm glad you've gone for it. Wish I were there with you. In our case one plus one equals ten!"

"I know, right?"

"Truth is, I'm jealous. You're learning more each day than I do in a month tooling around online and rotting out here in the burbs. Guess there's only one way to escape the bubble: pop it and run for your life!"

"I'm dead. When you're ready, we'll wedge you into Movement House, hang a hammock from the rafters if need be. Or stick ya in the closet. Whatever it takes."

"We'll see. Not going anywhere until mom is good and ready. She's always been so strong, but she's lost her one and only. Thirty-seven years they were together, through thick and thin. And while it pains me to admit, there's one thing me and the muggles agree upon: family comes first."

"Facts."

"By the way, whatever happened to Heather? I figured with you moving into town you two would--"

"Would what? Anyhoo, I got a text from her a few weeks ago. She graduated from U of M and decided to move back to her parents' place in Grosse Pointe for now. Another life on hold."

"Totally sucks. Did she say what's next?"

"No, just that she's spending time in Detroit volunteering at a community garden. That's a huge thing there, don't cha know. I think she's met someone."

"Cam, I don't know what to--"

"No need, I've had a sense it wasn't meant to be for a while now."

"You and I are for always, you know that."

"You are pure gold."

"So, what's the tea? Wait, let me guess: BLM declared the blocks around the burned-out precinct station an autonomous zone."

"Nah, we're not into copy-catting the left coast. Besides, I hear the Battle in Seattle didn't go so great. The Paris Commune held out twice as long, and last year the Zapatistas added eleven more autonomous zones in Chiapas."

"Well, Paperboy Prince says love is the answer."

"How basic. Thanks for sharing, pretty boy."

"C'mon, he's *really* cute. As telegenic as they come!"

"Please."

"Bet you right now he's going to end up in the White House someday."

"Get a grip."

"Obama broke through! Anything is possible."

"I see you've been dipping into the bourbon early."

"Fine, but don't forget what Oscar Wilde said about why socialism never works."

"Do tell, my dear."

"Takes up too many evenings!"

"Ba-dum-bump! Later, my love."

Two months had flown by since Cam first flung herself into the uprising. Early on, she joined Shoveling for Racial Justice, a white-ally group that supported BLM by taking up the less glamorous, behind-the-scenes work all healthy movements require. By late July she had moved back into climate-justice activism, joining Extinction Rebellion's local chapter. XR's symbol, an hourglass within a circle signifying how time is running out for myriad species, conveyed the urgency of the historical moment. She was taken with the direct-action group's novel disruption tactics and communal structure, designed to prefigure real democracy and frustrate the authorities. The spirit of the Levelers reborn.

Sustained pressure from BLM throughout June had pushed the city council to re-allocate funds toward community needs more pressing than crowd-control munitions and Kevlar vests. A willingness to recognize and grapple with the Minnesota Paradox—severe racial inequality sitting uncomfortably next to liberal sensibility—was growing. Still, not everyone in the cities and surrounding suburbs was on board. Cam sunk deeper into her bean bag as she perused comments on a piece in the Strib that chronicled the growing backlash. Most were defensive, unfair or downright cruel, though a few had a point:

Soberton

If protestors continue to mob every scene of police activity, even when the police action is more than justified, their sword of outrage will turn rusty and dull.

CandyLander

I'll happily take all the cops from your city and let them work in mine. Then you can have your utopia, where criminals run free and street justice is handled by whoever is quickest on the draw.

Spam the Maam

These malcontents should move to Wakanda. Obviously, this wretched country is not where you belong. And please take Ilhan Omar with you, it's high time she returned to her "roots"—or should I say the mother ship.

PrizmWard

Whaddya say BLM, shall we tally up? Police station and apartments for low-income people in cinders. Check. $500M in damages to 1,500 properties in 3 weeks, most small businesses not big bad corporations. Check. Thanks guys!

Effin Write

The inmates are running the prison in Minneapolis. Wait until the economic contributors move to the suburbs. The city will be left with the lifelong losers and a woke city council that ran out of other people's money.

Greek Geek

Good cops are retiring way faster than they can be replaced. That is what happens when socialists try to re-engineer society overnight. Earth to libs: re-read the myth of Icarus before it's too late. You have nothing to lose but your hubris and over-inflated idealism.

She closed her computer and stared up at the ceiling. What if the sound and fury is never-ending? Was there any way get people past their fear and loathing? A long minute went by. Nothing coalesced, just a jumble of half-formed thoughts floating above the despondency now welling up and threatening to drown her. She lurched forward, straightened her spine and blinked at the blank white wall several times before battening down her eyelids. Stay calm…feelings come and go…just breathe…. This much became clear: the defensiveness and hostility of many white folks, whose self-image and security felt threatened by BLM's insistence that being a "good person" wasn't good enough, exemplified a broader tendency to resist change and maintain privilege. But what if progressive whites in particular stopped posturing and started to accept feedback on their unconscious racism? What if college grads toiled for a year in a factory, warehouse or dollar store to learn what life is like for most workers? What if men didn't deny their sexism, and cis people dealt with rather than ran from their transphobia? What if the neuro-typical and abled-bodied acknowledged a wider spectrum? Wouldn't those changed mindsets contribute powerfully to social reform? Facing the music, asking for forgiveness, figuring out how to repair the damage—how rare these abilities were….

"*¡Vamos!*" Diego's bark startled her. She gripped both sides of the bag before falling back into the crater her body had created. A moment later Maya poked her head in. “You look like hell, girl. PMS if ever I saw it.”

“Uff-da, you *didn’t* just say that.”

“Truth hurts. Sure you still want to go? Everyone’s waiting.”

“Sorry, I’ll be out in just a minute. Don’t leave without me!” Maya walked over, offered a hand and pulled her up. Her firm grip reminded Cam of the first time she had tugged her to safe harbor and administered baptism under fire, the sloshed milk on her frightened face a balm she would never forget. Once on her feet, she fell into Maya’s arms and held tight.

“Whoah, you’re cuttin’ off the circulation!” Cam released her and laughed nervously. “Not sure where that came from…”

“You know I like dancing with you, but now is not the time.” Maya smirked and nodded toward the door. “Let’s roll. And don’t forget your water bottle.”

A few minutes later she came out. “Where’s Rayna, isn’t she coming?”

“Nature called, *again*,” dead-panned Diego. Three women and only one bathroom was torture. If only they knew what the name of this house really meant! One time Maya had caught him pee-hopping in the hallway and laughed so hard she nearly peed herself. Ever since he’d used the wait-time to hone his salsa technique, though most nights he just ducked out back and found a bush. His post-covid dream: making it into the Top Twenty on *So You Think You Can Dance*.

The plan was to bike together to a march hastily organized by United Renters for Justice, a neighborhood housing-rights group formed a few years back by Hispanics sick of the slumlords. Diego knew Miguel, one of the organizers and an old friend of his father Emilio. Both were second-generation immigrants whose Mexican parents had picked sugar beet in Red River Valley before the Depression. They had worked together for almost forty years at the railyard just around the corner from Movement House. Miguel had offered Diego a job after high school, but he preferred cutting grass at the publinks course a little further up Central and tending bar at Lumpy's, a popular dive in the arts district. He could bike to both workplaces in less than ten minutes.

Once he memorized the contours of each green, Diego's daybreak job at Columbia GC could be done in his sleep. At night he came alive. A born comic and a magician with mixers, regulars referred to him as the Jesting Juggler. Mix two parts George Lopez with one part Anthony Gatto and—voila!—you had yourself a J&J. Pre-shutdown he pocketed more in one night than he made all month riding the mower. Often keyed up after a late-night shift, he'd flick the Iron Maiden's flippers till dawn, smoke a joint and then trim one to eighteen just so while staying a hole ahead of the first foursome. Occasionally, PC and Nick the Stick gave him hell if he forgot to put a flag back or stuck a pin too close to the fringe. Everyone bitched about the sixth, a short par 3 guarded by a tall oak known to locals as Manute Bol with limbs that loomed over half the green. Sometimes he'd tuck the hole front right just to tick off Jacko, Little Jerry and Horse--none of whom could hit the crisp knock-down cutter that curled sideways after a short hop and gave you a chance at birdie. Most days he'd be done by eight-thirty and snoring soon after. He'd roll out of bed around two and go play an afternoon round with CJ and Dom, both single-digit handicappers like himself, though some days his door stayed closed until dinner.

After being laid-off from the bar, he had taken PC's advice and worked more on his short game, setting up his own nine-hole putt-putt indoors. A nifty design, the mini-muni started in his bedroom, doglegged left into the hallway and down to the bathroom, then hooked around into the living room and through the foyer and dining room before doglegging right into the kitchen, where you could grab a hot dog and beer after the round. Most pins were chair legs. If a ball settled under a couch or table or too close to a wall, you were entitled to relief. Still, the course proved difficult because doors and throw rugs were red-staked; any contact at all with either incurred a one-stroke penalty, and you had to play from point of infraction. Every hole had subtle breaks from the slight warps in the Tigerwood floors. The par 31 track tape-measured 63 yards and had an un-official course rating of 28.6. Only twice had he gone low, once with a 25 and then two days later with a course-record 23. That night he'd bragged about it while half-drunk and with his zipper undone. The women started calling him J-Lo after that and kept at it until he finally made good on his threat to stop mixing drinks.

Usually, he could sail through his nine-holer in eighteen minutes flat unless a human rain delay held him up at the notorious number two, a par 3 requiring a delicate bank shot off the side of the tub if one hoped to hit the plunger in back of the toilet for a hole-in-one. "I scheduled a pee time an hour in advance!" he'd yell, but they only cackled like hyenas and told him to get a life. Management sucked at this place. Often the door to the hole would remain closed for a half-hour or more due to heavy showers. Most rainy days he'd grudgingly card a 3 and move on.

After puttering around the house, he tried his hand at day-trading with crowd-sourced advice gleaned from a popular sub-ribbit. The uprising came just in time. Without a re-direct into something more righteous, he might've lost every penny he'd somehow managed to save. Maya kept ribbing him about the epic losses, if only to keep him from backsliding into the gamified e-trading app that made millions enticing millions to chase millions. At least the time he put into perfecting his putting paid off. Once Columbia opened in April, he shed three strokes from his handicap in no time. He had less success with the winter weight.

"Let's see, Diego, in just a few months you've gone from J&J to J-Lo to Robinhood or Bust. What's next *amigo*?" inquired Maya with mocking grin.

"*Que gacho.*"

"Testy today, aren't we?"

"Don't mess with me, *chica*. Not in the mood."

"You're a prince to come along. We're so grateful."

"Gonna pay my respects to Miguel and demand my rights. You gotta problem with that?" Diego hated being played, but Maya had his number and they both knew it. He was a founding member of Movement House only because he thought, once upon a time, he had a shot with her.

Rayna finally returned, adorned in the usual: hand-painted high-tops, tight denim shorts and bell-sleeved blouse. She must own a dozen identical outfits, Cam surmised, since she never seemed to do laundry. Maya called her Rayna Bell, or simply Bell, for the flowing sleeves and ringer on her vintage Schwinn she often rang for no reason. Always the same wig style, long and straight with bangs. Only the hair color varied, today neon pink instead of emerald-green, dark purple or copper red. Though four years older than Cam, she looked four years younger. Never any jewelry, but her one visible tattoo—a Bashō haiku with kanji characters strung like beads around her long neck–was the hottest choker she'd ever set eyes upon. She teased her on occasion about her shoelaces. Suggesting the need for a new pair triggered an adamant denial followed by a detailed account of the proper lacing and tying technique for maximizing their longevity. Anything for a little attention from awkward aspy girl, whose height and figure mirrored Heather's--and hers.

"Ah, there she is, our manga princess," announced Cam.

"OK, I'm ready. Thanks for waiting, ladies. You too J&J."

"It's what I do. Born to wait on the ladies."

Maya was not so patient. "Time to go, y'all. Past time, in fact." To escape Rayna's ring-ring-ring she pedaled hard and kept a brisk pace. In the lead was where you'd find her most of the time. Upon arriving they padlocked their bikes and waded into a small sea of millennials and the newly graduated, many waving past-due notices. Diego spotted Miguel near the makeshift podium and went over to say hello. Speeches called for an extension of the state's eviction moratorium, set to expire next month, and ran the usual list of renter woes: cracked concrete and sprained ankles; leaky roofs and overflowing buckets; backed-up commodes and ruined rugs; cheap fridges and spoiled food; broken locks and break-ins; doubled security deposits unreturned for no good reason. A few slumlord dummies swung in the breeze, having been hung in effigy. The march ended at a dingy real-estate office, notorious for never returning calls or making repairs. As expected, organizers found the door locked; they taped a petition over the Out to Lunch sign and thanked everybody for coming out on such short notice.

After treading the pavement under a mid-day sun and biking another hour back home, everyone was wiped. The three women retreated to their rooms. Before coming in, Diego trundled down the walkway and picked up a plastic bag stuffed with ads and coupons laying close to the curb. From the street,

Movement House wasn't much to look at, he had to admit. An aging bungalow painted pea-soup green with anemic patches of grass, three shrubs on life support and two old, diseased oaks that looked for all the world like a pair of Ents. Out front only dandelions felt welcome. Around back another world beckoned, a riot of color and lush growth surrounding a spacious deck. He made himself useful one time laying down some all-weather linoleum. Chez Diablo, they called it, the hottest dance floor in Nord'east! Luxuriant flowers bloomed from May to October. Along the deck's railing a row of vases held asters and day lilies. Down below the chrysanthemums and begonias brightened shady spots, while the coneflowers and petunias drew butterflies, the latter also attracting hummingbirds. In the evening its perfume wafted up through the deck boards. So many marigolds the backyard seemed ablaze through spring and summer. In the fall the flame would pass to the Japanese maple as its leaves turned jacinth. He kept two birdfeeders filled, a chore he dared not shirk lest the black-capped chickadees, blue jays and dark-eyed junkos jump ship. A long thick wall of bamboo, kept in check by his machete, hid the cemetery's barbed-wire fence and sea of gravestones from sight. *From Edina to Eden*, Cam had said the first time she stepped out back.

After the Fourth the fireworks had crackled across the sky for another week and then died down. So did the nightly protests. Evenings were now spent on the deck, usually with something home-cooked and occasionally with carry-out, pizza being the default. That and anything Asian. Diego stocked the cooler religiously, conjured big carafes of sangria on demand and conducted surprisingly good salsa lessons. Maya brought her Haitian *konpa* and Argentine tango to the floor, both of which Cam fell in love with instantly. She found tango more difficult to learn than salsa, especially the lead. They practiced most evenings and switched roles often. Blessed with nimble fingers but cursed with two left feet, Rayna was content to DJ, doodle and munch on puppy chow. Her preternatural ability to track down bops and jams in multiple genres was legendary. In a heartbeat they'd be free-styling to "Billie Jean" or faux-jitter-bugging to "Sing, Sing, Sing" or shaking it all out when she threw "Twerk" into the mix. Nina Simone's "Feeling Good" was their anthem, the one song that got all four onto the floor. It was hard to imagine a better place to ride out the pandemic.

Over a stuffed deep dish that night they planned to debrief the day's event. No one wanted to cook or dance after all the biking and marching. Around eight Diego's older brother Jorge, just off a shift delivering 300 Primo packages, paid them a surprise visit.

"Jeet?" asked Cam.

"Not yet." Maya ordered another pizza, this one a large thin crust with extra cheese. Diego handed him a beer and gestured toward the cornhole board. "Throw some?"

"Nah, kinda beat." He wondered how Jorge and his wife Juanita were handling the shutdown. She was still recovering from a difficult pregnancy. In between caring for four-year-old Victor and three-month-old Ora, she watched Univision and studied English. With the parks and malls closed, they seldom left their two-bedroom apartment in West Side. Jorge worked all day and kept his distance at night as a precaution. Little Victor was born to rumble, just like his papa, and he could not imagine how she coped day in and day out.

On occasion, when both kids were napping, Juanita dealt with the stress and isolation by touching herself. Long ago she had found other uses for her grandmother's rosary beads. As a child she loved to play with the crazy lace agate stones, one of the few indulgences allowed an orphan in a poor village. All fifty-nine agates were fascinating. She spent countless siesta hours tracing the swirls of color, each marble a portal to another world. In her teen years the rosary's silver crucifix served as a handle. She would run the round beads across arms and legs, around neck and ears and eventually past nipples. Sometimes she wondered whether any spots eluded her. One afternoon she found another, more alluring than the rest, wet and wonderful.

The day she left drought-stricken Sinaloa, her grandmother pressed the cool, glistening gemstones into her dry hands and simply said, "*El agua es vida. Ve a buscar agua.*" Walking west the first water she found was the Gulf of California. She hiked up the coast to Guaymas, where she took a chance and jumped in the back of a pick-up heading north to Hermosillo. A nun at the shelter there said cartel operatives patrolled the main roads looking for lovelies; she was lucky to be alive after such a stunt. Better to follow on foot the railroad track and river as far as Benjamin Hill. Along that route she could fill her plastic jug more easily, and nothing was more important when crossing desert. Along the way she waved on occasion to fellow migrants atop freight cars. Honduran daredevils! The last leg to Nogales had to be along Route 15. She traveled from early dawn till noon, then took a siesta among the shrubs before continuing until dark, the jug her only pillow. Whenever it ran empty, she managed to find a tap and a cheap tortilla. Avoiding pimps, coyotes and other predators proved trickier, but with each glaring come-on rebuffed she gained a little more confidence. Still, sister was right: forced abductions were all too common in this territory. All she could do to avoid that fate was stay out of sight at night and, when possible, tread the many miles with others as poor and vulnerable as her.

It took three weeks to get from Hermosillo to Nogales. She arrived with only a few pesos left in her pouch. At the border town's edge, she met a young couple as determined as she was to reach the other side. Enrique couldn't shake a nasty cough. "Bad air in the maquila," he replied when she asked him about it. "Gotta get outta this shithole before they bury me here." Days they scouted terrain and evenings studied the sky. When a full moon finally arrived, they followed a trail that meandered often but always kept returning to a course set by the North Star. Three days later a sanctuary group found them before the Border Patrol did. Curled up like a stray cat, an emaciated Juanita was rocking back and forth slowly, her rosary beads held tight with hands tucked between thighs.

Now here she was years later, with a roof over her head and food in the fridge, a good husband and two healthy children, yet often feeling as forlorn as Hagar wandering in the wilderness. Was the pleasure the rosary provided sinful? Who wrote the rules for self-care? She doubted the desolate figure on the cross, whose eyes she always shielded with her palm, would pronounce judgment. And these days, what could any priest or bishop say about it! Only God and her grandmother could speak. The former remained silent, and the latter had passed away not long after she left. "*Perdóname, abuela, me siento abandonada,*" she said to herself before sliding the beads and climbing heavenward.

After the fireworks frenzy subsided the summer days seemed even more lonely. One afternoon during a hot spell, while the kids slept, she showered and began to run the beads across her wet body while lying in bed on her back. Soon she closed her eyes and let them fall from her hand. In a deep reverie she saw her grandmother, hair pinned up and stout as ever, wearing a long cotton dress dyed ruby-red and embroidered at the edges with sunflowers. She was standing in front of her tiny cottage cradling a large wooden bowl filled with her granddaughter's favorite fruits: mamey, pitaya, cherimoya, prickly pear, jocote, mango and pomegranate! Juanita's mouth watered. Something in the eyes of her *abuela* said all was forgiven. None of the fruit was forbidden. It never had been. All at once a wall within, one built long ago to ward off wounds and limit hopes, was washed away by tears of joy that flowed continuously over temples into ears and down the neck into her thick brown hair. Down to the marrow, through every sinew and corpuscle, across every synapse a healing energy flowed. "*El agua es vida*," she repeated to herself quietly. Never had she felt so alive and yet so at peace. What was an orgasm—even a string of them--next to this bliss! A Fullness beyond compare had rushed in, set her free and at the same time somehow brought her home. *Aguas de la vida*.

An hour passed before a little boy appeared at her side and confessed sheepishly that he'd wet his bed. Her joyous outburst startled him, but soon he was laughing too as she raised him high and whirled him round and round in her arms. He had never seen his mother so happy! Their jubilation woke Ora, who was ready to nurse. The soiled sheets would have to wait.

Juanita and Jorge played by the rules and received in return a food-stamp card that loaded with $242 on the sixth each month. They paid $185 monthly for a high-deductible plan found on the state exchange, which meant the bill stating they owed five grand for Ora's complicated delivery was on them. Pay the hospital $175 monthly through 2024. Pay the minimum each month on the maxed-out credit card for who knows how long. Keep paying or see an already low credit score sink lower. Don't even think about savings.

Jorge worked harder than ever as an Amerizon driver speeding, running stop signs and parking illegally to stay on the break-neck schedule. Most days he didn't stop for lunch. Slurp down another PBJ and keep rolling. He dreaded the hurry-up texts that popped up whenever he fell behind. No wonder they called his device a *rabbit.* Peeing in a milk jug and ignoring the seat belt saved time too. At least he didn't have to go tinkle in a trash bag like the women drivers. The company's subcontractor always blamed them when packages went missing, so he never skimped on taking a pic of each one he placed on the doorstep. He almost quit last December during the holiday rush. Seven hours into his eleventh shift in twelve days he jammed his hand badly in the van door. As it swelled into a Michelin-Man paw he called his super. Don't come back until the van's empty, he said. And don't be late. After slipping on an icy walkway while trying to balance a thirty-five-pound box in one arm, he reluctantly cut his shift short. When he showed them his throbbing hand, now bundled in an ace bandage provided by a customer, they laughed and said only girls and faggots don't finish runs. He toughed it out and now relied on his one good paw to open jars, tighten screws and bear the weight of heavier items on each day's rack. In May a two-dollar bump in hazard pay put him at $17.20 an hour before withholding. Sometimes they stiffed him on the OT. A gig driver told him the feds fined the company sixty-one million dollars for thieving their tips. No surprise.

When the pizza arrived Jorge, though starving, refrained from wolfing down too many slices. He endured Diego's lie about leaving his little brother to drown after pushing him off a pier when they were kids. Reluctantly, he had come over to ask for a loan. Eating off food stamps and bumming rent money was humiliating, but he had no choice after his old Camaro blew a piston that cost a fortune to fix. Men in their family took care of business, no matter what it took. At least he hadn't done anything stupid and landed upstate like some guys from high school he knew. Despite the grueling sixty-hour weeks he just wasn't bringing home enough, and it was eating him up inside.

"*Hermanito, hablemos en el frente*." From his crisp tone, Diego knew something was up. Jorge gave the women a warm smile. "Ladies, *muchas gracias*. It was good to see you."

"Likewise, Jorge. Say hello to Juanita for me," replied Maya. Before the shutdown, they had come over on occasion for dinner. Little Victor had a big crush on Maya, who used to babysit him now and then pre-covid.

The Ramírez brothers walked to the street. After a brief exchange Diego pulled out his wallet and handed Jorge $300. "A dollar tip for each delivery today. You lucky I just hit the ATM, *hermano*."

"You lucky I fetched your sorry ass out of the water that day you fell in," retorted Jorge. "I'll get this back to you next month, no lie."

"I'm good, *hermano*. You got the wife and kids to worry about. Of course, if you had bought Bitcoin a year ago like I said you wouldn't be standing here with your hand out."

"*Siempre el culo sabio*. How you survived all these years I'll never know."

Diego chuckled. Jorge had saved his hide more times than he could remember. Now he had just given him a chance to give a little back. "You look tired, *hermano*. Still sleeping in the living room?"

He nodded yes. "Not taking any chances. Rona's no joke." The lumpy couch made for lousy sleep, and he missed roughhousing with Victor, taking

Ora for a stroll and cuddling with Juanita. He didn't miss diaper duty, though. Covid imposed what amounted to a prison sentence, only no one could say for sure when he'd be released. Still, he had it better than Ivan, his best friend from high school who picked orders off shelves and stuffed boxes all night in the Shakopee warehouse. He said the walk to the vending machines in the break room was eight football fields long, so he brought a thermos and two doughnuts, one for each of the two short breaks, and found a wall close his work area to kick back on. His fitbit tracked him at eleven miles one night; it must be broken, he thought, until others confirmed the distance. Cameras tracked the flows 24/7. The device clipped to his belt counted every step he made in the orthopedic shoes he bought after a month of blisters. By jogging to the john and back he avoided a dock in pay. Some of the older guys snuck into the stacks nearby. Why walk another half mile and risk not making rate? Everyone knew where whiz alley was and steered clear if they could.

Treat every package like it's coming to your house, team leaders repeated endlessly. Jorge always snickered when Ivan mimicked the training video showing a young girl bawling after a picker had grabbed the wrong doll off the shelf and ruined her birthday. It was no laughing matter that only two of the three dozen employees he started with fifteen months ago were still around. Given the hectic pace he hardly spoke with the few who stuck it out, much less the many who came and went quickly. You could go a week in the warehouse without saying a word to anyone. Zombie work by design. Most who left got injured or succumbed to arthritis, asthma and other chronic ailments aggravated by the grind. Several quit because of hearing loss from working too long and too close to so many noisy machines. He found it hard to get the incessant forklift honking out of his head after a shift. Several were fired for failing to make rate.

One oft-shared meme--Work Hard or U R History--mocked the company slogan. Three reprimands and an algorithm sent you packing, as it were. He had two strikes against him. High pollen levels had left him lethargic in the spring. One night he forgot his inhaler. On another he just felt too weak to keep up. Past allergy season he upped his game. A super doled out $20 gift cards to the week's "top rate" winner. By early August he'd pocketed three. Back in the day, he and Jorge were guard and tackle on the varsity's offensive line. Play through the pain, coach always said. He used the cards to stock up on Vitamin I, which kept the sore knees and back-aches at bay.

Wearing a special vest that kept stacked Kivas from running him over made him feel like roadkill in waiting. Bots and pushy managers were the least of his worries, though. The surge in orders from covid and free one-day delivery translated into bumper cars on the floor. Before the pandemic, workers joked another week on the graveyard shift at Shakopee left you one step closer to it. Now it was two. After pushing bowling balls and prom dresses out the door, he busted a gut when corporate claimed essential items were top priority. Last summer Muslim employees had struck for six hours on Primo Day demanding time to pray. The same month workers in five European countries and India went out on strike. At the time he'd spoken on the sly with a salt named Bashir, one of many East African immigrants working there, but decided it wasn't his fight. They canned Bashir and two other salts soon after the walkout. Now every worker's life was threatened by the latest hiring spree and speed-up. No one knew who was infected, and the managers refused to say. During the uprising they added insult to injury by handing out Juneteenth t-shirts and stopping the flow for nine minutes. The next time the Somalis walked out, he'd be right behind them. Jorge said they also were organizing at the delivery station in Eagan and talking with workers in Chicago, San Bernadino and other cities. Some of the geeks in Seattle might even join them. Imagine that.

"How's it going at work? Them *pendejos* still running you ragged?" asked Diego.

"Dudes in charge are a disgrace. Completely unorganized and playing favorites all the time. I've gotten to know a few of the Somali drivers. There's a plan brewing to strike on Primo Day in October if things don't change."

Diego recognized the steely glint in his eye. Whenever Humboldt High needed three yards for a first down, everyone knew the call was dive left. Jorge and Ivan seldom failed to open a hole for the fullback, even though his brother was small for his position and had better hands than the pretty-boy tight end next to him. Both grinders had more than one game ball, the most coveted prize beyond the league trophy. Before covid put a stop to the Brazilian jiu jitsu classes that kept him sane, Jorge had earned a brown belt. He rarely lost a match, even when pitted against the academy's most advanced. Messing with Jorge was a mistake.

"Sounds like you gonna jump in if they make a move."

"Strength in numbers. But don't tell nobody about it. Last thing I need is you and your loose lips gettin' me fired."

"I ain't sinkin' no ship. Just call if you need back-up."

"*Buenas noches, hermanito.*" He hugged Diego, fired up the Camaro and drove off like a drag racer. At the stop sign he left a long skid mark. Just enough steam let off to make it through another day, thought Diego, as he lingered on the sidewalk and fell into a favorite daydream: he and Jorge, badly outnumbered, brawl their way out of serious trouble…he always strikes the decisive blow that leads to victory…sometimes the punch saves Jorge from a knife stab that spells certain death.

Three brewskis in, Diego was on a roll. "Tell me, what does this moratorium get us? Doesn't mean jack, that's what. At some point the man's gonna want his money--all of it. So what if some of us are paid up and still gotta few bucks left from unemployment. *Los culeros* in DC turned that hose off yesterday, right?" He paused just long enough to twist open another top, take a swig and make a show of shoving his free hand into his blue jeans. "Say we keep payin' rent outta pocket and covid keeps kickin' our ass." He pushed his hand down further and was now listing sideways, like a stick figure coming unglued. "Well, this pocket ain't as deep as they say!" He yanked out his hand, turning the pocket inside out, a white flag now hanging from his hip. He froze in mock shock, mouth agape and arm extended. In his palm lay the bottle cap. The three women laughed whenever he resorted to sloppy slapstick, sometimes just to support a fragile ego and sometimes—as in this moment--because it worked.

Audience in hand, Diego kept rolling. "Landlords ain't the only ones knockin' on the door. Half us *pendejos* been takin' for a ride by Stage Coach and the rest of them robbers. They chargin' people twenty-four-effin' percent to use a credit card, for Christ's sake! Re-po man is havin' a field day."

"Usury rears its ugly head yet again," commented Cam. Before she could elaborate on the historical and cultural transformation of usury from vice to virtue under early capitalism, a digression she thought might interest Rayna, Diego re-poed the talking stick. "What if covid spikes again in November, like they say, and we're all still outta work? Then what? Come Christmas my nephew Victor's gonna be cryin' in his milk when there's nothin' under the tree, that's what. Can't even play with his own papa now cuz of covid."

"On the day after Christmas the other hose, so to speak, gets turned off," noted Rayna the resident policy wonk whose fingers never let the keyboard rest. A recent U. Chicago grad, she'd double-majored in Japanese and philosophy. Diego and Maya put up with her manga fetish and occasional zone-outs not only because she was the finest DJ around, but also because she could find anything online fast and cut through the alt-fact crap quickly. She'd spent much of her adolescence immured in her room, sketching esoteric figures and watching every anime film ever made. Reddish-brown eyes glued to the screen, she continued: "That's when the clock for twelve million on unemployment runs out. Most laid-off workers only get around four hundred dollars per week, and the extra six hundred they've been receiving from Uncle Sam just ran out, as Diego said."

"Positively Dickensian," chimed in Cam, hoping to impress her. A slightly raised eyebrow suggested it might have. "Or should I say social Darwinian." A faint smile signaled more. Game on.

Armed with the facts, Diego again took back the talking stick: "Tiny Tim on every corner! I'm tellin' you, we don't light a fire soon, a big-ass bonfire, them *chingados* in Washington ain't gonna spray the infield no more. If they don't pay, I say we don't pay. Housing is a human right. Am I right? Tell me I'm not right."

Maya had heard enough. "Don't light the torches just yet, Diablo. Jimmy's not the CEO of Stage Coach, he's just another mom-and-pop landlord with bills stacking up like everyone else. And he's done right by us the past two years. If we don't pay rent, it's not just him taking a hit. He's the lifeline for his daughter and her three kids."

"They already lit, *chica*," replied Diego as he waved his empty bottle at the tikis, then put it down and lit a joint, its smoke rising over his dark moustache and drooping brown eyes. Drain one too many and Diablo was his name-o. If his fearlessness and loyalty was his strength, his weakness was all too obvious. More than once, Maya had stepped in all sassy just in time to keep him and the other guy from going at it. What saved him was a willingness to stand down when she said so.

"But Stage Coach *is* evil." The sop she tossed his way drew a snicker from the other two. "Diablos!" seconded Cam. Then all three in unison: "Diablos!"

He drew the last Surly Darkness from the cooler, slumped back into his lawn chair and took two long slugs before belching. "Fine, but you haven't told me how all of that back rent gets paid. Moratorium just kicks the can down the road. Nothin' but a band-aid. We gonna bleed out, you watch."

"Time for a Rent Jubilee, yah? Forgive us our rent, as we forgive those who…" After her third glass of sangria Cam could not find the words to finish the thought, but it didn't matter. The idea was inspired--if a bit fuzzy.

"Rent forgiveness gets complicated, but I think you're on the right track," noted Rayna, glancing furtively at Cam before resuming another search. She danced over the keys in double-time. "OK, the National Low Income Housing Coalition says it'll take $100 billion to clear accounts. Send cash to renters, that's the simplest and most effective way. Congress includes that number in the next relief bill and Trump signs it so he can play sugar daddy and win a second term."

"No doubt his signature on every check," snarked Maya.

Diego stared in disbelief at Rayna. "Let me get this straight: the only way outta this fiasco is to put up with that *pendejo* four more years? Talk about a hosing!"

"Point taken," she replied with furrowed brow. "Maybe it can wait until after the election. Even if Trump loses, he'll still want to go out looking like Santa instead of Scrooge."

Maya looked at Diego and wiped a fake tear away. "I can see the joy lighting up little Victor's face now." Even when tipsy Cam never missed a cue. "God bless us, everyone!"

Rayna wasn't finished with her forecast. "If we do dump Trump and he tries to salt the earth on the way out, the governors can extend their moratoriums. Worst case, they circle the wagons and wait for the cavalry to arrive in late January."

Cam was surprised she had missed the fly in her ointment. "What if McConnell still controls the Senate? Then we're scrooged. People won't end up on the street right away, but without another round of relief they'll be buried in debt. That's Diego's point, don't cha know." Rayna turned quizzical and then withdrew into a strange, trance-like state that reminded her of Giles lost in his fork.

"Off into the ether again," observed Diego. "She'll snap out of it. We just never know when." Maya looked at Cam and shrugged. What prompted Rayna's return to the living remained a mystery to all.

"Well, Mitch *is* the mother of all Scrooges," noted Maya. "Maybe we should put some effort into Tina Smith's campaign. Winning the Senate is a reach, but you never know. BLM has to morph into BVM if we want our work on the ground to pay off at the national level."

"*Oh Dios mio*, not another effin' acronym," whined Diego. "Let's see... BVM stands for...blood-sucking vampires moonlighting."

His elocution (or was it the burb immediately following?) somehow broke the spell over Rayna. "Smacks of purple prose yet shows promise. But can we *please* drop the gerunds? They're a plague on contemporary literature."

"What the hell is a gerund?" asked glassy-eyed Diego. "Sounds like the shit I put in some fancy-ass drink after the preppy *pendejo* jams his phone in my face and asks, 'J&J, can you make me *this* one?'" Before she could respond, Cam grabbed a tiki torch in one hand and a left-over kabob stick in the other. Hoisting both high, she advanced upon her. "How about blood-drenched Viking marauds."

Diego raised his near-empty bottle. "*¡Esa!*" He hopped up and poured Cam another glass.

"Yes, that's more like it. The thrust of that image compels. God, I'm getting all goose-pimply," blushed Rayna. Cam ran the tip of the stick across the length of her thigh to raise more goose bumps. "Yes, that's it." Then she slid the wood spear between her legs and twirled it. "Yes, that's--"

"We heard you the *first* time," broke in Maya, annoyed the foreplay was morphing into getta-room. Cam withdrew the point but continued to hover over a quivering Bell. Teasing her from on top was pleasurable, no doubt about it, but she wondered whether she in turn was succumbing with intent or merely transfixed by a novel sensation. Either way, things had become more interesting.

Diego glanced at Maya and waved his now-empty bottle toward Cam. "Yo, *chica*, you gonna contribute to the writer's circle or what?"

"Give me a second, this is definitely not my forte...OK, I've got one: banal vacuous manuscript."

"Ooh! Mic drop!" exclaimed Cam as she held out the spear and let it fall onto the deck where it settled into a groove between two boards.

"So, who's this Tina Smith chick anyway?" asked Diego. "She a singer?"

An incredulous Rayna stared at him dead-eyed. "Surely you jest, J&J. Senator Smith is up for re-election in November. Please tell me you're registered to vote."

"Uh, I've been busy. But don't worry, I'll sign up tomorrow first thing. I'm down with blue vote majority. That's it, right? BVM, count me--"

"Enough said, Diablo. You're flagged," announced Maya. The three women rose at once and went inside, leaving him to put out the tikis and clean up. He stood up and scowled at the mess. "*Me cago en la leche!*" He picked up three empties and began to juggle, adding two more once warmed up. After a minute or so he caught one and then another, placing each onto the card table without a clink as the others remained afloat until the air was empty.

"*¡Esa!* Still got it, *chicas*!" he shouted through the screen door. All three howled as one. "*¡Vete al infierno!*" Always outnumbered he was.

"Diego!" hollered Maya a minute later. "Don't forget to put the can out, tomorrow's trash day." Now in her attic room, Rayna opened the back window and proceeded to play "Garbage Man Blues" just loud enough for Diego to hear.

8

CALIFORNIA ON FIRE

The next day Cam woke as usual around nine. She plucked an apple from the fridge and a handful of vanilla wafers from the donation jar before mounting her bike. Breezy and still cool, she took her time riding down quiet streets before stopping at California Building, the oldest arts haunt in the neighborhood. A notice said galleries were open by appointment only, so she settled for a chamomile at Hobo Coffee next door. The server, an Adonis out of place, handed her the cup in one hand and a glossy orange-red flyer in the other. "No Burning Man this year, sad to say, but here's an upcoming event that might interest you." After he vanished suddenly through a curtain of beads, her eyes fell upon the promo:

NORTHEAST ARTS ASSOCIATION PROUDLY PRESENTS:

CALIFORNIA ON FIRE

Join us Labor Day Weekend for an
Arts-on-Fire Festival
at Boom Island Park
A Fundraiser for Climate Refugees
(Masks and Social Distancing Mandatory)

Burning Man by the Mississippi, how inspired! And at her favorite spot no less! How had she not known? She finished her tea and pedaled down to the park. While keeping an eye out for Godol, she ate her apple by the river and imagined herself in the northern Nevada desert among thousands of ultra-hip creatives. Rayna said Burners make art a way of being in the world, prefiguring for a week what life in a fully actualized flow state can be. If only the rest of us could be free of all our anxieties and allow natural joy to flow unhindered! She had read Spinoza and Rousseau and Csikszentmihalyi and *A Thousand Plateaus* in her Continental Thinkers course, so she really knew.

A few minutes into her reverie she polished off the wafers. Among the cloud formations what seemed a dragon's head caught her eye. She looked upriver and now envisioned herself atop the lighthouse with a commanding view of the cities. In a flash it came to her: Rally her Extinction Rebellion group around the idea of replicating Lightship Greta, which XR folk in the UK were busy building. They planned to launch the red-and-white float from the beach town of Brighton and roll it into London to kickstart their early September offensive. What if XR-TC crowd-constructed her twin at the festival and then tugged it to the capitol building in St. Paul? There they could demand the state go fossil free by 2030, beginning with cancellation of Kilridge's pipeline project up north. Bringing Greta II to life and launching her down University Avenue would be the perfect follow-up to California on Fire, would it not? Arts on fire to change the world! She grew giddy at the thought and began to fill her journal with sketches and notes.

A half-hour later she looked up. Godol was already at the south bridge saying goodbye to his birds. A twinge of guilt came and went as quickly as the many pigeons soon flying overhead. She stood up and stretched, her arms reaching toward the sun. Just then a dropping landed too close for comfort. She looked down and saw the splatter on her tennis shoes. Instant karma! Tomorrow she would deliver unto Godol a double portion without fail. Meanwhile, there was much to do. She dipped her dirty shoe toes in the water, wiped them clean on the grass and raced back to Movement House in record time.

As participants in XR-TC's strat-chat popped onto the screen, Cam could not wait to share her lightship vision:

> **brianna:** Greetings, fellow rebels! [waves and smiles all around] Before we do a whole person check-in, any new items to add to the agenda? It's a busy one!
>
> **cam:** Hi Bri, hi everyone. [more smiles and waves] I have a totally awesome action idea to run by you all, don't cha know. The timetable is tight, but I—
>
> **brianna:** I'm sure we'll have time at the end for you to tell us all about it. Jasper, can you be our time steward today? [obligatory nod] Thanks so much, Jasper. [obligatory smile] And Helga, can you be our equal-voice guardian? [obligatory nod] Really appreciate you, Helga. [obligatory smile] Now, who would like to share how they're feeling first? And remember, we use the MEPS check-in method. Tell us how you're faring mentally, emotionally, physically and spiritually. [many obligatory nods] And don't forget to mute yourself when you've finished speaking. [more obligatory nods]
>
> **muna:** I'll go first. I have to say I'm really struggling mentally and emotionally with the stress of covid. Physically the distancing is next to impossible. People invade my space again and again and I feel so vulnerable. [several hearts and roses] The masks reveal our spiritual condition, right?

isolated and powerless. How can we protect other species if we can't protect ourselves? [Jasper signals time; many claps and fires]

kadijatu: That was so beautiful, sister Muna, thank you. My people in Sierra Leone already were suffering so much before the pandemic and now things are even worse. [hearts and roses flood screens] My country ranks third in its vulnerability to climate change. We have no time to lose. I am Mandinka, as you know, and so I am not just a survivor, I am a fighter. Today I am feeling very strong. [claps and fire fill screens] The will of Allah must be done. We have to— [Jasper signals time; a few open mouths appear; in the group chat an impromptu discussion over radical Islam and Trump's ban on migrants from Muslim countries breaks out]

pierre: Kadijatu, you are so inspiring. [one joy emoji pops up] I was feeling really down before you spoke, but now I am ready to take on the world! How do you do it? I really want you—

brianna: Excuse me, Pierre, but please follow the MEPS method and speak to all four aspects of your evolving self. And try to focus on you rather than Kadijatu. [many thumbs-ups; private chats proliferate, mostly spilt tea over Pierre hitting on other women in XR-TC before stalking Kadijatu]

pierre: Oh, right, I forgot. Well, let's see. I miss working out daily at the gym. Physically speaking I'm not where I want to be. I just can't seem to— [Jasper signals time; private chats continue, mostly pop-psychological takes on Pierre's narcissism]

brianna: Thanks for sharing, Pierre. I see we're already a minute and forty seconds behind schedule, so let's all offer namaste to those who did not have an opportunity to share before we turn to the first action item. [folded hands flood screens] Thanks, everyone. [obligatory smiles] Coltan, can you brief us on your sub-group's progress? How ready are we for Living through Eco-Apocalypse Root Camp? It's just two weeks away! [many claps and open mouths]

coltan: Yah, so, we've secured a large room in the U of M Student Center and two smaller ones for break-out sessions. Veggie potluck each day. No bottled water or straws allowed. Going to be super strict about that. [fire and thumbs-ups fill screens] Sinead, can you tell everyone about the energy flow we want to create?

sinead: Sure thing. We've been inspired by a practice our sister organization Earth Roar pioneered. They've been ending actions with a primal scream. We feel a ginorm--

sam: Wait, I heard some geezer croaked last year when they did this primal-scream thing. [many open mouths]

bruce: And a primal scream isn't exactly pioneering, Sinead. I believe primitive is the word you're looking--

helga: Sam and Bruce, stop right there. I sense a micro-aggression in motion, one magnified by the two of you in rhetorical lockstep. You must allow Sinead her fully allotted time. [many thumbs-ups; Sam and Bruce go off-screen] Guys, need I remind you that going dark after an accountability call-out also is micro-aggressive? I'm issuing you both a yellow card. [Sam and Bruce return a few seconds later and more thumbs-ups follow]

sinead: As I was saying before Bruce started mansplaining, we feel it's essential to begin each day of Root Camp with a ginormous release of primordial energy. A barbaric yawp is what we're aiming for, only much more intense than what old Walt had in mind. We'll survive the coming eco-apocalypse only by summoning the deepest— [Jasper signals time; some fire and claps pop up]

brianna: What do you all think? Floor is open. But remember, we take a full-consensus approach to decision-making, so please keep your comments constructive and conciliatory. [obligatory nods all around]

claude: Interestin'.

cam: I've been at a few Earth Roar actions. Primal screams profoundly empower. Sinead is right: we need to help Root Campers find their inner-- [Jasper signals time; three thumbs-ups]

kadijatu: I must take issue with this proposal. It strikes me as ethnocentric. Sinead, did your sub-group discuss the possibility that a so-called barbaric yawp might be disrespectful toward gutturally expressive cultures? [open mouths flood screens]

muna: I have to agree with my sister on this one. Frankly, I find the suggestion demeaning. Dredging up your inner reptilian is not the way to cope with coastal cities under water, multiple breadbasket failures and the mass hysteria heading our way. Leave the yawping to the yahoos who voted for a president that pulled the U.S. out of the Paris Agreement. [Jasper signals time; many claps and thumbs-ups]

pierre: Doing what ER does is copy-catting. We don't want--

helga: Pierre, you've already had your turn. You know our equal-voice rule is sacred. Without it we'll never--

sam: Isn't it called Robert's Rules of--

helga: Sam, don't interrupt!

sam: I was just asking a ques—

helga: Do you want a red card to go with your yellow? [open mouths fill screens; in several private chats, all agree Helga hasn't gotten over Sam dumping her last year]

bruce: That sounds like a threat, not a warning.

sam: Felt like a threat, fer sure.

muna: You two are ganging up on her. I'm issuing you both a red card on her behalf! [more open mouths]

brianna: Back to business, eh? Now, we haven't reached full agreement on the sub-group's idea, so I'd ask that they re-convene offline and crowd-source other options we might consider--along with the barbaric yawp, of course. Do we have a consensus on that? [nods and thumbs-ups all around] Great! Let's move to our next action item. We're now five minutes and a second behind schedule, so I'd ask that each person speaking limit themselves to fifty-one syllables at the very most. Successful rebellions require strict discipline. Guido, can you step in for Jasper? [obligatory nod and gratuitous smile] Excellent, Guido. I knew I could count on you. [private chats proliferate, mostly conjectures about what Bri could possibly see in him]

cam: Bri, remind us again why it's fifty-one syllables rather than, say, thirty seconds?

brianna: Our by-laws say so.

cam: Yeah. Sure. And do tell: what's the rationale behind this by-law?

maddie: I know! It's XR-TC's way of expressing solidarity with the Fifty-One State Movement.

marco: Is that a thing? Since when?

maddie: Of course, silly! DC plus Puerto Rico equals fifty-two, minus Hawaii after their secession movement succeeds. We went over this in detail in my Political Math class last semester. Professor Shomptsky was so-- [Guido signals time; three thumbs-ups]

marco: You must be joking. And you paid how many tuition dollars for that? [open mouths flood screens]

helga: Hold up, Marco. That put-down just earned you a yellow card. [many thumbs-ups]

brianna: Let's move on, shall we? Emma G, can you update us on the I-94 banner-drop sub-group's wordsmithing project?

emma g: Certainly. I'm pleased to report we've reached consensus after only four months and twenty-seven days of deliberation. Next month our message to all driving down I-94 will be— [Guido signals time] Bri, may I finish? [thumbs-ups all around]

brianna: We just reached consensus! [many claps] Please continue, Emma G, but be brief!

emma g: Wait for it.... Climate Change Is Mass Murder.' [some fire and claps]

bruce: I'm sorry, but this ham-fisted attempt to evoke the Holocaust is ill-conceived. [several open mouths] Did you all come up with that one after consulting with Ted Kaczynski? [in the group chat a spirited debate over the Unabomber's anarchist philosophy breaks out, with opinion divided]

helga: Halt! That was way too snarky, Bruce. You know the drill: first accountability call-out is a yellow, second is red, third is white-out. Three micro-aggressions constitute group-emotional abuse, even when the victims are separate-- [Guido signals time; Bruce signs out]

marco: He goes, I go! The tyranny of Minnesota-Nice-meets-PC-on-acid must end! This isn't parrhesia we're practicing, it's God-damned groupthink! Get a grip, peop— [Guido signals time; Marco signs out; many open mouths, followed by a tada emoji; in the group chat Emma G posts a link that explains the Greek term in-depth and includes a commentary by Cornel West].

manu: I move to ban both Bruce and Marco from all XR-TC strat-chats until they issue a formal apology. [several thumbs-ups along with two open mouths; another vigorous debate—this one around free speech within the movement--begins in the group chat]

brianna: The motion passes! Our first one this month! [in the group chat, free-speech advocates express outrage; private chats ponder replacing Brianna as facilitator] I see there's a buzz in the chat. Unfortunately, we're at the half-hour, and as you know our by-laws—not to mention the limitations of our corporate subscription—require me to close this session on time. But I'm sure you'll all agree this meet has been one of our most productive ever! See you tomorrow! [obligatory smiles and waves]

cam: "Wait! I've got a killer idea for-- [Guido signals time; all sign out]

During the next two strat-chats Brianna aborted every attempt Cam made to share her Greta II plan with the group. Both meets were consumed with the energy-flow question for Root Camp. Opinion remained divided, though the choice had narrowed to three: a barbaric yawp, an *Anjali Mudra* bow or a full-monty streak from Mondale Hall to the Student Center. Cam and Emma G's favorite idea—a skinny dip in the Mississippi at sunrise—was rejected early. The meditative *namaste* option drew support from moderates, positioned as it was between two bolder proposals. Cam decided to get Rayna's take and was not disappointed. While sharing a bowl of puppy chow, they discussed the possibilities.

"The underlying issue is as much metaphysical as it is motivational," opined Rayna as she delivered a sugary tidbit to Cam's tongue with her chopsticks. "What are the deepest energies a human being may tap into, attune with and channel toward the co-creation of value and beauty amidst an unfolding plenitude within a universal history that, in any given epoch, may be in a transition phase and thus appear as dissolution-destruction? With the advent of the Anthropocene, such is the situation we face, is it not?"

"Yah, you've put your finger on it." Cam fingered the smacks and smothered Rayna's tongue with it. "Take your time to savor…"

Ten seconds passed before Rayna swallowed. "Clearly the extreme options—yawp and streak—allow for maximal release of an atavistic-amygdalic life-impulse appropriate to the existential threat facing the species." She paused, plucked another piece of chow and delicately inserted it between

Cam's esurient lips, slowly withdrawing the sticks. "Both wild screaming and running naked are fitting responses to the insanity of this world-historical moment. At the same time, an *Anjali Mudra* bow brings our evolving being into alignment with energies at once bodily and spiritual while enhancing focus and other higher mental functioning. The latter capacities will be critical to any resilient, adaptive response to the coming eco-apocalypse."

"Oh my God, you're so on spot!"

"Perhaps both yawp and bow are needed to maintain optimal flow. I suggest you propose that option to the group." Cam drew close to her, took the sticks from her hand and began to nibble on her ear. Only a sapiophile would do, and no one was smarter than Rayna.

They never did finish the bowl.

On the daily strat-chat Cam attempted to make the both-and case, but only Emma G and Sinead seemed open to it. Everyone else stuck to a single Way and dismissed all others. She shared her growing frustration with Rayna, who replied that one-dimensional thinkers are far more numerous than those attuned to the multiverse. "Relationships with the latter are far more interesting, though often high maintenance," she added. Cam had no doubts about that.

By end of week, no consensus had been reached and no one had any idea what Lightship Greta II was about. Bri took perverse pleasure tapping Cam to close the Friday session with a 5.1 second wolf howl, claiming disingenuously in a private chat that all the group needed was a little priming. On the deck that night she told her sad tale of Burning Man on the Mississippi and a dream deferred. Her housemates listened patiently. Diego had heard many a sob story at Lumpy's and was confident he knew just what to do.

"*Chica blanca*, that fire festival and lighthouse-on-wheels sounds awesome. Them *chingados* don't know what they're missing! What you need is more sangria." Before she could decline, he'd filled her glass again. "*¡Esa!*" He checked the cooler. Only one Surly Darkness left? He went inside to fetch a six-pack and a joint. Upon return he found another tiki out. This place was more work than the bar. No one tipped either.

"Sounds to me like too many cooks in the kitchen," observed Maya. "Perhaps only the Quakers have figured out how to decide by consensus and be social activists at the same time."

Rayna, who always wore her red wig when thirsty, cleared her throat as she nudged her device toward Cam.

"What's this?"

"Bosch's *Ship of Fools*. Painted five hundred years ago, it now hangs in the Louvre, a reminder to all that democracy without skilled, virtuous leadership is doomed. The problem you've had getting heard goes back to Plato. In his allegory a murderous crew quarrels over who should steer the ship. One clever fellow convinces them to get the captain trashed. Soon some idiot wrests the wheel from him while the rest empty the wine barrels. The mutineers bumble along, oblivious to the dangers of being at sea. They ridicule and then ignore the lone seaman among them who's qualified to take the helm."

Diego sat up in his chair. "Shipwreck's next, right?"

"That's what Plato implies. My point is that Cam's XR-TC crew may not have what it takes to navigate even a mild tempest, much less a perfect storm. But at least they see it coming and are trying to deal with it. That's the intent behind Root Camp, I take it. A creative survival boot camp for the sane."

Cam handed back the computer with an admiring smile. "Yah, we need to prepare for the massive upheavals ahead. It's like Bell says, during this exceptional time we've got to tap our deepest energies and accelerate optimal flow."

"Take up new flow arts and other forms of deep play not yet discovered," added Rayna as she wrapped a red lock around a finger.

"Bump up the superpowers," chimed in Maya, not wanting to be left out.

"Bump-and-grind, baby!" grunted Diego. Under their glare he sunk deep into the lawn chair, like a beach crab crawling back into its shell, and drained his Surly.

"Root Camp is about unleashing potential," said Cam. "Who knows, XR and its allies might even be able to wind the Doomsday Clock back a bit!"

Rayna clicked three keys. "Less than two minutes before midnight, the Atomic Scientists say. Never been closer."

"But if we're too late—and we may be--at least we'll learn how to row lifeboats. Maybe we'll build a 21st-century ark."

"Wait a minute," said Diego as he stood up. "You gonna make some lightship or ark to ride out the flood while the rest of us *pendejos* drown?"

"XR is taking direct action in the hope of getting governments and the public to face up to a truth so frightening that most are still mired in denial. At this point climate change can be mitigated but not stopped, and only if bold collective action on many fronts is taken."

"You're losing me, *chica blanca*. Talk normal English." He sat down after snagging another Surly from the cooler and dropping the cap into his collection can.

"Let me translate into Diegolese. Serious shit is going to hit the fan, and the question now is how much. If it turns out the countries polluting the most don't get it in gear by 2030, then it makes sense to start getting ready for the horror show. Unless we get hit by a drunk driver, all of us sitting here are going to be living that nightmare. *Comprende, amigo*?"

"So…it's like at closing time when you gotta cut off the schnookered dude and take his keys if you can. But if not, then it's good to have EMTs out there just in case."

"Not a bad analogy, Diego," said Maya. "Oh, and I've been meaning to ask: did you register to vote yet?" The query sent Rayna and Cam into an uproar.

Diego lifted up his bottle. "To my fellow democrats, *vete al infierno!*"

"To El Diablo!" toasted all three with glasses held high.

"Let me guess, now you *chulitas* want another pitcher. Am I right?"

"White sangria this time, J&J."

"With a little more pinot grigio, yes *chulita*?"

"Si, señor."

"You got it." Diego marched inside and went to work. When Maya said pour, he always asked how high.

"Bell, are you taking requests tonight?" asked Cam.

"Always, what's your pleasure?"

"Isn't there a song called "Ship of Fools"?

Rayna clicked as quick as ever, despite having imbibed more than usual. "Whose version? Quite a list here. From the seventies there's Bob Seger." Cam and Maya looked at each other and shrugged. "Bob who?"

"Never mind, you didn't miss much. From the eighties we have a track from World Party's album *Private Revolution*, which I recommend. And 1988 was a banner year. Three releases, plus a short story with that title written by the one and only Ted Kaczyinski. He was in his prime, so to speak, when he published--" Cam and Maya stared at each other aghast as she stopped mid-sentence, clicked and began to read intently.

"I don't think so, *chica pelirroca*!" yelled Diego from the kitchen. He had golden ears, heard every footstep, whisper and zipper in the house. It was a superpower he kept to himself, since knowing what women want depended on hearing every little sound they made.

"After that *pendejo* dies in prison he's going deep south to get bent over and ripped a new one by El Diablo—and *that* mofo don't *ever* finish!" Diego rarely went the theological route but when provoked could be as formidable—in a backwoods circuit-rider sort of way--as any Mather or Edwards. Indeed, no sinner wanted to meet his hangry God or fall into the hands of his hairy Satan. A Guadalupan Catholic, his tender devotion to the Empress of the Americas turned fierce in defense of the underdog, especially Mexican underdogs. In his room hung three revolutionary flags, one from 1810, another from 1910 and a third from 1994. On all three was *La Virgen Morena*. So what if he wasn't registered to vote. What mattered was street politics, and for that he showed up. For all his flaws, Maya always had his back because he always had hers. Provide drinks and laughs, protect the women and children, dance till you drop. Other than lowering his handicap, nothing else was that important.

Lost in the short story, Rayna did not hear a word he or anyone else said. Didn't some of the best writing occur *in extremis*? As a matter of hermeneutical principle, she agreed with Barthes on the separation of artist from the work of art. Readers make meaning in an un-choreographed dance with the text. The event of reading fiction is just that: an event without a pre-determined path or end. Barthes said the author is dead, and so readers are free to assign meaning—or none at all—to a text no longer controlled by any stable, definitive interpretation. That the artist might be a monster matters not a whit. Rayna didn't care whether Wallace was dead from suicide, as he was, or still alive and threatening revenge upon the ex-wife he'd abused. In either case she could lose herself in his *Infinite Jest* again and again. Ditto when it came to dancing with the Unabomber—if his prose was any good. Only one way to find out.

Diego returned with a full pitcher. "*Oh Dios mio*, voodoo girl's gone again. Definitely cutting her off." He filled Maya's glass and then Cam's. They sat in silence, as if attending the wake of a relative no one really knew. Minutes later Rayna closed her laptop and fell into a frozen state. Cam sipped her sangria slowly. Maya went through two glasses. "Now what?" he finally asked. The two looked at each other and shrugged. "Some events you make happen, and some events happen to you," said the latter.

While they were cleaning up, a very tipsy Maya dropped one of Diego's empties on the deck floor. As the bottle rolled away a screech owl began its bounce song, the even-pitched trill repeated several times. Rayna came to suddenly a second later. "What time is it?" she asked.

"Almost midnight," replied Diego with a sly look, like that of a stow-away hidden amongst the barrels below.

The following Monday, Cam finally had a chance to pitch her lightship project. She found fifty-one syllables quite a constraint but took on the challenge without complaint. Once the flame was lit, she was sure a bonfire worthy of Burning Man would rise quickly. She spoke concisely and with eloquence, but the proposal was shunted off to a vision-vetting sub-group co-chaired by Muna and Emma G, the only XR-TC member to speak in favor of the idea. At this point, Greta II hadn't a snowball's chance in hell and time was short. Desperate to pull her brainchild out of the bureaucratic bathwater, she decided to foment a rebellion within the rebellion.

hi emma g
wanna form
a new group
freed from
the red tape?

yeet, yeet!
when do
we begin!
[fires]

right here
right now!
r u down with
greta ii?

totally ldi!
[hundred points]

[three thumbs-up]

do we have
a name yet?

think up
one later
so much to do
labor day only
3 weeks away

k ill loop in javin
he does set design
will luv this project
and namid too
he does amazing
multimedia work

sweet ill contact
the festival and pitch
our idea asap

wait did we just
get more done in
1 min than xrtc
gets done in
2 months?

lol lets roll!
[sparkles]

Gertrude Himmelgard, the festival committee chair, wasn't budging. Deadlines are deadlines, she kept repeating firmly, and August 1st had come and gone. That one installation space was still available was beside the point. Frau Himmelgard wasn't just German, she was a Kantian. Rules were broken over her dead body. Cam turned frenetic after three days of pleading to no avail. Maybe Goldie could help her find an end-around. She was more than a little chagrined by how quickly her best friend cut to the chase.

seriously how can
u not see the hag is
holding out for $

im an idiot

camster the hamster

total newb

no u r the shit
im still so jealous
just get your dad
to fork it over and
u r in like flynn

omg you didn't
just say that

hes my dads idol

cute but don't
spill the tea
about greta ii
just say its
a fundraiser
for refugees

u r the best!
[goat]

secure the bag!

Three days later Cam free-mo'd $3K to Gertrude, a donation so generous she promised a plaque in her father's honor on one of the California's concrete slabs. Foundational support, she called it. And tax-deductible, of course. While as far from the water as one could get, the last space was theirs after her committee quickly passed a resolution extending the deadline. Permit in hand, Cam outsourced the other paperwork—forms, waivers and what-not--to her calc-man Charles, who was bound for accounting glory at U. St. Thomas in a few weeks and always more than happy to help Cam out. His mad crush on her had no bearing whatsoever on the decision to recruit him, she told herself. He was fine with learning the new group's name later, though having neither that nor a tax ID likely put him in legal jeopardy. When you're blue-eyed and blonde, fools for love are easy to find, Goldie said.

After some deliberation Cam and Emma G thought it best to announce their splintering action through group text and invite others to defect without rancor or resentment. The week-long uproar that ensued wound up derailing final preparations for Root Camp, an unintended consequence seen only in retrospect. Chastened but not undone, the two mutineers forged ahead. They had to face the furies—Brianna, Helga and Muna—who mounted a relentless campaign to cancel Emma G Brutus and Cassius Cam, as they were now labeled online. Distraught by the cyber-onslaught, Cam reached out again to Goldie.

they r on a jihad
and wont stop till
we r toast!

block the bitches
and move on
by labor day
no one will
remember
or care

u dont get it
they r going to
other groups and
blackballing us!

mccarthy failed
and so will they
going to blow over
so don't let it knock
u off your horse

k omg I so wish u
were here with me

got your back
go kick ass!

im on it!

Soon things were looking up. Cam's father forked over another $3K, presumably to double the number of refugees aided. Javin and Namid joined the project once promised full artistic control; the latter also demanded and received group naming rights, a concession he felt more than fair after what his people had endured for five centuries. That he was one-fourth Chippewa made the deal more than worthwhile, Cam figured. Authenticity was in high demand these days, and he agreed to lead with XR and limit what followed to a brief phrase relevant to the festival theme. Handing design of the lightship over to the two of them was a harder pill to swallow. Would they remain true to the vision? Meanwhile, Sinead from XR-TC joined the fledgling fast-action team, and so now they were six.

When a week later Namid announced the name—XR-AF—without explanation the initial response was bafflement. If Arts on Fire was too obvious, as everyone but Cam insisted, what could it be? An anfractuous ID quest ensued. Emma G suggested it might stand for Anishinaabe Forever. Sinead's best guess: Ars Faber. Amidst the rampant speculation—Cam found the thread so long it threatened to blow her data budget--the only point of agreement was that it didn't stand for Antifa or anything crude. Still, it might! What made the guessing game never-ending was the discovery by Charles of a list: 2,112 famous people with the initials A.F. After three days the number of plausible candidates had dropped to fifty. Then Javin, who'd hardly weighed in at all, suddenly pronounced with unusual conviction that Fatima Al-Fihri—a ninth-century Tunisian Muslim woman credited with founding the University of al-Qarawyyin, considered the world's oldest university still operating by such authorities as UNESCO and Guinness World Records—was the answer to the riddle, though beyond pointing repeatedly to her resume he couldn't say why. His claim, while rejected after much debate, did fuel another vetting frenzy that narrowed down a Top Ten. All the while Namid maintained a mystic silence on the matter, a stance that with each passing day elevated his status within XR-AF to that of high priest.

August days melted away more quickly than Greenland's glaciers. XR-AF avoided time-wasting sectarian strife with a snap decision to side with the Four Demanders, an easy call to make since every other XR chapter in the U.S. had agreed recently, as an act of solidarity with BLM, to add a fourth demand to XR-UK's original manifesto. Cam's slightly more concise version, which she planned to hand out during the festival and solidarity sail, read as follows:

EXTINCTION REBELLION – OUR FOUR DEMANDS

1. The Government and media must tell the truth about the climate and wider ecological emergency, and they must immediately communicate the urgency for change to persons, communities and businesses.

2. The Government must set policies to reduce carbon emissions to net zero by 2030 and cooperate internationally so the global economy runs on just half a planet's worth of resources per year.

3. We cannot trust our Government to address this existential threat, and so we demand a Citizens' Assembly to oversee the changes necessary for our collective survival.

4. We demand a just transition to a post-carbon economy and society, a transition that prioritizes the most vulnerable people and indigenous sovereignty; establishes reparations and remediation led by and for Black and Indigenous People of Color (BIPOC); establishes ecosystem rights; and repairs the effects of ongoing ecocide to prevent extinction of human and all species.

While Namid and Javin only had $3K for materials, they had worked together before and knew how to make magic out of next to nothing. All agreed on the community-build concept; a modular design allowed for easy assembly. Same red hull as Greta I, but the lighthouse would mark Greta II as a distinctly American revolutionary vessel, matching the Boom Island beacon's blue-and-white colors and holding a liberty bell within its lantern room to draw attention to the float's broadside message: Sounding the Alarm – Climate Emergency.

Meanwhile, Emma G secured permits for the ten-mile solidarity sail—a tricky bureaucratic task during shutdown. Except for the wire-rimmed spectacles and darker hair, she was Goldie's double: compact in figure and just as fiery. Both budding writers. What distinguished them quite starkly was attire and all that said about two very different upbringings. Emma G's limited wardrobe was an indie-style mash-up of consignment shop purchases made with her own hard-earned cash from serving tables. On her feet low-budget tennis shoes from the Payless outlet, though she did lay out once for leather boots and didn't regret it. A layer-flapping chic-commie drip with an outta-my-way-bitch stride to back it up. Daughter of a divorced social worker, she was blingless and proud of it.

Goldie inhabited another fashion galaxy altogether: seven pairs of, well, everything for each season, along with all the accoutrements. Not quite past Juicy velour but getting there. Fifty-plus color schemes and shade options to cake up on every occasion, meticulously manicured from toenail to eyebrow. In shoe collection, not quite Infamous Imelda but getting there. Ms. Bling even had a dressing room she'd insisted upon when her parents had custom-built a Wright-style family abode a few years back.

For Gertrude and other festival organizers, landing permits for California on Fire wasn't easy either. After all the arson following George Floyd's death, they had to wait over a month before final approval in late July by city authorities, who at first imposed a strict ban on setting anything ablaze at the park but eventually condoned one fire pit near the water and a scaled-down version of Burning Man's final ceremony--the lighting of a wooden effigy to honor the dead—at the boat launch.

XR-AF's largest hurdle was left for Cam to clear. Bolting from XR-TC meant more than getting trolled. Fair or not, and Goldie's dismissal of the danger aside, word was out among local activists that Emma G and Cam were not to be trusted and that XR-AF was a faddish off-shoot soon to flame out. How to re-build relationships and enlist support for Greta II's sail to the state capitol? Only a year ago the Climate Strike had brought thousands to St. Paul. What if only a few dozen die-hards showed up this time? It obviously was the perfect follow-up--in Cam's humble opinion—but having a big idea guaranteed nothing. One thing was clear: a strategy for mending fences and marshaling troops called for the Goldie touch.

"Not sure what to tell you on this one, Camster. Karma's a bitch, don't cha know. Maybe you can make new alliances. Your fourth demand seems tailor-made for outreach to BLM. Get them and you can leverage your white Shoveler contacts. I'd also make a play for the local Burners. Their page has over two thousand followers. Scroll through it and you'll find abundant evidence of the Woodstock Syndrome."

"Geez, aren't we scathing today. Not even going to ask what *that* is."

"Call me a Hebrew snob, but I really don't expect the next major advance in humanity's moral and spiritual consciousness to quantum leap out of Black Rock City. Mostly New Age nonsense on stilts. Don't get me wrong, I love what they do with their installations. Incredibly creative. Anyhoo, the local Burners are a natural ally. They'll show up in droves. Mobilizing BLM may be harder."

"Fer sure."

"Wait, I know. At Burning Man they end the event by mourning the--"

"Of course! We'll make the wooden effigy into the likeness of George! Oh my God, it will be *so* amazing!"

"*We*, kimosabe? Are you on the festival committee? More importantly, do you have any idea how black people, not to mention BLM activists, will react if you do something like this without getting full buy-in from the beginning?"

"Maya has clout within BLM and will love this. If she goes to Gertrude with her posse, she'll rubber-stamp it in a heartbeat."

"Don't be so sure. There's a history here. Plus, you don't have much--"

"No time to waste! Golda Bloch, I don't know what I'd do without you! Don't go shuffling off to Buffalo."

"Hey, I'm not the one who's at risk of catching covid. Quarantine is my middle name these days. Just keep your mask up and keep six--"

"Yes, mother."

It was a Saturday night in late August and Chez Diablo was hopping. Cam had conspired with Rayna and Diego to throw Maya a surprise birthday party. On the guest list were three friends of hers--Rodney, Huey D and Angela--hardcore BLM activists Cam knew from the uprising, a moment that felt like just yesterday and at the same time seemed like it had happened half a century ago. Diego was dishing out drinks, Rayna was fielding requests and the floor was full of sweat. The cigar-sized joints lit by guests burned longer than the tikis. Maya knew something was up the day before when Diego lugged in two extra cases of beer and a box of booze with brands he never bought. His unsolicited remark about stocking up before the city closed the liquor stores again sounded like government cheese. She had played along anyway and impressed both Cam and Rayna with how well she feigned surprise earlier that evening. Now she was getting down with Huey D, while Cam chatted with Angela about the latest buzz within the movement over events in Kenosha, Wisconsin where a white teen had shot two protestors dead and injured a third.

Cam's plan was simple: wait until everyone was stoned and danced out before floating the idea of burning George the Man in honor of him and all other victims of police violence. Around midnight, as everyone sat around the card table, she came right out with it and held her breath. With each second of silence, she could feel her heart pounding harder—right before it went south fast when Maya shook her head and then looked right through her with a sudden sobriety Cam could not fathom.

"Girl, you know I love you. And you know I don't get tongue-tied easily. But *this* shit has left me speechless." Cam hung her head and fought back the urge to bounce up and bound away into the night, never to be seen or heard from again.

"Hold on, Maya, maybe Cahmie is onto something," suggested Angela.

"Say what?"

"For real, now. Hear me out. We've been talking for years about how to broaden the movement, and this might be the ticket. Obviously, making the Man look like George is total BS. No offense, Cahmie. But she's right about the ceremony's power, and it will be even more powerful this year if we get our people to show up. Just being there will send a message, and it might become an event that widens the circle."

Maya looked at Rodney and Huey D, both of whom remained poker-faced at first. Then they began to nod their heads slowly. Maya joined in a few seconds later. When Cam let out a sigh of relief loud enough to wake the neighbors, they could barely contain themselves.

"Strength in numbers!" proclaimed Maya, once she stopped laughing. "Question is, what will the cops do if we raise the roof? They gotta know black folk party when someone passes. In New Orleans we take our coffins to the street and stomp!" A moment later the joyous jazz-funeral standard "Feel So Good" lifted everyone's spirits. Maya fist-pumped Rayna. "That's my Bell, fastest fingers in the Midwest! C'mon y'all, let's do this!" All rose, formed a second line and buck-jumped around the card table. Somehow Cam had escaped her own funeral.

9

ALTERED FOUNDING

Despite XR-AF's late entry into the festival, the team landed a sweet spot close to the boat launch with a picture-perfect view of the lighthouse, a coup orchestrated by Charles after he discovered violations of the state's disclosure requirements for nonprofits in the mountain of forms Gertrude sent to him. It seems Frau Himmelgard had overstepped her bounds in wanting to know the citizenship and immigrant status of group members. That impropriety alone was enough to bring her to the table.

"Our favorite mentat is going to go far, don't cha know," chirped Goldie upon hearing of the upgrade, adding that anyone fool enough to mess with one of Friezelda-St. Mitt's finest would have their head handed back to them on a platter. "At the very least you owe him a peck on the cheek," she teased. No doubt, launching Greta II from the new locale, adjacent to the main walkway near the water and not far from the parking lot, would be much easier. Cam made his day with a gushing thank-you text full of sparkles.

Despite the tight deadline, Namid and Javin flawlessly executed the fabbing of modules and even managed to rig the liberty bell to a remote. Not to be outdone, Emma G conceived a children's make-your-own-lightship activity and with Sinead's help pulled the requisite supplies together in no time. Two first-rate boatswains! Cam spent the days before the festival running copies of Four Demands flyers and mounting a last-minute marketing campaign that yielded e-RSVPs from eighteen Shovelers with deep-green sympathies, twenty-three local Burners yearning to translate art into action, eleven Quakers true to their tradition and five women religious in Sister Yoda's octogenarian-activist network who knew better than most that time to turn things around really was running out.

California on Fire commenced the next Friday at six pm. Cam took the clear skies and warm breeze as a good omen. Short-sleeved festivalgoers poured in the first hour. "Looks like the early-bird discount is working."

"Never underestimate a Midwesterner's cheap streak!" snarked Emma G. Attendees had to mask and distance, of course. Orange-red dots every six feet. Attendance capped at five hundred. To allay public fears, Frau Himmelgard added an unusual covid-prevention measure: roaming Distance Keepers, each outfitted with a wood pole. DKs underwent assiduous baculine training. Nicely ask the non-distancing to comply and offer a kindly reminder followed by a more pointed one. If ignored repeatedly, then use the felt-tipped rod—dubbed a Himmel Barb after its designer—to reinforce the six-foot rule. "Remember, only administer polite nudges to protect public health. Ethics begins with etiquette," she told her charges before sending them forth.

By six-thirty the XR-AF team had handed out nearly a hundred flyers and invited each recipient to join in the fun of bringing Greta II to life, beginning at seven. Four eager beavers arrived early, and by seven-thirty the volunteer count had doubled. Javin was charged with managing the build-out, while Charles made sure all t's were crossed and i's were dotted before amateur hands took up tools and paint brushes.

At the crowded kiddie corner, Sinead and Emma G soon realized they had too few DIY kits to meet demand. Namid came to the rescue, distracting disappointed youngsters with the Anishinaabe tale of Mishipeshu. A fearsome underwater panther few mortals had seen and fewer still had survived, Mishipeshu had the body of a lynx, the horns of a deer, sharp scales on its back and an exceptionally long tail. Guardian of the earth's vast riches, this master of the deep engaged in perpetual battle with the Thunderbirds, lords of the air. One time four Ojibwe braves dared to enter its abode in a bid to secure copper, used by their people to heat water. Copper in hand, they launched their canoes only to find the ferocious beast in hot pursuit. Like a roaring river its hiss invaded their ears and cut close to their hearts. Mishipeshu growled menacingly, accusing them of stealing his children's playthings. Only one bloodied warrior made it back to the village, living only long enough to tell the tale before he breathed his last. Gesturing dramatically, Namid cried out: "Any second now, Mishipeshu might leap out of the Mississippi right over there!" When Cam saw both kids and parents shrink back in terror, she knew the acquisition of such an authentic voice had been more than worth it. No one had a clue what XR-AF stood for, but at this point who cared?

With all cylinders firing smoothly, Cam gave herself permission to take some me-time and tour the grounds. She hated to miss the sunset concert at the boat launch given by Lady Midnight and Maria Isa, Latina performers raising awareness and funds for the Stop Line 337 movement, but she couldn't do everything. Before heading out she climbed Javin's stepladder to survey the scene. Maya's imprint on all she beheld was breathtaking. In negotiations with the festival committee, she had warmed up with a demand that BLM activists pay half price, an expense that evaporated when a well-heeled donor offered to cover the full cost. She then demanded that a quarter of the installations speak to the climate crisis, a quarter to the sixth great extinction unfolding and another quarter to the uprising in their midst, leaving a fourth full artistic freedom. In return she promised to bring out her base. Done. Her final demand: two-thirds of the funds raised for climate-refugee relief must go to victims in Global South countries. Also done. All that Cam now took in from her perch had Maya's stamp on it.

She decided to walk along the river toward the south end and then loop around. Her first stop, *Key Toter*, was one of two installations touted by Namid. The unassuming sculpture, made entirely from old locks and keys, seemed a cross between Gumbi and Giacometti. About her height, the blue-grey figure's flat face had only one feature: a keyhole. Towing a large key behind him, his thin arms indistinguishable from the chain draped over his shoulder, he had come to a fork in the road. One way led to two model rockets, Tusk's Falcon 99 and Bleudough's New Buzz, each shooting tiny sparks from thrusters, the other to a ring of miniature teepees, each sheltering a small flame with little puffs of smoke rising through open flaps. After a few minutes she chose not to ponder further the path *Key Toter* might take. Did it have to be one or the other?

Further down the walkway, she came across a black diva. Assemblers titled the sixteen-foot figure *Afro R-Evolution* and fashioned her out of steel rods and balls covered in stainless steel mesh. She pulsed brightly as her long legs straddled the ground, eyes closed, arms at each side and palms open, a *wankandaste* presence at once beyond this world and a commanding presence within it. She sent a pic to Goldie, Rayna and Maya with a *gotta see!* text.

At her third stop Cam gaped at *Blowout*, a mesmerizing triptych worthy of Bosch's *Garden of Earthly Delights*. The dazzling work depicted in turns an epicurean bliss that made one's mouth water, an orgy of industrial excess sickeningly familiar and finally an eco-apocalyptic wasteland reminiscent of Alberta's tar sands. She lingered over its middle section, which featured a twenty-three-foot-tall oil derrick wrapped by spiral stairs with Rich Uncle Pennybags plopped on every fourth step bidding the ambitious to step over him while grabbing cash from his hand. Pics of this installation went to Sister Yoda, Vibol and Mr. Pierwink accompanied by a quotation from Pope Emeritus Benedict XVI: "The external deserts in the world are growing, because the internal deserts have become so vast."

Cam's next stop almost turned out to be her last, it left her so upset. An unknown artist titled the work *Six Feet.* Two fetal figures, both masked and each encased in a heavy thicket of wire, glowed brightly for a minute as they reached for one other, fingertips nearly touching. Then the silence was broken by a vacuum-like sucking sound. Their light faded gradually as the distance between them lengthened until all was pitch black and again silent, the extinguishment taking about three minutes. She sent several pics to her mother, whom she was beginning to miss these days.

Now near the footbridge where she'd last seen Godol, Cam found herself face-to-face with *THE EGO BOX*, another disturbing installation she would not soon forget. Made of trophies glued together, each gold letter stood nine-feet tall with both width and depth at six feet. Random passers-by were handed a golden ticket, congratulated and coaxed into one of the spaces separating the big letters. It was Cam's lucky night. As soon as she stepped in between E and G two Chippendale types hoisted panels into place, one covering the back side and another the front, enclosing her within a 6x6 fun-house mirror room festooned at its top edges with blue ribbons. They then sang in perfect harmony a mock hymn called "How Great Thou Fart". Afterwards, they removed the front panel and invited her to walk down a red carpet two other buff bowties rolled out, striking up the hymn's refrain while showering her with confetti. At carpet's end she was handed a pink rubber whoopee cushion and thanked profusely for her participation. All the singing and laughter from onlookers made her nausea from the warped mirror images worse. The amusement ended abruptly when she fainted a moment later. Luckily a first-aid station was close at hand. After smelling salts and a ten-minute breather she went on her way.

At her sixth stop she barely escaped the bite of *Big Croc*, a massive reptilian figure with jaws agape and snout aimed skyward as it sunk inexorably into a marshy muck labeled Dying Everglades. She climbed the installation's stairs and was passing through the beast's immense maw to the back side when suddenly she relapsed and stumbled headlong toward its sharp teeth. An alert attendant grabbed her by the arm and yanked her back, but not before her fav tie-dye caught one of the fangs. The rip measured thirteen inches, reaching from her belly button to her lowest rib. The attendant, a lanky young lad whose vanity mask said Try Me, escorted her down the stairs.

After three harrowing exhibits in a row, she was tempted to cut her tour short. She knew Giles would love *Big Croc* and posting pics for him always made her feel better. Mom said he had weathered her abrupt departure but lately was not doing so well. He spent the summer trampoline jumping, fish feeding and basement dwelling without saying more than two words at a time during dinner. Texts from Tramp usually arrived daily--*no guppies cannibalized* and other reports on the state of the fish tank, plus the usual twenty questions about her latest enthusiasm--but in August the flow had slowed to a trickle. Most worrisome was the tone: a listlessness had replaced his lively curiosity. She snapped shots from several angles and added a mid-riff selfie with the caption *narrow escape!* in hopes of provoking a lively exchange. Crickets. Lingering nausea gave way to gnawing guilt. Time for a geographical cure, she thought, as she stepped off an orange-red dot and moved on.

Soon she came upon *Bliss Dancer,* a welcome respite from her dis-ease. With exquisite balance the fourteen-foot-tall steel figure--another black diva, only more curvaceous—spun effortlessly on one foot to her right while the toe of her trailing foot pointed toward a sky that had turned crimson at dusk. Her ripped torso swiveled just so for the pirouette. Both arms were extended diagonally and both palms were bent back fully to form a ninety-degree angle at each extremity. Cam, and every other awed onlooker around her, found the sweeping symmetry astonishing. The ten minutes she spent in rapture seemed a millisecond. Below the pic sent to Rayna it read *flow incarnate*; below the one to Chano she shared the title and *thought you'd like it, hope all's well.* She laughed when he sent back [five fires]. They'd stayed in touch, despite the cancelled trip last spring. Cam introduced him to the latest emojis while he chronicled growing unrest on the island. He always began his updates with the same absurd title—To Blue-Ribbon Borlaug: On the Revolution within the Revolution—an ego stroke she never grew tired of receiving.

With darkness descending the installations' varied light schemes grew more vibrant, giving the park an appearance at once ethereal and carnivalesque. At her eighth stop she was taken aback by the title: *Amor Fati.* Was that *it?* Before her stood a black male figure made of dark steel that immediately reminded her of Wiley's *Simeon the God Receiver* in his dignity, luminosity and tattooed beauty. At the same time, he was altogether unique in visage and comportment, more a cool dude angling for a smoke than a cradler of the golden child. While both were tall and muscular, the one in front of her was bent slightly at the waist and knees, a crooked piece of timber yet sturdy nonetheless, half-naked and a little tense but not going anywhere either if trouble found him. Head cocked but not cocky. The other in her mind's eye, still on exhibit in Montreal, stood up straight in his bright-white cargo pants, utterly fearless and with strong arms ready for whatever might come to him—or at him—for he was unmistakably a warrior. The longer she stood there gazing, though, the more she saw of Simeon in his less regal yet no less magnificent double. Weren't his gesturing hands, and most of all his searching eyes, ready to receive as well?

A balloon pop broke her contemplation. The bent figure facing her now brought back memories of young black protestors she'd stood with amidst the flash grenades, tear gas and rubber bullets. There they had crouched, pants low and fists high, chanting boldly and ready for whatever might come at them because trouble had found them long ago and taught them a street-savvy version of the revolutionary patience Dorothee Soelle spoke about. That paradoxical notion, said Sister Yoda, had nothing to do with Nietzsche's *amor fati*. All was *not* necessary, *not* fated, even if all you could do under heavy fire was shoulder those in shock while falling back to bandage the bleeding and pour milk into burning eyes. Seared in memory were lines from Soelle on her teacher's wall: "If the wounded are to be healed, it is our hands that will heal them. If the maimed and the terrified are to be comforted, it is our embrace, not God's, that will comfort them."

One more stop she had to make, the other installation Namid said was a must see. She laughed when she saw the title: *Altered Founding*. Was *that* it? By far the largest structure—fashioned by five talented Native artists who'd started construction two weeks early—it featured a huge turtle that appeared to emerge from an ocean of blue crepe paper. The giant terrapin faced west with mouth wide open, allowing for entry by all who might venture within on all fours. Tribal flags occupied each scute of its broad carapace: a purple-and-white field for the Iroquois flag, with two boxes on each side of a white pine; an orange field for the Cherokee flag, their Great Seal surrounded by seven yellow stars, with a black star in the upper right corner symbolizing those who died on the Trail of Tears; a red field for the Oglala Sioux flag, with nine stylized white tipis forming a circle, their triangular doorways forming a red dwarf star at the center; a copper-tan field for the Navajo flag, with four differently-colored sacred mountains surrounding a map of the nation and a tribal seal, all situated under a rainbow. At the shell's south edge there flew a Kanaka Maoli flag. Overlaying the nine green, red and yellow stripes was a green shield bearing a coat of arms with a Hawaiian feather *kahili* in between crossed canoe paddles. From the north edge flew a four-colored American Indian Movement flag, twice the size of all the others.

Eager for a higher view, Cam climbed one of the totem-pole ladders placed at four corners. More scutes with flags than she could count. Each flagpole doubled as a spear with tips made from bone, obsidian and flint. Rising up from the center of the carapace a structure shaped like the U.S. Capitol but made of white steel and carved in the fluid style of the Chinook, its imagery replete with stylized sea otters, red-tailed hawks, salmon and eagles. The dome's open, airy design afforded anyone at the top of a spiral staircase a bird's-eye view of the festival. Presently a dark-haired girl appeared, and they exchanged waves.

After climbing down Cam entered the turtle's mouth and once inside discovered she could stand. Lying face flat next to the staircase a replica of the Columbus statue that AIM activists had pulled down at the state capitol back in June. Directly above it a large poster of Prince leaping with wild abandon into an enthralled concert crowd; in this case, it looked like he was stomping gleefully on old Christopher. Spotlights lit walls filled with copies of broken-treaty documents, a page from Termination-era text House Concurrent Resolution 108, AIM's original Twenty Demands, the UN Declaration on the Rights of Indigenous Peoples and a line from Subcomandante Marcos: "We're sorry for the inconvenience, but this is a revolution." Streaks of fake blood ran across the broken treaties. She heard light footsteps on the stairs and a moment later the girl who'd waved was staring at her bug-eyed, as was the Fraidy Cat on her pullover. She couldn't be more than nine.

"What happened to your shirt?" asked the girl.

"I fainted and Tick Tock almost ate me."

"You mean Mishipeshu." Her bulging eyes darted every which way. "Have you seen him?"

Cam decided to play along. "Can't say that I have. How about you?"

"No, I've stayed away from the water and out of sight." She pointed to the staircase. "I went up there to keep a look-out. I got spooked a minute ago when a drone flew past. Mishipeshu might be a shapeshifter. Or a Thunderbird might have gone over to the dark side and now be in league with him." Fraidy Girl might have nine lives, but by God she wasn't going to lose one of them tonight.

"That was a scary story you heard. But just a story, right?"

"Some stories are true. My father went hunting up north last year and came back with a finger missing. That's *never* going to happen to me." She grabbed a fistful of cotton cloth, mangling the freaked-out feline on her chest. "Why is there blood on the walls?" she asked. "And why would someone knock Christopher Columbus over and stomp on him? That's just mean."

Cam didn't know where to begin. "Ask your teacher if she knows who the Zapatistas are. If she does, then tell her all about the exhibit and keep asking questions."

"What if she doesn't?"

"She might not."

"Then what?"

"What do you think you should do?"

"Go online and read about them myself."

"Atta girl. Search for Zapatistas. With a Z."

"I have to go now. It's not as safe in here as I thought."

"OK then, take care."

After Fraidy Girl clambered out, Cam ascended the spiral staircase. Turnout was bigger than expected, in good part because Maya had delivered. Earlier the pole-toting DKs seemed to be everywhere, but now they were gone. The installations she'd seen weren't even half the show. Something for everyone, from those in strollers to those with walkers. Glorious. Nearly a third present wore tie-dyes, as if she'd sent a memo to all Minneapolis. She spied the snack at Hobo who'd told her about the event and then disappeared faster than Houdini. How could she ever thank him enough? In the north parking lot sat a patrol car, and another in the grass near the south end. No paddy wagons in sight, only the required ambulance. Two cops strolled along the main pathway near the water. Everything was perfect, even the security!

She turned her gaze toward the river and saw the Man, a facsimile of

Black Rock's space-alien figure made of wood and suspended in the air by metal cords. Imposing at twenty-six feet in height, yet modest compared to the towering structures recently built and burned out west. Nearby, flame-tossing Burners circled the fire pit. Around them ten drummers, one making a djembe talk, two stroking bongos, three beating congas and four playing dunun with curved sticks. The rich percussive sound carried across the park to the canoe rental where talented hoop dancers had a sizable circle of their own gathered around. Poi-light performers also attracted much attention. When the drum circle took a break Rayna, tapped by the festival committee for Friday-night DJ duties at Maya's suggestion, played one great selection after another. Business still brisk at the admission gate. Lines not too long at the concession stands. She spun three-sixty after gazing again at *Bliss Dancer*.

"Hey, can I come up?" someone yelled from down below. Ganga smoke wafted up into the dome. Time to go. Past time, in fact. Cam looked for Greta II, hoping to see her half-built by now. An ambitious goal for opening night, all had agreed. Instead, she saw the float ship-shape and ready for tugging to St. Paul first thing Sunday morning. A second later she heard the liberty bell ring. It rang two more times. People began to congregate around the lightship, like riverboats lost but now found. Emma G and Sinead could not hand out flyers fast enough. How many dreams bite the dust? Too many to count. Yet there she was, looking down upon one on the verge of coming true. "Right here, right now," she kept repeating to herself as she emerged from *Altered Founding* and snaked through the crowd.

While her crew had not mutinied, they weren't at all amused by the disappearing act during rush hour. "Where have you been!" scowled Emma G. "We ran out of flyers. Didn't you bring a bunch extra? Where are they!"

"We sent Charles out to track you down, and now he's MIA too!" wailed Sinead. Javin shoved a utility belt into her stomach, which suddenly felt queasy again. He looked knowingly at Emma G and walked off toward the concessions.

"I am so, so sorry ya'll. No excuses. I got caught up in the installations—they're incredible!—and I *totally* lost track of time. Greta looks sensational! I can't believe what you all have accomp--"

"Put a lid on it, Cam," snapped Emma G. "Tomorrow, if there's a deck that needs swabbing, you-know-who is on it. *Capiche*? And right now, we could use more flyers." She fetched them quickly and presented the pile.

"No, I don't think so. From now until closing, *you* are handing them out. And all day tomorrow too."

"Fer sure, I owe you guys big-time."

"Don't forget to ring the bell," added Sinead, pointing to the remote. "We're going to look for Charles. Not that you care." And off they went in a huff.

Namid was nowhere to be seen. Cam finally spotted him near the riverbank, presumably keeping an eye out for Mishipeshu. An hour later, all the flyers gone, the remote's batteries dead and most attendees on their way home, she walked over to him.

"Namid, I really am sorry about--"

"No worries, we forged ahead without you."

She shuffled feet and looked about, not knowing what to say next. "By the way, have you seen any of Gertrude's pokers lately?"

"Apparently the prod squad was disbanded after several incidents turned testy and complaints of civil-rights infringement hit double-digits."

"Yah, they were a bit much." She glanced over at Greta II, her high-gloss finish still a bit sticky. What a red-white-and-blue beauty! "I can't believe you finished the build so fast."

"Three guys with skills knocked out the assembly with Javin. The rest painted. I had stencils and made sure they didn't mis-spell anything. Unfortunately, we did have one spill." He pointed to a big red splat on the concrete. "You'll need to get that scrubbed early tomorrow morning before it bakes in."

"I'll take care of it."

"I'm sure you will. And in case you're wondering, I posted lots of pics on our page. Two video clips went out on Flitter."

"So, you did my comms job." She pulled out her phone and scrolled through shots of lumbersexuals piecing out the parts, wielding power drills and hoisting the lighthouse into place. One pic showed a mortified volunteer splattered head-to-toe in red paint, looking as if she'd been mauled by Mishipushu.

"Nice. I'm glad you--"

"Tell me, what did you make of *Key Toter*?"

"Well, it seemed a bit too obvious, don't cha know. The way of technology versus the way of--"

"Fair enough. But do you know the Seven Fires prophecy?" His voice now more animated and his eyes afire, she regarded him with growing curiosity. "Sorry, can't say that I do." His intense look told her she was going to hear it, whether she wanted to or not.

"When the seventh prophet comes, he tells the people about a possible rebirth of the Anishinaabeg. His oracle will come true *if* the New People arising during the time of the Seventh Fire listen to their inner voice and re-connect with the Elders. The other part of his prophecy, as you said, is more obvious: the light-skinned ones must choose between techno-philia on steroids and a slower, more earth-sensitive path. If they choose the right Way an Eighth Fire will be lit, a flame that symbolizes an era of peace, love and widespread prosperity."

"But if not, then we end up with *Blowout*."

"Yes, the two installations make the same point. A friend of mine created *Key Toter*. We had long conversations about its thematic. Her design choices suggest she really heard me."

"I can see that." Was this the same guy who hadn't said more than five words over the past two weeks, the keeper of the AF secret? Where did chatty boy come from?

"And what did you think of *Altered Founding*?"

"Oh my God, you were so right. Amazing."

"That's the work of a collective I often collaborate with. They consulted extensively with me before--"

"Yah, the work has your fingerprints all over it." Cam took a step away from him, sensing he was getting a bit too big for his britches. "Inside the turtle I met a young girl you thoroughly traumatized with your tale of a terrifying panther. I doubt she'll sleep tonight."

Namid's lip curled slightly for a second. "I'm asking about the historical project. Don't you think, after five hundred years, the time is right for the tables to turn?"

"Well, that's rather a tall order, don't cha know."

"From Nanavut to Patagonia, Native peoples are rising. What is happening in Chiapas and Bolivia is just the beginning. Look at how much the *Via Camp-*

esina has grown since Porto Alegre! The markets for organic food and alternative energy are exploding, the demographics are shifting toward a world of color. Everyone under thirty is joining BLM or the climate-justice movement. We're talking paradigm shift."

She found herself staring in bewilderment at Namid, who was now swaying back and forth slowly as he star-gazed. Was he Delphic or deluded? Sure enough, the long black ponytail, high cheekbones and sleek physique got to her. He *was* Hiawatha reborn, or better, a modern-day Tecumsah. How could she have projected her own pettiness onto him just a moment ago? It was time to salute the chief and ride home.

"I'm grateful for what you've accomplished in so little time. And I'm intrigued by what you're saying and would love to hear more, but it's been a long day. The festival opens tomorrow again at noon. See you then?"

"Yes, sleep well. Oh, and take this with you." He handed her a dreamcatcher. Where had that come from? "I suggest hanging it over your bed or by the window, anywhere good energy flows."

"Thanks." She smiled at him and then lifted the gift up for a better look, noticing for the first time a full moon about half-way up in the night sky. She adjusted the dreamcatcher's position until the moon came to rest fully inside its spider-webbed hoop, like a telescope so precisely aligned and focused on a distant star it seems only a mile away rather than millions.

"Dreams come in all sizes, Camilla. And some people dream bigger than others."

She offered another smile and then looked again at the moon through the hoop. Perfect fit. A moment later she turned to say goodnight but found him gone. "Namid, wait! I forgot to ask you about AF!"

10

CHILDREN OF LIGHT, CHILDREN OF DARKNESS

Early the next morning Cam arrived at the park with brush and bucket to clean up the paint spill, a chore that took twice as long as expected. She hustled back home, showered quickly and slipped on her sky-blue pair of running pants and another tie-dye. Before leaving she looked over the flyer one more time. One side had XR's Four Demands, the other provided details for the solidarity sail and September offensive. Their strategic plan would unfold over several days. Beginning on Sunday with a nine-am launch, lightship and crew would head down University Ave. and stop at Raising Cane's across from U of M for a mid-morning snack, warm-up rally and last-minute recruitment blitz, then pick up the pace and detour slightly over to South St. Anthony Park for another rally at noon. By one pm the Greta II gang would be lunched-up and ready to tug due east, accompanied by a flotilla of marchers. All would arrive no later than five-thirty at the state capitol. After resting on Labor Day, a green brigade would unleash a barrage of texts and calls to the governor and state representatives, while a 24/7 occupation of the capitol by the direct-action team would ratchet up the political pressure to amend Minnesota's climate-mitigation law and stop all new pipeline construction. Soon Kilridge's dreaded Black Snake would be cut off at the head, saving the Mississippi and its tributaries from defilement. Given how stirring the liberty bell had been the night before, her hopes for a spontaneous up-welling of support ran high.

Another big crowd came out on Saturday to enjoy the festivities. Near closing the night before, Emma G and Sinead found Charles captivated by an installation titled *Medusa Gone Mad*. Some thought it one of the event's best, though it was considered suspect by the thematic compliance sub-committee chaired by Gertrude herself. Out of a large neon-purple head, cracked open like a safe, sprang ten bobble-heading Alfred E. Neuman's, each one more hilarious than the next. One snaggle-toothed Alfred sucked on a watermelon rind, juice dripping off a stubbled chin; a second with ears out-flapped bore more than a passing resemblance to the last POTUS; a third had that surprised WTF look so often struck by Richard Pryor; a fourth had Alfred's middle finger shoved so far up a nostril he could scratch an eyeball; a fifth was head-spinning exorcist-style while the rosary beads he held close flagellated his red-raw neck; a sixth looked more like Hitchcock than Hitchcock himself; a seventh pulled off the perfect impersonation of Batman's butler; an eighth wore the Lone Ranger's Stetson, but had the eye mask pulled down over his mouth; a ninth was Putinesque in visage and toying with the strings of a POTUS puppet; and the tenth, a Charlie Brownish character, had a softball-sized blue marble cradled in his oversized mitt. From a speaker set amidst the bobble-heads came startling sound fragments--cuckoo clock, demagogic tirade, trumpeting elephant, heavy-metal guitar, dog whistle, car crash, howling monkey, leaf blower, cat fight—followed by a thrice-repeated retro commercial soundbite: Wendy's Grandma wanting to know where the beef was. Charles, it turned out, had made a fast friend that talked him into toking up, a milestone for the math-obsessed altar boy who still wore what his mother bought for him on sale.

"Got more bat-trees for the remote," announced Cam once the team assembled. With lightship built there was little to do except ring the liberty bell and enlist the interested.

"Have fun handing out flyers," sniped Sinead. "Emma G and I have better things to do."

Back by popular demand, Namid re-told the story of Mishipeshu and the Ojibwe braves every half-hour. Emma G and Sinead attracted a following of their own with a red-white-and-blue balloon chain that quickly rose and swept high over the festival, providing the event a patina of patriotism. Those signing the Four Demands petition could add a balloon to the chain. It was hard to say whether the bell, the tale or the balloons drew more people to the lightship and their cause.

Just before seven, Cam handed out the last flyer. Charles, who had shown up uncharacteristically late, reported 172 petition signatures with forty-one asterisks indicating serious intent to join the sail on Sunday and eight double asterisks for those committing to occupy the capitol 24/7 starting on Tuesday. Counting herself and Emma G, the shock troops for XR-AF's September offensive now numbered ten.

Stars aligning, Cam felt free to meet up with her fam for the evening. In a show of support, Rayna wore her green wig. Goldie arrived double-masked, a request her mother had made. Vibol and Elijah received invites as well, but the former already was off to Emory and the latter back in the Big Apple. The final ceremony wasn't until ten, so they had plenty of time to explore the grounds.

They lost Diego early on to the fire jugglers. "Meet you later," he promised. Now a foursome, they waded into the heart of the festival where, rumor had it, several hidden gems had eluded Frau Himmelgard's sub-committee. At their first stop they were not disappointed. Titled *U-Chthonicum*, the tent-housed phantasmagoria scrambled hidden corners in the human psyche, inducing uncanny moments and intense feeling-states for all who dared to play with its bewitching objects.

Past the tent flaps a psychedelic light show of astounding quality ran continuously and incense of incomparable rarity burned continually--a milieu so alluring it made ingestion of any controlled substance prior to entry seem superfluous. Dimpled balls of different colors and sizes lay in one corner inviting players to pick them up, roll on them, kick or lick them or toss them about, the only rule being that all objects had to remain in that corner. Touching any magic ball triggered novel sensations, some of which were pleasant and others not. Contact with one left you a little dizzy, another evoked a mild euphoria, still another triggered a somewhat sour taste and yet another invigorated as well as any Peppermint Patty.

The second corner contained a daedal object made of ropes, cords, strings and fine threads of differing lengths and textures intertwined densely through a jumbled maze of metal bars varied in thickness and height, its over-all shape that of a wild bush. When players stuck an arm into it, they felt in turns prickly or passionate or piqued, or they smelled delicious aromas from world cuisines, or they heard bizarre noises from beyond the world of the living, or they felt themselves floating in mid-air. Those who held hands while immersing arms might find themselves suddenly detesting or desiring one another sexually, or find each other's odor now disgusting and now enticing, or find the embarrassing sensation of wetting themselves at the same time to be odious one moment and exquisite the next.

Plopped in a third corner were four 21st-century versions of Woody's famous plaything. Intensity more than compensated for lack of originality. When fondled the new-fangled device released pheromones and evoked hormonal effects that made its predecessor seem sleepy and old-fashioned by comparison. Players found withdrawal from this corner most difficult. Pleasure moans reached decibels that put the priciest porn stars to shame.

In the last corner, which appeared empty, extreme sensations and feeling states shifted abruptly. With each step you entered a new world, sometimes heavenly and sometimes hellish. Step into the field and you might suddenly feel the most soothing mists on your skin. Take another step and you might see, hear and feel rats and other vermin crawling up your legs and arms. After a third you might hear celestial harmonics beyond all known acoustics. Dare a fourth and you might taste and smell the most hideously foul meat ever. Few players took more than a few steps upon entry. Many passed over it entirely after observing its potent effect on others.

Players were tagged and limited to twelve minutes of total exposure with no more than six minutes in any one corner. If you overstayed a corner two Umpa-Lumpa types quickly led you back to the neutral zone in the middle. When your buzzer went off, you had to exit the installation promptly. If you dawdled more than six seconds, two goggled geeks with the letters OOO on their white coats arrived to escort you out. They made Vaderesque hissing noises at anyone who continued to linger.

Upon exiting the four women were informed by the Triple O Men, whose gravelly voices really were as scary as Luke's father, that no two persons ever reported having similar experiences. Several rounds of sharing confirmed the claim. How could this be? The hyper-subjectivity of the place(s) and, above all, the impenetrable quality of its strange objects appeared to validate Harman's object-oriented ontology. Or so said Rayna in a post-tent monologue that went on far longer than six seconds, much to the very real annoyance of Maya and Goldie. As usual Cam was utterly taken with her learned discourse, which climaxed with a reference to Morton's dark-ecological concept of the hyper-object and several salient examples--an iceberg, Australia, a Gulf oil spill, an ocean called the English language–and closed with her imploring them all to read his *Realist Magic* cover-to-cover no matter how long it might take. With nothing more to be said, at least for now, they went in search of something more grounded.

At *Shroom Crossing* entrants were promised delectable treats and the best back rubs ever on an island paradise said to exist just beyond an imposing moat and tall stone wall. From the other side one heard well-known Pink Floyd tunes playing. Just swallow the green pill and an imposing drawbridge would fall to permit entry into the elysian abode. Opinion was divided over whether to ingest or not to ingest.

"Always one shady character among the lot," declared Maya. "I'm taking a pass." Cam and Goldie nodded in agreement. Still ruminating on the postmodern implications of *U-Chthonicum*, Rayna was more open to the offer. "Heaven can't wait. I say we take the plunge. The last installation stimulated, did it not? Altered states of consciousness, whether induced by drugs or tantric positions or--"

"Vote is three to one, Bell," interjected Maya as she turned and began striding briskly away. Cam and Goldie scurried along close behind. Rayna sulked a few seconds before catching up.

All four loved the next installation, a medley-style homage to modern social dancing titled *Close Embraces*. Every half-minute a carousel would turn and present a new dancing pair--actual dancers of considerable skill, not mannequins. The show ranged across genres without much attention to the history, though it did begin appropriately with waltz and polka. Cam had grown fond of tango from lessons with Maya, and both were entranced by the sophisticated couple who made time itself stop with their interpretation of Piazolla.

"How good was that!" gushed Cam.

"Believe it or not I've seen better. And more than once," said Maya.

"No way, when and where?"

"In DC. Every Saturday I went down to Eastern Market for the lessons and *milonga.* Once a month they brought in teachers from New York or Philadelphia. Sometimes a touring couple from Bueno Aires. They gave a performance at the dance around eleven."

"Well, I won't be dancing in DC anytime soon."

"True that, but something tells me you're going to love it there."

"Hey, can you two zip it," snapped Goldie, gesturing toward the carousel. "The show goes on, don't cha know." They watched a dozen more demos. Rayna's favorite turned out to be salsa, which gave her something to measure Diego by. Goldie was drawn to swing's energetic tempo. The homage ended with a film snippet featuring the incomparable Astaire and Rogers.

They skipped buoyantly over to *Wheel of Fortuna* next. The ferris-wheel fabrication reaching twenty-four feet in height had eleven seats numbered one, ten, twenty on up to one hundred with those seated depicting each age, from a newborn to a ten-year-old on up to a centenarian. All but two of them had a companion. The baby was in mother's arms, the kid held hands with a BFF, the new adult kissed a lover and so on until one came to a middle-aged woman, alone with her head buried in her hands. From sixty to ninety the aging had a spouse, daughter, nurse or priest by their side, but there was no one to comfort the last frail figure looking down at the empty picture frame he held limply.

At ground level a sparkly game-show hostess, assisted ceremoniously by two female bodybuilders, took their cue from three older men, all sharply dressed alike as executives but varied in height, who were drawing ticker tape from a retro main-frame and snipping it at intervals with their bare teeth. Whenever the flow of tape stopped and was bitten off, Vanna and the two Chynas brought the giant wheel to an abrupt halt, at which point the exec walked the severed tape-thread over to the base of the wheel and placed it inside an open coffin. He then wrote down the seat number closest to the coffin on a clipboard, stepped over to an old PC and clicked the mouse, increasing the numerical figure on an over-sized electronic scoreboard by one. After four or five snip-clicks the pattern was clear: the tallest executive did most of the biting and most of the seat numbers he recorded were 70 and above. Goldie was the first to figure out what the scoreboard's running tally—now at 183,691—was meant to signify.

"Goldie, are you OK?" asked Cam, who noticed the slumping shoulders and sad eyes.

"Just thinking about my dad. He would have turned seventy-one last week. It's been almost three months since…" As her voice trailed off Cam gathered her in and rocked gently.

"What was it like for him?" asked Rayna. Maya and Cam frowned at her, but the question seemed to bring Goldie back to life. In fact, it was the first time anyone had asked.

"Do you really want to know?" All three nodded yes. "My mom took him to ER because he was having trouble breathing. It became harder and harder, and he was breathing faster and faster, gasping and in a panic."

"They say it's like trying to breathe through a very narrow straw," observed Maya. She'd spent many a summer hour studying the pandemic's impact globally; it was topic number one, two and three in her graduate program. "Patients say it feels like a band across their chest or that their lungs are on fire. Some say it's like a swarm of bees stinging them inside their chest. For others it's the sensation of being smothered."

"Yah, he told us it was like someone was holding a pillow over his face. It got so bad he started to badger the nurse for an overdose."

"An overdose?" asked Cam.

"To put an end to it all," said Rayna. Goldie nodded yes and continued. "Can you imagine the sense of impending doom? I've tried, but I don't think any of us can really know."

"So many who get sick end up isolated," said Maya. "Were you and your mother able to be there with him?"

"Too risky, they said, but we kept the video calls going as best we could. The nurses were great about that. They made it part of the care from the get-go. Even so, it wasn't long before he was on his own."

"How did the illness progress?" asked Rayna. Her clinical tone bothered Cam, but Goldie seemed to appreciate her direct, no-nonsense manner.

"On day two the delirium began. We'd be talking to him and suddenly he'd get really agitated. The difficulty breathing never let up. We could see the fear on his face. Sometimes he didn't know where he was or didn't seem to recognize us. That was horrible." Goldie began to waver, and Cam held her tight. "I've got you, love. I've got you."

"Maybe we should pick this up later," suggested Maya.

"No, I want to tell you guys. I need to tell somebody." Cam loosened her hold but stayed close.

"How did the nurses treat the delirium?" asked Rayna.

"They sedated him when it got bad."

"Perhaps that was better than being alone," said Maya. "Patients only see their caretakers covered head-to-toe in PPE."

"Martian care."

"Yep, they say ICU nurses can work alongside colleagues for years but not recognize them at the holiday party."

"When was the last time you saw your dad?" asked Cam.

"Just before my mother drove him to the hospital. He waved to me before getting into the car. And then he was gone. On day three they hooked him up to a ventilator. My goodbye was in the driveway."

"Once they put him on the ventilator, what happened next?" asked Rayna.

"That didn't seem to help, so they tried a heart-lung machine. It pumps blood out of the body into a device that oxygenates it; then back it goes. At one point the nurses flipped him onto his stomach to get more air into his lungs."

"Proning," observed Maya. "They medicate the patients heavily so they can't move. The nurses turn them in bed every couple of hours to make sure their skin doesn't break down."

"They also worried about kidney failure, so they put him on a dialysis machine. He had catheters and monitors stuck everywhere. They were going to inject remdesivir, but he waved them off. He knew his time was up, and he was right. He died at 2:21 am on June 9th."

For the first time, Cam really understood why Goldie was so reluctant to leave her mother. She silently vowed to be there for her always no matter what.

"I'm sorry for your loss," consoled Maya.

"He was an amazing architect," she replied. "His firm worked with Jean Nouvel to design the new Guthrie Theater that opened in 2006. It's not far from here, on the other side of the river."

"I love that space!" blurted Rayna. "The promenade overlooking the water is incredible. Last fall I saw *Lucia Mad* there. What a story! Not even the famous Dr. Jung can help the brilliant but disturbed daughter of James Joyce. When he tries, Lucia toys with him like a cat flipping a mouse about. Again and again, she makes a play for her father's protégé, the young Samuel Beckett, but he is clueless and overwhelmed by it all. Pathetic, really. Let the fool wait forever for Godot, he missed his chance at heaven! The young actress playing Lucia, an exceptional talent just out of Oberlin named Llewie, left the audience stunned. The standing ovation seemed like it would never end. I'll never forget it." Cam was surprised by the passion with which she spoke. Where had it come from? Just a moment ago she was the clinician. Then she remembered how Giles remained reserved for weeks or even months at a time before the dam broke.

"Creating spaces for those kinds of performances is what my father lived for," said Goldie, the pride in her voice palpable. Cam fondly recalled the many plays the two had seen at the Guthrie: *Harvey*, *A Christmas Carol*, *An Enemy of the People*, *West Side Story*, *Metamorphoses*, *Leaves of Grass – Illuminated*, *Cabaret*. Her love of theater and acting ability owed so much to these shows. If only they had seen *Lucia Mad*!

Over the weekend only one other flyer circulated widely at the festival: an invitation to visit the Empyrean Temple virtually. At the boat launch, not far from the Man, stood a circle-shaped platform with a sidereal compass rose painted on it. Upon arriving the women saw four stylish Burners standing at the four cardinal points along the platform's perimeter, all facing its center and all focused on their phones. The flyer described three phases of what its creators called the Ethereal Empyrean Experience:

> Empyrean is an inclusive, healing virtual Temple space where visitors can share, express, process, grieve and heal during this transformative time. Empyrean represents the region just beyond our physical realm that is the highest center of wisdom and source of energy-consciousness. At this highest point one can interact with one's own concept of the divine.
>
> **PHASE I – CREATE A VIRTUAL OFFERING**
>
> Offerings can be created through Burn Week 2020 and seen during the Ethereal Empyrean Experience. Visitors can choose from a variety of "venerated objects" that encapsulate personal texts, images and audio messages. You can select where your offering is placed within the Temple and choose whether it is private or publicly viewable.
>
> **PHASE II – VISIT THE VIRTUAL TEMPLE**
>
> All are welcome to visit the virtual Temple free of charge via device. Each visitor will experience a solo Temple journey, immersing themselves in a way that is uniquely meaningful to them. The Temple flame burns a loving light for you. Please join us.

PHASE III - ATTEND THE VIRTUAL TEMPLE BURN

The virtual Temple Burn Ceremony is meant to inspire connection, contemplation, regeneration and transformation in a trying year. Through this experience in the virtual multiverse, we can defy space-time constraints and share in this collective catharsis.

Not surprisingly, Rayna expressed the most interest. Which made it interesting to Cam. After a brief discussion they decided to leave Triple E for another day. After all, an actual Burn was about to take place. Instead, they visited the porta potty and then stopped by the lightship. An ebullient Charles lofted the petition clipboard high. "Sixty-nine percent of festivalgoers signed and nineteen more asterisks for tomorrow!"

"Fabulous! Any more frontliners for the Tuesday offensive?" asked Cam.

"Two more double asterisks."

"That makes twelve."

"The dirty dozen!" exclaimed Emma G, whose protest rap sheet ran several pages.

Over two hundred distancing attendees formed a semi-circle around the Man. Diego was nowhere to be seen, though, nor was he responding to text. Cam and crew found dots not far from Greta II, while Namid and Javin went over to hang out with friends at *Altered Founding*. The finale began with the drum circle bringing its beat to a crescendo and falling silent. Then a fire juggler carried a large torch from the pit over to the Man while the other jugglers, joined by several wing-light performers, danced around him. The spectacular swirl mesmerized all present. After a Wiccan high priestess blessed the fire all eyes fell on the Man, now lit and beginning to blaze. One old Burner, bent toward the multiverse by LSD, raised wrinkled arms skyward to welcome a host of ancestral ghosts he saw rising from the Big Muddy. On each side of Burning Man, security guards stood ready to intercept anyone who might rush into his arms. For the ritually-ensconced the only sound was of crackling flames.

Meanwhile, a horde of unmasked, Hawaiian-shirted boogaloos crossed over the north footbridge and began to storm about, brandishing torches and lofting an array of flags. A torrent of posts on 2can over the past two weeks had identified the festival as a mortal threat to American Christian society. The night before a boogaloo mole posted pics of two installations in particular: *Altered Founding* and Greta II. Rabid calls to rid the earth of such filth flooded the boards. Frothing militia from as far away as Idaho, Nebraska and Indiana vowed to rendezvous with their brothers at the Spam Museum in Austin, Minnesota on Saturday night. From there they would convoy to Minneapolis and cleanse the park in defense of the right to bear arms and breathe free.

As the boogaloo bellows grew louder, terrified festivalgoers ran to their cars and soon were snarled in a parking-lot jam that left horns blasting, bumpers dented and middle fingers flying--an unusual departure from Midwesterner decorum. When the beer-belchers finally stumbled upon *Altered Founding*, they found the turtle demon guarded by a BIPOC army twice their size. As soon as the invasion had begun, BLM and AIM activists came running. Fifty-one warriors stood at the ready, each holding a flag-spear that Namid, Onawa and her Native collectivists had passed down from the terrapin's carapace. Among them were Rodney, Huey D and Diego, who earlier had suffered a nasty burn after a miscue with a fire baton and had been holed up at the first-aid station until now. Arriving just in time, he asked for something in green, white and red but gladly accepted the Yavapai-Apache flag-spear after Onawa gave him a maybe-later wink and said she found him the splitting image of Geronimo.

The philistines grew restless as four more police cruisers pulled in and event security amassed on their flank. Seeing they were outnumbered, their mole redirected them to Greta II. Torches and flags lifted high, they howled wildly and began a sixty-yard charge toward the lightship screaming "Drown the witch! Drown the witch!" Having retreated from the first skirmish of what local historians would later call the Battle of Boom Island, the frustrated pack was determined to dump the float into the river.

Cam shook her head in disbelief. Though the Man was still ablaze, most Burners bolted at the first sign of trouble. Apparently, the multiverse was calling them elsewhere. The whites of rage-filled eyes now in sight, she ordered her crew to abandon ship. Sinead and Charles cleared out, but Emma G refused to leave her post and kept ringing the liberty bell in hope of rallying earnest petition-signers to their side. Where were they when it mattered? She and Cam looked at each other a moment, like Thelma and Louise, and then turned to face the crazed Caucasian mob with arms locked.

Goldie and Maya suddenly appeared and grabbed each one by the arm. "Let's go, now!" barked Maya. Cam knew that when she said move, you didn't ask how fast. The four women scrambled out of the way just in time and then watched aghast as six barbarians rolled the lightship into the river while the others guffawed. Three of the troglodytes waded in and kept pushing the sinking vessel further away from the bank until beacon and bell disappeared under the water.

Maya tried to hold Cam back, but it was no use. She tore free and seconds later sent one of the vandals gasping headlong into the river with a g-forceful flying kick. She bounced up and felled a second brute with a swift knee to the groin and a blinding eye stab. Another slob came at her and soon went fetal, clinging to his crushed jewels. Still another charged and seconds later was choking on dust and dislodged teeth. Two more lugs lunged at her but quickly were wailing in agony as well. Six down, only eighteen more sorry sacks to go. Half their weight but twice as quick and far better trained, it would take four or more of the slugs to subdue her. And now here they came. She targeted the biggest thug, knocking him flat with a wicked roundhouse kick before the others overwhelmed her. Just then Diego jumped the one bear-hugging her from behind and wrestled him down into a chokehold. Seconds later, several boogaloos rushed in and began a brutal payback. The chump to Cam's right fell unconscious with a hellacious hook kick. Eight down. To her left a punk gasped for breath after a vicious punch to the Adam's apple. Master Moon had preached discipline in self-defense and the proportionate use of force, but she wanted vengeance. She took a step toward the wheezing dolt. He was terrified and she knew it. Good, let the pathetic puke tremble in his boots. She took another menacing step as he staggered backwards. Time to end him right here, right now.

Maya again saved Cam from herself, jumping in between her and the dazed boogaloo. "That's enough, Cahmie. Let it go. He isn't the real enemy." BIPOC troops now ran to their aid, pulling the bruisers off Diego and holding them in custody. Two old AIM warriors were not far behind, carrying their flag into battle. They formed a human shield in front of Diego, flanked by young braves. Maya and Cam passed through them to see to their friend, on his knees holding his side and coughing, his face puffing up from the blows and broken nose bleeding profusely. Brass knuckles had gashed him open just above the right eye. He looked up at them and grinned before buckling. Maya caught him just as he was about to face-plant into the concrete. Cradling him in one arm, she yanked off her shirt with the other and held it firm against the gushing wound. In a fury Cam looked about for more perpetrators to punish. Maya let go the shirt, caught her by the pant leg and would not let go. "They aren't the real enemy," she repeated. Cam looked down at Diego and quickly came to her senses. She pulled off her tie-dye, knelt down and gently pressed.

The police finally stepped in and began cuffing some of the instigators, who congratulated themselves while the other goons gathered up their wounded and headed back toward the footbridge chanting "The witch is dead! The witch is dead!" The four arrested disappeared into the back seats of cruisers and were driven off. EMTs rolled a stretcher in for Diego. Maya accompanied him to the ambulance and rode shotgun to the hospital.

Cam went to check on her crew huddling near the water's edge. Goldie comforted a weeping Sinead while Emma G spat obscenities. Charles stared across the river, mouth open and every bone shaking. Upon seeing their captain's approach, they pulled themselves together as best they could. They had watched dumbfounded as she shredded one attacker after another, a wildcat unleashed and unvanquished. Sinead lurched forward into her arms sobbing, and soon they all were consoling each other and crying.

11

GRETA 2.0

Tears turned into coughs when the smoke from a now cindered Man reached the mourning crew. Surveying the grounds, Cam spotted the petition clipboard on the pavement, its many signatures buried under the muddy footprint of a size-thirteen jackboot. Just as well, they were as worthless as the pansy-ass liberals who'd turned tail and ran as soon as the rabble had rumbled in. She would take one Diego, one Emma G, one Maya, one Goldie over ten thousand of them. Her days of wearing tie-dye were done.

"Where's Rayna?" No one knew. They fanned out, and a half-minute later Emma G whistled everyone over to the Triple-E platform. She sat at its center in lotus position, palms up and facing toward where the Man had burned, her eyes fixed straight ahead and gazing intently, as if he were still aflame. Cam still had not picked the lock on these trances, though she had a hunch the key was uniquely audible in character rather than some riddle one might decipher. Beyond semantics to pure sound, yet nothing ever as simple as a hand clap or finger snap. With Giles she had tried this and that odd noise, sometimes tumbled two together, but over the years had learned from many trials to be patient and wait. Autists dance to their own drummer.

Beholding Rayna--a cover-girl for *Yoga Today* with legs tucked, spine straight and breath even—Cam thought back to the night she had fallen into the Unabomber's literary embrace. After finishing his version of Plato's allegory--a broadside against liberal myopia and conservative cunning that doomed the ship's fools to the fate of the Titanic—she had closed her laptop and froze up, just sitting there like one of Kaczynski's it's-all-over icebergs. Was it the rolling bottle, the bird song or the two randomly in tandem that un-thawed her that night?

"I better get going," said Goldie. The others agreed. After goodbye hugs they walked away slowly. The smell of burnt wood lingered in the air. Above the park lights sat a full moon serenaded by crickets no longer drowned out by lovely drumbeats or the ugly outbursts of angry white men. Other than a few staff milling about, not a soul remained. The river seemed as still as the one sitting cross-legged on the compass rose. After such madness, how could it be so calm?

Cam stepped onto the platform and sat down beside Rayna. She tried not to think about the sunken lightship and was delivered from a flashback by Namid, who appeared out of nowhere and was now right next to her. They sat in silence for several minutes before he pulled out his phone. A familiar smirk fell over his caramel-brown face as he watched the video: two dozen rampaging pseudo-patriots, two brave young women locking arms to meet the idiotic stampede, Greta II's liberty bell ringing before going under, a flurry of fierce Cahmie-kazie kicks felling the flabby left and right, warriors ancient and new running to a fallen comrade's rescue, unrepentant cretins crowing as they left the scene of their crimes. Two minutes and forty-three seconds of Mississippi Mayhem, as the incident was now tagged, had gone viral. Way viral.

"What's with the shit-eating grin?" asked Cam. In those striped pants and that athletic bra, she looked ready to run again, run through anyone. He handed her the phone. She stared blankly at the view count: 170,242 and rising fast.

He stood up and began swaying slightly and humming low as he surveyed the night sky. She noticed him rotating the bracelet on his wrist, as if the position and movement of all celestial spheres depended on it. Each round piece of white-shell polished, a ring of glistening moons as lovely as the full one above.

He looked down at her. "Do you know what that number means?"

"What the hell are you talking about?" she shot back. "Diego was beaten to within an inch of his life, and our float is at the bottom of the river!"

"What they did to him was awful, but he will recover and grow stronger." He crouched down and gently removed the phone from her hand. "Over 170,000 views already. By noon tomorrow it will be one million. You and Emma G, but especially you Camilla, are about to become heroines of the movement. It's an elevation moment."

"A what?"

Namid nodded toward the north sky, home of Lynx, Corona Borealis, Leo Minor and other members of the Ursa Major family. "Come winter, remind me to tell you how Little Bear came to join Big Bear in the heavens."

"Whatever."

Then he pointed to where Greta II had gone down. "Out of these waters will rise the White Panther." He offered her a hand up, and now the two of them were star gazing. "I had a dream last night, and in it you were--"

"Namid, did you toke up over at *Altered Founding*?"

He found the question amusing but off-point. "We all say we want a leaderless revolution, but inspiring leaders still make all the difference. What just happened wasn't political theater—except that it was. And of the very best kind. You were the real deal, hopelessly outnumbered yet staying with your ship until the bitter end, your loyal lieutenant by your--"

"Her name is Emma G, remember? This is *totally* ludicrous."

Namid grew more animated. "And then there you were, feet and fists flying, thrashing through one villain after another. Camilla, you *are* the White Panther."

"Don't call me that, it's ridiculous."

"Well, it's better than calling you…oh, I don't know…Cam of Arc."

"Uff-da, you *didn't* just say that."

"You're right, I didn't. In my dream you were a pow--"

"Enough with your dreams and messiah-making! I can't even get Rayna to wake--" Just then a siren wailed. She popped to her feet and smiled at them, refreshed and full of life.

"See! You just raised a dead girl!"

"That's *so* not funny."

"Look, I know this all sounds far-fetched, but before you walk out onto the water and raise up Greta II from her watery grave, I want you to check your messages. It will serve as confirmation of my--"

"Fine, give me a second." She found hundreds of texts waiting for her, all of them ultra-superlative and most first-person plural.

cam we luv u!!
u totally rock!!!
[hearts and sparkles]

cam we r so
not worthy
u r the bomb!!
[tears of joy faces]

wig!!!
cam done slam
the spam man!!

wanna own

a boogaloo?
call cam!

cams the shit
boogers done split!!!

cahmie-kaze
kicks ass!!

wam bam
thank u cam!!!

where do we send
$ to rebuild greta?

whats the plan cam?
whatever it is
were in!!

cam we'll go
to hell and
back with you!!!

captain cam
in command
run for your
sorry-ass lives
boogaloo
bitches!!

how many cams
does it take to drop
eight boogaloos?
just one!!!

cams midi-chlorian
count is higher than
anakins any day!!

way to rip
the boogs
a new one
cam!!!

On and on they went. After reading about twenty she turned her astonished eyes toward Namid, who spared her the I-told-you-so look.

"What did you mean by…what did you call--"

"An elevation moment. It's when an authentic leader emerges. Think David dropping Goliath."

"Without a vision the people perish!" gushed Rayna, who was beginning to grasp the enormity of what she had missed and couldn't wait to hear all about it.

"Sleeping beauty weighs in," snarked Namid. "In any event, things are going to move fast now. Be ready to go big."

"*Carpe diem*!" exclaimed Rayna, now feeling all tingly and trembling slightly.

"I'm not sure I really get--"

"Don't worry, my handler's fee is very reasonable," he joked. "Star-making isn't that much different from performance art and multi-media. All you need to do is embrace the role. From now on you *are* the White--"

"Stop calling me that!" Her head was spinning. She'd been up since dawn and had barely eaten anything all day. Dehydrated as well. Time to take a bow and exit the stage. "I don't know where all this is going, but I do know this: we *are* going to re-build our lightship and set sail for St. Paul soon."

"That's the second act of the play. Going to be epic. Paradigm shifts require a mythic-symbolic element that activates the collective unconscious."

"Huh?" Cam hated it when the conversation sailed past her. Postponing college was beginning to look like a bad idea after all.

"Never mind, we'll talk tomorrow." He placed a small packet in her palm. She recognized the gold foil but not the oval shape. "Open it and take a whiff." She found the moist black flakes pungent, a dark and sweet aroma that reminded her of the Red Man chew her uncle Olaf loved so much. "Ojibwe offer the leaf out of gratitude, and to mark the beginning of a significant venture." She inhaled again before pocketing the second gift he'd bestowed in as many nights.

"Rayna, make sure White Panther gets some rest tonight."

"Who?" He gave her a patronizing grin and turned to go.

"No, wait! Which AF is it, *Altered Founding* or *Amor Fati*?" She was tired and didn't find his smirk funny at all. "C'mon, give it up. My stomach is growl--"

"Neither."

"I don't believe you. Just tell me!"

"When the time is--"

"Tell me now!" Her ego depletion complete, she lunged hard at him. He deftly side-stepped her, and she stumbled toward the platform's edge. There was more than one panther present.

He decided to ignore her splenetic display. "Well, if you insist, let's all have a look," he said while motioning for them to come close. Together they watched a music video he pulled up. "Las Amigas del Fuego" opened with a moony solo guitarist atop a large rock by the foamy sea before cutting to his fire-juggling girlfriend on stage. Rayna found it charming and thematically on point, but she could tell it was a big let-down for Cam.

"Really, Namid? *That's* what the *mysterium tremendum et fascinans* is all about?" Drawing on her four years of Latin with Mr. Fizz and Doc Scanlot felt good. "And I'm supposed to let you turn me into some kind of legendary leader?"

"Cam, don't you think you might be--"

"Button it, Bell."

"Immerse yourself in the lyrics," he replied, not shaken in the least. "Maybe they'll grow on you. But if not, then we'll just say AF stands for Arts-on-Fire and move on."

"I said that was it from day one, but everybody else thought it too obvious!" She paced around in a circle and held her head, now pounding with a headache.

"First thought, best thought," said Rayna with an eager smile. They looked for Namid, but he had vanished into the night. Not once have I ever seen him coming or going, Cam thought to herself. How annoying!

"Let's go home before my head explodes."

Things did move faster, as Namid foresaw, though it took two days to reach a million views of Mississippi Mayhem, now often referenced online as 2M. Invitations for interviews with Pox, The Young Lurks and other outlets hot-on-the-scent soon poured in, making the rest of Labor Day weekend one non-stop media event. GBS and other last-century, geriatric networks soon followed with breathless requests. Through the week Cam spoke with writers from *Roll a Bone*, *Vanity Hair*, *Jacobinista*, *Spired*, *ZEIT* and other hip 'zines calling every five minutes. Rumor had it that Netrifix and Ripple TV Triple+ had started a bidding war for rights to fast-track production of a mini-series. Were calls from Jimmy Kimmel, Oprah and Trevor Noah next? Just texting *thx luv u 2* [heart] in reply to the avalanche of adoring messages now took almost two hours of her day. A vastly expanded circle of friends wanted a blow-by-blow, as it were, and that took another hour. Flitter followers skyrocketed from 491 to 783,000 only six days after 2M. Up to that fateful Saturday night she'd never had headaches, but now they dogged her daily. Fast fame's a screechy-needy bitch, Goldie said.

Namid assumed the role of Mar-Comms Director, a paying gig established soon after a flood of donations through Fund-Upped left XR-AF flusher than most players on the World Poker Tour. As platforms overseer and gatekeeper for Cam's media engagements, he remained laser-focused on the paramount objective: branding her as White Panther and making sure the framing of 2M amplified her voice and image. Early on, he quickly suppressed a spontaneous attempt by wildcat admirers to dub their heroine none other than Cam of Arc. On an unauthorized stan site, they claimed she'd quoted the fifteenth-century martyr and saint--who once declared "I am not afraid, I was born to do this"--alleging she had uttered these very words just after Greta II sank and just before she buried eight boogaloos. All it took was a flit from White Panther herself denying the attribution. Meanwhile, the alt-fact king Alex Jones lit up InfoBores, 2candom and other far-right echo-chambers by labeling Cam and Emma G the Most Dangerous Zoomers in America, a charge Namid skillfully flipped into 767,000 mocking re-flits in four days. Greta herself sent a congratulatory note on being so named, joking she'd never been jealous of anyone until now.

On every bridge and wall Banksy and countless other graffiti artists immortalized White Panther and G-Force, as Emma G was now known, making the two ubiquitous symbols of the fight to save the planet. In the emerging iconography G-Force, while relegated to minor-heroine status, often appeared at White Panther's side, the two fierce young felines locking paws. Her renamed blog Hear Us Roar became wildly popular. She quickly established herself as a lively contrarian voice within climate-justice circles. On the stump she was as articulate as White Panther and more informed when it came to policy issues. Single-handedly she revived the intra-movement debate over Jeff Gibbs and Michael Moore's controversial *Planet of the Humans*. While readily conceding that technological advances in alternative energy were missing from the film's outdated presentation, she argued its main thesis remained valid: "green growth" within the current system is a fallacy too many well-meaning enviros cling to mindlessly, a very inconvenient truth that aging technophiles like Al Gore were still in dangerous denial about. At least Tusk admitted the raison d'être of Zestlah is to fund the colonization of Mars before it is too late. Ozzie Zehner's *Green Illusions* deserved a much wider reading among the faithful, given its sober view of clean-tech's limits and the need for a revolution in cultural values and lifestyles that—however improbable—remained the most realistic pathway toward a sustainable future.

Namid commissioned the obscure songwriter of "Las Amigas del Fuego" to lionize the two heroines and contracted with notable Minneapolis Sound musicians to record "Ballad of Boom Island" at Wild Sound Studio not far from the now-famous park. Once the song took off, soon becoming more popular than Fatboy Slim's Greta-speech remix of "Right Here, Right Now" had been a year earlier, XR-AF had a second very healthy revenue stream. A third flow of cash came from dolls, caps, buttons, posters, bumper stickers and myriad other merch. All contracts, waivers and such were placed in the capable hands of Charles, who was elevated to CFO. His father, a patent attorney, provided invaluable pro bono support behind the scenes. Goldie served part-time as advisor-at-large.

By unanimous acclaim Cam was appointed Prowler-in-Chief with Emma G and Sinead co-serving as Vice-Prowlers. Namid handed Sinead the job of replying to the torrent of fan texts, freeing up Cam to focus on setting sail for the capitol as soon as possible. All crew members received the same pay, a locally adjusted living wage of $18.85 per hour. Overhead was minimal, and so ninety-plus percent of the huge sums pouring in went to climate-refugee relief, donations to BLM and a war chest for launching Greta 2.0.

Overnight, Cam's status within the local movement went from suspect to first among equals, a glow up that paid big dividends. When she invited MN350, Sunrise TC, Earth Roar and kindred groups to attend a strategy retreat in mid-September--an event that would include BLM, AIM and Chicano activists--all responded enthusiastically. In the run-up to the retreat, she and Emma G worked tirelessly to build relationships and forge a consensus. XR-AF's position was clear and principled: the solidarity sail should go forward and aim to achieve its stated goals while respecting the agendas of other groups. Reaching agreement on a date and joint statement proved difficult, to no one's surprise.

During the retreat a breakthrough occurred when younger BLM activists and older AIM leaders agreed to Namid's proposal that Greta 2.0 set sail October 12th on Indigenous Peoples' Day. XR-AF's mission aligned with Red America's defense of Turtle Island on behalf of all humanity, he said to the latter. Turning to the former, he acknowledged the uprising to thunderous applause and thanked them on behalf of the Anishinaabeg for their courageous defense of *Altered Founding* and their fallen brother Diego. When he invited them to become honorary members of the Ojibwe bear clan, Native elders rose as one in affirmation. As Maya, Rodney and Huey D stepped forward, other delegates took a knee and raised a fist. Each received a copper ring etched with a bear claw. "The Ojibwe bear clan protects the people, as these warriors demonstrated so valiantly at Boom Island," pronounced Namid. "They also are healers." Standing next to him, Cam felt a little uneasy yet also proud of her new friend, who was on the verge of uniting forces so often scattered. He presented Maya with another ring. "Sister, please give this to Wrestles with Boogaloos. Tell him our prayers will not cease until he stands strong among us once again." Another huge applause broke out.

Ward Means, the eldest and most respected AIM leader present, now raised a hand. All fell silent. He gestured for Maya to come closer and then regarded her for what seemed an eternity. "You are the one they call Maya." She nodded yes. "I am told you led your people with courage and skill after they killed George Floyd. Welcome to the *Makwa*. If ever you call upon your clan brothers we will come to your side, no matter who your foe may be. We trust you will do the same." As Maya and elder Means embraced, he slipped a small pouch into her hand. "*Ginebig* for Wrestles with Boogaloos," he whispered to her. "Just a sprinkle heals wounds fast." Cam glanced at Namid and saw his lip curl. She didn't know what kind of theater this was, she just knew it was of the very best kind.

"Let us now feast in celebration of our unity and shared vision!" cried Namid. A hearty applause followed. "We will re-convene for a brief closing session at seven-thirty." As everyone went off to eat, he motioned Cam and Emma G over. He was all business. "Let's mingle and make sure everyone feels good about October 12th. Focus on anyone who seems to be on the fence. We'll re-group at seven to go over Cam's final address. We want to lock this down tonight. There won't be another opportunity as good as this one."

At the appointed hour Cam and Emma G reported in. "I pow-wowed with five climate-justice allies, and they're all stoked," said Cam. "Same here, the date's a lock," concurred Emma G. He flashed a knowing smile and handed them a piece of paper. "Take a minute to read it over. I want to check-in with Sunrise before answering any questions you might have." They turned toward each other and shared a giggle. Before they knew it, he'd slipped away.

Emma G thought the speech needed to close with a bolder call to action, but otherwise was just the ticket: a compelling vision of how the solidarity sail would unfold and the roles various actors in the drama could play if they chose to get involved. Classic soft sell, with plenty of room for listeners to fill in the blanks themselves and scratch their own contribution itch. Cam agreed, except she thought the ask at the end--a simple invite to attend a follow-up planning event—was just right for this choir.

Namid returned looking more confident than usual. "I just talked the Sunrisers into pushing for AOC's presence. She's tight with Ilhan, and if we're lucky we'll score the entire Squad on 10/12. Cam, you may need to join that call. You're the catnip, after all."

"I'm what?" She planned to major in international relations at Georgetown but now thought communications a better choice.

"So, superhero one and two, any edits? We have ten minutes." Emma G pitched the idea of a more inspiring close, but Namid wasn't convinced. "We're holding all the marbles. All we need to do is ask for volunteers to help us roll them out."

Cam read over the text once more, identifying moments for a natural pause and eye-contact. During the delivery she barely looked down. All clapped warmly in agreement. After a short Q&A the event ended with a collective wolf howl led by White Panther.

The following Monday, Namid presided over XR-AF's strat-chat:

namid: I think we've waited for Charles and Goldie long

enough, let's get started. [four thumbs up] Sinead, what's on tap this week?

sinead: OK, so tomorrow we have White Panther and G-Force appearing at Earth Roar's annual die-in at the art museum. Emma G, you blogged about their corporate campaign last week, yah?

emma g: I did indeed, and an expanded version came out as an op-ed in the Strib yesterday. [three claps]

namid: What's the piece titled?

emma g: Wait for it...Warbill Poisons the Mississippi Watershed. Dumping of petrochemicals into the tributaries is worse than ever, as is the dead zone in the Gulf. We're linking ER's world's-worst-company agenda to XR's Fourth Demand and calling upon Big Mack to pay reparations to Cajun fisherfolk and Cancer Alley victims. We're also taking a page from Ecuador's constitution and demanding the Mississippi be granted legal personhood under federal law, with guardianship going to a citizens' assembly. In Quebec recently a municipality and the Innu of Ekuanitshit granted the Magpie River legal standing to protect it from hydro development and other threats. So we think--

namid: Excellent, going big on this one. And the byline?

emma g: White Panther and G-Force, who else?

namid: Music to my ears, super number two. Sinead, please continue.

sinead: On Wednesday we're virtually hosting the volunteers for the Greta 2.0 sail. Namid, I assume you're facilitating?

namid: That I am. Herding cats is my specialty. Javin, how's the new build coming along?

javin: I've assembled a crack fab team. Only change is proportional: Greta's new hull and lighthouse will be larger, and her liberty bell will be louder.

cam: Hear us roar! Love it! [Charles signs in, all glassy-eyed; a private group chat begins, mostly conjectures about how often and how heavily he is toking up]

namid: Kind of you to join us, Charles. Sinead, what's next?

sinead: Cam, on Thursday you and Emma G are mending fences with XR-TC. Rain or shine, they're dropping a banner off the bridge over I-94 at noon.

emma g: Are they still going with Climate Change Is Mass Murder?

sinead: So I'm told. It's the only thing they've reached consensus on since we split.

namid: You don't say.

emma g: I can work with that. Explore the dark side of the Anthropocene, call out the particulates crisis and compare its annual six-figure death toll to covid's. Blog post will be up by noon tomorrow.

namid: Good, and let's get a long-form piece in next month's issue of ***Gaianda***. They can't get enough of G-Force.

cam: Atta girl, super number two! [Emma G flips Cam the bird]

emma g: No byline for you, zero. [laughs all around; Charles coughs and goes off-screen]

namid: Camilla, I've booked you for a talk with Roger Hallum on Friday. Part of XR-UK's Rebel Now! podcast series. By the way, how did their September offensive go?

cam: When Lightship Greta rolled into London the bobbies confiscated it. Thousands marched on Parliament Square. XR folk blocked roads, staged sit-ins, glued themselves to bridges. Six hundred arrested. Bobbies kept warning protestors they risked big fines if they didn't obey the rules against gatherings of more than thirty. G-Force blogged on it last week, don't cha know.

namid: Sorry, I missed that one somehow.

cahmie: Yah, you should go back to it. She argued the chance of catching covid during an outdoor demonstration is quite low, and for those under sixty the small risk is worth it since direct action will be more effective than electoral politics in getting governments to meet XR's demands.

namid: Fascinating. Sinead, anything else?

sinead: Just the weekly update on financials. Charles? [he comes back on-screen]

charles: Hey, sorry to check out, had to go number one. So, another record-setting week. "Ballad of Boom Island" still near the top of the charts. Merch sales up eighty-eight percent, donations sixty-seven percent. Cost controls in place. Bottom line: we're good! Oh, and I took the liberty of sending our friend Gertrude $3K to cover legal fees in a civil suit against her arts association. Seems one of the Himmel Barb boys triggered someone's PTSD. [three open mouths] And before I forget, did everyone get their pay last Friday? [thumbs up all around]

namid: Thanks, Charles. [obligatory smile and nod] I believe we are adjourned. [obligatory smiles and goodbye waves]

Afterwards Cam called Goldie. "Hey, why didn't you join the meet today? Everyone wondered where--"

"Cam, I've been meaning to tell you, I decided last-minute to start classes at Columbia, all virtual obviously. You were so caught up with the festival, and I just thought--"

"That's great! You can study and help us with Greta 2.0, all from the comfort of the Silver Queen!"

"If only it were that easy. I'm already buried with assignments and need to spend time each day with my mom. She's not doing so well."

"Oh my God, did she test positive?"

"No, she's not sick. Grieving takes time. Depression, anxiety, loneliness—it's all part of it. Just because society treats death like a hiccup doesn't mean it is. I need to be present, and it feels like XR-AF is a distraction. An enticing one, fer sure, but it's not what matters most right now. I didn't want to let you--"

"Don't even say it. We'll be fine, don't cha know. The solidarity sail is set for Indigenous Peoples' Day."

"Let me guess, a Namid-engineered event."

"How did you know?"

"Takes one to know one, Borlaug. He's one smooth operator. Keep your wits about you and make sure he always knows the Prowler-in-Chief has final say."

"Aye, captain."

"Don't even."

Near the end of the solidarity-sail planning meet, Cam urged everyone to attend an emergency-response rally at the state capitol that night. BLM-TC Metro, the Shovelers and other anti-racist groups were coming out in solidarity with counterparts in Louisville who had taken to the streets denouncing the kid-gloves treatment given to Breonna Taylor's killers. She read from a flit just posted: "Cop on trial only charged with Class D felony: wanton engagement in the first degree, maximum term of one to five years in prison, $15,000 cash bond. No other officers charged. This is AmeriKKKa." Later, she and Maya reached out to allies. Members of the *Makwa* promised to show up.

During the rally, Cam gave a short speech that Emma G drafted hastily. "The terrible swift violence that claimed Breonna's life is of a piece with the slow yet equally awful violence against poor people of color living in the Bronx, Flint and so many other sacrifice zones. Tonight, we say "*¡basta!*" We stand as one to say "*¡basta!*" Led by White Panther, all gathered chanted "*¡basta!*" for another minute.

Afterwards Cam chatted with friends from the uprising. They still called her Cahmie. Everyone in BLM knew White Panther had two meanings, one historically grounded and another fabricated by a talented Chippewa whose projection worked for them because she embodied the militant-sixties legacy as well as anyone. Long before white allyship became trendy the White Panthers had shown the way. According to Maya, it was Diego who summed it up best the day after the festival when he interrupted a pale-faced nurse who kept yammering on about the violence, appalled that a nice girl from Edina had been involved, and asked her a simple question: "Who do you want in the foxhole with you, White Panther or the frickin' church lady?"

Just before the evening ended a buzz went through the crowd. In Crystal City, Virginia another Amerizon van had exploded not far from the company's new HQ2 construction site. The driver was at his last delivery, a luxury high-rise for young professionals and employees working at the Pentagon nearby, and luckily in the building at the time. Several pedestrians suffered mild concussions. Debris struck a jogger. Live coverage showed the van's remains still smoldering. The blast, more powerful than at Palo Alto, damaged several parked cars severely and obliterated a bus-stop shelter. An already ugly year had just become uglier, Cam thought to herself as Maya drove the two of them home. Diego was on the phone with Jorge when they arrived.

"Time for a new line of work, *hermano*. Or find some other company to drive for. You gone from Primo delivery to prime target!"

"Don't freak me out like that. You know finding a job that pays $17 an hour ain't so easy."

"You and the Somalis gonna do something?"

"I just gotta message from Amerizoners Unite. They're adding safety inspections to the list of demands. Each local has its own issues—simple stuff like clean drinking water and porta potties--along with everyone's two big gripes: slowing down the work pace and getting the truth about who's got covid. Primo Day is just a few weeks away, and we gonna walk out if Bleudough blows us off."

"Maybe the bombings will get that *chingado* to sit down with you all."

"Or maybe the company will ignore us and make a play for sympathy.

Nothing like a terrorist threat to distract people, keep them in line."

"Them *pendejos* might try to frame the workers, make it look like they planted the bombs. Sounds insane, but after what that dude Snowden brought to light you gotta wonder."

Despite all the cameras, after a week local police, the county sheriff and federal law enforcement still had no leads, nor had authorities in California arrested anyone yet in connection with the first bombing seven months ago. Experts had deemed Palo Alto a one-off solo job, some estranged employee gone postal. Soon worried sick about the virus, the public had forgotten all about it until now. Within days Bleudough announced a new group, Amerizon Security Services, and partnerships with ISYS, Pinkerton Consulting & Investigations and other top names in the surveillance-industrial complex. He vowed to ferret out the culprits. The newly appointed ASS CEO--a former national-security advisor to Obama, advisor to Black Hawk Investment and chair of a high-level commission on enhancing national cyber-security--told the press no node in the net would go unsearched.

The only clue from the recent bombing was a large unmarked white envelope, dropped three days later into a postal box four blocks from the HQ2 site. Within it a blue marble, an iron cross and four shreds of cardboard, one with the capital letter B written on it and three with the numbers 1, 6 and 8. In early March a similar envelope had been found at F8, a trendy retail outlet for the latest tech gadgets located four blocks from the first van explosion. That envelope also contained four shreds--one with the capital letter M and three with the numbers 1, 5 and 6—but no marble or cross. After Crystal City bloggers soon suggested a connection to Bleudough's net worth--$186 billion as of September 2020—and the price he paid for a Beverly Hills mansion--$165 million—early in the year. Various theories regarding the identity of the perpetrators circulated through social media, most of them wild guesses at the meaning of the blue marble and iron cross. Questionable associations were made to Kaczynski and members of eco-fascist groups with whom he was alleged to have corresponded over his many years in prison, despite his repeated disavowal of all such groups.

While at the XR-TC banner drop, Cam took an unexpected call from her father, who had been alerted to the Strib op-ed by colleagues at work.

"Cam, your mother and I are livid about this editorial. We also heard through the grapevine that you went behind our back last fall and led an embarrassing protest at Mr. Leland's house. Don't you realize your grandstanding might affect my chances of promotion? I'm on the short list for SVP of North American operations!"

"Dad, I can't give Warbill a pass, I'm sorry. You were wrong about the company's ESG credentials. They're bogus, nothing more than greenwash. After what happened at the festival, I have a responsibility to--"

"Stop right there, young lady. We need to talk about the festival. I gave you six thousand dollars, and you gave the world Mississippi Mayhem!"

"The money did support my group's participation, and the event did raise thirteen thousand dollars for climate refugees."

"Climate what?"

"Climate refugees are those who--"

"Enough, I heard you the first time. Honey, listen to me: this white-panther persona they've created is a charade. The fact is, you're being used. Your mother and I think you--"

"Dad, if it's about the money, Charles can write you a check."

"It's not about the money! You're playing a game with much higher stakes than you realize, one that could cost both you and this family a great deal. The more attention this larger-than-life character gets, the more likely you'll get hurt. Not some plastic action figure, the real you."

"Well, I'm afraid it's too late to say the empress has no clothes."

"Uff-da, you *didn't* just say that."

"Wait, that's my line. You can't steal my line like that."

"This isn't funny. Some say the line between theater and reality is illusory, and you seem to think so too at times. But there's more to it than that. Your mother and I don't feel like we can trust you anymore. At the very least, apologize to her for hiding what happened last fall."

Cam hesitated and then agreed to call soon. As awkward as the conversation was two days later, for Giles's sake she readily ate humble pie. Even a mild rift with her parents would stress Tramp, and she was no longer there to manage a meltdown. Nothing else kept her up at night. Mom was merciful with penance, demanding only that she not find herself too busy saving the world to join them for dinner at Thanksgiving and Christmas. After hanging up, several minutes passed before she deciphered the message her mother was trying to convey toward call's end, a message layered into her mildly wistful tone, assurances that dad's promotion was a lock and the giveaway: how much she reminded her of Leo. Not only did she miss her daughter, she also was proud of her for risking harm's way and not backing down when it really mattered.

In August XR-TC had cancelled Root Camp amidst the organizational upheaval surrounding Cam and Emma G's splinter group. Still, there remained a desire to take up spiritual practices that could help rebels become more resilient and sustain their sanity during the long emergency ahead. Despite a hectic schedule, Cam decided to attend a walking meditation event sponsored by XR-TC and two sangha groups on the Sunday before 10/12. She and Rayna biked to Como Park on a perfect fall day, crisp and sunny and bursting with vibrant colors. At the carousel they listened with thirty other seekers to instructions on how to walk mindfully along the trails. Muna smiled as she handed them a sign to carry, a peace offering Cam accepted graciously. She held hands with Rayna during the walk. Best of all, no one made anything of her presence, although two kids wearing White Panther earmuffs came up to her afterwards and asked for an autograph. Playing a public figure already was old.

On the back deck that afternoon they watched the clouds roll in while munching on falafels, red peppers and hummus. The first R&R in six weeks, and not a moment too soon. Tomorrow was going to be huge. Her team wisely spared her the last-minute details. At ten pm Emma G sent a brief text confirming all was in place for the launch. By eleven she was asleep in Rayna's arms. Around one a gentle shower began to pitter-patter upon the roof. Only Diego heard the soothing sound.

A hard rain fell on Indigenous Peoples' Day, much harder than forecasters expected. Sticking to the original script, XR-AF's skeleton crew christened the lightship and set sail at nine am sharp. Outfitted in yellow raingear, they looked the part as they tacked right and towed the float southward on University Ave., a dozen boomer-age activists walking in their wake. Cam donned her dad's old bucket hat and wore her now thread-bare sweatshirt. She sent him a selfie, his favorite number ten front and center. His two thumbs-up reply tickled her. Since when did he emoji?

Support for the solidarity sail was washed out, there was no denying it. Just as petition-signers had run for cover five weeks ago, many who had pledged to participate now remained under cover. The police escort dwarfed them and likely would discourage others from joining along the way. Adding insult to injury, Javin couldn't locate the back-up after the liberty bell's remote stopped working, and the team soon found his low-hung hull design made the ship hard to tug over potholes and through puddles, a brummagem if ever there was one. Pulling up at Raising Cane's for a few chicken fingers, Cam realized her small crew wouldn't come close to completing the ten-mile trek on time.

Luckily a brief lull in the downpour allowed for a last-ditch recruitment effort at U of M, just across the street from the snack shack. Enlistment would be more difficult due to the school's shift to hybrid classes, which left fewer undergrads on campus. Yet when students text-flared that White Panther herself was in their midst asking not what Minnesota could do for them but what they could do for Minnesota, Greta II soon had a stronger crew, albeit one considerably more male Caucasian and scruffy-looking than Namid envisioned during the event-optics projection the week before. Five wore maroon-and-gold sweatshirts stamped with a large M. Cam sent Emma G a pic of the new recruits.

our golden gophers

u storm the capitol
with the crew you got

please

were desperate
dontcha know
[eyes-lips-eyes]

Just before noon Sinead reported in from South St. Anthony Park: only two volunteers had shown up for duty, and the park remained as empty as a refrigerator after the Super Bowl. At least they knew the planned detour was out, a fact in their favor at this point. Charles calculated the Gopher squad's yardage gained per hour would not be enough to hit pay dirt by five-thirty. Arriving late was not an option. Working with MN350 brass, Sunrise leaders promised to deliver AOC and Ilhan to the capitol at that time, but the former only could stay for twenty minutes since she had a seven pm flight to Chicago. Show up on time or don't show.

Cam told Charles to keep her apprised of the lightship's pace. At twelve-thirty the totally drenched crew was grumbling for lunch. She glanced over at the Black Coffin Tattoo shop, closed for the holiday, and then up at a dark rumbling sky. Any minute a bolt of lightning might be the end of it.

"Charles, coordinates?"

"Six miles from the capitol zone. We *have* to pick it up." What was the call? With no time to stop for lunch, Cam handed off XR-AF's corporate credit card to three fleet-footed undergrads and sent them ahead in search of provisions. They would have to eat and tug at the same time, assuming the gatherers scored some grub soon. They returned twenty minutes later with bags full of fries, Big Macs and bottled water. During a short time-out to catch a breath and take a few bites, she told her huddled crew only a strong ground game during the second half would get it done. Time for the Gophers to grind. They raised plastic bottles high and yelled "Ski-U-Mah!" as one.

Now wearing maroon-colored bucket hats hurriedly bought at the Bullseye nearby, Team Greta drove block by block through the heavy downpour. Two attractive wet t-shirts were assigned to feed the lead tuggers their burgers and fries on the go. She could hear Namid now, railing about the optics, but she was in catch-up mode and that was that. Testosterone plus glucose mattered most now. At two-thirty they went off-tackle left at Wendy's and were now at the four-mile mark heading due east. The MPD escort peeled off at this point. Where were the St. Paul cruisers? Waiting on the cops was out of the question. They would have to lay out their own buoys to ensure public safety. Cam sent a special team of marshals down avenue to do just that. After the fast-food re-fueling her young crew's pace had improved. Charles reported the storm front should clear by five. Momentum seemed to be swinging their way.

Four blocks later the float met unexpected resistance at Denny's, where counter-protestors began to line the crosswalk and block University. Cam's lead marshal held up a permit and pled with eighteen wide white women from the Iron Range who held signs decrying the witch Greta's sins against God and guns and all that was good about an America they would make great again. The lightship pulled up close to the thick boogala wall. What was the call? Seeing no secondary she barked an audible--captain's sneak—and rushed two middle-aged mamas caught completely off-guard. When they tried to block her, she faked right and then cut hard left. Both went down with easy sidekicks, flustered but unhurt. Four strong marshals quickly pulled them aside as a fired-up frontline hauled Greta through the gaping hole. With number ten at the helm, the Gophers seemed capable of anything.

Since two a cam-equipped drone had been streaming the unfolding drama, courtesy of former XR-TC members Bruce and Marco. How the former navigated the drone through the deluge was anyone's guess, but there it was covering the action. After White Panther's bold rush-call at Denny's the livestream went through the roof, jumping from 4,110 viewers to 78,340 in ten minutes. A half-hour later 234,360 were cheering every yard Team Greta gained against the torrential downpour. Marco reminded everyone of the deadline the intrepid crew was up against. At three-thirty the viewership reached 691,700 and twenty minutes later spiked to 1.7 million. Word was out: White Panther was on the prowl with her posse, come hell or high water.

Visibility remained low and storm run-off kept rising as a soaked Gopher squad sloshed onward, aching ankles and all. Sprinting ahead block after block, Cam's marshals held cross-street traffic at bay. While honking car horns helped maintain morale, by four the bucket-hat brigade was running on empty, the rain relentless and their only respite since lunch a brief pause before busting through the eighteen wheelers. Charles reluctantly informed her that at the current pace five-thirty wasn't doable, despite the herculean efforts of her muscle-cramping crew.

What was the call? She texted SOS to allies. BLM mobilized immediately, as did young AIM Turks. Diego called Hector, a Chicano community organizer in West Side, and sent him intercept coordinates. He promptly dispatched three Latino hunks to the Popeyes at Lexington and University. Six BIPOC studs poured in just behind them. Dozens of other activists arrived minutes later. All eyes looked west in hope of sighting the lightship through a wall of water, a wall more daunting than any the Iron Ladies had thrown up.

As soon as Cam received word reinforcements were in wait, she snatched the megaphone and went to the front of the float. "Suck it up for four more blocks, boys! There's a back-up team at Popeyes ready to relieve you. All the Cajun Crispy Shrimp you can eat on me! Lean into it on my count. Hut, hut, heave! Hut, hut, heave!" Rallied by White Panther, the exhausted undergrads somehow kept the drive alive. Now but a block away, they heard a mighty roar and reached deep within for the final eighty yards, urged on by their captain. "Hut, hut, heave! Hut, hut, heave!" Fifteen yards from the intersection they collapsed in a heap. Pulchritudinous females tended to the fallen tuggers, quenching their thirst with Surly's Furious IPA and plenty of pop. Bent over and heaving on the sidewalk, every marshal was shot.

"Charles, what have we got?"

"Two miles to go with fifty-one minutes left on the clock." Cam huddled with her replacement squad and ran through the drill. Be respectful but act like you own the streets, she told the fastest, and off they ran to halt traffic. The strongest she sent to the lightship.

"Take your positions!" she cried. "Ropes up. Ready, set, GO!" Now in flying-wedge formation the new crew quickly had Greta hydroplaning across the concrete, like Ahmad Rashad blowing past double coverage as Tarkenton's long toss began its downward flight for another Vikings touchdown. Three million viewers hung on Marco's every word and went berserk upon seeing how fast the float flew. At ten of five Charles flashed a smile. The rain was letting up. A few minutes later Emma G confirmed AOC and Ilhan were en route to the capitol. Still, once inside the ten-yard line the defense always tightened. Armed with fresh muscle and what was now an all-ages armada of activists at their back, Cam ran through end-game scenarios. Be ready to scramble if the boogaloos came with a last-minute blitz. Stay calm if the cops appeared and halted play on a parade-permit technicality. Form ranks and resist nonviolently if they attempted to seize the lightship, as the bobbies had in London last month.

By five after five the rain had stopped. Cam called a thirty-second time-out so her crew could re-hydrate and mop off. Roused by Marco, thousands were flooding onto the capitol grounds. At twenty-five past the swelling throng erupted upon glimpsing Greta's beacon, now but a block away. Dozens of police officers appeared, along with two phalanxes in full riot gear. National Guard troops and armored vehicles began to amass as well. Keep driving hard down avenue, Cam told herself as she scanned the perimeter for trouble. Megaphone in hand, she led BIPOC crew and crowd in a chant:

"Power to the People!"

"The People got the Power!"

"Hear us roar now!"

"Stronger by the hour!"

"Power!"

"People!

"People!"

"Power!"

The multitude parted to let Team Greta 2.0 advance toward the base of the capitol. Many brought bells that now rang loudly. Cam saw AOC and Ilhan coming down the steps with the state's lieutenant governor to meet them, escorted by Emma G and Namid. At arrival she turned to her triumphant shipmates, raised a fist and wolf howled. A collective roar rippled out in all directions, reverberating around the world as 4.8 million ecstatic viewers joined in. After leading another chant, she took off her bucket hat, swept back her blonde mop and approached the politicians. They stepped forward as one to greet her with a warm hug. Namid rushed over to remind them that distancing was mandatory. They released her, stepped back and enjoyed a laugh as the crowd continued to clap, howl and ring bells all around them.

Marco wisely refrained from color commentary and continued his flawless play-by-play coverage:

> "Again, if you've just joined us, we're live via drone-video at Minnesota's state capitol where thousands are celebrating Indigenous Peoples' Day. Lightship Greta 2.0, captained by the phenomenal White Panther, arrived minutes ago after a grueling ten-mile slog through torrential rains and an imposing right-wing roadblock. The twenty-foot float was tugged ably most of the way down University Avenue by U of M undergrads recruited at the last minute. At a Popeyes two miles from the capitol they were relieved from duty by strong BIPOC replacements that sped the protest float to home port where they were met by leading politicians. The sun is beginning to break through as Lieutenant Governor Peggy Flanagan, a member of the Ojibwe White Earth Nation, prepares to address the overflow crowd from a podium at the top of the capitol steps. At her side are AOC and Ilhan Omar. They are joined by White Panther and G-Force. Let's listen now to what the lieutenant governor has to say on this historic day."

The next sound heard wasn't the lieutenant governor's voice. From twenty steps below a gunman fired off four rounds with a Glock G19 pulled from his coat pocket. One shot grazed White Panther's shoulder. She spun and ducked into the shadows. People fled shrieking while others dropped to the ground. Those on the podium retreated toward the building's front door as national guardsmen rushed past them to confront the shooter, who looked more like a model for a Father's Day ad than a psychopathic killer. He bounded up the steps screaming "death to all witches!" but soon fell under a hail of bullets. Screams were followed by the wail of sirens, crying teenagers and a police bullhorn ordering the few still present to disperse immediately. St. Paul's finest, now ubiquitous, swept the area but found no other threats. Blood gushing from the bullet-ridden body streamed down step after step before forming a large pool below. Soon yellow tape was strewn everywhere.

A stunned global audience of 5.7 million gasped during the eleven seconds of terror. Now they held their breath. Flanked by national guardsmen, White Panther and the politicians finally emerged and waved to all from the top step, the late-afternoon sun lighting up their resolute faces. At the perimeter a huge roar went up and kept rippling outward. White Panther pressed a palm against her wound, now bleeding profusely, while G-Force stood close and waved on her behalf.

"Not feeling so good," murmured Cam to Emma G. Exhausted and dehydrated, she fainted a moment later. EMTs swept in quickly, placed her on a stretcher and rolled her out of sight, Emma G and Namid following close behind. The politicians were escorted off the premises under heavy guard and left the scene in unmarked cars.

His voice trembling, Marco did his best to narrate the unfolding horror. Friends with Emma G, he texted her and then informed his audience, now at 6.2 million, that White Panther's condition would be relayed to him as soon as possible. Fifteen minutes later he heard back from her and shared the news:

> "I just received word from G-Force that White Panther is OK. I repeat, White Panther is doing fine and is in good spirits. She suffered a surface wound from a gunshot and

> will need stitches and anti-biotics to ward off infection. After fainting she was revived with smelling salts. G-Force says White Panther thanks everyone for their support of XR-AF and the Greta 2.0 solidarity sail."

At six Pox led with the assassination attempt. Other national media picked up the story by seven. That night the InfoBores site and 2can boards went ballistic on White Panther while showering praise on the shooter, who died instantly after five bullets to the skull and nine to the trunk. A true patriot all Americans should honor, they said. Defense of the homeland requires such sacrifice. Against the godless all is permitted. We will finish what he started. No one kicks mama and gets away with it.

Widespread condemnation of the violence by political leaders across the state and country came quickly, with the chilling exception of Trump, several QAnon-crazy House members and Texas senator Ted Cruz, who demanded the FBI investigate the left-wing instigators he claimed had created a climate of lethal violence. The commie White Panther's brutal, unprovoked attack on two God-fearing mothers, both loyal customers of America's Diner with as much right to cross the street in their own good time as anyone else, must not go unpunished.

Sympathy texts took Sinead three hours to wade through the next day. She noted messages from notables and sent a [paw clap] to the rest. That evening Cam responded to nearly two hundred texts from friends, relatives she hadn't heard from in years and a slew of movement leaders, limo liberals and lefty politicians. Both AOC and Ilhan sent kind notes asking about her health and inviting her to come visit them when she arrived in DC for school next fall. Near midnight she was still burrowed in her bean bag pecking away when Maya stopped at her door.

"Sorry to interrupt, Cahmie, but you should get some rest after what you put us all through yesterday."

"Yes, mother."

"For real, all this drama *will* catch up to you if--"

"The bastard shot me on the side I like to sleep on!"

"How inconsiderate of him. Next time he should--"

"Oh my God!" She grabbed a pillow with her one good arm and let it fly. When Maya ducked it landed upside the head of Diego, who happened to be heading for the john.

"Yo, *chica blanca*, what the hell did I ever do to you--except pour you drinks and save your life!" Maya picked up the pillow. He was half-way down the hall when it bounced off his backside. "*¡A la chingada!*" he yelled back before ducking into the bathroom. Both women burst out laughing.

Around one Rayna came to Cam's door, barely ajar. Her light was still on, and she peeked in. Cam lay on her futon in panties and a baggy t-shirt, eyes closed but restless. "Close da light and come here once." She flicked the switch, walked over to the bean bag and dropped her clothes on it. Soon the two peas in a pod were sleeping soundly.

12

MISHIPESHU AND THE BLACK SNAKE

XR-AF began its next strat-chat with a de-brief of the solidarity sail, now widely known as Monsoon Monday or M2:

namid: Our post-M2 optics analysis using Bruce and Marco's superb footage clearly shows White Panther and her two crews acted responsibly under difficult conditions. The St. Paul police will have to explain their absence at Denny's. We will ***not*** be the fall guys here. That said, let's contact Earthjustice and assemble the best legal team possible, just in case. Sinead, can you handle that?

sinead: Of course, number one—er, Namid—I'm on it.

namid: Thanks, Sinead. [obligatory smile] Let's look forward, shall we? Charles, with so much sympathy cash coming in, can we bump our collective pay-rate up to $21 an hour? [obligatory nod]. Appreciate it, Charles.

emma g: That seems excessive.

sinead: Many frontline workers are getting hazard pay increases, so I think it's justifiable. What we went through at the festival and the capitol was very traumatic. [three thumbs-ups]

emma g: Charles, keep mine at the current rate. And cancel our Primo membership while you're at it.

namid: Given Marco's exemplary work on our behalf, I've taken the liberty of hiring him as Associate Director of Optics and Amplification. [Marco comes on-screen; all wave].

charles: Welcome to the team, Marco. Going to send you some papers to sign. Waivers, an NDA, background check, a non-compete—the usual on-boarding sort of thing.

marco: Sounds good.

namid: Marco and I have been thinking about how to capitalize, as it were, on White Panther's stratospheric rise in popularity post-M2. So far, her theatrical prowess amounts to an untapped asset. We need a music video for the ages and an Emmy-Award-winning mini-series. A bidding war for production rights to both is raging as we speak. [three thumbs-ups] Camilla, can you handle all that in addition to your heavy schedule of speaking engagements? We'll hire a make-up manager and a--

cam: It might be better if we focus in coming weeks on the campaign against Kilridge's Line 337.

namid: I'm confused. Didn't I just see you click thumbs-up *twice* a minute ago? I suggest we go really big with--

emma g: She clicked the wrong emoji by mistake, *right* Cam? [two open mouths]

cam: Yah, we really don't need more publicity right now. Current revenue is record-breaking, and we're getting a ton of free press as it is. [three claps]

namid: But these hyper-elevation moments are the rarest

of all! Windows of fame close so quickly these days, we'd be foolish to waste--

emma g: Namid, listen up. White Panther just said our priority is cutting off the Black Snake's head. Last time I checked she's still the Prowler-in-Chief, correct? [Emma G glares at Namid through the screen; two open mouths]

namid: Yes, of course. White Panther versus Black Snake, another epic narrative we'll serialize at some point. Need to think long-term--

emma g: In the *long-term* we're all toast if we don't deal with the climate crisis. Namid, I gotta say, I'm really beginning to wonder what your real ag-- [more open mouths]

cam: Both of you, just stop. We've been a great team because we've used common sense, supported each other and put the mission first. The minute we don't do that, the bickering begins. Let's not go there, OK? [claps all around]

namid: I couldn't agree more. G-Force, I'm sorry if I got carried away projecting White Panther out to--

emma g: Apology accepted. [two hearts] Now, how about we do the weekly run-down. Sinead?

sinead: OK then. All that was *way* more drama than I can handle, but I'll do my best. [two more hearts] So, let's see... White Panther and G-Force are booked solid. Next big action date is Halloween. It's on a Saturday and MN350 is organizing a Line 337 protest at the governor's mansion. Emma G, you'll blog on the event soon, yah?

emma g: As always. Going to expose the false choice Trudeau, Trump and the construction industry present.

This isn't about jobs versus owls. Tar sands oil is now unprofitable, but pipeline supporters falsely claim otherwise.

cam: What's the specific demand MN350 is making?

emma g: There's a mid-November deadline for the water permits. If they're approved, Kilridge will start construction this winter. Governor Walz can deny them, but if he doesn't the Black Snake will slither ahead. Approval would violate Ojibwe treaty rights.

namid: What storyline is MN350 using? Are they leveraging Halloween imagery?

emma g: Not sure. For years their slogan has been Keep it in the Ground. Their Go Fossil Free divestment campaign got a huge boost from Greta, Sunrise and the Climate Strike Action last year. They do awesome work, just not super-creative when it comes to direct-action design.

marco: May I make a suggestion? [smiles and nods all around] Perhaps we can work with MN350 and the Native collective that created ***Altered Founding*** to put on an outdoor play villainizing the Black Snake, which we can depict as a Count-Dracula-meets-Smaug figure. We'll have a cast of hobbit-like characters rise to the challenge, led by White Panther and our good governor. An action thriller with a satisfying end. [claps and thumbs-ups all around]

emma g: Geez, that's ***really*** good!

namid: Epic! We've got just enough time to pull this off, I think.

cam: Marco, let me just say you and Bruce slayed it on

Monday. Glad to have you on board. [thumbs-ups explode across screens] And the play idea is lit. My only reservation, after what we went through a few days ago, is the weather.

charles: If we go blank check on budget--and right now that's no problem since we're more loaded than a Saudi sheikh--we can rent a large indoor space as a back-up, one that can accommodate distancing. In fact, we could do two shows, a matinee at the guv's house and then a Halloween-night performance indoors.

marco: Yes, and we can augment our indy livestream with a PBS live special on TPT.

emma g: Yeet, yeet!

cam: Now *this* is the kick-ass team I know and love! Let's roll! [fires and claps explode across screens]

Between non-stop speaking engagements, co-writing with Emma G and rehearsing for the play Cam barely had time to sleep, much less take morning strolls through her favorite park. She missed Godol and wondered how he was doing. Headaches kept cropping up. Giles's birthday almost slipped past her; only mom's reminder text saved her from eternal shame. As a present, she promised to take him to the Halloween matinee.

Since the festival, he had coped as best he could with his big sister's newfound fame. Now in seventh grade at Our Lady of Lost Lakes, he signed three fake autographs right after 2M went viral before deeming it unethical. One gaggle of girls, all wearing masks that said Hear Us Roar, still hadn't forgiven him the demur. How dare he deny them! The parochial school had chosen to go hybrid, which helped limit his exposure to the Pantherines, a tween stan club that most of the student body quickly joined. Late in September the cub club took out its claws and threatened to go on strike if a casual Friday dress rule wasn't put in place so they all could wear their White Panther and G-Force gear. They also were determined to have the dynamic duo visit the school. Giles did not like getting leaned on. "Please, pretty please Giles! We just know they'll come if *you* ask! We've collected $283 in lunch money, and it's all yours if you do us just this one favor!" When he suggested they donate the money to XR-AF and re-direct their energies toward demanding that Lost Lakes declare itself a slave-free chocolate zone, they threatened to never speak with him again. After he asked whether they'd put that in writing, they stormed off and reported him to the arch-director of discipline for verbal harassment.

As expected Namid took control of play production, hiring a script writer whose credits included *Zafira and the Resistance,* a play the Guthrie had put on a year ago. Cam had no trouble convincing MN350 to collaborate, provided there was space for other activist art already in the works. The director hit it off with the fab five from the Native collective, who were beside themselves when they heard money was no obstacle. Javin was tapped to lead set design despite his miscues with Greta 2.0. A chance at redemption, the Prowler-in-Chief declared, was a core value of XR-AF.

Mishipeshu and the Black Snake premiered on Summit Avenue in front of the governor's mansion. Under cloudy skies a costumed crowd watched the mythic panther of Anishinaabeg lore tangle with the evil serpent Killagua, whose head was indeed black but whose scales mirrored corporate colors. After being wounded, Mishipeshu retreated to his copper-lined cave and all seemed lost.

The rapacious Killagua, bitumen dripping from its gold tongue, finally was brought low by White Panther and her brave hobbitsy band, among them a ruddy-faced figure wearing a purple cape imprinted with the state flag—the only hokey element in an otherwise nuanced and beautifully-choreographed show. What made *Mishipeshu* memorable was neither the dragon fight, exciting as it was, nor the feel-good ending. Rather, two dozen blue-light performers left the audience spell-bound by creating the most convincing illusion that everyone—cast and audience alike—was under water the entire time.

Giles loved every minute. Just getting out of Edina for the first time since Cancun was present enough. Dying for some distraction, Goldie drove them into town. Both wore the best costumes ever: touched up with a toothbrush moustache, Tramp wore a vintage vest and sported a bowler hat and cane; Goldie caked her face super-glossy for another convincing Wonder Woman performance. Giles traded his old cane for her lasso of truth and spent the afternoon trying to rope his big sister. After the play and a banana-split at Sebastian Joe's their magical day together was done. His good-bye hug left Cam tearful. She clung to her pillow for an hour and took two aspirin before heading to the evening show. Occasional shutdowns aside, Giles was always right there while she was praying most days to St. Eligius for deliverance from too much to do. Would she ever find time to be with him, with her parents, with Godol?

Saturday night's performance was held at the Armory. Formerly the home of the Minneapolis Lakers, the venue had a pre-covid capacity of 5,600 and now held 700—all masked and standing on dots after making donations. More spectacular than the outdoor opener, the show included sonic thunder-booms and a massive backscreen that flashed appalling images of Mordor-like devastation, Alberta's boreal forests and other pristine wildlands ravaged by fossil-fuel barons. The floor became a sea, the afternoon's blue-light dancers now joined by two dozen more. During the final battle, the audience gasped when a dark tar-sands lord astride Killagua wounded White Panther with a spear. They cheered wildly when rider and beast succumbed at last to the plucky resistance. A dozen more dancers appeared and began the victory celebration by ringing bells. Ushers rushed to hand out bells, and soon the Armory was one big bell reverberating far beyond its walls. Asked by one critic whether it wasn't a bit overwrought, Namid replied that sometimes killer special effects and the near-death of a heroine at the hands of an arch-villain are the whole reason to watch. *Mishipeshu and the Black Snake* set the Twin Cities theater world abuzz for weeks afterward.

After a tremendous ovation, the post-show pitch commenced. White Panther and G-Force took the stage accompanied by 350.org founder Bill McKibben, who had come from Vermont to stand with frontliners up north. Emma G said McKibben's *The End of Nature*, a Thoreauvian meditation on the Anthropocene written a decade before the term first appeared in the scientific literature, ranked in significance with Leopold's *Sand County Almanac* and Carson's *Silent Spring*. Microphone pinned to coat, he summarized the case against Kilridge and then closed with a call to action: "Sign the petition on the way out. Call the governor Monday morning and demand he revoke the permits. Be ready to hit the streets next week and amp up the pressure if he doesn't do the right thing. And for God's sake, vote blue on Tuesday!"

Governor Walz did not watch the production out his window, nor did he attend the evening performance and applaud his do-the-right-thing double. The election came and went, followed by the kettling and arrest of six hundred protestors the next night on the I-94 bridge. Another protest was held at his official residence two weeks after the Halloween event. The following Monday he refused to rescind the water permits.

The next day Cam received a text from Vibol, busy as always finishing up his first semester at Emory.

hi cam sharing some
scary breaking news
an amerizon truck was
blown up in druid hills
close to my campus

big yikes
vib r u ok?

im fine but a guy out
walking his dog was
taken to the hospital

driver ok?

yep ringing doorbell
when van blew
cars nearby toast

dog?

didn't make it

[crying face]

been 3 now

ikr and no
one caught

bet bleudough will
offer $1B bounty

when r u
coming back?

staying here
to volunteer
for warnock
and ossoff

yes! run off is
jan 5 right

sure is

so awesome!
did u vote

absentee ballot glad
tina smith won

now u r
gonna get us
to 50 in ga!

gonna work
my ossoff

vib made
a funny!
[clown]

haha

jk luv u!

cam be careful u r
a big deal now
cant tell u how
proud i am

xoxoxo!

i tell people i used
2 b your chauffeur

my man alfred!

[skull]

She was disappointed he wasn't returning for the holidays but glad he was joining an all-important campaign. It could open doors down the line. Several members of Congress started out this way. His quiet, respectful manner had never fooled her. More than once, she'd seen the tiger in his eyes, a fierce devotion to truth and justice he channeled as well as anyone. In Cambodia the Phan family had endured more terror than most, only to find they were forever foreigners in the states. The relatives he'd introduced to her carried themselves with a dignity and grace she greatly admired.

Two days later, after an ill-focused strat-chat left XR-AF's next move in doubt, Cam fell into her bean bag and began to read Emma G's latest blog: "Kilridge now has a license to wreak havoc up north, and a new front has opened in DC where the incoming administration will be pressed to cancel not only Keystone XL but also DAPL and Line 337. Meanwhile, direct action by Giniw Collective and other sister-resister bands will disrupt any new construction. Stopping the pipeline requires--" She stopped reading, closed her eyes and conjured a fanciful image of pudgy little Ewoks ambushing Kilridge's bulldozers with trip ropes, log rolls and hurled rocks before scurrying back into the woods. If only.

According to Charles, XR-AF had spent $137K to execute their Cecil B. Demille strategy. Other than paychecks, rave reviews in local theater rags and a job offer in New York that Javin just couldn't refuse, they had nothing to show for it. Festival, sail, play—all demonstrated that moving works of art moved people only so far. Reality remained a mule that kicked back hard. Corporations flipped politicians with dark money and tied up opponents in endless lawsuits. Look at Amerizon. Despite the Primo Day protest and PR hit, the vans kept rolling without any concessions to workers. How many more bombs had to go off before someone died or Bleudough blinked?

Cam stood up and stretched for a few minutes before ascending to the attic where she found Rayna sitting cross-legged on her mattress half-dressed. Without a wig her pixie cut, fair skin and coy smile reminded one of Tinker Bell. She walked in, pulled Rayna's shirt off and tossed it to the floor. She got naked, climbed in close and ran her fingers the length of Bell's lithe body.

"Lay back," said Rayna. Looking up, Cam saw nine circle figures pinned up on the angled ceiling above her, each made with a single sweeping stroke of an ink pen, a stroke remarkably like the one Bell's tongue was now making. None of the circles were complete.

"What kind of figures are they?" she asked, now caught between curiosity and creamy delicious.

"*Ensō*," replied Rayna after another orectic swirl.

"Why are the circles all open?" Cam didn't mind waiting longer this time for an answer. Once she finished, Bell crawled up beside her, extended an alabaster arm toward the ceiling and began to re-trace each *ensō* in the air with her index finger. Cam's lips moistened as she watched her digit loop around counterclockwise to one o'clock and linger.

"An unfinished circle symbolizes movement toward perfection and the beauty of imperfection. *Wabi-sabi*."

"Wait, are you talking about the paste we put on--"

"No, silly. *Wabi-sabi* is a Zen concept. One realizes that everything is transient, ephemeral through and through.

"Always an open circle."

"Right." She traced another circle figure. "*Ensō* expresses the reality of what Buddhists mean by *anicca*: the impermanence of all that pretends otherwise. For Plato the circle represents perfection, the Ideal Form. Few escape the cave to see it."

"One big ship of fools."

"Pretty much. In the West only Heraclitus, Epictetus and Whitehead come close to grasping *anicca*. Whitehead's felicitous phrase is the "perpetual passing away of all things."

"Into oblivion, nothingness?"

"Well, for him a very unorthodox deity gathers up all that has manifested value and beauty through time and preserves it somehow. All occasions of positivity, one might say, end up in the everlasting arms of the Godhead, presumably a bliss as ineffable as *nibbana*. Mystics in the apophatic tradition use images of negation, not this and not that, to convey their glimpse of the Ultimate."

"States of consciousness beyond the ordinary," remarked Cam as she ran her fingers across Rayna's thigh.

"Yes, that's it."

"Tell me, master," whispered Cam. "Is there a technique involved with these strokes?"

"Indeed there is, padawan."

"How exciting. Will you show me how?"

"I already did."

"*¡Esa!*" yelled Diego from down below. He looked heavenward and whispered *gracias* to the Virgin for the gift she had bestowed.

13
AMERI-BOMBERS

Since Crystal City, Jorge and every other Amerizon driver had wondered whether their van might be the next to blow sky-high. Druid Hills ratcheted up the anxiety several notches. Four days after the mid-November bombing another envelope was found, this one on the doorstep of a synagogue nearby. Again a blue marble, iron cross and four shreds; again one with a B, but this time the numbers 0, 1 and 8. Immediately the blather-sphere connected Bleudough's reported net worth of $186B in September to the current number: $180B. Investigators had interviewed countless people linked to activity at the gadget store, postal box and now the synagogue. Still no solid leads. Whoever was blowing up the trucks knew their tech and was very good at covering their tracks.

In the weeks following both Crystal City and Druid Hills the national media were long on opinions but short on facts. While unconfirmed by independent sources, one major news outlet reported just before Thanksgiving that the FBI, ATF and other agencies involved in domestic-terrorist incidents were closing in on a secretive organization identified as the Unabomber-inspired Sons of Ted and instantly dubbed the Ameri-bombers across cyber-space. Allegedly the cabal hid within crevices of the Sierra Nevada and Appalachian Range. Cells supposedly communicated face-to-face through rare clandestine meetings nothing at present was known about. Meanwhile, many blogger-heads played up the iron cross and race, noting that all three delivery drivers were minorities while the Jewish synagogue receiving the third envelope was in Druid Hills, a wealthy neighborhood that includes Emory University where Senate candidate Jon Ossoff's spouse Alisha Kramer worked as a physician. The Jewish power couple met as teenagers at The Paideia School, also in Druid Hills. Supporters of this theory said the blue marble signified a rejection not only of industrial technology but also the globalists who financed it. One left-leaning ribbit thread made much of Bleudough's space company Feather Flite and his stated intention to spend as many billions as it took to get off a dying planet. If that meant crushing unions, stiffing towns on tax revenue needed for essential services and outfitting governments to surveil the populace systematically, so be it.

Come Thanksgiving it was more difficult for many of the laid-off to put turkey on the table. Almost four months had passed without the extra $600 a week in unemployment relief. With Lumpy's and other bars in the cities still closed, and with Columbia's greens now covered in snow, Diego dipped into savings to pay rent. Skyrocketing cryptos tempted him to get back on the day-trading app. Instead, he listened to Maya and returned to his short game indoors while branching out beyond salsa, what with tango lessons on offer. Rona exposure during trips to the store was enough risk for now, she said. And while she'd friend zoned him long ago, who knew where dancing tango on cold winter nights might lead.

On Black Friday a text from Emma G caught Cam's attention. The link she sent opened to the day's lead story: Amerizon workers at multiple locales had walked off the job and were vowing to stay out through Cyber Monday if the corporation continued its refusal to discuss safety, working conditions and other pressing issues. An Amerizoners Unite spokesperson in Sacramento called out the company and its billionaire CEO: "It's past time for Mr. Bleudough to care more about protecting the people that make him rich and less about rocketing into space." Cam soon had livestreams running simultaneously; on screen were job actions at nine U.S. sites with five solidarity events in the EU and two in India, twice the number of walkouts in mid-October. At the Shakopee warehouse 435 pickers had packed it in at noon, and another 390 were set to follow suit at midnight—Jorge's line-mate Ivan among them.

"Diego, you gotta see this!" After missing a birdie putt in the dining room, he stomped into the kitchen. "This better be good, *chica blanca.* I was about to go three under before you broke my—" His eyes popped at the sight of so many workers on strike in so many places. Picketers held signs that read We R not Robots, Make Amerizon Pay and Protect Essential Workers. Wearing orange safety vests, striking Amerizoners in Chicago chanted "Shut it down, clean it up!" *Gilets oranges.*

"How about Eagan? You see my brother?"

"No. They said 120 drivers walked out, was he among them?"

"Hell yeah! *¡Basta!*"

"*¡Basta!*" echoed Cam. A minute later she texted Aalia, who sent a vid of the march around the Amerizon Spheres, biophilic-designed structures used for an employee lounge and workspaces in Seattle. Over 850 tech workers, nearly all millennials, were circling what local media called "Bleudough's Balls" chanting "Look for the bombs, not just the bomber!" The most common sign read A Primo Idea: People over Profit. One wag's placard said Grow a Pair and Pay Up. Most cars passing by honked in support. Aalia's brother Fitan was one of several demonstrators interviewed by local reporters. "We support the just demands our fellow Amerizoners are making. With the pandemic still raging and a mad bomber still at large, the customer-comes-first mantra no longer works. It's time for safety first."

Since the Primo Day walkout only a few local demands—a water cooler here, a porta potty there--had been met. The company did release aggregate figures on U.S. covid cases--20,000 workers with coronavirus since last March—but shared no site-specific numbers. They also were dragging their heels on van safety, arguing that daily inspections would delay delivery of essentials to the homebound. And they continued to ignore demands to abolish the meat-grinder make-rate system and heavy surveillance of workers. The rabbits must keep running, regardless of how many vans blew up or frontliners went limp or deaf or caught covid.

"We should boycott them *chingados*," said Diego.

"One group is trying to get sympathetic Primo members on board by starting a threshold campaign," noted Cam.

"Never heard of that. Why not just boycott?"

"Many don't succeed, unfortunately."

"The grape boycott worked for Chavez and the farm workers." At Humboldt years ago, Diego had been famous for juggling, dealing weed and getting suspended after another fight. Since no one expected him to graduate, much less go to college, he didn't even look at the brochures. Other than a few teachers, no one knew about the A's he'd earned in his history classes. On the windowsill in his room a row of Carlos Fuentes novels, all Spanish-language editions he loved to read. Ask him about Mexico's past, and he'd hold forth until distracted by a dare to keep a six-pack's worth of empties afloat while belting out the national anthem, "Mexicans, at the cry of war".

"You're right, and it worked in Montgomery too, but those are exceptions that prove the rule. In most cases customers lose interest after the first wave of publicity, or they figure others will boycott and so they take a pass, or they assume not enough people will join them and so why bother? A threshold strategy is designed to overcome these problems. The campaigners ask a question: Would you quit Amerizon if one million other people did too?"

"Sounds like a no-brainer."

"Right? And when support reaches the one-million mark, pledgers are urged to drop Primo quickly."

"A big wake-up call."

"Then the company is confronted with a list of demands that must be taken seriously."

"What if Bleudough doesn't bend?"

"Then they set a higher threshold and the campaign goes to round two."

"Keep raising the stakes till he folds."

"That's the idea. Unfortunately, most people want their packages on the porch right away and couldn't care less what it costs workers and local economies and the planet."

"Convenience is king," added Maya as she walked in and joined them at the table. "And the libs are the biggest blue-pill poppers of all."

"What if the Ameri-bombers start blowing up the bigwigs, not just their trucks?" Diego conjectured. "During the revolution, my man Zapata blew up trains to defend the peasants against state thugs, but he never put a hit out on enemy leaders the way they did with him. Judas kissed him goodbye."

"Back in the nineteenth century, some anarchists tried to jumpstart general rebellions with political assassinations. And the list of terrorist groups in the twentieth century is long. Their track record is dismal. They get ratted out or infiltrated, sooner or later. Maybe a show trial first before the firing squad," observed Maya.

"XR and the threshold campaigners base their strategy on research showing civil resistance works if you can get sustained participation from 3.5 percent of the population. A lot of dictators were toppled that way in the last forty years," added Cam.

"I'm intrigued by the threshold idea, but as soon as folks catch a whiff of inflation they'll run back to the cheapest provider. Under covid conditions especially, I can't see a million Primo members pledging anytime soon."

"Yah, not holding my breath on that one either. It's up to the workers themselves."

"Then again, if more trucks blow and people start dying a frightened public may demand that Bleudough pay up or they'll jump to Stallmart and Bullseye."

"You saying Jorge has to play Russian roulette for the sake of the revolution?" asked an indignant Diego.

"Of course not, but don't forget his hand never healed right. No golf for him."

"That's a low blow, *chica*."

"Just sayin'. We all know the grunts get maimed or die prematurely every day because health and safety take a back seat to prof—"

"*¡Basta de hablar!* We're taking food to *mi hermano* and the strikers now!" Cam and Maya rose instantly and began to pull out leftover turkey, stuffing and gravy brought back from the family feast in Edina while he made iced tea. They cut up carrots and tossed bananas, apples, nuts and chips into bags along with a few PBJ sandwiches. No one knew what the Somalis liked to eat. And besides, there wasn't much else in the fridge.

By Cyber Monday only three walkouts of any size were still holding. Amerizon released a statement assuring Primo customers that no delivery delays were expected. In TV interviews Bleudough appeared astonished that some employees had turned their back on the company. "It wasn't Congress that delivered a living wage of $15 to workers, we did that." He reiterated the vague claim that authorities were "very close" to catching the Ameri-bombers. During the disruption company share prices, already at record highs, dipped momentarily but soon rebounded. Firings at every action site sent a clear message: cause trouble and you are history.

On the Fourth Sunday of Advent, Cam watched Holy Qurbono at St. Maron's from her bean bag. Since leaving Edina she rarely attended Mass, virtual or otherwise. Near the park she'd spotted the Maronite Catholic church. She loved the incense wafting everywhere, the way chorbishop Maroun held a hand cross most of the time and the haunting tonality of the Syriac hymns, which sounded like they came from a mosque rather than a church. A few months back she'd watched a gospel Mass with Maya livestreamed from St. Aloysius, located a stone's throw from the capitol in DC. While at Howard she'd fallen in love with the Jesuit-run parish and its raise-the-roof choir. Cam had asked her, half-jokingly, if the parishioners got drunk beforehand. Maya just laughed and reminded her of rabbi Yeshua's water-into-wine miracle and what some cynics from out of town had said about the Spirit-filled disciples praising the mighty acts of God in many tongues during Shavuot.

After Mass she took her time biking down to Boom Island, grateful the roads were cleared after the big snow and winter winds weren't whipping. Almost five months had gone by since she'd given Godol an offering. The day before Thanksgiving she'd visited the park in hopes of seeing him, and two more times since then. Perhaps today she might get lucky. Petitioning St. Anthony, preacher to fish and finder of lost things, couldn't hurt. In her backpack a baggie full of oyster crackers, extras from the corn-and-chili chowder Diego had made two nights before, and half a sleeve of fig bars pilfered from Rayna's shelf. For the first time in her life, the idea of indulgences almost made sense.

When she arrived Godol was a few steps from the south bridge, his large flock gathered around. She pedaled fast, racing past the boat launch where White Panther had risen from the river to fame. Sixty yards away and pumping hard, she looked up and saw him turning to go after tipping his beret to the birds. "Wait!" she yelled, just before her front wheel hit black ice and she slid out of control. She tried to break the fall and tumbled across the concrete to the river's edge. Now on her butt facing the water, palms stinging fiercely and right knee throbbing, she looked over her shoulder for him but couldn't see above the snowbank. Still dazed, she hoisted herself up somehow, hop-turned and looked again. She'd never seen him do anything but saunter along slowly with his bum leg and found his giddy-up amusing, a black-bereted duck waddling as quickly as he could toward her, a legion of rock doves flapping above him. He still had forty yards to go, and she prayed again to St. Anthony not to let him land on his bottom too. She glanced to her left and flashed back to the festival fight. There was Diego under a barrage of brass knuckles, then on his knees wobbling, face swollen almost beyond recognition but with a Cool-Hand-Luke grin that said it'd been worth it.

Godol finally pulled up, a bit winded, his avian entourage stomping as they landed and cooed all around him. "You OK?" he asked, his face scrunched up out of concern.

"Not sure. I banged up my knee pretty bad." She tried to put weight on it, but it hurt too much. He bumbled over, placed her arm over his shoulder and helped her to a bench. Her phone lay near the bike, and without asking he retrieved it. Maya said she'd be there in fifteen minutes with Diego. While waiting they watched the pigeons feast on the largesse spilling out of her backpack. She sat there, embarrassed and in pain yet happier than she'd been in a long time.

"Ya'll, this is my friend Antoine," Cam said upon their arrival. All smiled and nodded to one another. She turned to Godol and gazed into his ocean-blue eyes a long moment before asking where he lived. He lifted an arm and pointed across the park in a northeast direction. "At Saint Maron's. I'm the janitor. Basement room there is not so bad," he replied with a smile, all the while never breaking eye contact. She wanted to fall forever into that light-filled cavern, but the wind was picking up and her neck was beginning to ache. They said goodbye and watched him make his way over to the south bridge, bid his feathered following adieu and cross over. Maya grabbed Cam's bike and backpack while Diego escorted her back to the car.

"Was that who I think it was?" inquired Maya as she turned onto University and drove past Godol's church.

"The very same. Haven't seen him in ages, don't cha know."

"That's the whitest dude I ever seen!" blurted Diego.

"All I know is, from now on I'm charging White Panther here a premium for search-and-rescue services," ribbed Maya.

"Me too," chimed in Diego. "I hear her crew's been rakin' in more dough than El Chapo."

"Speaking of drugs, tell me we have some Vitamin I back at the house. My knee is blowing up."

"I'll make you a Bloody Mary that numbs you good, *chica blanca*, don't worry."

That evening Cam checked in with Vibol, eager to hear about the run-off campaign in Georgia.

"Y'all gonna pull off a miracle down yonder or what?"

"We're cranking. They sent me to Gwinnett County where there's a big Asian American and Pacific Islander community. No one has ever knocked on their doors before. Stacey Abrams has been reaching out to the Korean pastors and other AAPI leaders for years, but they've been invisible to everyone else."

"Crazy number of different constituencies, yah?"

"Sure are. A lot of Chinese, Koreans, Vietnamese and Filipinos own small businesses, and many are conservative Christians, so they aren't a lock for Democrats. But most did vote for Biden. The second-gen immigrants are better educated and less susceptible to the red-baiting that Republicans still use down here to good effect. We've had success with multi-language campaign lit and, as I said, we've been the first to show up in person and ask them what they want."

"And what is that?"

"The end of covid, like everyone else. At last count the number of U.S. deaths was at 320,750. They can't open their shops or go to church. They've heard how South Korea and other countries have handled the pandemic much better than Trump and want to know what Dems will do differently."

"Sounds like a winning issue to run on."

"As I said, we're on a roll. I was a little nervous talking to strangers at first, but I'm getting the hang of it. Just be real and really listen. That's what people want most of all."

"Listening to you, I'm beginning to wonder if all my play-acting has been a waste of time. We still haven't stopped Line 337, and Warbill is tougher than Killagua to take down."

"Tell me you're kidding. If I had a dollar for every White Panther t-shirt and cap I've seen out there, I'd buy an island!"

"That's just a pop-culture thing, not real politics. I'm flavor of the month."

"Yes and no. Your street theater and my door-knocking mean little if it doesn't translate into electoral gains and policy changes, but that inside game needs our outside game. And you are the boogaloo slayer everyone knows and loves. The easiest vote I get going door-to-door is the one with White Panther and G-Force bobbleheads in the window. I show them a pic of you and me at Friezelda-St. Mitt's and it's a lock. Cam, you are a change accelerator. As the demographics shift it's transformative figures like you who--"

"Hold up right there, Vib. I've been labeled so many times lately I've lost count, don't cha know." She wanted to be spared the commentary. Why she wasn't at Georgetown yet was beyond her.

"Let's just say you *are* the bomb."

"After what happened last month in Druid Hills, let's not use that expression either. Earlier today I was bombing along on my bike and wiped out. My knee looks like a soccer ball."

"What size?"

"Haha." Both sensed it was time to wrap up. "Stay safe out there, Vib. Mask up!"

"Always. So, once you mend, what's next?"

"Looking like direct action up north. We've been sending supplies to the front. Biden said he'll cancel Keystone XL but hasn't said a word about other pipelines.

"I have an idea: how about you take time off from Prowler-in-Chief duties and get your driver's license."

"Uff-da, you *didn't* just say that."

"On second thought, just keep riding your bike over black ice and leave the driving to me. I ask you, what's a superhero without a chauffeur?"

"You're so fired, Alfred. Don't come back to Minnesota, ever!"

"Not planning on it. Sunny and seventy down here."

The governor's refusal to stop Line 337 opened a rift within XR-AF on strategic priorities. Cam made it clear that milking White Panther's mystique only made sense if they had a clear goal that required lots of cash. Emma G identified two options: commit to influencing decisions made in DC with a national campaign or stay focused on the local struggle against Killagua. Namid and Marco argued for the former while Cam and Emma G pushed for the latter, leaving Sinead and Charles undecided. For Namid it was all about amplifying Cam's star-power and shifting public opinion; politicians with their fingers in the wind would follow. Emma G insisted direct action and movement building should take priority over PR, and she remained deeply uncomfortable with the commodification of White Panther and G-Force. One spoke of influencers and polls, the other of direct democracy and people power, the two of them talking past each other.

Ambitious plans for a Greta 3.0 sail from Chicago to DC went nowhere. Every time the team mapped a national trajectory the scope of operations weighed too much upon them. Scaling up would require re-organization and a level of professionalization no one wanted. XR-AF could stay true to itself best by joining the resistance, said Emma G. She and Cam would go up north while the rest of the team broadcasted the battle against Black Snake. Namid begged to differ. After Thanksgiving they should focus short-term on selling more merch, time being of the essence. The added revenue would go toward another pay increase for all XR-AF associates and fund a marketing study he considered critical to their long-term success. After Emma G told him to go to bourgeois hell and went off-screen, the team's future seemed more uncertain than ever.

Cam confided in Rayna late one evening as they listened to Brandi Carlile, watched a gentle snow fall outside her attic window and refined their *ensō* technique.

"What Rith said about my clout on the campaign trail supports Namid's position, yah? Both believe White Panther is becoming a force for good on a global scale."

"Fame is fleeting. Isn't Greta herself going back to school? Neither of you are messianic figures."

"You can say that again. But this thing has taken on a life of its own. Lately I've felt like I'm on a runaway train and just want to jump off."

"So, why not jump?"

"Because it's about the mission, not me! What if they're right and I throw away a golden opportunity to reach millions and really make a difference?"

"Move mountains through record sales of stuffed dolls and paw gloves."

"Haha. White Panther is about giving ordinary people hope the fight against corporate elites and authoritarians of every stripe is winnable. In India now, 250 million small farmers are rising up against a strong-man regime that wants to roll out the red carpet for Warbill and other agri-biz giants."

"Not to be too cynical, but isn't Beijing tightening the noose on Hong Kong? And sadly, hasn't the Arab Spring come and gone?"

"Yes, democracy is dying! I'm not going to sit around watching one more Netrifix original while it all goes down the drain."

Rayna clicked the music off. "What a heavy burden. Perhaps you should be called Cam of Arc after all."

"Now you're mocking me. Great, just when I need emotional support."

"Autists don't do that sort of thing. Or haven't you noticed."

"Yah, but you do hold me tight sometimes." Cam nudged closer, tucked her head under Rayna's arm and buried her face into her chest. She swirled a finger around her nipple.

"You're improving, padawan." Cam swirled again. "Yes, that's it." A moment later Rayna interrupted a promising practice session with one of her characteristically blunt queries: "What are you going to do about XR-AF?"

"That ship of fools I captain?"

Her self-deprecation drew a smile. "Maybe it's more like a raft for crossing rivers, and the time has come to let it go. On the other side, you need thick gloves, a warm hat and snowshoes, perhaps, for a long winter's journey."

"So *that's* your take on all this! I should ditch the team and go up north.

Why didn't you just come out with it?"

"Because it's not my decision. You know I don't want you going anywhere except into my bed each night, but that's just my *tanha* talking."

"The second Noble Truth. Slay the ego, otherwise it won't matter what dragons we face out there."

"You've been reading those sutras, I see."

"It's the cure—renouncing all desires—I can't swallow." Rayna grew silent. Had she slipped once more into her vast interior? Finally, she reached across the mattress, took hold of a large sketch pad and flipped to a sheet bursting with geometric shapes and bold colors, all set within several concentric circles, an elaborate and vibrant world with four entry portals, deities by the dozens, rings of jewels warding evil away, lotus leaves beyond number. A Buddha's abode. Cam imagined an architecture arising, as when one turns the page of a pop-up book and beholds the unfolding of a magnificent structure in miniature.

"What a beautiful man--" Suddenly Rayna ripped the sheet from the sketch pad and began shredding. Soon a small heap lay before them. She lifted a candle from her side table and held it still. Other than the rising smoke and falling wax the only discernible movement was the flickering flame, now positioned between her and the pile. A long minute passed before she spoke. "One extinguishes the fire by following the Path."

Cam held up a fistful of shreds and let them flutter down into the sheet. All were scattered now, a shattered rainbow. "That fourth one is easier said than done. I don't want to be anywhere else but right here, right now."

"Me too." She put the candle aside and fell back into the bed with Cam, cradling her in her arms. The two peas in a pod nestled further into the embrace. Above them only a few circle figures remained.

"Yesterday I read a haiku that made me think of you," said Rayna.

"Are you saying you *weren't* thinking about me before?"

"That's right, *you* don't exist at all until some image, word or sensation tickles my fickle mind. You appear a moment in waking consciousness—mirage-like--and flit away soon after."

"Wow, that's true love. And now you want to share a poem with me?"

"I memorized it. Do you want to hear it? It's written by Charles--"

"Wait, you don't mean--"

"Not *that* Charles. And now I can't recall his last name…Beuck, Charles Beuck."

"Well, you *did* think of me once you came across the haiku, so…"

"First, close your eyes and listen to the snow." After giggling, Cam grew quiet and tried to honor the request. Ten seconds passed before Rayna began to recite:

> Ice white snow falling
> Deep night and wintery snow
> The hare flees the fox

Cam suppressed another giggle and did her best to let the snow tickle her inner ear somehow. A moment later she stuck a pinky finger in and flicked out a bit of wax.

"Such crudity shows just how far you have to go."

"Maybe it does and maybe it doesn't." Then she sat up and looked Rayna in the eye. "I do know this: I'm going up north to fight Killagua, come what may."

"Hare and the fox. Yes, I have foreseen it." Cam grabbed a pillow and thumped her hard on the shoulder.

"Anger will be your undoing, pada--" Another blow landed, this one a little harder. Rayna started laughing and pointed at her mockingly. Cam jumped off the mattress and hurled the pillow as hard as she could, but she raised her knees up in time to block it and now was howling maniacally.

"Yo, *chica loca*! Some of us are trying to sleep!" yelled Diego from below. He cursed the demon who made every sound audible and amped some so high he sometimes wanted to tear the ears right off his head.

Still at an impasse, the team made one last attempt at reaching consensus. During the strat-chat, Cam kept her decision to head north in January to herself. With holiday merch sales humming, she hoped Namid and Marco would reconsider the resistance plan and Emma G would refrain from impugning their motives. Sinead's boredom worried her most. Her title might be Vice-Prowler, but day-to-day she played gopher to Namid, sifted through endless stan texts and tended to other menial tasks like one more mechanical Turk. As it turned out, Charles made the meet's bombshell announcement. Effective immediately he was resigning as CFO and disassociating himself completely from XR-AF. Then Sinead said she was quitting too. Not surprising. Neither offered an explanation. Each simply waved and signed out after dropping the load.

Afterwards Cam called Charles, who confessed to trouble with his parents after flunking two courses. Mr. 4.14 GPA with *two* F's? In no known universe did that occur. She pressed him about life at U. St. Thomas, knowing he had opted for hybrid mode and been on campus regularly since late August. Or so he had said. After a few minutes he broke down and told her about the pothead he met at the festival and how he blew off classes to hang out with several girls who found his role at XR-AF and growing e-trade portfolio fascinating. One of them, a business major named Maxine with a modest 2.42 GPA but outsized ambition, had just told him she was pregnant. A staunch Catholic, she said abortion was not on the table. He had to man-up and do the right thing, she declared flatly. White Panther mania and bitcoin had made him rich, so what was the worry? Besides, just because it was a shotgun wedding didn't mean it wouldn't be a blast!

Cam hardly knew what to say. She wanted to ask whether Maxine was the only one with child but thought the better of it. She also wanted to know whether XR-AF's finances were as clean and healthy as he claimed, though that could wait. After leaving him with a vague assurance of support she called Goldie, her crisis-management guru.

"Get a handle on the financial situation and re-confirm copyright and trademark status for White Panther and G-Force. If this ship is about to sink, find a lifeboat and row hard."

"What about Charles?"

"No gold-digger is going to ruin his future. I'll call him myself."

"And tell him what?"

"That he can't even wipe his own butt much less a baby's, for starters."

"What's he supposed to do?"

"Not buy her a ring. Take her to an adoption agency. Either that or an abortion clinic."

"*This* is the guy you were sure would go far in life?"

"Even the best among us go too far at times and regret it later. If she keeps the kid, then he ought to contribute financially. But he doesn't have to fall on the marriage sword. I believe it was you who said a chance at redemption was a core value of XR-AF."

"Yah, I did say that, didn't I."

"He screwed up, but that doesn't mean she gets to suck him dry. She'll catch these hands if she doesn't like it." On these matters Cam had more questions than answers, but of one thing she was sure: when the bombs started falling you wanted a sharp, scrappy chick named Golda Bloch in your foxhole.

That evening Cam plopped into her bean bag and read Emma G's latest post: "Beware the Ally Industrial Complex. Leaders of progressive groups are tempted to advance their own careers off the movements they claim to serve. While building organizational capacity and increasing individual influence, they hold themselves out as 'champions' of the oppressed without understanding what collective struggle and mutual support is about. The problem plagues all liberal nonprofits established and controlled for the most part by privileged elites." She put her laptop down and grappled with what felt like an accusation. Mostly she found her rock-star status tiresome, a burden she wanted lifted. Still, was it helping her more than the movement? Was Emma G offering a confession of sorts and ready to renounce her G-Force fame? Just then a text from her arrived.

did u read it?

still processing

dont take it
personally

hard not to
dontcha know

remember how we
started last august?

rebellion within

the rebellion
[skull]

time for another one

ikr lets go
up north

yeet, yeet!

14
UP NORTH

The next morning Cam let Namid and Marco know it was time the team folded. Going forward AF would stand for Ally Foundation, its commercial assets now overseen by trustees. No new spending on advertisements and promotion. All residual revenues would go to non-profits dedicated to climate justice and conservation of biodiversity. In her note to Namid, she invited him to join the new board and closed with a reminder: "Come winter you were going to tell me about Little Bear joining Big Bear in the sky. Still want to share?" He replied a few hours later:

Dear Camilla:

You were born to be the White Panther, whether I showed up or not. Here's how one version of an old Anishinaabe story goes...

A young brave named Niigaanii asked his grandfather Niimi, where do the moon and stars come from? Who puts them there? Long ago, he replied, no stars existed. Only two moons and the sun dwelt in the sky. On Turtle Island a boy named Little Bear lived with his grandfather, while his father Big Bear lived unseen behind the clouds above. Why do we only see one moon now? asked the boy. For eons, his grandfather said, two worlds existed side by side and shared the sun. All was equal and people lived in harmony with each other. Then evil crept over one of the worlds like a snake. The good people there tried to flee to our world, while the evil snake followed close behind, slithering and hissing. Many who could not escape became evil as well; the venom of alcohol and selfish desires sank deep into their veins.

Overwhelmed by the evil ones, our people cried out to the Creator for help. The Creator took pity on us and sent the evil people back to their world, far away from the sun. He hid their beautiful moon from their sight and left them in darkness. The Creator then told our people that one day a child would come who would have the power to heal and make a place in the sky for people of both worlds. After his task on earth was finished, the child would take his place in the sky beside his father, Big Bear, who would finally come out from beneath the cloud cover.

Little Bear was fascinated and often thought about this story. One night he had a disturbing dream about his bow and arrow. The next morning Little Bear asked his grandfather about its meaning. He remained silent a long time and finally said: you must get ready for what is to come. Your destiny awaits.

Then one day, Little Bear felt compelled to climb the mountain looming over his village. Taking up his bow and arrow, he kissed his grandfather good-bye and ascended to its peak. He stood up straight, drew an arrow from his quiver and took careful aim at the brighter of the two moons. With all his strength he pulled back on the bowstring and let the arrow sail through the sky. Once struck, the moon shattered like broken glass into a million pieces, the explosion vibrating through both worlds and lifting the veil of doom from the dark world. In utter amazement Little Bear beheld a sky filled with countless new stars and one full shining moon.

After gazing in wonder at the starry sky awhile Little Bear looked down at his grandfather's lodge and whispered good-bye for the last time. The excitement he felt made his heart race as his spirit rose toward the heavens and his father, Big Bear, who now appeared in the sky alongside him.

Look up north any clear night, and you will see them.

Andopawatchigan.
Fondly,
Namid

For Christmas Giles and dad went overboard with a front-yard homage to White Panther. While tinsel was still tacky, a riot of multi-colored lights festooned every tree, shrub and pole in sight. Near the front steps a giant stuffed feline with ferocious eyes loomed over a large replica of Lightship Greta 2.0 flanked by Native warrior figures. Cam knew mom found the display beyond gaudy and appreciated the cheerful smile she feigned upon her arrival. She also cringed at what Giles had done with the crèche: magi and shepherds out, White Panther and G-Force in. Only little Lord Jesus, ox and ass made the cut, both animals dwarfed by a monster Mishipeshu that appeared ready to make them its next meal.

Dinner-table discussions, which had ceased for the most part after Cam's departure months ago, now resumed in earnest. When Zoe declared the nativity scene sacrilegious, Giles mounted a spirited defense: the gospel light must shine, he announced boldly, in and through the characters and stories of one's own culture. Religion without relevance digs its own grave, said his Lost Lakes theology instructor Mr. Hobanski. In the moment his mother judged a stand for orthodoxy too risky and let the matter drop. She knew Cam would never forgive her if Giles disappeared into his fork for a week. At least he had dressed the Norway pine as perfectly as ever, the only change several White Panther and G-Force ornaments on higher branches and the crowning gold star replaced with a lighthouse.

"White Panther's pics of the crèche and tree were re-flitted 104,723 times already, don't cha know," announced Giles a few days later. "That shows tradition needs to be re-invented now and then for it to stay fresh." When dad asked whether that was his view or Mr. Hobanski's, he fell silent. With her one good leg, Cam kicked her father under the table. They held their breath as Giles sat stone-faced and then reached slowly for his fork. A moment later he was munching heartily on a hunk of ham. Mom gave her a saints-be-praised look that said Mother Church would outlast the idols of the age once again.

Zoe had collected pinecones and waited until Cam arrived to help her make the front-door wreath. The sap of tradition, sticky and fragrant. Working at the kitchen table with her mother, she recalled climbing the tallest white pines at Lake Vermilion, the bark rough and needles prickly but always enough limbs within reach to get close to the tip where one began to sway in the wind. Belief in God came easier at that height.

The days back home went by slowly, which suited Cam. Her sprained knee still needed a few more weeks. She kept up with holiday wishes from fans and forced herself to sit with Giles in the basement where they piled up points blowing away bad guys with their thumbs. Gathered around hearth, the family cheered when Jim Carey's Grinch got the girl and wept when Jimmy Stewart's George saw how wonderful life was. *A strange normalcy*, Cam wrote in her journal.

After dinner the Borlaug clan played Jenga. Kids versus parents. Whichever team won more nightly matches before the ball dropped at Times Square would hold bragging rights for the coming year. Late in the deciding contest, with the oversized set's fifty-four wooden blocks now towering almost to the chandelier above the dining-room table, Zoe stunned everyone when she sized up and then carefully placed her fingers on a lone block eight levels below the highest layer.

"Hold on, hon', sure you wanna go for broke?" said Erik. "Ya got safer plays, here and here. With that one block, ya gotta pull perfect or else. Awfully risky. Don't ya think the timing's bad? Maybe you should—"

"No, the time is right," she replied with a sense of conviction she hadn't felt in the longest time. Cam's phone camera upon her, she yanked it clean away to let the fifteen odd blocks above land on the single-block level below. All held their breath while the whole thing jiggled a moment—as if in slow motion--before settling into a precarious balance of a sort. Zoe's heart-clutching scream a second later nearly undid the improbable feat she'd pulled off. Giles held the table firm, his eyes fixated on the teetering tower as if all civilization depended on his willing the unlikely edifice to remain erect.

Cam's vid of the epic block-snatch exploded across White Panther Nation. For the proverbial fifteen minutes, her mother was more famous than her.

What to do with the block in her hand? Over another reddi-wipped slice of pumpkin pie, they reached agreement: the match was declared a tie. No one, and most especially Zoe, could bear the thought of what might happen if she attempted to complete her turn and place it atop the tower, which now seemed to be listing toward its imminent demise. Giles came up with the perfect excuse for suspending play: the rickety structure's proximity to the chandelier made any more block replacements dangerous, given that players—including one with a sprained knee--now had to stand on a chair to reach that high. Pleased with their plausible out, all retired to the living room to watch *Scrooged*. Five minutes into the show, they heard civilization end noisily. Cam snapped a pic of the ruins for documentary purposes but refrained from sharing it with her admiring public. Why kill the happy-holiday buzz by revealing the tower's fate?

Still in her hometown of Cleveland visiting family, Rayna missed New Year's Eve at Chez Diablo. Unable to dance, Cam subbed as house DJ and stuck to the fab playlist she sent. Angela, Rodney and Huey D showed up, joined by a few friends of Diego's from West Side. Maya reached the seventh heaven well before midnight dancing tango with Gaspar to a trio of blues jams. Only a few flashy figures, and only when well set up. She relished the tight whiplash *boleos* he led and sweeping *rulos* he drew for her. Perfect timing on back *sacadas* and breathtaking *volcadas*. Always on the beat, he knew just how to compensate for her miscues and thus maintain a supple, sensuous connection throughout each song. When he brought her to *la pausa*, that still moment pregnant with possibility, her smile said it all.

"His dancing hits different," remarked Cam afterwards.

"A Cadillac ride," replied Maya as she fell into the couch fully satisfied. One *tanda* with Gaspar was better than sex; at a *milonga* he made love to seven lucky women. None cared that he was balding, a bit pudgy and had a hook nose.

Throughout the evening Diego entertained guests with remarkable juggling routines and generous pours, stopping only to salsa with Dulce, a buxom light-skinned Latina who signaled interest early and often, a signal that no doubt improved his game that night. At midnight they all bid the worst year ever good-riddance and wolf-howled the next one in. Diego borrowed Maya's car the next morning to drive Dulce home. 2021 was off to a good start at Movement House.

Five nights later an impromptu party was thrown in celebration of the improbable Democratic victory in Georgia. Cam texted Vibol to congratulate him:

omg yall
did it!!

bedlam here still
can't believe it

way to make
history vib!!

stacey abrams and
fair fight action
made this happen

new south rising!

lucky perdue and
loeffler were ripe
for the picking

petty plutocrats
swept aside by
the blue tide!
whats next

sleep 3 days

[skull]

been asked to
help with a
union drive
in alabama

so exciting!
whats your role

support workers
reaching out to
the unconvinced

youll slay it!
semester off?

no i will
drive to
bessemer on
weekends

taking on
biggest beast
of all!

wp inspired me

xoxoxo!
wp will
keep telling

everyone to
cancel primo!

inside game
needs
outside game

[fire]

The next day Cam sat with Rayna at the kitchen table and watched the sickening assault on democracy at the nation's capital. During the week that followed denial about the disgraceful incident ran deep among red staters. Most preferred to mimic Sen. Josh Hawley's obscene fist-pumping support for the rabble. Oregon's GOP had the temerity to claim the attack on the Capitol a false-flag operation designed to discredit the outgoing POTUS. Republican officials in Texas slung about the slogan "We are the storm," a QAnon locution pointing ominously to the day of judgment when all liberal pedophiles will be liquidated. Planes used to get hijacked, now it was parties.

Cam and Emma G received an invitation to join the Giniw Collective on the condition they respect decisions made by the Native women leading the group. As white allies they could share ideas freely but must do so in a spirit of humility and service. Neither had to think twice before accepting the offer. Once at full length the Black Snake would belch as much greenhouse gas as fifty new coal-fired power plants. Kilridge had ramped up the wreckage of wildlands and moved more personnel and equipment into place. Braving bitter winds and icy temperatures, water protectors clogged thirty-six-inch pipes with their bodies, occupied standing trees for days at a time, scaled forty-foot bi-pods to block access roads, chained themselves to machines. They played a piano positioned to block the bulldozers, their lyrics indicting fossil fools for crimes against all inhabitants of the home planet. Many now faced criminal charges for acting to protect the sacred *manoomin*. Soon she and Emma G would join them, two more bodies on the front line.

Less than a week after the storming of the U.S. Capitol a fourth Amerizon van exploded. Parked outside a stately abode on Moreland Boulevard in the affluent suburb of Edina, Minnesota, it blew sky-high around seven pm. The Latino driver was at the front door and so uninjured. Incredibly, no evening strollers were hurt by a blast clearly more powerful than the previous three. Soon a white envelope, wrapped lightly in cellophane and camouflaged by the snowbank it protruded from slightly, was found six houses down the block. It carried the same contents as September's envelope: blue marble, iron cross and four cardboard shreds marked with a B and the numbers 1, 8 and 6. Surveillance footage from 4:23 am showed a jogger wearing a black face mask appearing at the spot and shoving the envelope into the snow. Video from other bombings revealed that SUVs had pulled up shortly before the explosions about a block from the Amerizon vans and then driven away immediately afterwards. A security camera at the corner of Moreland and Ridge captured the same activity. In all four cases, however, the make, model and color of the vehicles differed, the license plates of each were covered temporarily and no one inside could be identified. Extensive analysis of data in all locales failed to indicate tailing of the Amerizon vans by the SUVs in question. How, when and by whom the explosive devices were planted remained unknown as well. Only the method of detonation, done by remote once within range, was presumed known at present.

What motivated the Ameri-bombers also remained a mystery. After Druid

Hills rampant speculation continued to revolve around the little-understood activities of eco-fascist cells said to be lurking somewhere in the mountains of northern California and Appalachia. Just hours after the Edina bombing, allegations against Earth Roar and XR-AF popped up online and spread quickly across 2can boards. These left-wing eco-terrorists, a host of alt-right haters claimed without evidence, had morphed from childish protests at Warbill CEO Mack Leland's house into something far more sinister. Hackneyed comparisons to the Weathermen and Earth Liberation Front accompanied the accusations. Radicalization had resulted from White Panther's reckless and often violent activity since Labor Day. Frustrated by lack of success in forcing utterly unrealistic policy changes on Minnesota's governor and state legislature, she and her Jew sidekick G-Force had recruited psychologically vulnerable youth to join a secret cell group that was responsible for the carnage. Devious in their methods, they planted the iron cross to throw authorities off the scent. The blue marble, of which a great deal was now made, gave them away. As for Bleudough and his billions, that was chalked up to socialist envy of all who make it big in America on gumption and good ideas. Despite the absurdity of these fact-starved theories, an Oath to Poach White Panther and the Ameri-bombers collected many e-signatures.

Other cyber-commentators linked the blue marble and Amerizon's huge carbon footprint to *Individualidades Tendiendo a lo Salvaje* or ITS (often translated as Individualists Tending Toward the Wild), a loose network of anti-civ radicals in Latin America inspired by the Unabomber. In Mexico ITS had bombed the national ecology institute, a federal electricity commission office, two banks and a university. Three years ago, a Chilean cell group claimed credit for injuring Oscar Landerretche--then chair of the board of state-owned Codelco, the largest copper producer in the world—with a gift-wrapped bomb. On this theory, ITS now had an active North American affiliate that was behind the slew of bombings. The iron cross wasn't a false flag; rather, it symbolized the death-dealing trajectory of all modern-industrial societies responsible for the Sixth Great Extinction. Just as IBM and other corporations had flourished under the Nazis, Amerizon was now positioned in Crystal City to make billions from lucrative contracts dispensed by the Pentagon. Consistent with Kaczynski's 1995 manifesto, ITS communiques over the years mocked the naivete of liberals and moderates who thought the present techno-industrial system capable of structural reform. Recent events seemed to confirm their critique: despite a minor slow-up in deliveries and brief lull in new Primo memberships during the four-day walkout in late November, company operations continued to expand without any significant changes in policies or practices. The threshold campaign only had 25,000 pledges. While Bleudough touted his Give it Up for Gaia Foundation more often, managers at a warehouse in Bessemer, Alabama were busy undermining a campaign to unionize the sprawling facility's mostly black workers.

Back in June, the Teamsters had declared that bringing the union to Amerizon must be priority number one. If left unchecked, the company's relentless expansion eventually would result in declining wages, cuts in benefits and lousier working conditions for the entire country's 5.8 million logistics workforce. Teamster organizers admired the militancy of Amerizoners Unite groups that stormed the manager's office with a petition and walked off the job when ignored. Nonetheless, to win significant gains a union with more resources and a broader strategy was necessary.

Just two days after the Primo Day protest in October, Bessemer activists met with local Teamsters and asked for help. The union had anticipated this kind of opportunity and was ready. Soon a cadre of salts from eleven different cities arrived in Alabama and secured plentiful warehouse jobs. They humped it to show bosses they were exemplary employees and earn the respect of co-workers. Amerizon kept its blue-collar employees isolated by design, but the salts formed friendships and stayed on the look-out for natural leaders. When the moment was right, they presented them with a choice: either unionize to bring about big improvements for everyone or go it alone within the current exploitative system. What made the salting difficult was the high turnover: even as the company brought in hundreds to handle the holiday rush, many of the worn-out and injured left. Despite all the coming and going, they managed to recruit dozens of worker-leaders ready to fight for a union.

When it became clear the walkouts on Black Friday had failed, the organizing committee went into overdrive. Countless impromptu chats and quick huddles during breaks and shift changes; blanketing of break rooms with flyers; a constant flow of flits, texts, emails and video meets; a virtual New Year's Eve party. By mid-January they had 1,612 union authorization cards signed, enough to petition the NLRB for representation though not enough to be confident of winning the vote.

Organizers also assembled a training and support team, which Vibol was joining. Once worker-leaders committed to the union, they needed help setting up and conducting house calls to those still on the fence. With labor law restricting union talk onsite and managers constantly fear-mongering during the captive-audience meetings they kept calling, these house visits would make or break the union drive. The recent spike in covid had shut down the outreach effort, but with vaccinations now available and case numbers rapidly declining the time seemed right to mask up and get out there. Both visitors and hosts felt more comfortable on the front porch or in the back yard, even on a chilly evening. Each time a recruitment team headed out, a retired Teamster who seemed to live at the union hall would say: "Just remember, if Georgia's Dems can pull off a miracle one door-knock at a time, so can we next door in Alabama!"

On the night of the van explosion in Edina, Goldie called Cam after sending her a link to the news report. She was still reading when the phone rang.

"Wow, the NSA, FBI, ATF, ICE and God knows who else have cameras on every corner and are monitoring every phone call, text and website in America, yet still no suspects."

"You are now a suspect."

"Wait, what? Oh, just because we spotlighted Big Mack at his house?"

"Right. Someone with a badge and a big gun will be knocking on your door *very* soon. Contact Earthjustice first thing tomorrow morning and line up legal representation."

"You are scaring me, don't cha know."

"No joke, Camster. A lot of folks who hate your guts are going to try and use this bombing to destroy you."

"Why does all this sound way too alarm--"

"No, I'm not pushing the panic button. What part of getting shot last October did you forget? With four bombings, with Trump's mob storming the capitol and his toadies still trying to steal the election—the country is on edge. There's a lot of pressure on the powers-that-be to find scapegoats fast. Red states are passing draconian laws aimed at making life miserable for environmental activists. They're moving to criminalize dissent. Anything to suppress another uprising."

"Congrats, you've succeeded in freaking me out totally."

"Lawyer up, pronto."

"OK then."

She called Earthjustice the next day. Two days later federal agents came to Movement House. They questioned her for over an hour, spent a half-hour each with Maya and Diego and less than ten minutes with Rayna, who took umbrage at their relative lack of interest. "You even wore your green wig for the occasion," teased Maya. Cam's attorney advised her not to go up north in a few days as planned. Any travel to hotspots could be misconstrued. Better to wait and find out whether Giniw Collective members also were being investigated and then compare notes. She chafed at the recommendation but agreed to lay low for a while.

On day one the new POTUS ordered the shutdown of Keystone XL but nothing more. Once cleared by advisors for travel three weeks later, Cam and Emma G were more than ready. With no end in sight to Line 337, the two prepared to remain at the resistance camp for months if necessary. Unless Biden or a Minnesota judge stopped construction, it would be complete by early fall.

Fat Tuesday became the obvious date for a going-away party that doubled as Cam's nineteenth birthday bash. Maya placed a large Fleur de Lis on the mantel and filled the front rooms with purple, gold and green balloons. Rayna obsessed over a tiered metallic table skirt dressed in the same colors and wore her most elaborate wig ever to match, the first and only time anyone had ever seen her off color. During the party she played songs from all of Maya's favorite New Orleans Krewes and, as always, fielded requests. Emma G asked for Arcade Fire's "Everything Now" and "You Get What You Give" by the New Radicals. In a fit of nostalgia Cam requested World Party's "Ship of Fools." Juiced by Diego's generous libations, she kept belting out *you will pay tomorrow* before Maya imposed more inclusive lyrics--*we're gonna pay tomorrow*—that everyone took up with gusto. Mardi Gras masques had replaced covid coverings, and for a moment the choral refrain gave the whole event a macabre feel.

Around ten Diego pulled out a huge *rosca de reyes* that disappeared quickly. When a boatload of colored beads appeared, Dulce sent necklaces sailing across the room to every reveler and then wrapped the many that remained around her neck and arms with elaborate skill, her jeweled splendor drawing not just Diego's attention but every other man's. Maya brought out painted coconut throws from the Krewe of Zulu. At one point Diego had everyone mesmerized as he lofted five of them into the air effortlessly. Dulce was smitten. If not for his bartending duties, he boasted, he would have broken Israeli juggler Ofek Snir's world record of two hours, forty-one minutes and twenty-seven seconds.

The next day, after sleeping in, Maya and Rayna drove Cam and Emma G up to the Giniw encampment at Long Lake, dotted by ice-fishing camps. After greeting Tara Houska and other collective members, they helped set up an A-frame not far from three teepees and six other tents. Before departing they spoke with Tara, an attorney and one of the group's founding members.

"What does Giniw mean?" inquired Maya. Tara knew who she was and so didn't mind the question. Word of the honorary bear-clan member's exploits during the uprising traveled quickly. She wasn't so sure about the red-wigged chick wearing touched-up high-tops in February.

"Giniw is an *Omishoomisimaa*, a grandfather who protects *Zíigwan*, the Springtime Spirit of the East that watches over all women of the nation. Giniw flies high, sees far and brings messages to the people. Soaring across the sky he carries prayers to the Great Mystery."

"Those who stand unafraid and put prayers into action," added Rayna. Tara looked the red-wigged one up and down: another wifty liberal parroting verbiage off their website. If not for Maya, she'd have told her to lose the wig.

Maya sensed her annoyance and tried a re-direct. "What does the eagle feather around your neck signify?"

"Carrying an eagle feather is a sacred act. To be given a feather from grandfather Giniw is the highest honor one can receive. One must earn it, and with it comes great responsibilities since the feather's power comes from the Thunderbirds." Tara then pointed to a small flock of sandhill cranes flying over the camp. "They flee when Kilridge's heavy machinery makes a racket." Rayna couldn't take her eyes off the richly embroidered blanket keeping Tara warm. To keep her toes from freezing, she'd started to hop from one foot to another, a dance that annoyed her Native host even more than the carrot top.

"Emma G told us Line 337 has caused division among the Ojibwe bands. What's going on with that?" asked Maya.

"An old story of divide-and-conquer. At Standing Rock, the First Nations stood together in the face of state brutality. Here in Minnesota the company creates division by pouring cash into local communities lining the pipeline route. They dole out donations and jobs, five hundred of them to our people. They pay for the county cops through a special fund set up by the state. What they call being a good corporate citizen I call legalized bribery. Sadly, it's working. Two bands decided not to oppose the project."

"How big is their operation?"

"Huge. Four thousand workers are now at five different along a pipeline corridor that runs across the entire state. Our Indian Affairs Council asked the governor to stop construction so that legal challenges can be heard in state court. From now until the end of March, they will push hard to get work done before stopping in April and May for the thaw and spring rains. They saw what happened to Keystone XL and are desperate to create a fact on the ground."

"We heard a lot of water protectors face criminal charges," observed Rayna.

"Over one hundred and thirty to date. We will use a necessity defense and argue that direct action is the only way at this point to secure our treaty rights to hunt, fish and gather on unspoiled lands. Back in 1991 the old pipeline that's still in use spilled 1.7 million gallons of crude into the Prairie River not far from here. Largest inland oil spill in U.S. history. Pipeline accidents occur across the country again and again. Line 337 is just one of many black snakes."

"What if just twenty thousand of the twenty million who rose up last June joined you? I bet you could gum up the works but good," mused Maya.

"Can't argue with that!" The three women shared a laugh. "Here's another hypothetical: what if a million people pulled their money out of Stage Coach, VD and other banks funding this project?" suggested Tara.

"I'm so busted!" cried Maya. "Tomorrow I'll close my VD account first thing!"

"Me too!" echoed Rayna.

"Ha! And you two better tell all your friends!"

Only a sliver of sun remained above the tree line, and the temperature was sliding downhill fast. Neither Maya nor Rayna wanted to leave, but the latter's numb toes were burning. Maya handed Cam a beautifully wrapped gift. "Happy birthday, *chica blanca.*"

"Uff-da, you *didn't* just say that."

"Well, it's from Diego and me. Wait until later to open it. And remember, your room will be waiting for you when you return triumphant. Of course, if you lose don't bother to com--"

"Don't even…" They laughed and shared an embrace. Then she and Rayna went for a short walk. She also had a gift but wanted her to open it right away. Cam ripped open the rose-colored tissue paper and giggled at the sight of a sketch pad with ink brush and jar.

"Really, a beginner's set?"

"Yes, padawan. Up here you're a tyro." After a long, tender hug and nose kiss the two strolled back to the car where Maya was waiting. Cam and Emma G waved goodbye as they drove off down the dirt road, their dust lingering in the arctic air. Soon it was time for a simple dinner by the fire. One of their new friends sipped on tea but did not eat; she was on day three of a hunger strike.

Everyone retired early. Tomorrow at dawn they would block an access road with a tall bi-pod and two old cars Native activists had arrived in from out of state. At their first water-protector action, Cam and Emma G would sing the Nibi Song and hold a large banner that read From the Headwaters to the Gulf: Rivers at Risk.

Cam burrowed into her sleeping bag with a flashlight and Maya's present. Emma G already was asleep. She closed her eyes and listened a minute to the snow now falling. Then she unwrapped her other gift, a first-edition hardback copy of Dorothy Day's *The Long Loneliness*, and dove in. Her resolve grew as she read Dorothy's own account of spending a month in jail and enduring the Night of Terror in which she and other Silent Sentinels were beaten mercilessly by prison guards. A week before she and other suffragists were brutalized, she had turned nineteen.

15
ESSENTIAL UPRISING

"Amerizoners Unite, what a joke!"

"Bunch of ignorant, over-weight whiners."

"Hey, did anyone see that memo last week? Stats show the warehouse employees only last three years before they wear out."

"Parts and labor!"

"More like collateral damage in the war to dominate the market. Not a few markets, mind you. *The* market."

"Swallow it whole!"

"Whole Foods!"

"Here's to winner takes all!"

So crowed four fit but loose-lipped execs in Seattle, caught unawares on tape after one too many at an unofficial holiday party. If you were robo-terminated, like the Army vet in Arkansas who busted ass delivering Primo packages for three years, don't waste time trying to get a human being on the phone to explain why. Site managers and corporate HR alike made being MIA their mission when it came to the froth thrown up by the churn.

One post on MakeAmerizonPay.com summed up the outrage provoked by the leaked audio:

Sans Savings

Yo, Ameri-bombers, why not give Feather Flite's New Buzz

> rocket a run for its money and send forty vans skyward instead of just four? Somebody's got to take the gloves off. We expendables would be much obliged.

Workers in Bessemer had a better idea: build a strong union capable of standing up against management's disinformation and thinly veiled threats. Their version of ready for take-off? When structure testing showed the union's strength had reached a level among the rank and file that made winning the vote on representation likely. Tests took several forms, scaling up in risk and significance as the campaign unfolded. How quickly were newly recruited worker-leaders able to gather union card signatures from their crews? How many were on board after a week? After four? Once signatures reached a majority, how many were willing to pose for a group photo wearing a pro-union sticker? Coming out together often flipped the undecided, which then made petitioning the NLRB a good bet. Still another test gauged community support. In Alabama and beyond the momentum was swinging their way. Buoyed by thumbs-up flits from superstars and statements of support from professional players associations, unionists convinced local sports teams and vendors to display Support Your Bessemer Teamsters signs at events. Ministers urged the faithful to post lawn signs, and soon neighborhoods were awash with them. At busy intersections on Valentine's Day folks from SWEET Alabama—a non-profit pushing for sustainable cities—handed out heart-shaped balloons that urged takers to Show Our Teamsters the Love. The number of Go Teamsters bumper stickers seen around town hockey sticked.

Four months of organizing came to a head on a Tuesday at noon in late February. Jericho trumpets played as two dozen buttoned employees stood at the main entrance holding up union cards and posters filled with pics of their comrades. Inside the warehouse, hundreds of Teamsters Stand Tall buttons now appeared on defiant chests. Other pickers asked to get pinned up, and with each passing minute more came forward. An exhilarating new energy pulsed through the giant building. Never had so many Amerizoners grinned at one another. All could feel the wall of fear crumbling before their eyes. Bleudough had no balls! From the stacks a few workers began to chant "Teamsters stand tall! Teamsters stand tall!" Soon the decibel count was deafening. This congregation knew how to raise the roof!

Grim-faced managers fanned out and shot disapproving looks at the buttoned now bursting at the seams. For months they had followed the standard playbook: lecture ad nauseum, flood the facility with anti-union merch and messaging, barrage every associate with texts. Mostly they targeted younger workers either confused by all the fuss or fearful they might be fired. For years corporate had done all it could to keep this day from coming. They hired Pinkertons, set up a secret unit at HQ1 to spy 24/7 on workers' private Facebook groups, deployed PR spin doctors across platforms of any consequence and closely tracked unionization risk with a heat map tool. Bessemer was Code Red. Now the fire was threatening to get out of control, and they knew it.

BLM-Birmingham activists, teachers, reps from union locals and two busloads of Teamsters all the way from Boston showed up in force the next day when the organizing committee announced the petition filing. Within twenty-four hours the union drive was page one everywhere. A flurry of celebrity endorsements soon followed. In DC the House passed the Protect the Right to Organize Act, a game-changing reform of labor law that faced long odds in the Senate. At a press conference, AOC and other Squad members wore Teamsters Stand Tall buttons and another that said Essential Uprising. They catalogued the contributions of frontline workers to keeping the country fed and cared for over the past year, despite the daily risks to their lives, and called on all people of conscience and good will to act in solidarity by demanding their senators vote for the PRO Act. Ilhan Omar spoke eloquently of the heroic organizing efforts of her fellow East Africans in the Twin Cities, among the first Amerizoners in the U.S. to stand up for their rights. The walkouts last fall, she noted, may not have moved Bleudough and the top brass to do the right thing, but they did move the needle on public opinion. Polls showed seventy-six percent of Americans in favor of the union drive in Alabama, including fifty-seven percent of registered Republican voters. Others indicated ninety-four percent disapproved of the attempt by Ameri-bombers to sway the public, ignite rebellion, scare Bleudough into making concessions or whatever it was they wanted to see happen, since in a year's time they had not issued a single public statement. Their enigmatic envelopes only pissed people off.

Creatives went to town with the Essential Uprising meme. In one short video gone viral, incensed nurses strung up an incredulous hospital administrator with blood collection tubes and spanked him with a bedpan until he cried "Uncle Joe, do something!" Another showing a beleaguered, pimple-faced Domino's driver flinging a freshly baked pepperoni pie into the face of a screaming manager fared nearly as well. Still another, which featured a convenience-store clerk holding late-night customers hostage with an AR-15 until they swore on a King James Bible to call their senator, did even better. Amerizon's PR team quickly marshalled an army of employees to counter criticism of the company on social media. Loyalists at the warehouse began to wear Mister Pickster mascot pins, usually awarded to associates with perfect attendance but now bestowed by panicking managers upon anyone with a pulse not wearing enemy pins.

Meanwhile, the Teamsters and other unions across the country received more requests for help in a week than they had the previous decade. Inspired by successful teacher strikes in West Virginia and elsewhere, Marry Lot's hospitality workers recently had won an important victory with their One Job Is Enough campaign. Was a blue wave beginning to rise? Too early to tell, but as the union-hall phone kept ringing the Ents among them began to stir in unfamiliar ways. Settled on barstools for decades, mumbling amongst themselves about NAFTA and other blows to labor's gut, they now had a look in their eyes that organizers half their age had never seen. Suddenly, talk of Flint no longer seemed nostalgic.

By mid-March the regional NLRB office had approved the bargaining unit at Bessemer, certified the petition and ordered a mail-in vote on representation to be completed within a month. A few days later the White House released a video of President Biden voicing his support for all workers fighting to win a union. In L.A. the city's labor federation marched outside Pinkerton offices to protest their union busting on behalf of Amerizon and other corporate titans. That same day Bessemer workers crowded around Danny Glover, who had come to deliver a message of support from L.A.'s workers.

"I'm starting to believe the whole world is watching," enthused one beaming picker as he pumped Glover's hand. Like Paul Robeson and other black actor-activists, Glover had stood with underdogs time and again—in many cases when the cameras were turned elsewhere. In 2013, he'd gone to northeast Ecuador to stand with local residents and environmentalists protesting against rampant pollution of the region's watershed by Big Oil.

"We're not just watching. We're standing with you. Millions are rooting for y'all. Good people know what you've done to keep this country running."

From the crowd came a question: "Hey Danny, did you promise to cancel your Primo membership if a million others do?"

"Hell yeah!" Caught on video, the posted exchange had 412,000 views by week's end. Threshold pledges more than tripled to 94,600 before the month was out.

Vibol and other veterans of the Georgia ground war continued to train worker-leaders, set up house calls and drive them from one to the next. Though he never said no when offered cake and cookies with sweet tea, at least in Gwinnett County the tea had been served hot, the sugar was optional and the dessert portions far more modest. A bit tubby from day one, since joining the Alabama campaign he'd put on ten pounds and come to the last notch in his favorite belt. Recruiters did all the talking. He was there to clean his plate with a smile, show the Biden video if asked and observe body language, often the best indicator of how a co-worker and his kin really felt about the situation. In between visits they sifted through talking points that worked and those that didn't, a learning curve some climbed more quickly than others. Improving their ability to sell the union, field objections and allay worries about getting fired became his raison d'être down south.

Too sluggish to advance past little league despite his love of the game, he remained a Little Piranha who'd spent years studying the small ball his beloved Twins had played so well when he was little. In recent summers he'd lived in the bleachers at Bullseye Field and still hadn't forgiven the team's front office for firing The Ignitor, hall-of-famer Paul Molitor, from his management post three years ago. While he couldn't catch, hit or throw much, he definitely had a knack for coaching others. In this case, coaching worker-leaders on how to help co-workers stay in the box when corporate came with the heat. In the deadly-serious game now being played, inoculating the skittish from company ploys was as important as getting them to sign a union card. Before employees mailed their ballot in a few weeks, hardball managers would be throwing high and tight or looking to buckle knees by hurling some wicked-scary curve at them. Some of the bastards might throw right at their head. Still, when workers *knew* what pitch was coming, they usually stood their ground instead of bailing. Moving from house to house, and coached in between, his worker-leaders began to deliver more persuasive pitches and chalk up more Ws for the Teamsters.

By mid-April he'd driven and coached a dozen pitchers on some 250 house calls. When it came to newly signed union cards, his "slugging percentage" was remarkably high for a chubby kid from up north, a cagey veteran organizer nicknamed John Henry joshed. "Vib, you alright. For a Canadian," he replied with a sly grin and husky voice each time Vibol tried to clarify the difference between Minnesota and Manitoba. Weekend nights in Bessemer he crashed on the former miner's couch after they'd pigged out on pizza and watched cable. Each morning a reveille roused him, followed by a boatload of buttered-up, syrup-smothered hotcakes with bacon and grits, a southern breakfast that grew on him. *Show'm how, like you do*, his host would always say on his way out the door to the union hall.

Having spent three decades underground in Tuscaloosa County's Black Warrior Coalfield, John Henry's geography might be a little suspect, but his stats sure weren't: worker-leaders shuttled and tutored by his boy had collected

144 signatures before mail-in voting began, and four weekends later they'd inked fifty-six more. No other field intern's performance came close. Based on their own polling, the Teamsters expected about 4,000 mail-in ballots by the Wednesday deadline, now only three days away. During the midnight drive back to Atlanta, Vibol checked the math: on 250 house calls his pitchers had secured 200 yes pledges, an eighty percent win rate that had brought the union ten percent closer to a historic victory. Totally spent, he overslept the next morning and later kicked himself for missing a PoliSci lecture titled Five Ways to Widen the Overton Window.

Fireworks flared across Bessemer and hundreds of other union towns throughout the land on Thursday night. It was close: 2,176 yes, 1,978 no. Organizers weren't sure the 198-vote margin could survive the many challenges company lawyers would hurl at authorities in coming weeks. Vibol received his first speeding ticket racing back to join the victory party and almost crashed the rental while responding to Cam's congrats text.

northern lights
r bright tonight!
yall r what
democracy
looks like!

so exhausted
but so fired up!

vib on a roll!
[goat]

yah just got
pulled over
doing 88
fines gonna be
more than that

my alfred

a lawbreaker
good thing
i fired you

ikr so stupid

get the union
to pay it

just might ask
btw hows your
dragon slay going

killaguans stopped
work last week
too muddy
up here

for how long

they'll be back
early june
well be
waiting
for them

school next fall?

depends

in for a dime

in for a dollar

As soon as he arrived, John Henry and another organizer known for playing pranks met him at the door. They plopped a crown, hastily made with stapled cardboard, upon his bewildered head. Then they hoisted his weighty frame up on their shoulders and paraded him through a union hall packed with new members and their supporters, all of whom were now raucously chanting "MVD! MVD!" After the victory lap, they placed him atop a table. "Speech! Speech!" cried several others in on the joke. The hall grew quiet and waited for him to say something. Anything. Still completely befuddled, he looked dumbly at John Henry and asked, "What's an MVD?" The whole place fell out.

A few minutes later, as cups of bubbly were going around, they still had him on the hook. "Vib, da numbers don't lie. You dis union's MVD, no doubt about it. We done the math, and your slugging percentage puts you up there with da Babe." All heads nodded vigorously in agreement. "Yessiree bob, you da Babe. No doubt about it." Another round of backslaps and bubbly followed. He tried to ask again, but they shot him an astonished, cross-eyed look that said *every* working stiff in the room knew what MVD stood for, so how could a college boy like him *not* know? A third polite request fell on deaf ears.

"Vib, you alright. For a Canadian. Now listen here, you da *MVD*, that's what *you* are."

"Yessiree bob, you da Babe."

"No doubt about it."

Enough was enough. Even Cambodian Catholic altar boys, who from their first rice bowl are bred to respect the giver, to never bite the hand that feeds, to maintain harmony in all social situations, had limits to their patience.

"Damn it all, just tell me what MVD stands for. *Now*."

A wry smirk fell over John Henry's face. Raising a boulder fist to his lips, he cleared his throat. "Don't get dem panties up in a bunch, Vib. You da union's Most Valuable Driver. Congratulations, son, dat's quite an honor." Everyone buckled over. He threw a bear-arm around the clueless young Canadian. "Vib, you alright," he said with a chuckle and a vice grip that left his boy sucking for air. Then one organizer and worker-leader after another came up and gave him a fist-pump.

"Welcome to the union, son."

Not one Teamster cared a lick about the champagne's modest pedigree.

Just hearing the corks pop was more than enough, though they did quaff every bottle quickly. A powerful and exciting sound, those pops, like a rocket shot off the bat of Hammerin' Hank giving his Braves the lead over the Pirates. "Game on, Amerizon!" they all chanted later that evening after a seamless transition to Pabst Blue Ribbon. "Game on!"

The next morning, after crashing at John Henry's, Vibol took it slow on the drive back to Atlanta. He thought about whether it was time to take himself out of the Bessemer line-up. So far, his spring-semester grades were nothing to write home about. His extended family had stepped up to the plate in a big way to make an Emory education possible. Even with all the aid, four seasons from now he'd be staring at a student loan number approaching $120K. Yet while whiffing at school was not an option, walking off the field into the corn rows of Alabama wasn't either.

For the Teamsters, gaining the right to bargain collectively was akin to a play-off berth: a beautiful thing, but really nothing to write home about unless they won the trophy. With only a narrow victory on representation, everyone knew management was going to contest the vote in court, double down on union busting and ignore requests to begin contract talks. The coming months of organizing would be as crucial to Teamster success as those now behind them. No less than a thousand no votes had to be flipped. Only then would the union be strong enough to call a strike and hold on if it all went into extra innings. Only rock-solid teams with gamers at the plate and strong bullpens won those grueling contests of will.

There was one other thing the union's organizers knew: a doughy Asian kid sent from the North Pole was the best coach of worker-leaders they'd ever seen, and they needed him in the line-up now more than ever.

By the time he pulled into campus, the choice was clear: in for a dime, in for a dollar. Only he could pay the ticket. No self-respecting chauffeur would do otherwise. And more importantly, no coach worth his salt would ever refuse to throw more batting practice, even if it was getting dark and it meant tossing beachballs to the shrimpy shortstop who might never leave the nine-slot or cross the Mendoza Line. No, a real coach kept on chucking even if his arm was falling off and the pay was so low he *had* to order Pabst after icing down and popping four more Vitamin I.

And if fifty-one more throws in the dark somehow increased the odds, even just a little, that during the top of the fifth a flare off the end of his broken bat might drop in and lead to a go-ahead run, a run that might end up being the difference one hot summer day, then you sucked it up and kept hurling them over the plate for the four-eyed whiff-kid to take another hack at. After all, he was one helluva glove and, you knew deep down, a gamer-in-wait who just needed someone to believe.

Play through the pain, coach always said.

Game on, Amerizon.

Game on.

16
TREATY PEOPLE

Each spring the Chippewa exercise their treaty rights and go sugaring on county, state and federal lands. Come first thaw the Giniw Collective doubled as a sugar camp. In between protests they tapped maple trees, sap running through sumac spigots into pails carried to the fire. Women watched over the syrup turning thick in the cast-iron kettle. Some they let cook longer to make hard candy.

"A certain sap collected from a secret grove near a remote river is by far the sweetest," said a visiting elder. "Long ago Nanabozho decided to dilute the sugar from all the maples on Turtle Island by sending rain upon them so that Anishinaabeg had to work for their syrup and show gratitude. He was distracted a moment by lightning and passed over those trees. Only a few know where they stand." Cam and Emma G heard this tale and many others while gathering firewood and cleaning out sugar-crusted pails. They made pancakes almost every morning before the first frog croak signaled the end of sugaring season.

As Sugar Moon gave way to Sucker Moon, abundant rain kept Kilridge's bulldozers at bay. "Just as Grandmother Moon looks after the waters of creation," said another elder one night as she gestured toward a sky filling with storm clouds, "women protect the waters of their people." At Long Lake the spring winds picked up and the days grew longer. Having trekked across the ice for miles when she first arrived, Cam now walked alone for hours along the water's edge, each step inching her away from White Panther mania and the weight of expectations she no longer wanted to carry. On her long walks she kept an ear out for the loons, now flying north from the Gulf coast to fill empty evenings with their yodels, hoots, wails and tremolos, a nightly chorus that would grew more vibrant with each passing week. They arrived with dull, reddish-brown eyes and dressed in winter's dark grey and white. By late May their marble-red eyes and breeding plumage had begun to appear, male and female alike donning a tuxedo covered by a black-and-white cape across the back. Elegant attire for a mating dance.

With the pipeline on hold, Cam and Emma G climbed tall pines as a warm-up for the tree-sitting to come. They rode shotgun on recon missions, mapping out the best spots for blockades. Once a week they bummed a ride to the nearby town of Park Rapids where they checked out books at the public library and then met up with Native women for Salsa Tuesdays, an awareness-raising event that never failed to raise their spirits.

One Tuesday just shy of shorts weather, Maya and Rayna paid them a surprise visit, with Diego in the back seat and two cases of Surly Darkness in the trunk. The Ojibwe grandmothers took an interest in the young Mexican with skills and wanted to hear all about the bear-claw ring. They wound up keeping him on the floor four hours straight. Only two Surlys left when he finally escaped their clutches and collapsed onto a bench.

"Wrestles with Boogaloos has met his match!" teased Maya on the way home. He wound up on the living-room couch for two days, ice packs on every joint and one atop the skull. The feet blisters hurt for three weeks. In Indian country, they talked about that salsa party for months. He wished it never happened. Better to get beat up by ten boogala mamas than dance with *those* women ever again.

While Diego and his new friends danced until they dropped, Rayna and Cam found a diner around the corner. The red-wigged one was thirsty. At this time of year, barely a third of the booths were occupied. Locals off work early or laid off cracked peanuts, sucked on pretzel sticks, nursed bottles of pop. The topic of conversation at one table: whether the state would allow moose hunting again. Eight years back the population had crashed but appeared stable of late. Three Ojibwe bands had allowed limited hunts, a treaty right the state honored. One kill brought seven hundred pounds of meat into the family freezer. It wasn't long before the talk turned to moose-call technique. Unlike the animals, that subject was inexhaustible.

Off in their own corner, Rayna and Cam shared a smoothie but said little to one another. Three months apart had been hard. After exuberant hugs upon arrival, the impromptu reunion soon felt strained. In recent weeks, they had texted less frequently. Neither was quite sure why. There was something about impotent longing that wearied the heart, a nameless something that gnawed away at the assurances conveyed by *miss-you* [heart] messages and old sayings. Yes, absence made hearts grow fonder, but there was more to it than that. Much more, yet not the kind of thing that found its way easily into words. Most attempts began to sag as soon as they left the tongue, like a punctured tire losing air while one kept driving along, utterly oblivious, until the bumpy-muffling sound that signaled a flat no longer could be ignored.

"Long-distance relationships suck," Rayna finally said. Stating it flat-out seemed to take the pressure off. Cam found herself able to breathe again.

"I'm going to be up here for as long as it takes, you know that." That too needed saying, if only to confirm what both already knew.

They sat in a silence broken only by the last noisy slurp. Cam sucked the plastic straw clean. "Did you bring your chopsticks? Maybe they have puppy chow at this place."

"Sorry, I left them back at the ranch. Besides, using straws just isn't the same." Before the awkwardness crept back in between them, she reached into a pocket and pulled out a folded piece of paper. She opened it up and took her time flattening it on the table. Cam could see it was a poem, four stanzas filling the page.

"I wrote this last week and was going to recite it to you, but now I'm—"

"Please do. I'd rather hear the words in your voice." She knew Bell never said no to anything; one had only to keep ringing. Still, she spent several all-too-annoying minutes trying to set expectations low, going on and on about her writerly struggles with rhythm, meter and the like, like a meter maid taking way too long to write up a wholly undeserved ticket. Cam just smiled and made encouraging noises.

"OK, but only if you close your eyes and listen a minute to me blinking," she said finally. Stifling a giggle, Cam honored her request and waited patiently. She heard her blink several times and sigh gently before she began to lilt her way through the lines.

What fate awaits true glimpse of gold
when days again grow tiresome and old?
What then becomes of deepest desire?
Does it hide, cry out, or just retire?

From sun-seared peaks of ecstasy
where souls afire run free

one falls back into normalcy.
There state and market hold the key,
lay all the grids and tell the many
to stay cool and take but a penny.

Though most comply to get by
the desperation they deny,
the void they try in vain to fill
with another win, another thrill,
still lingers all the dreary days,
still haunts them in so many ways.

Among the beaten and abused
we the unbowed will light a fuse.
So quick! guard the grids--if you can--
go execute your master plan.
Until the powerful do pay,
we rebels will never go away!

Be content with just a simple day,
masters across the ages do say.
Let go now your every desire,
for only then may you quell the fire.

Cam sat still and resisted the urge to gush over the modest literary effort. Rayna knew trite-and-too-cutesy when she heard it. Speak only if one can improve the silence, she reminded herself. Easier said than done.

"The last two lines are taking me back to the attic. Tell me, master, are you going to shred this poem before my eyes a second from now?"

"Come on, that was the right thing to do at the time."

"Yah, it really was on point. I think about it often on my walks. A daily reminder of you."

"Cam, you've made the right choice coming up here. Let's let things unfold as they will, knowing we won't be together anytime soon—if ever. I'd rather dwell in that truth—painful as it is—than cling to false hopes."

"The master speaks from across the ages."

"Seriously, since you left it's become very clear to me how different we are."

"What are you getting at?"

"Some DJ, some dance. I'm an attic dweller, at home in the life of the mind, content with my sketchbooks. You are much more than that, a player on big stages, not a backstage type like me.... It's better to accept that and all that it means for the future."

"Am I the crazed rebel in your poem?"

"You tell me."

"I think I'm going to run out the door screaming any second now."

"Or you can stay and let me hold you a little while."

"I thought autists didn't do emotional support."

"Fine, you can hold me, then."

"When you are near, I do." Cam nestled up close and gave her a nose kiss. "When you are not, I hold you in my heart."

"Are you turning sentimental?"

"What's a girl up north to do?"

"You know I miss you. After that, there's not much more to say."

"Perhaps your poem has more to tell me. When I'm ready."

"Keep it then."

"I will, thank you."

"And let's make a treaty, just between you and me, to always hold each other in our hearts, come what may."

"Now look who's getting sentimental."

"Are you in? If so, we can seal the deal with another nose kiss."

"All in." This time they met each other in the middle and let the warm touches linger.

"Yes, that's it."

That evening, after the dust kicked up by Maya's car had settled, Cam walked toward the lake in hopes of hearing the loons calling to one another in the distance. Sounds beautiful yet strange, deliciously familiar yet still mysterious, close yet far away...

Just like Rayna.

Not long after construction had resumed in earnest, a tornado ripped through one Kilridge work site like a warning from the gods. The collective re-located twenty-five miles north to Namewag Camp, closer to a stretch of pipeline about to be laid. Water protectors issued a call for Treaty People to gather at the headwaters of the Mississippi in early June to support frontliners risking arrest. Amidst a record heat wave two thousand activists from dozens of states, Canada and Puerto Rico poured into Pure Bliss Ranch, a White Earth Nation meeting ground, for a day of training. After hours of role plays and practice sessions the sun-beaten assembled under a large white tent to hear Anishinaabe leader Winona LaDuke. Her casual delivery, in turn folksy and sardonic, belied a fierce determination. She spoke with a moral authority grounded in decades spent defending Native lands from despoilment.

"No one chooses to make a career out of stopping stupid, dangerous development schemes, and at my age--" Her sudden pause and darting eyes evoked laughter. "The last thing I want to do is chain myself to a foreign corporation's equipment and get arrested for trespassing on lands my people have inhabited for centuries. But until the treaties are honored, we will hold our ground." The Treaty People, dripping with sweat and waving hand-held fans, clapped and wolf howled in assent. "The state pays us $13 million yearly for all the fish caught in our lakes and rivers and then washes its hands when these sacred waters are threatened by another pipeline even its own commerce department says makes no economic sense." Boos rumbled through the big tent. "The politicians keep talking about local jobs. Really? Go to any man camp and you'll see mostly out-of-state plates on the pick-ups," she quipped to knowing laughter. "Over the past fifteen months a lot of folks have re-thought what is essential to human flourishing and what isn't. Clean water, clean air and healthy soils are on everyone's must-have list, and for good reason. Only from a warped, narrow perspective is more fossil-fuel infrastructure 'essential' to this state's prosperity in coming decades. Treaty People protect the earth from the greedy, the *windigos*, because they know what really matters. Thank you for coming from the four corners to stand with us."

As everyone clapped and wolf howled again Winona's eyes rolled across the crowd and came to rest a moment on Cam, who stood at the tent's edge. Only the gazes of Godol, Chano and Rayna reached as deep, reached across time and space and all the boundaries that egos and authorities erect. Winona gave her a faint, knowing smile and nodded. Perhaps she was acknowledging the presence of White Panther, but that meant nothing next to two caring souls coming close. In an instant she knew right here, right now, was where she was meant to be.

The Treaty People, two thousand strong, marched the next day down Great River Road. Above them flew hundreds of dragonflies and a few journalist drones. Police kept their distance as the demonstrators came to occupy a concrete bridge spanning what appeared to be a small, winding creek. Below them was the not-yet-mighty Mississippi beginning its southward flow and 1,450-foot drop in elevation over 2,550 miles to the Gulf. A merciless sun drove some and then many into the shallow, muddy waters. They splashed about, took selfies, freed themselves from bras. Winona herself took a dip. Some of the unwet chalked the bridge with demands while others chanted:

"Pipelines are poison!"

"Hey ho, hey ho, the 'dozers got to go!"

"Kill the Black Snake!"

Two hundred yards south of the bridge a corduroy road met the little Mississippi. Over its wood beams Kilridge workers with horizontal direction drills soon would rumble to the river's edge and begin dredging--unless Native women making their way on foot through the tall marsh grass to set up a prayer tent got there first and refused to cede the territory. From the bridge Treaty People cheered the re-claiming. Fire Light Camp, now occupied by six original inhabitants, stood between the Great River's humble headwaters and Killagua's fiery breath.

Winona came up from the water and was handed a bullhorn. "Pipeline supporters say I'm all wet. For once they're right! Joking aside, Kilridge recently received permission from the state for massive drawdowns of water from our lakes and rivers. Despite a severe drought the initial permit granting use of 540 million gallons was revised to allow for five billion. That, my friends, is what corporate capture of the state looks like." A chorus of boos followed.

Meanwhile, just off Route 71 thirty miles away, Native activists had blocked an access road with an old motorboat, above which hung a large banner: Relatives Not Resources. A quarter of a mile back, water protectors halted construction of a pumping station by crawling into unlaid pipes and gluing themselves to the steel, human plugs hard to remove. Cam and Emma G chained themselves to an excavator. Others locked onto backhoes and belly scrapers. Medics and monitors kept a close watch. At noon a large contingent of county cops in riot gear began to move in and order the two hundred protestors off the property. Soon they were hacksawing through the chains and carting away bodies gone limp. Mid-afternoon a Border Patrol copter buzzed in low and sent dirt and debris flying everywhere. Demonstrators hunkered down and waited out the dust storm. That evening, without warning, police fired a sound cannon that sent piercing sonic waves across the site, like a car alarm only more intense, inducing nausea and headaches among the remaining resisters. Past midnight a severe thunderstorm drenched everyone. Caked with splattered mud and shivering, Cam could not get the ringing in her ears to go away. She dozed a while a few hours before dawn. Runners kept her and other frontliners hydrated through the next day. Supporters chanted whenever the hacksaws fell silent, while Jane Fonda gave interviews and hoisted a Stop Line 337 sign high. By early evening nearly seventy had been arrested. Cam and Emma G were among the last to be hauled off to the county jail where they and many others were kenneled, strip searched and held for two days before being released on $500 bail.

Work at the pump station resumed. Media attention soon turned elsewhere. After the Treaty People gathering, county sheriffs decided Minnesota Nice might not work after all. They had studied Standing Rock and prepared to do likewise. In late June thirty deputies lay siege to Namewag Camp, located on private property but now subject to illegal harassment. No cars in and out. Drone surveillance 24/7. For resisters arrested at Shell River and other sites, bail was jacked up to five grand. More worrisome for the movement was the stalling of momentum. Calls to join the resistance failed to produce the surge of new recruits needed, though some brave souls continued to show up at Red Lake and other camps. None of the solidarity actions at the branches of VD, Stage Coach and other banks around the country drew more than a hundred demonstrators. Time was running out. Come late July a company press release claimed the pipeline was sixty-five percent complete and on track for completion by mid-September.

Water protectors had only one small victory of late: a state judge ordered police to back off Namewag Camp, noting that Kilridge's operating permit banned the use of corporate counter-insurgency tactics that infringed on free speech, peaceable assembly and other civil rights. Angered the siege had been lifted by a liberal judge, a bunch of boogaloos on ATVs arrived at the camp's edge late one night and taunted its residents. Invites to come party with the boys and make them happy incensed the women. Three years earlier Shania, a collective member, had been abducted by three drunk whites, gang banged and then dumped on the side of the road where tribal police found her dazed and half-naked the next day. No rape kit on hand when needed, no arrests after the county DA's lackadaisical investigation. To protect her now, they put beeswax in her ears and sat with her in the sweat lodge.

Cam walked laps around the campfire and stoked it with kindling from branches snapped hard over her knee. Emma G could see White Panther was itching to pounce. "Remember what Maya said, the real—"

"I know, I know, these cornholes aren't the real enemy."

"It's true, they aren't."

"Tell me, then, when *do* we get to face those most responsible?"

"Maybe sooner than you think," responded Tara, joining them at the fire.

Cam shot her a quizzical look. "What do you mean?"

"I've been talking with Winona and other folks. We need to draw a lot more people into the movement and cause a big ruckus soon—real soon—if we want to get Biden's attention. Unfortunately, he's our best hope now."

"And how do we do that?"

"When you joined us back in February, we thought it best if the whole White Panther and G-Force thing went onto the back burner. But we're almost to August and our back is to the wall now. Time to try something different."

"Like what?"

"You two fly to the four corners and recruit like crazy, then head to DC and raise as much hell as you can. We have contacts with solidarity groups in many cities that will set up events. What do you think?"

"Isn't this the 'white savior' play all of us wanted to avoid? I'm glad no one has mentioned White Panther for months, don't cha know."

"A good point, and one we discussed at length. Here's why we think this is different: in Indian country, people know you're a warrior and have been up north five months on the front line. You've earned trust and can speak with authority as a powerful ally."

"What if people have forgotten—"

"No, they haven't. When they hear White Panther is once again on the prowl, they will remember the uprising and your boogaloo busting and your brush with certain—" Tara stopped suddenly and stared ominously at Cam. Then all three burst out laughing.

"Seriously, you're the one to fan the flame. Look at the ongoing strike in Bessemer. They have Bleudough and a lot of other bosses running scared." It was true: when Amerizon refused to negotiate a first contract in good faith, the new union had re-doubled its outreach to the unconvinced. Vibol stayed on as a summer intern, coaching fired-up pickers as he ferried them to the houses of co-workers. Each week a few more Teamsters Stand Tall buttons appeared on the warehouse floor. Soon after management imposed a new shift schedule that made life even harder for associates with school-age kids, organizers almost ran out of buttons. On Juneteenth, with ninety percent of the workforce on board, the strike had begun with a massive walkout that was now in week six and holding strong.

"Been almost seven months since the last van blew," noted Emma G. "I think the Ameri-bombers just wanted to light a fuse."

"And if we fail?"

"Win or lose, you will be in DC to start classes. That's another reason we want you to land there by end of August. Cam, you are going to be shaking trees for a long time."

"I thought I was going to be tree-sitting." She looked over at Emma G. "What about you? I thought all things Washington made you ill."

"I'll serve as liaison to our allies on the Hill," she replied calmly. Her poker face never did work.

"You, an inside-the-beltway operative! You've been in on this from the get-go. We both know you can't lie to save your life, so don't—"

"Guilty as charged. In fact, I was the one who got in Tara's ear a few weeks ago," confessed Emma G as she pushed pine needles about with a big toe. Seldom did she avoid eye contact, and never had she gone behind Cam's back.

"She's looking out for you on this one," said Tara. "Everyone agrees that getting you back to school is important."

"Hold on a second. This is a proposal, not a directive, yah?"

"Of course! Who are we to tell you what to do? If you want to stay here and see this struggle through, then do it. White Panther may or may not turn the tide by going on tour, but either way this is one battle of many to come. We're taking the long view here, and that's why we all felt strongly that DC is the right direction for you to go at this point."

A long silence ensued. Emma G glanced pleadingly at Cam, who was toeing pine needles as well now. "Sleep on it," Tara finally said.

Tara's proposal, and an unexpected text from Giles, kept Cam up all night:

cant go outside
too much smoke
from fires out west
edina air quality
worst ever

tramp u ok?

dad says itll
blow over idk

keep your
inhaler close!
stay up

wp keep fighting
promise u will
never give up

never!! love u
little brother!!!
[hearts]

They drove to Minneapolis for a demonstration and then rendezvoused at Standing Rock with the Totem Pole trekkers from Lummi Nation who were heading next to Michigan to support the protest against Kilridge's Line 5 project. After successful events on the left coast, they rolled east through Denver, Chicago and Cleveland where they were met by bell-ringing supporters, the bells growing louder in Boston, NYC and Philly before they arrived at the nation's capital. Eleven stops over twenty-seven days in a van transformed into the likeness of a leaping wildcat and driven by Red Road Woman, a DAPL protest veteran and trucker whose head-to-toe tattoos Cam found fascinating. Trailing close behind two cars carrying Native warriors ready to defend White Panther with their lives. At several stops they joined divestment activists staging mock oil spills and die-ins at major bank branches. In Chicago and NYC, they re-enacted the final scene of *Mishipeshu and the Black Snake*, vanquishing Killagua with the enthusiastic help of kids drawn from sizeable crowds. Emma G revised Cam's stump speech daily to include news of another flood, another fire, another huge chunk of ice splitting off from Antarctica. Inane, post-space flight comments from a starry-eyed Bleudough and his boosters proved the perfect foil. Pledges of resistance grew in number.

On the first Saturday in September a bike parade led by White Panther rolled down Rock Creek Parkway to Lion and Tiger Hill at the National Zoo.

Joined there by a blue-monkey brigade, they zig-zagged through the neighborhoods of Mount Pleasant and Adams Morgan on their way to Malcolm X Park for a rally. Onlookers waved, clapped and snapped pics while drivers honked their support. Kids sporting White Panther gear head-to-toe darted out of alleys on bikes and joined the parade. At the park all gathered around the Joan of Arc Memorial. Soaked in sweat, Cam mounted the top step to address the large crowd: "In the Persian Gulf the wet-bulb temperature now reaches 95 degrees Fahrenheit. At that number you can't sweat enough to avoid overheating, organ failure and eventual death even if you're young, in great shape and sitting in the shade with a tall glass of water. If this pipeline and others get built, it will bring us closer to the day when going for a bike ride, or just sitting outside in the shade, won't be possible. The world house is on fire. Let us ride now to the White House and sound the alarm!" Bells many brought rang loudly.

Bikers and blue monkeys headed south on 16th Street, stopping for nine minutes at Black Lives Matter Plaza. Then it was on to Lafayette Square for a grand rally at which a 337-foot long Black Snake made of light cloth coiled its way through the crowd and, at White Panther's command, was ripped to shreds, its remains gathered up into a big burlap bag. All turned to the White House—just a hundred paces away but walled off from the public by a tall iron fence—and took up a thunderous chant:

"Pipelines are poison."

"Kill the Black Snake!"

"Pipelines are poison."

"Kill the Black Snake!"

Later that day Piscataway and Powhatan tribal members joined the drum circle at the square. After Chief Billy Tarac reminded everyone of what was at stake, local musicians vowed to keep the beat going 24/7 until the POTUS shut down Line 337. In a blog post, G-Force dubbed them the Determined Drummers.

In mid-August Janelle Monáe had released "Pounce". A timely statement with a frisky beat, the bop shot to the top of the charts. From NYC an Alvin Ailey dance troupe soon showed up at the square, handing out paws and offering free lessons on how to do a fast-and-funky jig named after the hit. Once White Panther joined in and the #PounceOnThis challenge went viral, the new song-and-dance quickly became the movement's signature. AOC and Ilhan stopped by to offer support, with the former pouncing in no time. That vid reached a million views in less than a day.

Toward summer's end several hundred Treaty People ready to get arrested flowed into the resistance camps. Sympathetic media coverage increased as did calls, flits and texts to the White House. Resisters young and old kept crawling into pipes--only to get carried away by the cops, whose numbers and impatience grew. Over 800 water protectors arrested in four counties. Yet all for naught. Despite the occasional disruption, thousands of Kilridge workers kept digging, dredging and laying pipe. In late September the company issued another press release declaring the project completed. State authorities fast-tracked inspections, and by mid-November tar sands oil was flowing across the North Star State on its way to the shores of Lake Superior for shipment to refineries.

After a bumpy start Cam settled into her first semester at Georgetown, with a dorm room overlooking the Potomac. A few dozen zealous undergrads joined her at the square on weekends—up to midterms. Determined Drummers kept the beat until the first freezing temperatures arrived. As hopes for a last-minute canceling of Line 337 faded, she found herself looking past the placards to the seven-acre park's still glorious foliage. Like a thousand other protests watched over by Lafayette's ghost, this one had washed in full of energy and then receded, another wave pounding sand before passing away. What remained were statues at each corner of the park, all well-guarded by sentinel trees with roots reaching under pavement that doubtless would receive another pounding. Would marches to come proceed past a fifth statue at the square's center--Andrew Jackson astride a horse rearing up on its two hind legs—or would he too join the ranks of the fallen?

On Veterans Day, a disconsolate Cam admitted defeat in a text to Chano:

taking the L so sucks
feel like a total fail

You fought bravely
and you fought well,
my blue-ribbon friend.
Proud of you.
[heart]

no green new deal
either my sunrise
peeps r just as
bummed as me

It can take decades,
and along the way
you lose some battles
and win others.

like the victory
just won by
small farmers
in india

Exactly!
Tomorrow the sun
rises and so will you.

happy warrior
along the way

Si, señorita.
[hundred points]

when can I
come visit?

Any time, once
we're all past
the pandemic.

feels like rona and
her mutant kids
will never go away

The vaccines our
doctors developed
are working, as
are yours. This
too shall pass.

u r good at
cheer ups thx
time to hit
the library

Adios, amigo!

As the Bessemer strike dragged on into the fall, union drives and walkouts at other companies across the country multiplied. Meanwhile, in what was called the Great Resignation, millions of employees simply quit their jobs, making it harder to hire scabs. The day before Thanksgiving, Teamster members voted to ratify the contract agreement with their employer. Jubilant warehouse workers reported back to work on Black Friday, knowing their union's major demands had been met.

Emma G became a roving correspondent for Vox, an indy news outlet. Visits to Hear Us Roar reached 760,000 per month by year's end and doubled in 2022. That same year, Minnesota's governor pardoned Winona, Tara and 127 other water protectors—most of them Native—who had begun to serve long sentences for trespassing, inciting a riot, terrorism and other trumped-up charges.

In 2033, Canadian-based Kilridge Corporation quietly shut down its pipeline operations upstate due to lack of demand for the product and mounting lawsuits related to a major spill six years earlier.

After being the second Borlaug to win a blue ribbon at the State Fair, this one for an exhibit exploring whether and how climate change increases the likelihood of earthquakes, Giles graduated magna cum laude from Friezelda-St. Mittens and went on to study geophysics and seismology at U of M while living at home. His first job out of college was with Twist Metals at its copper-nickel mine in northeastern Minnesota. From his parents' cabin at Lake Vermilion, he commutes to work each day in his electric car, a graduation present.

Upon completing her grad studies, Maya worked as a program manager with the Planetary Health Alliance at Harvard and eventually became a senior administrator in the World Health Organization. Her extensive travels allow her to dance tango in many great cities.

Once Maya left for Boston, Diego and Dulce took over the lease at Movement House. Two days after she told him she was pregnant, he proposed. Everyone from the old days came into town for the wedding. Rayna DJ'd the party at Casa Diablo, of course. A roar went up when the newlyweds did the

Pounce. Diego went into bar management but kept cutting grass part-time so that Dulce could stay home with little Pablo and the other two tikes that arrived soon after. When Jorge landed a job at the railyard nearby, he and Juanita moved in with their kids. Casa Diablo was renamed Casa Niños and is still hopping. Over the old linoleum on the back porch they laid wrestling mats, on which no-longer-little Victor now gives both his dad and uncle a run for their money.

Rayna moved back to Cleveland and worked in coffee shops and bookstores a few years before landing an administrative staff position with a local theater, where she met someone who reminded her of the actress Llewie, star of her all-time favorite play *Lucia Mad*. They're still together.

Emma G turned out to be right: the fourth van bombing was the last. Federal investigators continue to search for clues that might reveal the identity and locale of the Ameri-bombers.

17

STATE OF THE UNION ADDRESS - 2034

After warm greetings and preliminary remarks, President Ocasio-Cortez broke with tradition: rather than trumpet her administration's first-year accomplishments, she recalled the long, decisive decade that made her groundbreaking approach to governing a diverse population of 358 million possible:

"Today the state of the union is stronger than ever because sixteen years ago, striking teachers in West Virginia, Arizona and other states launched a Red for Ed movement that made a quality education for every child, not just the privileged, a reality. In 2021 Congress established universal pre-K and authorized $750 billion over ten years to upgrade and decarbonize every public school in the country with solar panels and green retrofits. Four years later the Excellent Education for All Act was passed. Test scores turned a corner as teachers in all counties, not just wealthy ones, received fair pay and began to be held in higher esteem by their communities. Today, our students are among the best prepared on the planet, and more of our most talented young minds enter that noble profession.

"We are stronger than ever because fourteen years ago young Americans took to the streets of Minneapolis, Portland and many other cities to demand structural reform. In the years that followed, they searched for ways to heal and transform a country riven by fear, resentment and gross inequality. Growing numbers went door to door, starting conversations with fellow citizens about what matters most and registering new voters. Many began to build a genuine sharing economy. Their collective efforts saved our democratic experiment from the corporate greed, misinformation and authoritarian impulses running rampant at the time.

"Today, the more vulnerable and less powerful among us are free from want and free from fear because a New Majority has showed that a politics of the common good can and should prevail over the monopolists and dream hoarders. Thirteen years ago, the improbable victory of striking black workers in Bessemer jump-started the union organizing that has driven a just transition to the post-carbon economy, a productive economy that has reduced the poverty rate by a third. A renewed labor movement also helped to propel the shift to cooperative commerce that swept the country after the Mega-Recession of '27 made clear the time had come for a new economic order, an order no longer dictated by one-percenters. Today nearly forty percent of our well-trained workforce is represented by the Alt Energy Workers, Caretakers United, Teamsters and other democratically run unions, while a record number of companies are now either employee-owned firms or producer cooperatives. Instead of closing shop, thousands of retiring owners helped their workers take over the business. What a legacy! And they succeeded because Congress established and fully funded the SBA's national network of Cooperative Enterprise Institutes.

"Amerizon and other corporate goliaths have fallen, the rules of the game no longer rigged in their favor. One David working behind the scenes in Bessemer was a first-year college student named Vibol Phan, recently confirmed by the Senate as the nation's first Secretary of Cooperative Commerce. Some say he's too young and inexperienced to lead such an important new agency, but I say anyone who began his public life as a frontliner during the covid pandemic, who knocked on hundreds of doors to get Senators Warnock and Ossoff elected, then knocked on hundreds more a few months later to win a union in Alabama and then kept on knocking at the door of change until it opened—again and again—during the most remarkable of decades, I say *that* door-to-door David is just the one we need to lead the boldest innovation in democratic governance we've seen in a century.

"A New Majority knows that neither prosperity nor health comes from Wall Street or Big Pharma or Silicon Valley. Our greatest days of innovation lie ahead, and the place to be these days is flyover country! The recently renamed Department of Agro-Ecology is led by Secretary Camilla Borlaug, a brave veteran of the many struggles that opened the way to a new and truly sustainable American future. Who else but White Panther could make carbon farming and meatless meals cool? Fifteen years ago, diabetes and other diet-related diseases were out of control, as was obesity. Today they are rare, and the hundreds of billions in healthcare cost savings have enabled us to fund a Freedom Dividend. We are less prone to another pandemic because she inspired thousands to go back to the land and create a new food system that, research has shown, better protects all of us from deadly pathogens. Along the way she lost her share of land-reform and other battles but never kept clawing, truly a cat with nine lives! Last century her granduncle, the great seed scientist Norman Borlaug, gave us the first Green Revolution. For years she has led the second Green Revolution, and I wager historians of the next century will consider her contribution to humanity even more valuable.

"Secretaries Phan and Borlaug are two of many new leaders re-inventing a federal government too long demonized by the Right. With my administration the torch has passed to the first truly 21st-century generation, a generation that has re-discovered the small-r republican truth that serving one's country is a great honor and the duty of every citizen. Last year a record number of volunteers entered the Climate Corps. On a massive scale we've re-directed talent and treasure after de-funding the false, wasteful wars on drugs and immigrants. In 2020 well over two million people were behind bars, but today less than a million. Every week another city reports success in transitioning to community policing and comprehensive care for the mentally ill and drug addicted. A respect for dignified manual labor and for the differently abled, darker skinned and those from another culture has taken hold, though we still have a long way to go. The waning forces of bigotry and religious obscurantism are no longer taken seriously even by their own children, who have left their communities in droves.

"At the same time, people everywhere can see that technology-driven affluence is a false god and are finding ways to re-connect with the sacred and each other. All four of FDR's freedoms still matter, not least freedom of worship. John Muir, one of our greatest environmentalists, found God in the wilderness. He called the forests he roamed cathedrals. Tonight, I am announcing my support for the Re-Wild America Act, which I urge Congress to pass quickly. Led by Interior Secretary Tara Houska, the National Re-Wilding Project will build on the success of the America the Beautiful Initiative, restoring degraded ecosystems and establishing biodiversity corridors in every region of the country. The Act also will provide the Native Treaty Commission with greater enforcement power to ensure the rights and sovereignty of First Nations are respected fully. And for the first time, a Native-led consortium will work cooperatively with Secretary Houska to care for both tribal and public lands.

"Going forward, we must continue to re-define our relations with other nations. Despite progress in reducing carbon emissions globally the climate crisis remains the single greatest threat to international stability. A decade ago, after Superstorm Mona left half our nation's capital under water for over a week, we finally realized a new grand strategy for national security based on sustainability was necessary. Sadly, too many countries have adopted a nationalistic and militaristic approach to the growing number of food shortages and climate refugees. But one Gaza Strip is one too many already. We cannot condone regimes that, ironically, study both the Nazis and the Israelis for lessons in how to manage so-called problem populations toward premature death. We must not waver in our commitment to build a new system of global governance based on three core principles: collective security, mutual aid and respect for human rights. The days of pretentious Great Powers wielding a big stick must end. Having narrowly avoided a major war with China over Taiwan, my predecessor went to Beijing and forged a Planetary Peace Pact that, among other things, cut global military spending by a third and banned nuclear weapons for all time. Across the globe our embattled democratic allies rallied in support of a new set of rules for governing the world community based on a more just relationship between the prosperous North and impoverished South. The success of the Global Minimum Tax, which has reduced both tax dodging and carbon cheating significantly, shows that international cooperation generates win-win outcomes.

"I want to close tonight with a tribute to several fellow Americans, each one a quiet hero whose shared story of community uplift became quite common in the 2020s but too often has remained untold. Thank you all for coming, and please stand a moment when I mention your name.

"For many years Freddie Donaldson's barber shop on Lake Street in Minneapolis was the kind of place that make city neighborhoods great, a gathering spot where card games, witty banter and back slaps made one's day a little better. Young bucks from all over town waited an hour for the former Army sergeant to give them just the right fade, despite the ban on devices and nothing to read but faded copies of *Jet* and *Ebony*. If anyone complained, his reply was always the same: 'You can shoot the breeze with the brother sitting next to you or ship out'.

"During the 2020 uprising Freddie's shop, already closed for months due to the pandemic, went up in flames. Six months later his wife, a nurse at the public hospital, died of covid. Insomnia and panic attacks followed her funeral. He told his friend Herb Markley the pills prescribed were too expensive, and he feared falling into depression. For months Herb kept tabs on him. They played checkers, walked the dog and found cannabis made Freddie's days a little better. When the city finally opened up, Herb's choir pal Jamie Givens, who worked at a community bank, paid Freddie a visit. She walked him through the low-interest loan process, and along with the insurance payout he was able to open a new shop in his old neighborhood and re-hire his cutters.

"Build Back Better was the slogan in those days, and that's what Freddie and many local business folks did. Soon after re-opening he got together with Cynthia Platt and other shopkeepers. They formed Lake Street Revival, a progressive business association on a mission to make the long-neglected commercial corridor a priority for city authorities, state agencies and the SBA. Their group adopted the local rec center while working closely with police, social workers and counselors focused on supporting young men caught up in the epidemic of gun violence at the time. Freddie and his associates volunteered in the after-school mentoring program. Over time things improved. Drive down Lake Street today and, block after block, you can see the fruits of their tireless effort. Gone are many national chains, which too often vacuum up local dollars and send them elsewhere. In their place over a hundred new businesses, half of them coops or employee-owned enterprises with apprentice programs for local high-school graduates, are thriving. Money circulates within a neighborhood that, little by little, keeps getting better. Oh, and lest I forget, three years ago Freddie and Jamie got hitched!

"A story too ordinary for this august occasion? I think not. Our best days are ahead of us because of exceptional lives and strong associations like theirs. Good night my fellow Americans, and God bless."

GLOSSARY
FOR ALL AGES

AUTHOR'S NOTE: A friend suggested others might benefit from a glossary. While piqued at first, after many months I conceded that posterity just might concur and even find amusing the annotative remarks added to a good number of entries. Besides, in a world awash in alt-facts, glossaries belong in works of fiction as much as anywhere else, do they not?

From A to Z, you'll find acronyms spelled out, observations on ironic [emoji] usage and elucidations of obscure terms along with use-at-your-own-risk translations of zoomer slang (ZS) and Minnesota Speak (MS). All omissions and errors are mine, except where I was led astray by some irresponsible website, of course. As for Diego's foreign-language invective, readers are on their own, what with this being a G-rated glossary and all.

A

andopawatchigan – An Ojibwe teaching: "seek your dream". A disciplined search for one's purpose and dedication to carrying it out. Over time, a sustained commitment to living the dream enables one to come into balance with all one's relations, where who one is related to includes all living things. The journey toward what cultural historian and eco-theologian Thomas Berry calls the Dream of the Earth never ends.

anfractuous – Replete with winding, intricate turns; what one expects in a first-rate mystery novel or memoir recounting an interesting, well-lived life.

avuncular – Genial, tolerant; like an uncle. Along with **pulchritudinous**, no other adjective so undermines its meaning simply by the way it sounds. In conversation, would you ever describe Uncle Al this way?

B

basic – ZS for unoriginal, banal. Also used often by over-worked, under-paid adjuncts in brief comments attached to B-grade undergrad essays.

bet – ZS for agreement with a statement or proposal; as in, *"Wanna play Grand Theft Auto?" "Bet."* Life's risky when you spend so much time thumbing your way through it. Bet.

bruh moment – ZS for a moment of failure. Not to be confused with an "OK, boomer" moment, despite the similarities.

brummagem – A lemon, i.e., something that looks glossy but grossly underperforms when road-tested. Examples: appliances in new rental properties, cheap hair dyes, Chevy Volts, some members of Congress.

C

cake eater – In MS, someone wealthy, privileged. That many Minnesotans love cake does not mean the state is full of cake eaters. Far from it.

catch these hands – ZS for get hit; as in, *"Mess with him again and you'll catch these hands."*

Cecil B. Demille – Many of the famous director's seventy films were epic in scale.

chill – ZS for cool. Applied by zoomers to parents, principals, police officers and other authority figures who stay out of the way or don't ask too many questions.

clap back – ZS for retort; as in, *"After he dissed her jeans, she sent me with that clap back on his hoodie."* Adam Grant, a noted authority on reciprocity styles, says that givers tend not to clap back, matchers clap back in like manner and takers clap first and keep clapping until someone claps cuffs on them.

[cowboy hat face] – Used by zoomers to indicate unease in awkward moments. Look at this emoji long enough, and odds are the aforementioned feeling will come over you. **Bet**.

Csikszentmihalyi, Mihaly – Hungarian-American psychologist who coined the concept of *flow*: optimal states of focus and high performance; moments when one reaches the peak of Maslow's pyramid. Received degrees from and taught at U. Chicago for many years before leaving for the left coast. Ironic that an academic with the world's most unpronounceable surname came up with *this* concept. **[cowboy hat face]**

D

deadass – ZS for "I'm serious"; as in, *"Did you really ace the calc quiz?" "Deadass." "What a mentat!"* One of several terse, emotive expressions vying to become the generation's letmotif. Rumor has it that Netrifix is coming out next year with *Deadass*, a black comedy-drama that will pick up where *Shameless* left off.

dooking – Laughing sound ferrets make when it's playtime. Fer cute.

drip – ZS for a hip/fashionable style in dress/appearance; it also can refer to a person's comportment. The blingy-pricey version: **drippin'**.

drag – ZS verb: to insult. Being dragged through the mud is no fun.

E

ESG – Short for environmental and social governance, another tag for corporate social responsibility. Advocates of "conscious capitalism" promote adoption of ESG policies and practices, while critics dismiss ESG as "corporate greenwash". **Bet**.

Ents – Giant talking-tree beings from J. R. R. Tolkien's fantasy world. Slow to move, but when they do, it's curtains for anyone who's incurred their wrath.

esurient – Hungry or greedy. Unlike **avuncular** and **pulchritudinous**, this adjective sounds like what it means without being onomatopoetic. **Facts**.

F

facts – ZS for strong agreement; "amen to that". Notice the collapse of the conventional fact – opinion distinction implied by this colloquialism.

G

Gloop, Augustus – One of Roald Dahl's best object lessons, Augustus is gluttony personified, and his golden-ticket-seeking father emblematic of America's dream-hoarding ten percenters.

glow up – ZS for someone who looks more attractive and/or "together" overnight. Root causes of a "glow up" range from shopping binge to mystical foretastes of the beatific vision, though the former tends to prevail in this secular age.

[goat] – ZS acronym: greatest of all time; often appearing in the form of a hollow-horned ruminant mammal. Only the biblically oblivious—and they are legion--could come up with this one.

Great Filter – A hypothesis advanced by Robin Hanson that seeks to explain why no ETs have been found, despite the (high) probability of their existence. Hanson posits various stages of evolutionary development likely to occur on many thousands of planets suitable for life. His Great Filter hypothesis: one or more of these stages—e.g., an explosive colonization of other star systems after a civilization with advanced technology has developed—must be improbable. One possibility is that advanced global societies with growing populations often fail to meet the energy/resource challenge and self-destruct. And in a vast, expanding universe the few that make it through the Great Filter and succeed in colonizing space may still be far, far away from Contact with homo sapiens and other less-evolved life forms.

gucci – ZS for cool, awesome. How far this descriptor travels colloquially beyond complimenting another's apparel/appearance is unknown at present, but ethno-linguists at Polytecnico di Milano won a grant from the company to find out.

H

Hammerin' Hank – With all due respect to Barry Bonds, old-school baseball fans still consider Hall of Fame home-run hitter Hank Aaron's 755 dingers the all-time career record. **Facts**.

hermeneutical – Pertaining to the interpretation of texts. While grossly over-simplified, the history of modern hermeneutics may be summed up as a turn to subjectivity, the Eliot-inspired and classics-oriented New Critics fond of "close readings" eventually eclipsed by Barthes and variants of reader-response theory. Bluntly stated, if the author is dead, then all manner of interpretation is permitted.

hits different – ZS for something that stands out or exceeds expectations. In intimate contexts the phrase becomes LGBTQ+ friendly and gestures toward a partner's flow-like performance.

Humanities – A zombie concept conveniently kept on life support by marketing VPs at U.S. colleges and universities; an extinct form of scholarly inquiry in U.S. academe, having been strangled slowly but surely by the corporate python that Princeton's finest political philosopher Sheldon Wolin calls "managed democracy" or "inverted totalitarianism".

I

I'm dead – ZS for "I'm dying of laughter". Whether this is irony ***in extremis*** remains a matter of debate among semioticians.

in extremis – Latin for under extreme circumstances, especially at the point of death.

Infamous Imelda – A notoriously corrupt Filipina First Lady and convicted criminal, Imelda Marcos and her dictator husband Ferdinand stole an estimated $10 billion from their fellow Filipinos before being deposed in 1986. She was said to own over 3,000 pairs of shoes. **Facts**.

interestin' – Means "I don't agree" or "I don't like it" in MS, where being indirect so as not to be offensive is Rule #1, 2 and 3 in social intercourse.

J

jams – ZS for an old song that's good. By "old" a zoomer means any tune from last month or later.

jeet – "Did you eat?" in MS. Not an offer to share a Slim Jim.

JAP – Jewish American Princess; one of America's most adaptive stereotypes.

For students of cultural history, cheap copies of *The Official J.A.P. Handbook* (1982) can be had online.

K

Kaliesque – Pertaining to Kali, Hindu goddess of death. If you get a Kaliesque look, then you are as good as dead. Likely sooner than later.

L

Laudato si (2015) - Pope Francis' groundbreaking encyclical on the environment is the latest installment of modern Catholic social teaching, which one wag called the church's "best kept secret". **Bet.**

lit – ZS for cool, awesome; still can mean drunk.

Little Piranha – A Minnesota Twins **stan** during the first decade of the 21st century, when the major-league team showed for the last time in MLB history that small ball works. **Facts.**

M

main character – ZS for a person who has charisma, someone confident and well-liked. *Be the Main Character in Your Life* lasted almost a month on Amerizon's best-selling self-help books list. **No cap.**

manoomin – Wild rice that grows among the many lakes inhabited by the Anishinaabe.

Mendoza Line – Playing for the Pittsburgh Pirates and other major-league teams, light-hitting shortstop Mario Mendoza failed to achieve a .200 batting average five times during his nine-season career. This record-setting incompetence notwithstanding, he was inducted into the Mexican League Hall of Fame. Note to front office: don't draft anyone who wears glasses.

mentat - Appearing in Frank Herbert's sci-fi classic *Dune*, mentat humans can calculate as quickly and accurately as any computer. Rumor has it that Booble's soon-to-be-released VR headwear will bring Herbert's fantasy to fruition and relieve millions of STEM-challenged students of the need to study calc and many other annoyingly difficult subjects.

MOA – Mall of America is the largest mall in the western hemisphere; located in the Twin Cities suburb of Bloomington, it includes a theme park and an aquarium. Its award-winning lost-and-found service routinely reunites children with their distraught parents. Being helpful is what Minnesota Nice is all about.

N

no cap – ZS for "No lie" or "I'm not lying". When used while under pressure in dicey port-district situations, the phrase implies that one deserves not to lose a knee cap. **No cap**.

no [heart] – ZS for "You are so cancelled". Or what happens at the end of the pier when "no cap" doesn't cut it.

Niebuhr, Reinhold – Mid-20th century public intellectual; wrote *The Children of Light and the Children of Darkness* (1944), a Christian-realist defense of democracy. Chapter 9 is titled after Niebuhr's treatise, and the entire novel may be read as an appreciative reply to his position.

O

OOO – Short for object-oriented ontology, a metaphysical view advanced by

Graham Harman and other speculative-realist philosophers. No brief gloss—least of all this one—can peel OOO back enough to offer even a nibble's worth of insight, but here's a timely passage on "banana-being" from Harman's Heideggerian-inflected tome *Guerrilla Metaphysics* (2005): "A police officer eating a banana reduces this fruit to a present-at-hand profile of its elusive depth, as do a monkey eating the same banana, a parasite infecting it, or a gust of wind blowing it from a tree. Banana-being is a genuine reality in the world, a reality never exhausted by any relation to it by humans or other entities" (74). **Facts**.

Ope! – In MS, a spontaneous exclamation similar to "oops"; used by hyper-polite Minnesotans when accidental contact occurs. Considered contemptuously anthropocentric when used deliberately while squashing bugs, swatting flies, flaying fish, etc.

Overton Window - The range of policies considered politically acceptable to the mainstream at a given time. In the short run, visionary practitioners of ***parrhesia*** often find themselves outside the window looking in. In the long run, what was once unthinkable and often laughed at becomes common sense, or what everyone now sees when they look out the window.

P

parrhesia – Not a trendy-spendy cheese served on Silicon Valley's ever-so-veggie pizzas; a Greek term for frank, honest speech or speaking truth to power. *Parrhesia*, Brother West tells us, is essential for public deliberation in a healthy democracy, and in its absence idiots and ideologues of every stripe fill the void. Sound familiar?

pulchritudinous – Good-looking, comely. Is there a greater waste of five syllables in the entire, thirty-pound tome titled the Oxford English Dictionary? I dare all comers to cite an entry that proves me wrong. Let the #UgliestAdjective challenge begin!

Q

Qanon – An example among many of what decadent empires vomit up. Suffice it to say, their conspiracist drivel is less interesting than the "Q source" (Q = German *quelle* = source) hypothesized by biblical scholars seeking to account for material—mostly sayings of the radical Jew Yeshua ben Nazareth—found in the later gospels of Matthew and Luke but not in Mark, the first canonical gospel written around 70 CE when Roman troops stormed Jerusalem and torched it after tiring of Zealot terrorist—er guerrilla attacks.

R

real one – ZS for a person you can trust.

rona – ZS for coronavirus.

rulo – In tango, a "circle of light" drawn by leaders with their toe, into which followers are invited to step. Each tango couple is a circle of light unto itself.

S

scabs – Slang term used by unionists; refers to replacement workers crossing the picket line during a strike. Scabs hurt. **Facts**.

schnookered – In MS, it means you're really drunk.

secure the bag – ZS for get the money. When used in dicey port-district situations while applying pressure to another's private parts, the phrase strongly implies that one expects to receive full payment soon—or else. **Deadass**.

Shavuot – Jewish Pentecost or Feast of Weeks, which celebrates Yahweh's gift of the Law to His Chosen People. To be clear, the feast in question only lasts for one or two days.

sisu – MS for grit, gumption. Whether *sissy* serves as an antonym to sisu is a hotly debated topic among participants in U of M's popular Local Living Languages program.

Ski-U-Mah! – A cheer used by U of M football fans.

Skol! – A cheer used by Minnesota Vikings fans, many of whom attend U of M.

[skull] – Used by zoomers to indicate laughter. (See ***in extremis*** above.)

slay – ZS verb: to do really well; as in, "*After the Golden Gophers slayed the Badgers on Saturday, losing only by two touchdowns instead of five, schnookered* ***U of M*** *undergrads ran naked all through campus screaming* ***Ski-U-Mah!***" **[skull]**

smacks – ZS for tasty treat. As in, *"Dat's lip-smackin' good, don't cha know."*

speedrun – ZS for trying to finish a video game as fast as possible. Results only valid when not under the influence of amphetamines or more than two cups of Caribou's dark roast.

Strib – What denizens of the cities call the Minneapolis Star-Tribune.

stay up – ZS for "Chin up, it'll be OK". Not to be confused with its boomer-male slang meaning: "Don't forget to pop a Viagra."

stan – ZS for an obsessed fan. Stans stand behind their (wo)man (or team), no matter what. Not giving a rat's ass that Britney is now free is anti-stan. **Bet**. Not giving a rat's ass when the Vikes or Twins don't make the play-offs is punishable by law in the North Star State. **Deadass**.

T

taking the L – ZS for going down to defeat. Changes in context may alter the phrase's meaning slightly; as in, *"Damned uber didn't show up, so now I'm taking the L to Midway. Probably gonna miss my flight! Ya just can't win these days."*

thicc – ZS for a hot, curvaceous figure. To date an ethno-linguistic mystery, though chances are good that some thousand-raids-on-the-obscure dissertation from a zombie **Humanities** program may shed light on the matter at some point.

thirsty – ZS for someone craving attention. Arguably the best re-purposing of an adjective achieved by zoomers to date. Keep it up, kids!

tyro – A beginner or novice. One ethno-linguist of some repute has traced the term's origin to Silicon Valley; as in, *"He's a tyro maniac, forever starting this and that new venture before failing fast and, well, you get the idea."*

U

umbrage – When one takes exception to, and is offended by, a comment or action seen as a slight or insult; as in, *"While at happy hour, she took umbrage at his admiring look, cancelled him online and—icing on the cake—abruptly ended his career with accusations of sexual assault neither plausible not provable but taken seriously by an ambitious DA up for re-election in a suburban county trending woke-blue."* @MeToo.

U of M – University of Minnesota. Famous alums: Norman Borlaug, Alan Page, Bob Dylan, Henry Fonda, Jessica Lange, Paul Molitor, Garrison Keillor and Yanni (who???) among others. Unofficial lists of Golden Gopher greats typically include no less than three failed Democratic presidential candidates. **Ski-U-Mah!** Not. (See also **Mendoza Line** above.)

V

Vaderesque – Presenting as super-scary evil, yet not beyond redemption. Does not appear in woke glossaries, since how you (re)present is WHO YOU ARE.

Volscians – Among the Indigenous tribes of Italy; long-time enemies of Rome and its imperial ambition. In *The Aeneid*, Vergil's warrior-maiden Camilla dies defending her Volscian homeland against Aeneas the invader.

Via Campesina - An international organization promoting small-scale sustainable agriculture and food sovereignty, i.e., local control over food production and self-sufficiency. *Via Campesina* is made up of peasant groups, agricultural workers, rural women and Indigenous communities.

Vitamin I – A reference to ibuprofen.

W

What's the tea? – A zoomer asking about the latest gossip/news; you oblige by "spilling the tea". Not to be confused with the code signal used by Tea Party activists to launch flash mobs and other direct actions designed to take down the federal government.

wig – ZS for when you're utterly amazed by something, so much so your piece flies off your head.

WWJD – Short for "What would Jesus do?" Most car owners sporting this bumper sticker believe they know the answer to the question. Steer clear.

X

xenophile – One attracted to foreign styles, customs, manners and so on. An extensive cross-cultural study funded by UNESCO estimates the ratio of xenophiles to xenophobes is on par with the odds of winning the lottery. (See **Great Filter** above.)

Y

yeet – ZS verb (1): to throw something; (2) to move fast. As in, *"Yeet that shit over the fence and yeet your ass before we land upstate!"*

yeet, yeet! – ZS for "Hell yeah!"

Z

Zapatistas – A revolutionary group controlling parts of Chiapas, a remote state in southern Mexico. Libertarian socialist in ideology, most Zapatista militants are of Indigenous descent.

Zs – A boomer injunction: stop reading and go to sleep.

CPSIA information can be obtained
at www.ICGtesting.com
Printed in the USA
BVHW060857110222
628683BV00001B/56